SANCTUARY OF ECHOES
BY
EVELYN KLEBERT

Sanctuary of Echoes
By Evelyn Klebert

A Cornerstone Book
Published by Cornerstone Book Publishers

Copyright © 2021, 2023 & 2024 by Evelyn Klebert

Cover Art and Interior Photographs by E.D. Poll

Cornerstone Book Publishers
Hot Springs Village, AR
www.cornerstonepublishers.com

Fifth Cornerstone Edition – 2024

ISBN: 978-1-61342-211-3

Dedication:

For Michael, Robert, and Jonathan who fill my life with inspiration.

And Corey who looks after us all

"When the oak is felled the whole forest echoes with its fall, but a hundred acorns are sown in silence by an unnoticed breeze."

— Thomas Carlyle

"Refusal to believe until proof is given is a rational position; denial outside our own limited experience is absurd."

— Annie Besant

Table of Contents

SANCTUARY OF ECHOES

PROLOGUE

"Do you think it's wise at this point, friend?"

He looked about the darkened parlor for perhaps the last time. Surely, he had no business returning here. The handful of men sitting near him, on the sofa, and in adjoining chairs didn't exactly move in the same circles as he. One he knew for a fact worked as the captain of a cargo ship along the Mississippi River. His business had kept him away for the majority of their gatherings. Another was from a very prestigious and wealthy old family in town — one that his newly earned wealth simply did not allow him to rub elbows with, at least under ordinary circumstances. And then there were others, perhaps only one that he, during his ordinary life, counted as a regular acquaintance. But there were seven here tonight, enough to open and enough to follow through with the business at hand.

He brought the glass of brandy lightly upwards to slightly graze his lips but didn't actually take a sip, just enough to rouse a weary mind. The week had been impossible, a heavy rush of nightmarish landscape as he buried his still young wife.

The physicians had no definitive answer for him about her death, a fever around the heart — "just a weakened constitution."

He lowered the glass. "Wise? I see no alternative. For myself, I am now the single parent of two young children. I have no time for such clandestine endeavors any longer."

"Clandestine? You insult us."

The heavy voice traveled to him from the fireplace where its author stood. And not for the first time, he felt a chill travel across his back. "I meant no insult. Perhaps I should have said secretive. The point is that the world is changing, and I see no benefit in continuing."

Again, the heavy voice, "But perhaps you do not speak for all of us."

And then from other quarters, "He speaks for me."

"And me as well."

And then, after a hesitation, one more voice. "I agree. The danger has begun to outweigh the benefit."

He leaned back in his chair, an unexpressed sigh of relief in his chest. That was four of them. All they needed was a majority to disband. But then the figure he distrusted most moved out of the darkness into the semi-light of the fireplace, that long, pale, pinched face. "There is so much that remains untapped. The documents we've acquired thus far—"

"Must be destroyed," he finished his statement.

"Destroyed? Are you out of your mind? We've only begun to scratch the surface. This city is filled with treasures we've yet to tap into."

"There is too much opportunity for abuse." And then he smiled kindly, trying to assume a less threatening pose. "My friend, power is a tool. Depending on whose hands it falls into, it can be used for good or ill. And speaking for myself, I wouldn't want to be entrusted with such a responsibility."

"Perhaps you are just weak. I have no such doubts about my capabilities."

"And that could be your greatest weakness," he remarked pointedly.

Another figure moved out of the shadows, a more welcome one. "He is right. It all should be destroyed. I can do it myself. The Ariadne is setting sail the day after tomorrow. I can dispose of everything on the voyage."

He nodded, "Buried in the turbulent waters of the river. That seems appropriate."

"You're all mad. We've collected a wealth of information, rare books of immeasurable value."

And then a different voice, an older man, frail, full into his seventies — at least thirty years the senior of every other member of the group. "Don't forget Joseph Marchand." A silence fell across them all at the mention of his name. He had hoped it wouldn't be necessary to bring him into this. But the resistance had made it unavoidable.

The old man continued, "The doctors say he will never recover his reason again."

"You can't blame that on us. The fool rushed things, tried things before we were ready."

"Do you honestly believe, Gabriel, that we could ever be ready for these kinds of forces? Ever truly be prepared?" The old man's voice had risen to a volume that he honestly didn't think he was capable of anymore. And it seemed to have squelched the dissenter.

He rose to his feet, "Shall we take a vote now?" It was true that all they needed was a majority. But the vote was unanimous. As he gathered his coat and hat, he knew he would never step foot in this house again and that his dear, sweet wife could rest easy now.

CHAPTER 1

OLD WOUNDS

She watched from a distance as he approached one of the stone benches in the park. He sat there waiting, and it chilled her. She must have contemplated approaching him for five minutes at least, five long, daunting minutes. It was inconceivable in some ways, the thought of opening this particular door again. It had been so long since they'd last met — ten years, perhaps longer. She'd changed in immeasurable ways and assumed he had as well. And it was indeed a chapter of her life that she had closed, albeit not so firmly as she'd liked. But circumstances as they were, well suffice to say necessity overrode inconvenience and all other considerations.

Slowly, she stepped from behind the pavilion and made her way to the stone bench. She felt sure that he knew she was approaching but didn't turn round to acknowledge her. He simply sat there quietly, waiting. She stopped at the side of the bench, silently determined that he would speak first. He rose to his feet, a foot or so taller than she. He was dressed nicely for their meeting in a brownish sports coat, light-colored shirt, and dark pants. But when she looked into his eyes, she flinched for a moment, feeling the jolt of an old connection that she instantly mentally blocked herself from. He wouldn't get the better of her. She eyed him deliberately with no flicker of emotion. It was best to establish distance right at the start. He sported a short, clipped beard, and his thick dark hair was ever so slightly graying at the sides, the signs of age.

And in that moment, she wondered with distraction how much age showed in her face now. "Corey," he murmured, the same low, graveled voice.

She responded with a cool deliberateness. "Iain, I'm glad you could meet me."

Then there was something in the dark eyes that rose to the surface, sparkle, challenge, something indefinable, "How could I refuse?"

She nodded, trying to appear detached but feeling acutely as if she were a fifteen-year-old girl again rather than the thirty-seven-year-old woman she'd become. There were benefits of age, benefits she'd become accustomed to — respect, an ease of being unconcerned with things that plagued her in her youth, a knowledge that she was past particular aspects of life. All these shields of age felt suddenly stripped away from her in the deep gleam of his Baltic, amber-colored eyes. She'd forgotten and, at this moment, truly hated how ill at ease this man had always made her. She crossed her arms in front of her, walking a few paces, and then turned to address him directly. She felt calmer, more secure from this vantage point. "How long have you been in the country?"

A slight smile flickered across his face as though she amused him, which rankled her greatly. She had accomplished much in her lifetime already and was well-respected in her chosen profession. What she didn't need was condescension from this particular man. "Actually, only a few months, I've been keeping a low profile."

Her heart felt uncomfortable in her chest at the underlying tension of their exchange. "Yes, well, you were difficult to track down."

"But you managed to do it." His words came fast upon her own. And then his eyes passed over her again with that slight smirk of amusement that incensed her. "Would you like to sit? Or are you more comfortable glowering at me from afar?"

She dropped her arms from their protective stance, suddenly feeling very foolish. "I'm not glowering. It's just that this is a little awkward for me. Surely, you can understand this."

He shrugged, "Well, let's endeavor to get the awkwardness out of the way. Are you still with that ignorant idiot, Morris?"

She jolted in shock, feeling as though the air had literally been ripped out of her lungs. How dare he? How dare he drag their ugly past into this bright, clean present when she had worked so hard to eradicate it from her life. She glanced away. There were children in the distance playing on a swing set. And for a moment, she wondered how it would be to start over, to start everything over. "Why would you ask such a thing?" she murmured.

"Curiosity, don't worry. I've ceased caring about any of that long ago."

"Then why bring it up?" She eyed him directly, but he met her gaze unflinchingly, calmly. And that had always been his way, never to avoid any confrontation.

"I wanted to see if it matters to you."

"I haven't seen him for over five years."

An expression flickered through his eyes that was so fleeting, then quickly replaced by icy detachment. "Well, my congratulations, at least you've begun to develop some sense."

And then something inside her hardened at his insult. A coldness enabled her to close off those places he could still reach. "Iain, my time is valuable, and I do not desire to waste it on things that don't matter. I have something serious to discuss with you, or I wouldn't have expended the time and energy to find you."

He frowned a bit, "Yes, Corey, always business with you. Well, it's a lovely October day. So why don't we take a walk, and you can tell me all about it."

Her fingers trembled as she attempted to bend the soft metal into place. It was so delicate that the gloves she wore felt cumbersome. This piece was too fine to manipulate from behind a shield. It was reckless, but she removed the gloves and then shaped the metal of the necklace with her own fingertips. It was a malleable piece, a rare silver alloy, yet oddly resistant to her will. It required her to use all the strength she had in her slim fingertips to force the issue, and then she dropped the whole ornament onto the softly padded surface of her worktable. Her index finger began to ooze dark red. A sharp edge had punctured her — so much for the rewards of trying to force things.

She leaned back in the leather, swivel chair with a deep sigh. Corey had thought working on some of her jewelry would relax her this evening or rather distract her. But thus far, it had only succeeded in feeding her frustration. She'd been a fool to think that Iain would be of any help to her.

She knew, and so did he, that there was entirely too much history between them.

Some things, her father had always told her, were simply not worth salvaging, and some things were simply dangerous to attempt to salvage. She reached across her worktable to its edge to retrieve a glass of brandy she'd poured earlier. It burned her throat as she sipped it, but it comforted.

Jewelry-making was a skill that her father, Clayton Knight, had taught her. It served as a hobby now and a comfort, although there were times when she did accept commissions from selective clients who needed a piece for a special purpose. For the jewelry she constructed was not merely ornamental. That, too, was a skill her father had passed on to her.

"*I'm curious. Why approach me with this Corey after all this time? Surely you have enough friends or just contacts that could help you.*"

"*I'm not sure any of them could be trusted with this.*"

"*What makes you at all sure that I could be?*"

She grimaced as she squeezed the still-bleeding fingertip. It should be attended to, but she didn't feel like dealing with it. The house felt peculiarly empty tonight, although she didn't mind living alone. After several years of a problematic marriage to Sebastian Morris, living alone had been quite soothing. Tonight, however, in contrast, rambling around the old family house felt strangely oppressive. But then he'd done this to her, disrupted everything.

She sipped her brandy and allowed her mind to return to earlier in the day. She'd been foolish to think that perhaps time had softened his sharp edges. Now, it was clear that they remained as razored as the metal that had cut her skin.

They had walked largely in silence through Audubon Park, a time which only served to feed her uneasiness. She wanted to get down to business, to separate them from the turmoil of the past. "So," he began, "you have captured my attention. I'm wondering exactly what could have driven you to contact me. I'm more than sure I wasn't your first choice. What about the others?"

Her throat seemed to tighten at his inquiry, although it was one that she more than expected. "Everyone has drifted apart. I'm sure you must be—"

"Aware? No, dearest, as it is, I've been quite detached from your little group for some time. Or does your memory fail you?"

It jolted her how vitriolic he sounded. Of course, she'd only hoped that time might have softened this. But clearly, all the old wounds had only festered. She swallowed, trying desperately to frame her questions carefully. "After you left Iain, things were not the same. Slowly, I don't know, it took around a year, maybe less. It all began to break down. Brae left for England, Quinn went up North, and Sebastian," she hesitated.

His eyes never met hers. He simply continued to stare forward as their pace came to a standstill. "Sebastian?" It was a question, although his tone was nearly devoid of emotion.

"Well, let's just say he's kept his distance after the divorce."

He turned away from her, staring off at the imposing church directly across the street from them. "Did I ever tell you I seriously considered becoming a priest as a young man?"

It was an odd disclosure for him to make now, considering the complete estrangement of their relationship. But it did summon the quick image of Iain Shaw as a young man, a fifteen-year-old boy, tall, thin with flashing eyes and that longish dark, brown hair. It made her smile. The idea of him as a priest seemed as ridiculous as she being a homemaker. "No," she simply stated.

He glanced over at her for the first time in many moments with a bit of a quick smile, "Yes, I suppose it was preposterous. But I was determined to dedicate myself to something." She glanced away from the intensity of his gaze. "So, the old group drifted apart. It doesn't seem all that tragic, Corey. I suppose we all grow up at some point."

"Yes, but as you know, our group went much deeper than ordinary friendships."

She looked back into his face, which had hardened a bit with the light of understanding. "What are you saying?"

Then softly, she explained, "It's been breached."

His eyes widened, then the expected question, "All of them?"

She shook her head, "No, not all Iain, but the Triquetra is gone."

He stared at her blankly for a moment, but then his jaw hardened. "My car isn't far from here. Let's go sit down, and you can tell me everything." He started walking quickly and deliberately as she struggled to keep pace. There was a familiar determination in his stride, one that simultaneously cheered and disturbed her.

It was more disquieting than she'd expected being this close to him again. "We could go to a coffee shop or a restaurant." She stammered a bit, hating the uncertainty she heard in her voice.

His face was set stonily — best poker face among all of us, Brae had always said. But that was back when Brae was enamored of everything he did. "Then we could be heard. That wouldn't do."

She glanced outside the car. They were parked in his white sedan along a small residential side street near the park. It wasn't particularly well-trafficked, and it did occur to her that she felt quite vulnerable here with Iain. There was a time, a brief time, when she felt he had the capacity for great violence. And the truth was that she scarcely knew him anymore. There had been so many years. Her impetuousness in contacting him very well could have been reckless.

She glanced back at him. He was watching her quietly with an unreadable expression. Her eyes widened as another unwelcome thought intruded. He'd shown signs of it when he was young. It occurred to her now that he might have further developed the skill while he was abroad. He might be canvassing her thoughts at this very moment. Corey deliberately went inward, erecting ancient barriers that she'd found unnecessary to use for many years. This was another disturbing thought, the possibility that she'd become quite soft.

Iain looked away from her outside the front window. "I thought they were to remain placed in a safe haven."

She blinked, taking a moment to reconnect with what he'd said. "Yes, they were."

He nodded, completing her thought. "Too powerful to be in anyone's control."

"Yes," she agreed. This was perhaps the one area where they could be in complete accord.

"Did you check on them, Corey?"

She shook her head, staring forward, feeling quite uncomfortable in engaging his gaze directly. "No, I didn't. I mean, I never really tried. There seemed to be a finality to everything. I didn't think this was possible." She hated admitting that to him. It felt, in a way, like giving the enemy your battle plans.

He looked a bit surprised, "Really? Not ever tempted?"

She stared forward, "No, it never occurred to me."

His hand brushed her arm, and it caused a further chill to steal through her flesh. "Then how can you know this, be so sure?"

She sighed, ceasing to debate how much to tell him. If she were to secure his assistance, she must be candid. "I had a visitor late one night about a month ago."

"Who was it?"

She swallowed, her throat quite dry now. To most, what she was to say would seem quite nonsensical, quite deluded, but then again, given all they had experienced together— "It was my father."

She heard him emit a sound somewhere between a sigh and a breath. She knew what he was thinking, even without having his talent. After all, her father had been dead for ten years, ten long, quiet years.

She expected some sort of response. Perhaps, in some odd way, she expected some compassion. But in retrospect, given what had occurred, his reaction should have been entirely predictable. "A month? Are you telling me you waited a month to act on this?"

It felt like a punch. In telling him about her father, she had opened herself to him, her feelings, becoming vulnerable and, of course, giving him his opportunity. "No," her voice sounded like ice in her ears. "I didn't wait."

"Ah," it seemed accompanied by a soft laugh that was hollow in its emotion, but then again, that might have been her imagination. "So, whose help did you seek first? I'm assuming you didn't travel outside of the original group."

"No, that would have been unwarranted," she answered quietly.

He smiled, but it was an ugly smile, a cutting one. "Yes, who?"

His tone continued to shake her. It almost felt like a command. "Brae, I spoke to Brae."

"Yes, naturally, dear Brae. How is she?"

She wrapped her hands around her arms. Moments ago, the car had felt stuffy, but not now. Now it was so cold. "She's made a new life for herself. She's afraid to get involved again."

"Yes, yes, she was always the brave one, wasn't she?"

"That's not fair."

"And you, you would defend her to me. How interesting. Who else, Corey, Quinn?"

Her breath felt sharp in her chest. It was like an inquisition. "Quinn, he's been ill. He couldn't help." She managed to get out.

"What's wrong with him?" Amazingly, there was compassion in his voice. But then it was true. He'd always had a soft spot where Quinn was concerned.

"A resurgence of the leukemia. I couldn't ask him to expend his energy on this."

"Of course not. I remember the last time." His voice had softened ever so perceptively, reminding her of the man he used to be. And just as quickly, that slight humanity was gone. "So, who does that leave? Yes, of course, our friend Sebastian. I'm quite sure he would have been more than happy to help."

That cold feeling crept around her heart again. "No, I didn't ask him."

"No?" he asked mockingly. "Why? He would be the obvious choice."

Her voice was controlled, measured. "Because I don't trust him."

He leaned back against the headrest on the top of his seat, and soft laughter came from him, "Well, I find that funny. Now, you don't trust him. Well, that's too bad, Corey, because I will tell you with no hesitation that hell will have to freeze over before I lift a finger to help you." And she knew at that moment that he'd spent the last half an hour with her just so that he could refuse her.

CHAPTER 2

BRAE

Iain watched coolly as Corey headed down the street back onto the grounds of Audubon Park. She'd taken it well, not as he'd expected. The girl he'd known would have fought with him. The woman he'd left behind would have raked him over the coals before she made her exit. But the figure he watched disappearing from his sight now was someone different — someone weary, someone guarding herself as though her life depended on it. He'd sensed it immediately, these changes, and it bothered him. He wanted an object to bestow all his grievances and all his old, justified resentments upon, but she didn't make it easy. It wasn't at all as he'd envisioned it to be.

When he'd first received her message asking for a meeting, he was outraged at her audacity. But she'd done it and certainly deserved what she'd gotten for it. His throat tightened. She'd said nothing when he refused her, just quietly left.

But he didn't feel triumphant or satisfied — just an old sadness that had set in some time after all the anger had left him.

Overwhelmed with frustration and disappointment, Corey abandoned her jewelry-making attempts. Sarah Brennan's tiger eye pendant would have to wait. It wasn't as if she were on a schedule. She wandered through the old house on Esplanade Avenue tonight, desperately wishing she were elsewhere. It had been her father's house. Her mother had died when she was only six, and an older brother, who was now rarely in contact with her, had left immediately after college. Samuel seemed more than driven to put his childhood behind him, while Corey seemed less determined to escape hers. Although she did leave for a while, there were a few years in her twenties when she'd lived with a friend in New York City. It was a harried but innocent time, an odd thing to say of that place. She'd spent time in a creative community, developing her love of photography. But then there was word that her father had become ill. So, as a good daughter, she'd returned and never looked back.

She sipped her brandy and sank into a large den chair near the unlit fireplace. She sat in the shadows, unable or unwilling to summon the energy to put on the lights. Claire, her friend from New York, had drifted away from her. But her other friends, she shivered although the darkened room was not cool, she had renewed her acquaintance with them.

She leaned back and closed her eyes, allowing herself to slip back into more pleasant times. It was easier to do this now rather than even begin to tackle what she was facing. It was Brae back then who had drawn her into everything — back then, when all seemed well.

They were meeting on Nashville Avenue. A party, reunion of sorts, Brae had told her. Brae Ryan was a vibrant redhead whose energy level had surpassed Corey's from the moment she'd met her, and that was years ago in the Ecole Issoire private school — an upper-class establishment where five troubled souls had somehow drifted together to forge a bond of sorts. It might have been their problems, that neediness, which drew them to each other. Brae's difficulties had been more obvious than others — divorced parents and a problematic relationship with a stepparent.

Corey had literally almost bumped into her in the French Quarter one sunny afternoon about two weeks after her father had gotten out of the hospital.

Oddly, Brae seemed elated. It felt unexpected somehow that her presence would be so significant to someone. "Corey, I had no idea you were in town," she began, hooking her arm in hers and leading her to a nearby bench in front of St. Louis Cathedral. Corey had wanted to get out of the house for at least a few hours. They'd hired a nurse, and her father had insisted. Her father had always been a curious mixture of good manners and belligerence. So, she'd taken her camera, determined for a precious little time of solitude and creativity. But then, all of that was sidetracked.

"Well, Dad's been ill." She glanced away, watching the artisans positioned with their stands along the side of the square, oddly envying them in the moment. "It's cancer, but the prognosis is good."

Brae smiled. She had a lovely, wide smile that exuded an infectious warmth. She was extremely intelligent, but that was a quality that some did not take the time to perceive, so distracting was her beauty. "So, are you staying on or going back to New York?"

She pulled her long dark hair back away from her face. It was hot. It was autumn here, but they were still sitting in the sunlight. "I don't know. I guess that depends on Dad. I can't just leave him on his own right now. What are you doing?"

"Working in the art gallery on Royal Street, sort of learning the trade."

Brae's family owned one of the city's older and more prestigious galleries, but she was surprised that her old high school chum had opted to be drawn into the family fold, problematic as it was. "Well, I'm surprised. I thought you were distancing yourself from the Ryan dynasty."

She laughed, "Yes, well, it seems I have a people talent. And once I learn the ropes, Dad has promised to let me go into the negotiating and buying portion of the business. It kills time until I figure out what I really want to do."

Corey's eyes were drawn again to the artisans lined up along the black wrought iron fence surrounding Jackson Square. "Yes, that's the trick."

Brae nudged her. It was so odd how they were slipping into that familiar high school banter of so long ago. She hadn't realized how she'd missed it. "What about you? Any grand passions in New York City? You never write."

She did feel a bit embarrassed refocusing on her friend. It was an odd thing that she hadn't stayed in touch. Deep down, she wasn't sure if it was deliberate or not. Perhaps part of her had yearned to start something new and cut ties to all that had come before. "Sorry about that, and yes, I did have a grand passion for Central Park and Broadway."

Brae laughed, tossing her shoulder-length red locks about, just as Corey remembered her doing in high school, "No, men, the men in New York."

"Were like men anywhere except maybe a little more self-absorbed and brusquer. And what about you, Brae?"

"Yes, I just broke up with another love of my life. But I do have some good news, something to stir things up a bit."

Corey felt an odd fluttering as though she knew exactly what Brae was going to say before she did. "There's a party tonight, gathering sort of. I want you to come with me." It was odd, a reticence in her to hear anymore. She glanced around at the quiet surrounding them, and part of her simply wanted to slip back into it, unnoticed by life. "The old group," and then Brae bent closer to her, whispering in her ear, "the Marguillers, we're all meeting at Sebastian's tonight. And some others. He has a fiancé now, but I think he brings her, so I won't be the only female in the bunch." And then she squeezed her arm, "But now that you're with us, that's not necessary."

She murmured, "Everyone will be there?"

She nodded, "Yes, all in the same city now. Although Quinn left for a while, but he's back. And you should see Iain. You'll scarcely recognize him. Not at all like you remember."

And her throat tightened, but she couldn't seem to utter the excuses that had risen to her lips.

She'd checked with her father several times before she left that evening. "It's not necessary that I go if you need me here tonight."

He'd shaken his head groggily. He was still on pain medication. The disease had spread quite extensively, and the corrective surgery had been rather radical. "I'm fine. Celia is just next door. You should go."

"I have my phone on me. You can reach me anytime."

And then his glassy blue-gray eyes had focused on her face directly. "What is it, Corey? You seem like you're looking for a reason to stay."

She sat down in the chair next to the hospital bed that had been set up in his room. "No," she muttered, a bit unconvincingly. "I'm just worried about you."

The hand still attached to the IV tube reached over and lightly patted hers. "There's no need to worry. I'm not going anywhere until it's my time, and nothing you or I do will change that."

She smiled, still feeling butterflies churning in her stomach at the prospect of reuniting with her old friends.

"So, it's just you and your Dad in that old house again?"

She sat next to Brae in her red Mustang, an optimum sports car for her vivacious friend. "Yes," she murmured. "Me and Dad. Does Sebastian live far?"

"No, just down Nashville Avenue. He has a townhouse there. So, Samuel doesn't visit?" Brae rambled on, seeming intent on digging up as much information as she could.

"Not often," Corey murmured in distraction. Her mind was whirling. She'd remembered Sebastian's parents had a house in the Garden District. And they were probably as well off or more so than Brae's father. So, a townhouse on Nashville Avenue, well, that did seem appropriate for him. From what Brae said, he had just finished law school at Tulane. Sebastian was the dedicated sort, not one to waste time to find oneself. It was odd to her. She was only twenty-five but felt as though much more time had passed. "What's Quinn doing now?" she asked.

She smiled, "I think learning the antique business. But I don't know if it will last. He's a bit of a drifter."

"Yes, I remember." She looked into the darkness as they turned onto a gated road beyond which were rows and rows of expensive-looking townhomes, lovely but curiously the same, not much to distinguish one from another. Brae stilled the car, talking to the man in the small guard house. She hadn't asked about Iain, which was curious because she did want to know.

It was Quinn who had unceremoniously opened the door as they reached the landing. Corey was cheered to see him. His smiling face hadn't changed much since they'd last met, which was about two or maybe three years in her estimation. Brae, with no reticence, hugged him gregariously, then spontaneously grabbed Corey's hand, almost dragging her across the threshold. "Look who I've got with me, everyone."

Her whole plan of making a quiet entrance at that moment was wholeheartedly thrown out the window. Quinn caught her in a warm hug. "You look amazing. New York must have agreed with you." She smiled at the delight in his soft brown eyes.

"Well, it's nice to be home."

And then, just beyond him, another figure slowly approached her. Sebastian was dressed casually, but she noted in expensive clothes. And she had to admit he had changed. She remembered upon leaving a young man with unruly, light-brown hair and always a bit of grizzle on his chin. But now he was clean-shaven, short, clipped hair, and well-dressed. He'd always been a bit rebellious of his parent's lifestyle, but it all seemed different. Now, he appeared to be embracing it. "Hello, Corey," he murmured, taking her hand and softly kissing her cheek. "You look well."

"You too," she answered, noting a pretty blond woman standing just behind him. He seemed to follow the direction of her eyes and straightened up, holding his hand out for his companion. "Um, sorry, Corey Knight, I'd like you to meet my fiancée, Amanda Carlyle."

She smiled immediately, taking in the way Sebastian's fiancée clung to his hand. Amanda, in response, spoke in a light but evidently cultured voice, "Glad to meet you, Corey. Bat has spoken so kindly about you."

The nickname Bat slammed home hard and threatened an unwarranted ripple of giggles to erupt somewhere from the deepest reaches of her soul. She raised her eyes and met Quinn's twinkling ones. And then, from across the room, she heard a deep but familiar voice. "Yes, well, maybe Bat would be so kind to get our friend Corey here a drink before she gets nauseous from all this reacquainting." With a frown, Sebastian stepped back a bit, allowing her to see the author of the jarring intrusion. Iain was across the room leaning on the mantle of a fireplace with a detached but amused grin. In the moment, he seemed the antithesis of Sebastian, dressed in blue jeans and a black button-down shirt. He was as she remembered, not as skinny, nor hair quite as long, but still bearing the essence of that very wild and unpredictable boy.

It was odd, as she remembered the feeling clearly now. Back then, she'd not connected its significance. How could she? There was nothing to compare it to. No one she'd ever met, not in New York, not in her years in New Orleans before that, had elicited such an odd response from her — as though he had actually physically reached into her heart and caused it to thump oddly, powerfully, nearly like a jolt. She couldn't say it was pleasant nor unpleasant, only that it had occurred.

She drifted toward him, a rush of a thousand teenage memories accompanying her. She tried to smile but wasn't at all sure if the task was accomplished. The odd moment had her manifesting off in some altered state where the normal rules of existence felt thrown out the window. "Good to see you, Iain."

And he was nodding but not smiling as he'd done at her entrance. He moved closer, close enough so their exchange could remain exclusive. His green eyes seemed much darker than she remembered, canvassing her deliberately, lingering on her face. And then he murmured, lowering his voice. "This suits you, Corey, this new world-weary aura you're carrying around. Evidently, the city did you some good."

She frowned, unsure how to take his assessment, probably a mix of a compliment tinged with his sarcasm. "Well, I did like New York, but it isn't home."

A slight smile flickered across his lips, "No, this place is distinct. So, what are your plans?"

Again, her heart gave that curious thump. She'd forgotten his directness. What took most people a destination of several hours to tactfully arrive at, he dove into in a matter of seconds. And then, from her side, Sebastian had suddenly appeared, slipping a glass of white wine into her hands. "It's a Chablis. Hope it's still your drink of choice."

She smiled at him. There was an ease in Sebastian's manner that seemed to diffuse any other tensions. "Thanks, that's fine."

"So, will you be here long, Corey?" Funny how Sebastian's question quite succinctly echoed Iain's but felt much less intrusive coming from him. Iain quite casually reached behind to the mantle where he'd left his schooner of beer, seemingly a bit less interested in her response now that his friend had posed the same question.

"Actually, I'm not sure. My father's been ill."

And then Iain's eyes darted back to her face. "Is he all right?"

It felt so odd, sharing like this. In the month that she'd been home, it had only been she and her father and a mass of doctors and nurses, strangers, who were the only ones privy to their deepest fears. And opening up about it all, now felt remarkably like prying open the rusty door to a dank, ugly dungeon. She swallowed, feeling oddly incapable of uttering a glossy version just now. "I'm not sure." She swallowed on a dry throat, "It's been rough. The cancer had spread, and they had to do some radical surgery, some organs," she said with difficulty. "Well, suffice to say, he won't have the same quality of life as before. He prides himself on his independence. I think, in a way, he hates me being here. He feels like he's a burden."

She felt Sebastian's hand on her shoulder, light but reassuring. "Look, Corey, if there's anything I can do to help. Hire medical people, anything."

She shook her head, feeling oddly exposed at her disclosure. "No, no, we have a nurse helping out and more doctors than I'm sure are necessary. It's just going to take time, that's all."

Then another voice intruded, "Bat, Brae was telling me there's a full moon tonight. Let's go out on the patio to see it." Corey saw an odd, fleeting expression that she could only describe as frustration flicker across Sebastian's handsome features.

Then, briefly, he reached out and squeezed Corey's hand. "So good to have you back," he murmured, then moved across the spacious room toward the glass French doors on the far side. Corey glanced back at Iain, who had distanced himself somewhat at Sebastian's appearance. He wore a distant expression as though he were studying something odd. "Seems like my old friend is going to have his hands full with that one," he muttered, his eyes still on the place where Sebastian and Amanda had left the room only moments before.

She took a sip from the glass of wine that had been chilling her fingertips for some moments. It was good but drier than she liked. She found it surprising to what degree Sebastian was now embracing this lifestyle. In the past, it had always seemed quite repugnant to him. "They seem to be an odd pair."

Iain looked at her, his expression quite amused. "You think so?"

She shrugged, "Not on the surface, I suppose, but in substance."

"But Corey, you've been gone for a while. Sebastian has only been interested in operating on the surface for some time."

His comment puzzled and disturbed her to some degree. Her eyes scanned the room. Brae talked with animation to Quinn, who seemed a complacent but slightly disinterested observer. Brae seemed frenetic, as though she were actively putting on a show, and in contrast, Quinn appeared disconnected. There was an element here that she felt amongst them all and, oddly, perhaps in herself as well. They'd drifted from their center. "You're seeing it." Her eyes flew back to his face, and she wondered about him, about Iain if it was the same for him.

"What do you mean?"

He smiled, "You don't have to be afraid of the truth, Corey. We've all drifted off course." Then, lightly, he brushed her cheek with his hand. "But our compass is back."

CHAPTER 3

OLD MR. KNIGHT

He'd thought of stopping at a nearby restaurant and having dinner on his way back home. But his mind was so engaged that instead he'd pulled into the driveway of the small house that he'd rented nearly four months earlier on Chestnut Street. It was not very far from where he and Corey had met in the park. It would've been easy enough to bring her to the house to talk, but then he'd known she would have been too uncomfortable. And if he was being honest, and he was not a man who engaged in the pointless activity of lying to himself, he didn't want her there. He didn't want her memory anywhere near the life he was leading now.

Iain felt grim as he stepped out of his white sedan. It was disconcerting. Things hadn't gone as he'd expected, not as he'd anticipated. He'd become more disciplined in the last ten years of his life. He'd managed to reign in the wild emotions he had so often allowed to take dominion over him. That was why he'd returned to the city. There was no family here for him anymore. Both his parents had died some time ago, and his one sister lived several states away. There was no reason for him to return, too many bridges burned. But he had done so anyway, to prove that he had mastered what was.

The front den was sparsely decorated, with a sofa and a few chairs — no artwork on the cedar paneled walls. He wanted it clean, stripped down. The room had become dusky in the fading light of the afternoon, but he didn't put on the standing lamp near the sofa or open any of the drapes. He sunk into a chair, dissatisfied.

Having some success had its drawbacks. He was a sculptor who now sold his work, whose work was now being exhibited in galleries — a fact that no doubt would have shocked his father if he were still alive to see it. But Iain had even managed to make peace with that as well. He had not spent his time idly. He had studied and learned from Masters.

He closed his eyes, and a face rose out of the darkness. It wasn't Corey's, although her presence still dominated his mind. It was someone else's — old Mr. Knight, Clayton Knight, with his intense, blue-gray eyes.

It hadn't been long before the old man died. He'd asked Iain specifically to come to see him, something that had seemed puzzling even to his daughter because, by that time, he and Corey were already at odds.

He closed his eyes, allowing the sensations of the memory to wash over him. That was how he triggered the past most acutely, its textures, smells, sounds. The room was too cold for a dying man. He'd been a little surprised to see one of the windows open, its light shears fluttering from a breeze. Instinctively, he'd moved to close it, but Clayton Knight raised an emaciated arm to still him. "No, it makes me feel connected to the world." He motioned to a chair beside the bed for Iain to sit. He remembered thinking how weak and hollowed-out the old man's voice sounded. When he'd first stepped foot in this place over a decade earlier, the master of the house's voice nearly reverberated through the halls, echoing with an intimidating power. Everyone seemed shaken by his presence, except Corey, of course. The brusqueness of her father's manner had always seemed unnoticed by her. Whatever everyone else saw when they encountered the imposing figure of Clayton Knight, she saw something entirely different.

"I was surprised you asked for me, Mr. Knight," he said quietly.

The man in the hospital bed nodded, his face ashen and nearly sunken. "I imagine so, my boy. But when your time comes, and you can feel the next world beckoning so strongly, you might also feel the need to put things in order before you leave."

He leaned back in the chair, caught up in a maelstrom of emotion, compassion for the old man but defensiveness concerning the obligation he now felt to allow private and sensitive issues to be aired. "Mr. Knight, I have great respect for you, sir, but I hope this doesn't have to do with Corey."

There was something that flickered across the tired blue-gray eyes but then was gone in an instant. "No, my boy, your personal life, with or without my daughter, isn't my business. You two will have to puzzle that out without an old man's interference. This has to do with another obligation altogether." And then he weakly pulled himself a little higher on the mound of pillows he was resting on. "You, my boy, and your friends, this group of yours, have taken on your shoulders a great responsibility, although I suspect some of you don't view it quite that way." The image of Sebastian quickly floated across his mind, and then on its heels, Quinn's smiling face. And in that moment, he knew exactly why he'd been summoned here.

"You're talking about the objects."

A smile briefly flickered across the gaunt face. "The objects, is that what you call it? What a benign word for something so potentially destructive."

"It's odd, Mr. Knight, that you would consider them destructive."

"It would be more than foolish not to. Anything, and I mean anything that has the potential for such power, can be used destructively. And the sooner you acknowledge this and act accordingly, the safer the rest of us will be."

"You think they should be destroyed." He jumped to the obvious conclusion, which, of course, was erroneous. Clayton Knight was many things but obvious was not one of them.

The old man sighed deeply, closing his eyes for so long that Iain thought for a moment that he might have fallen asleep. But then they flickered open again, radiating the bright life force that this powerful soul still clung to. "Destroy? I don't think any of us have that capability."

He felt a little puzzled, "You don't?"

Again, a smile, and as he remembered now, it had been a bit of an indulgent one, "You still really don't know what you're dealing with, do you, my boy? That's all right. We'll chalk it up to youthful arrogance." He bristled a bit internally at the comment, which did not go unnoticed by the elderly man in the bed. "It's all right. No one had more of it at your age than I did. Unfortunately, life tends to beat it out of us and humble us. But not to worry, you're not quite there yet."

"What do you want me to do?"

"Yes, yes, best to get down to business. You'll find the plans I outlined for the safekeeping of the objects in the top drawer of my bureau. I'm putting you in charge of this, Iain. Of all of you, I feel you can be most trusted."

His words of trust he found oddly chilled him rather than cheered him. "I don't understand. Surely your—"

"Yes," he nodded. "Corey is such a strong woman, but not to be accused of being biased, I find that women tend to sacrifice themselves too much. She has that capacity, unfortunately, even if it means betraying her essence. You, I believe, are a pure soul. That does not make you particularly good, but I do not believe you would ever compromise who you are, Iain. So, if I have your promise, I can rest easy that these plans will be carried out."

He didn't bother to ask about the others, Sebastian, Quinn, or Brae. And he didn't bother to ask why he was now taking such extreme steps. It was clear to him and the old man that, like the Roman Empire, the Marguillers were decaying from within. And such power should not remain with those with divergent and conflicting ambitions. Within a week, Corey had eloped with Sebastian, and before the close of the month, the old man had died.

There had been one last gathering of the Marguillers. With their help but not their knowledge, Iain had followed Clayton Knight's plan and placed the items out of their reach, all their grasp, for all time — or so he'd believed. His eyes flickered open in the shadows of the room. But he could still hear the old man's voice in his mind. "I do not believe you would ever compromise who you are, Iain." And he, at that moment, realized that old Clayton Knight was right. He had not compromised who he was, not once, and he had traveled a difficult and lonely road because of it.

· CHAPTER 4 ·

QUINN

It had only been several days after Sebastian's get-together on Nashville Avenue that it began. Looking back, Corey hadn't expected much contact from her old friends. The reacquaintance had felt a bit awkward on many levels, as though the friends of youth had evolved in such divergent ways that the old bonds had disintegrated. But then, upon reflection, that was comfortable for her to believe. It would reaffirm her desire for distance, for an odd need to withdraw from the familiar. As it was, however, this inclination was taken out of her hands.

"Hello," she'd answered the phone. The housekeeper and the nurse who had been hired to make things easier in her father's convalescence evidently were out of pocket for the moment.

"Corey, it's Iain."

Her heart thumped a bit at hearing his voice. A strange flush swept over her as well tucked away memories from high school seemed to gain a new life. "Hi," she murmured, still feeling a bit surprised at the sound of his voice.

"How's your Dad today?" Again, direct, with purpose, she thought.

It was nearly eleven in the morning. Already, the nurse had gotten her father out of bed for a brief walk down the hall. "He's doing all right, sleeping now. He had a busy morning."

"Well, I'd like to spring you for a while. I'm working on a new project and need some inspiration. Thought you might want to bring your camera."

She swallowed tentatively, "What sort of inspiration?"

"Can you be ready in a half hour? I'll buy you lunch."

"Where are we going?" she continued to inquire.

And this time, there was laughter in his voice, "You'll see."

He picked her up in a truck, a well-used, superficially nicked, and dented pickup truck. But it made her smile. Iain was what he was. When he knocked on the door, he was dressed in blue jeans and a loose plaid shirt that looked a bit dusty, as though he'd been working on some sculpture up until the moment he came to get her. She'd dressed casually as well, jeans and a black fitted sweater she'd picked up during her time in New York. She'd swept her long dark hair into a ponytail, just out of convenience.

When he walked into the house, his eyes swept over the foyer for a moment with an odd expression and then back to her face. It was like the other night at the party. His gaze was so direct — unlike many people she'd met while she was away, who were furtive and malleable. There was a slight smile, "It's been so long since I've been here. It's strange."

"I know. I had that feeling when I came back. But I think it had more to do with how I'd changed rather than this place."

Focused now on her, he took her hand in his. "Changed, have you, Corey? Then it will be interesting finding out how much."

A bit surprised, she pulled away, and he only smiled at that. "You didn't say where we were going."

"No, I didn't. Are you ready?"

She felt a bit of reticence sweep over her. "I have to check on Dad before I go."

He leaned against the door. "Fine, I'll wait for you and trip down memory lane while you're gone."

She headed down the hallway toward the staircase, murmuring, "Don't hit your head while you're tripping along."

And behind her, she heard that deep laughter that was unique to him.

He knew exactly where he lived, in a renovated shotgun house on Magazine Street. Once he'd returned to the city, he did take the time to find everyone's whereabouts, just so that he could, at the very least, avoid contact. Iain had no desire for reacquaintance, although several times he had considered visiting Quinn Murdoch. Out of all the old group, he was the one he'd felt no resentment toward. Quinn was an odd type, to say the least. He'd always managed to be involved and yet keep himself at a healthy emotional distance — no small task in that group. But then there had always been his health, sporadic bouts of illness since he was a teenager. And in some respects, Iain supposed, this had become the focus of his life, leaving little room for other centers.

He hadn't called first because the whole visit was an impulsive one. Yesterday, after meeting with Corey, Iain was determined not to get involved. This morning, after a fitful night of restlessness and dreams, he had found there seemed to be little choice but to do the opposite. But the question became where to begin.

He'd parked his car on the street and walked down the block to Quinn's house. Breathing deeply and allowing no hesitation, he rang the doorbell. It was some moments before the wide, light blue painted door swung open, but when it did, it took him by some surprise. The face was gaunt, and the frame very thin, akin to emaciated. But a brilliant smile illuminated his visage, finally echoing the man he had once known. He was holding a cane, but he let it drop to the side as he moved to embrace him. "Iain, I can't believe it."

A flood of warmth reached into that cold buffer he had cultivated around his heart. "So good to see you, my friend, so good."

The den was warm and cozily decorated with paintings and collectibles throughout the room. If Quinn was anything, he was a collector and had always been looking for the odd item that would appreciate in value. And up on the white mantelpiece of the fireplace sat the sculpture that Iain himself had done long ago, a period piece — *Cavalry Man on His Horse* but done with the odd sweeps and curves that gave it a modernistic twist. It was carved in a large piece of brown limestone that he'd come into possession of just a year before he'd left New Orleans altogether. Quinn had always admired it, and Iain had given it to him as a going-away present as he had expected never to see him again. It was a valuable piece now, but at that time, he had desired only to divest himself of the past.

Quinn appeared in the doorway, his hands holding two steaming mugs of tea. "Hope you can stomach chamomile tea. I'm off the caffeine for now. New reports that it interferes with the chemo treatments."

"You're taking chemotherapy now?" he asked, as Quinn handed him one of the steaming mugs and indicated he sit on the rose-colored Davenport antique sofa.

He nodded, sitting down near the fireplace in a matching bergère chair. He had to admit he found the décor more akin to an old-fashioned tearoom than a bachelor's house. "Yes, the doctors thought a bone marrow transplant this time around probably wouldn't be any good. I have had two over the years, you know. One early on and then while I was away up North."

"They didn't help?"

He smiled that wide, whimsical grin he remembered as a boy — the one that seemed to be laughing at life's cruel ironies. "Sure, for a while, but nothing seems to stick permanently. Right now, we're just trying to drive the beast back into remission. Give me a few years, maybe just months of peace." He sighed deeply, "But not to worry. It's my dragon to fight. Done it all my life. It's you I'm interested in." Again, the smile, "The prodigal son returns. Never thought I'd see the day, my friend."

He leaned back on the uncomfortable brocade sofa, "Yes, life takes interesting turns."

"Yes, and then we tend to orchestrate some of those turns."

Iain glanced away from the bright, interested gaze of his old friend. Again, a bit perplexed by the décor, his eyes passed over a wide vase of fresh flowers on an ornate lemonwood end table near the tasseled damask drapery of the window. "So, not to knock your decorating, Quinn, but even this seems a bit on the fanciful side for you."

He nodded in agreement, "Yes, I know. It's nearly nauseating. But it's a business move. I don't get out as much as I'd like, so I bring clients here, searching for odd collectibles, unusual antiques. And many are older women. They like the Victorian feel. Gives them more confidence in my capabilities."

"Finally, put your packrat instincts to good use."

"Yes," and then he pointed over his head to the sculpture on the mantelpiece. "I've even entertained some amazing offers on that. Now that you've become bankable. I knew it was only a matter of time, but I haven't had the heart to let it go." And then the smile faded a bit, "But being sick is expensive. One day that may win out over nostalgia."

He tried the tea, ignoring the slight scorch of his lips at the heat. "I'd rather you make good use of it than letting it collect dust."

"Yes well, I'm still holding out for a miracle. After all, you're here again, and ten years ago, I would have declared that an impossibility."

"Yes, as would I."

Quinn sipped his tea, seeming to relax a bit. "So, you never told me. What was the inspiration for that piece? It did seem unique even for you."

He leaned back. His mind was being forced to furrow into painful areas. "Actually, a tomb at one of the old cemeteries in town."

"Ah, St. Louis."

He hesitated for a moment, considering if it were appropriate at all to open this particular door. "No, it was Metairie Cemetery. I went there with Corey, well, in the early days." Just the mention of that cemetery, let alone Corey in conjunction with it, dropped an awkward chill upon their reunion.

Quinn forged on, seeming reluctant to acknowledge that this place had been mentioned between them. "Have you seen her? Corey, I mean, since you've come back."

It was a bit startling, the casual way that Quinn had inquired. Dangerous ground they were skimming across today. "Briefly."

Quinn eyed him with curiosity in that prying way as though he'd found something interesting to pick at. "Well, I have seen Corey just a few weeks ago as well."

"You did?" Iain made himself sound deliberately disinterested.

"Yes, it was out of the blue, not unlike your visit. We have spoken every few months since I moved back, but more rarely lately. I have to say I have been concerned that she's becoming a bit of a hermit. She's still a very beautiful woman with a lot of life ahead of her. It would be a pity if she allowed a bad marriage to be the end of her."

"What did she want?" he asked, pointedly sidestepping the rest of Quinn's comments.

"Oh, you mean recently. I don't really know. It was odd. She seemed anxious but never really let on to what it was about. And, of course, she was concerned about me, the health and all."

As Quinn spoke, Iain was beginning to get a sense of that conversation. He could feel her here in the room, not see, but clearly feel. He breathed in deeply, aware of the pressure of her body on the couch next to him. She'd sat here but more toward the arm of the sofa. He could feel heat emanating from where she was, as well as the anxiety seeping out of her.

Quinn's voice droned on, "She did ask about Brae. Brae is still in England, you know. If I'd heard anything from her and about you also. She seemed hesitant about that. I think she was digging for something. But never really said what."

The emotions were clear — upset, worry. He let his hand drift on the sofa, more to the area where she'd been. It sent a strange rush to his head. He could feel himself touching her hand. Almost, almost — she'd almost asked Quinn, but she couldn't. He looked so frail. She couldn't burden him. He pulled his hand away, yanking himself perhaps a bit too harshly into the present. Quinn was watching him closely with no expression. "All right?" he asked.

"Yes, never said what it was all about?"

He shrugged, "Never said. Is that why you're here too?"

"What do you mean?"

Again, the slight smile, as though it all were amusing, "About whatever was never said?"

When he left Quinn, he hadn't intended to head in that direction, hadn't intended, but then again, curiosity took hold. Although some of the city seemed remolded from the years after the storm, the road leading to the Metairie cemetery seemed largely untouched. He drove past its iron gates and made a left into the old section. He could have driven through. There were dirt pathways available for vehicles, but he found a place to park, as he had no particular destination. The leaves crunched beneath his shoes as he began walking toward the area he had no intention of going. It was a row of tall tombs, family crypts decorated with angels, religious effigies, and other symbolic monuments housing many generations — all unique and individualized. He breathed deeply in the air as the memories wrapped around him with a force he hadn't anticipated, those things he hadn't allowed himself to recall for fear of damage. The anger he could remember, the betrayals had become even palatable, but not this, not this — so much more toxic.

"I feel drawn in here as if I can feel the emotion all around me."

"You're very sensitive, Corey."

She turned back to him with a curious smile. "Now, that's not something people usually accuse me of."

"Then they're blind."

He walked on, the memories slamming into his chest.

"She's weeping."

"Do you think?"

"What do you think?"

"Just allowing the desolation to take her over."

He stopped in front of it, the tomb, his eyes passing over the inscription. Several steps led up to the small structure's closed doors. But that day, they'd been open.

She'd walked up the steps, but in his gauzy memory, it seemed as though she'd glided, hesitating on the threshold.

"What's the matter?" he'd asked. But he knew, felt it in his skin, felt her in his skin.

She shook her head, "I don't know. I feel afraid."

Then he'd walked behind her, leaving his sketch pad on the ground, and placed the palm of his hand on her back. He felt a slight tremor pass through her; then she moved forward. She knelt beside the statue of the prostrate angel who was bent over an altar and lightly touched the cold statue's hand. He stood next to her, hearing her breathing. And then she looked up into his eyes, the soft brown eyes fired with lights. "It feels powerful," was her whisper.

He refocused on the present, mounting the steps with purpose. And placing his hands on the iron pulls that opened the tomb. Within was, as he remembered, a beautiful statue of an angel draped in sorrow dramatically over an altar. He reached into his pocket, took out a soft felt pen, and marked the symbol inconspicuously in the angel's cold palm. He felt a thread of sharp yet old energy pass through him. He straightened up, taking one last look. He braced himself, reigning in the old memories. He'd made a choice now, and there was no turning back. He strode purposefully back to his car, allowing himself to spend no further time wandering in the past.

CHAPTER 5

THE HOUSE ON ESPLANADE

They spent what little was left of the morning roaming through the Greenwood and Odd Fellow cemeteries at the foot of Canal Boulevard. Someone who didn't know New Orleans might think it was an odd destination bordering on macabre. But once one began to travel the silent pathways between the tombs, it became readily clear. The places were dripping with artwork — statues, carvings, silent aesthetically crafted monuments paying homage to the departed.

She'd brought her camera, while he'd brought a simple sketch pad and pencils to mark out his impressions. "This all right?" She thought she'd heard him murmur, but she was already drawn deep into her impressions and all the stories that echoed through the hallowed grounds.

"You're kidding, right?"

"Are you taking pictures or not?"

He'd squatted down next to the bottom steps of a tomb, lightly brushing away debris from an aging inscription. *"Death shall have no dominion and will not take her from us."*

"I can't stand hearing that kind of stuff." He glanced up, his eyes reflecting the first signs of concern since he'd brought her through the gates of the Metairie Cemetery.

"Because of your Dad?"

She shook her head, although that was a thought. On the surface, one might think Mr. Iain Shaw callous for bringing her here after her father had had such a close brush with death. But she knew better or perhaps felt it. He came here with purpose and thought perhaps to share his purpose with a kindred soul. "No, that's not it. It's the pain in the words. It tears at me."

He nodded, glancing down again while slightly brushing his fingertips along the surface of the carved stone. "I don't feel it in the words, but I can feel it here, in the stone itself, as if it holds that pain."

She stared at him, feeling a chill ripple through her. That was why he sculpted. The stone spoke to him. "Do you want to go?" he asked.

She frowned explicitly. They were stuck here somehow in this moment, and they had to walk through it to somewhere else where there was air again to breathe. "No, let's suck dry what this place has to offer."

And then he laughed, "That's my Corey. My emotional carnivore."

She couldn't remember if she smiled at him or just began to take photos. Some photos were in an album, locked away — maybe in the attic, in a closet, out of reach where they could no longer make her feel the weight of all she had lost.

Corey felt a chill pass through her. She pulled the woven shawl she wore more tightly around her. It was late in the day, and she'd spent much of it dragging around the old house just taking care of small, time-consuming tasks. She was trying to avoid dealing with the present, dealing with the dilemma she had lying at her feet now. Of course, she could go on and avoid the whole problem, which at present seemed a plausible course. Her father should have given someone else this monumental responsibility, laid this at someone else's feet, someone more capable, more willing — who had more to give.

She picked up a mug of hot tea, slowly sipping it. Now that Iain had closed the door on her, there weren't many tangible options. Brae made it clear she had no intention of lifting one finger to help, and Quinn— She sighed deeply, remembering their last visit. He was so frail. It seemed unfair to draw him into this. But then again, she hadn't been so desperate then.

A familiar face rose in her mind, one that caused mixed feelings, disdain, guilt, and, yes, undeniably some abstract kinship — a maelstrom of conflicting emotions. It had been several years since she'd even laid eyes on him. And she preferred it that way. The last time she'd been walking down Royal Street after leaving a meeting with a prospective client interested in having a piece of jewelry custom-made. Her mind had been occupied, but she felt the shift in energy at his presence. She stopped and looked across the street where he was standing, watching her. Sebastian appeared remarkably unchanged. Not unlike the day she'd left their marriage. Her immediate impulse was to keep moving, walk away, and he would, she thought in that moment, have deserved as much. But her feet felt rooted deeply into the French Quarter sidewalk. When he reached her, he wasn't smiling, but his dark eyes were wide.

"Corey, it's good to see you," he said softly. His face was clean-shaven. He hadn't sported a beard since those early days after college. "How are you?"

She didn't even manage a smile. At the moment, it seemed too arduous. "I'm well. But I have an appointment."

A smile flickered across the aristocratic face. Most women found him very handsome, but the word cold and, at times, detached had always accompanied her estimation of him. "Poised to flee." It was an assessment rather than a question.

"I'm sorry, Sebastian. I can't pretend things are harmonious where they're not. I don't have that kind of energy."

And then the warm eyes hardened in a way that had become all too familiar in their years together. "I'll always be here for you when you need me."

"I won't." It was the last thing she said before she turned and walked away.

He made it so easy, damn him. She was sure he would help. He would help and wouldn't drag her over the coals as Iain had gleefully done. He would make it easy and make her pay for it later. But later, she might think of a way around it. Vaguely, she heard the front doorbell ring. She was alone in the house and in no mood for visitors, so she tried to ignore it. But again, it chimed, and quite without thought, she drifted toward the front hallway. She wasn't expecting any visitors, and the housekeeper she employed came in only twice a week now. Without bothering to check who was there, she slowly swung open the massive front door to find Iain waiting outside with a disgruntled expression.

"Didn't think you were going to answer."

She frowned, stunned at his jarring manner, "Maybe I shouldn't have. What do you want?"

"Now, I think I'd like a cup of coffee," he stated rather matter-of-factly as though they had parted on the best of terms.

Her throat tightened at his glibness. "Look, I'm not in the mood."

And then she saw that old sparkle in his green eyes, "Now, is that any way to treat an old friend who has decided to help you."

It took a moment for his words to penetrate, and while she should have felt relief, that old anger flamed up inside her. "Oh, I hadn't noticed. Has hell frozen over?"

And then he smiled with some enthusiasm, "You know, my dearest. I think perhaps it has."

The house felt different and yet the same. The bombardment of sensations nearly smothered him as he made his way into the parlor of Clayton Knight's Esplanade mansion. The atmosphere in this house, as he remembered, had always been dense, but the years that had passed had layered it with a new thickness that he now found oppressive. He wondered distractedly if this was something recent or if his years away had sharpened his sensibilities to the point that he could now discern what had always been. And on the heels of that contemplation, he wondered, with a degree of concern, how Corey could stand living here, given her highly intuitive and reactive nature.

She silently handed him a white mug of what he assumed was his coffee and made her way across the room, resting her cup on the fireplace's mantle before turning to him with a deadpan expression. Besides being taught with restrained emotion, her face seemed drawn and pale. It bothered him that he had not noticed this during their conversation in the park the other day. He had been so intent on his emotional tirade that he hadn't taken the time to truly absorb what was before him. Her brown eyes seemed cloudy, wary, and defensive. But then that was the reaction he'd cultivated at their initial meeting. "I'm not sure why you're here, Iain. If it's more of the same, I have to tell you now that I'm in no frame of mind to entertain anymore of your recriminations."

He nodded, "That's not why I'm here. What's past is over. This concerns the present."

An eyebrow raised, the brown eyes narrowing. Clearly, she didn't believe him or trust him. "Quite a change of attitude."

He sipped his coffee, bitter and strong, just as he liked it. "I've been to see Quinn."

"What did you tell him?" Concern flickered across her restrained features.

"Nothing, although I did feel he knew something was going on. He's a smart guy."

She looked away, "He has enough to deal with. He doesn't need to be drawn into this."

"What did Brae say when you told her about the Triquetra?"

Her eyes widened, "What's the point of this, Iain? You've already told me—"

"Yes, I know," he interrupted. "Let's say I've reevaluated things."

"What does that mean?" she asked pointedly.

He put down his cup and walked across the room to her. It worried him, so pale, but she stared him down unflinchingly. "I'm going to help you."

There was no relief in her expression, just wariness, guardedness that he wished wasn't there. "Why? I thought you hated me."

He shook his head, "No, but I feel an obligation, a responsibility."

She nodded, "Fine, I don't care why you help. Let's just do whatever is needed so we can go our separate ways."

Again, he smiled, seeming somewhat amused at her distress. "You always did know how to make me feel welcome."

CHAPTER 6

ECOLE ISSOIRE

The hallways felt cold, even in the spring, and spring in New Orleans, more often than not, was like summer everywhere else. But the long hallways of the Ecole Issoire private school were always cold, and on reflection, she thought, perhaps that was to keep its enrollees uncomfortable and slightly intimidated. What it did, however, was create an agitation and feed a growing spark of rebellion in a select few.

Corey Knight was what, unfortunately, could only be described as a troubled, reclusive teenager. Her mother had died when she was nearly six years old, leaving her and her older brother in the strong, capable, but, yes, slightly calloused hands of Clayton Knight. They, the whole family, on a level, were outsiders. For reasons they'd kept very close to the vest, Clayton and his young bride relocated from Massachusetts to the city sometime in the early 1960's. Anyone, upon reflection, would consider it an odd choice. They had no family in the area, no business connections, no real reason for coming, except that they did. Clayton, always an imposing figure, was not a rich man. But he became one quickly through business investments, stock negotiations, and partial ownership of a successful chain of antique souvenir shops. The list of where he had his business dealings was endless, and within several years, Mr. and Mrs. Knight purchased the small mansion on Esplanade Avenue. It was clear there were areas of society that the Knights would never penetrate. New Orleans was an old city, still riddled with its invisible social barriers, and the Knights, no matter how wealthy, would always be *nouveau riche*, a local term meaning, in an unflattering fashion, "new money." But that didn't stop Clayton

Knight from placing his only daughter in one of the city's more expensive and exclusive private schools where she could rub elbows with many who would never accept her.

"Corey, come on. You need to get to your class." Samuel, her brother, was a tall boy built broad in the chest with his father's fair looks. On the other hand, she was also tall for her age but slim and dark. In her family, she seemed a bit of an aberration with large brown eyes, but then she was reassured by the photos in the library that she was simply an echo of the missing link in the Clayton clan. In resemblance, she took after her poor, deceased mother, who was barely a shadow in her memory. But Samuel, in contrast, was personable, well-liked, and, at least in her first year at the school, might serve as a buffer between her and the world around her.

"I don't like it here. It feels creepy."

He bent close to her ear, still wearing a dimpled smile for any onlookers. "Don't say that too loud. It will make the powers at be develop a dislike for you."

She sighed, "Why would they care? It's just a building."

He let out a short laugh of disbelief, "Trust me. They consider you greatly honored just for you to place your undeserving little feet on their hallowed concrete. Come on, sis. Play along. Be humble, grateful, and gripe quietly where no one can overhear you." He straightened up, pointing to a series of doors down the long hallway. "That's you. Play nice." And then he'd turned on his heel and disappeared into a mass of uniformed students.

Again, a chill passed through her. It wasn't so much she disliked the place. There was something wrong with it. She felt it in her skin like cold hands lightly brushing its surface. She knew this wouldn't work. Dad would have to listen. Somehow, she could make him see.

She slipped into the classroom that was already largely filled with students, some standing, some sitting, talking as if renewing acquaintances. In a very keen way, it made her heart drop. There would be no familiar faces for her here. She'd spent the last several years in a small private school on the city's fringes. It had been a choice made for her by her father in conjunction with a therapist. Corey was a person who, as they termed, was highly reactive to her environment, which was why this decision by Clayton Knight had entirely floored her. One evening not so many weeks ago, she'd been summoned into his private study, a room on the furthermost northern corner of the house. He gestured for her to sit in front of the rather large mahogany desk that had been there, she secretly believed, since the beginning of time. She did sit, feeling a crisp tenseness in the air but having no inclination of what was to come. And then it happened, "I'm sending you to Samuel's school, Ecole Issoire."

She literally felt a noose tighten around her neck. "What?" was all she managed.

"It's an excellent school. You'll get a great education there."

"But Dad—"

"Corey, I know this seems abrupt, but I also know you have to find a way to get on in the world, to adjust. Hiding out isn't the answer."

She stood up, feeling anger suddenly pouring through her. "That's not fair. I haven't been hiding out. Doctors that you hired recommend a different environment."

He nodded, "Yes because they think it's all in your head. All these feelings you get. I don't."

The anger subsided. She could see the expression in those wizened blue-gray eyes, the pain. "Dad, I can't."

He stood up, walking around the desk to strongly take her hands in his. "Corey, you have to toughen up, find a way to live in this world. Your mother—" And then he stopped. She could feel the emotion in him, but he was a gruff man, uncomfortable with expressing it. "Your mother," this time his voice was steely, "she was vulnerable like you. And I think I protected her too much. Maybe if I hadn't, she'd have been stronger."

"That's not true," she whispered. Her voice choked up with the emotion she felt in him.

He let her hands drop, "Well, whatever the case. I've decided, and you'll just have to find a way to live with it."

And here she was on this stark, barren day, staring around her cold English Lit classroom, trying to find a way to live with it.

Her inclination was to choose a desk at the back of the room, but she forced herself to opt for somewhere in the middle, the middle heading toward the back. The room itself was large, with a remarkably high ceiling and two massive windows spanning the outside wall. Pulling her books out of her backpack, she glanced about furtively. An older, petite, gray-haired woman had entered the room and shuffled papers on a podium at the front. The other students were beginning to settle into their desks. She breathed deeply. For the moment, the coldness was receding. At least that was comforting. Suddenly, she felt a hand softly gripping her arm. It was startling, and she instinctively looked up into a pair of rather long blue eyes and a truly dazzling white smile. The voice was a husky whisper, "Can I bum a pencil off of you?" The girl was sitting directly to her side, although she hadn't noticed her before. She reached behind to her backpack that she'd hooked on the arm of her desk, pulling out the required item. "Thanks," again, a wide smile and a look of curiosity. "I'm Brae, Brae Ryan."

She smiled, feeling a flutter of light in this dismal predicament. "I'm Corey Knight."

Again, the girl grinned back at her, but they were interrupted by their instructor's voice ceasing all friendly interactions.

"Corey Knight, now that sounds like something out of a book."

Brae Ryan carelessly flipped a lock of her long red hair, whipping it behind her ear artfully, even if she didn't mean to. In the few short hours of their acquaintance, Corey had noted the girl had a grace, not a subtle grace, but definitely, an untutored one that made awkward moments smoothed into something more sublime. She'd pulled her long dark hair back into a loose ponytail this morning. There hadn't been much thought to her appearance. She had been so wrapped up in anticipation of the ordeal to come. Shrugging in response to the comment about her name, "You think? I'd never thought about it that way."

They sat on a granite bench in one of the many courtyards strategically placed alongside the Ecole Issoire buildings. The first two classes of the day, it turned out Brae and Corey shared, but after this mid-morning break, they would be going their separate ways. Then Corey would be left to fend for herself. Brae smiled again with that wide smile, but also an expression in her eyes that told Corey, for some odd reason, that she found her a curiosity. "You don't know many people here."

She shook her head, "No, outside of my brother, you're it, and we've just met."

"You know, I could tell just looking at you. You act differently. Most everyone around here has been rubbing elbows since kindergarten, with a few exceptions."

"Hmm, maybe you should tell me how everyone else acts so I don't stick out so much."

The girl next to her laughed, again sweeping wayward locks of red hair behind her ears in her smooth, unruffled fashion. "You not stick out! Have you looked at yourself lately? Why don't you ask the Mona Lisa just to be a landscape? Ain't going to happen."

Corey felt her heart sink a bit, "Is it really that bad?"

Again, the brilliant smile as if to say, what planet are you from? "I didn't say it was bad. You're just not ordinary. Hey, don't fret about it. Some people scrape all their lives not to be ordinary, and they still can't manage it. Embrace it." She still felt dubious, but her heart lifted just a slight measure at Brae's offbeat encouragement. "Now let me see your schedule again. Maybe we can rendezvous at lunchtime. Corey smiled at her new friend's take-charge attitude. In some respects, she was feeling a bit as though the girl had adopted her, but just at the moment, that felt fine with her. It was much better than just drifting aimlessly along.

She checked her watch: nearly twelve. She breathed deeply — her head still pounding with a low, steady pain. Glancing up, the teacher at the front of the long, cold classroom continued to write on the board. Her hand ached painfully from taking notes nearly throughout the entire hour. It seemed insane to her on the first day of class to be proceeding at such a pace. But then again, this school had a reputation to uphold as one of the finest in the city, and evidently, some, though clearly not all, of the instructors took that challenge to heart. Focusing on her notebook, she felt her eyes glazing over with fatigue and, again, that keen claustrophobic feeling surrounding her chest. Last period in American History, she felt sure she could cope with her new circumstance, but this hour had unraveled all her confidence. Freshman Chemistry had a classroom that felt something akin to a cemetery vault. She'd glanced around the room when she'd entered. There were no friendly, engaging faces like that of Brae Ryan's, and as the hour progressed, the expressions became only more distant, more dour. No doubt she wasn't the only one who'd found this particular time challenging.

"Now, quickly, before class is over today, I'm going to assign each of you a lab partner for the experiments you'll be doing this year." Mr. Andrews, a middle-aged, slight, spry man who had just spent the last hour torturing them with a monotonous voice and demanding attitude, had now clearly jolted everyone back into alertness. His small eyes appeared to narrow, although Corey couldn't be sure because she was strategically seated toward the middle, drifting to the back segment of the classroom. "I've randomly paired you all together." And then, there was a thin smile that she felt sure could have been mistaken for a grimace. "Besides learning some Chemistry this year, you might just get the opportunity to make a new acquaintance. Make sure you exchange phone numbers before you leave. Now Adams and Maqueda, Barrett and Garfield—"

As the sound of Mr. Andrews continued to drone on and the class slowly became a milling mass of students as each one connected with their recently discovered counterparts, Corey collected her books, poised to make a quick escape as soon as they were released. Her headache had inspired nausea, and now all she wanted was to try to duck out and get some water before anything escalated. Vaguely, she heard the anticipated pairing jump out at her from the front of the room, "Knight and Shaw." She looked up, glancing around at faces focused elsewhere. Clearly, some recognized their other halves, and some were as lost and clueless as she was. What was the name again? Shack, Shore — something or other. And then beside her, a rather low voice for the age of fifteen corrected her thoughts, "Shaw."

She turned abruptly, confronted by the green eyes of a rather stony-faced youth. It struck her immediately. Not eyes like Brae's that were filled with light — eyes that were darker, more tumultuous. And then, to his name, he added the blunt statement, "You looked like you didn't catch it."

She frowned, a little taken aback at his directness. "There were a lot of things I didn't catch today."

He was taller than she, at least half a head, maybe more, with dark brown hair, a bit on the straggly side, which set off a rather interesting face. "Oh, don't worry about that. It will only get worse. I'm Iain," and then he smiled a bit as though he'd found something rather funny. "I guess I'm going to need your phone number." His demeanor, the odd smile he wore, the fact that her head was continuing to pound, and basically the whole day had irritated her somewhere past her endurance point. "Do you have a name? Or should I just call you Knight?"

She grabbed her backpack and swung it over her shoulder, "Corey."

He nodded, what expression he'd worn seconds before now having dripped completely off his face. He glanced around the room and then looked at her straight on. "Let's go outside. We can finish this there."

Without another glance, she headed toward the door, not checking if Iain Shaw was following her or if the ceiling of classroom 155 was crashing in. She just wanted out, wanted out and wanted home so she could talk her dad into getting her into another school. She kept walking once she made it into the hallway. But then, she was stopped by a somewhat firm hand that she felt on her shoulder and a whisper in her ear. "Take that door on the side," was the instruction. Still feeling light-headed she was relieved to see that it led outside, blessed outside with trees and sky and no old cement rooms that felt heavy and clammy. She breathed in momentarily as she walked down the three steps leading into the courtyard. And she forgot, completely forgot, who'd directed her here. Just for a blessed moment that was, "Is this better?" came a voice from behind her. And then he was standing next to her.

"What do you mean better?"

"You looked sick Corey Knight, like you might pass out in there or worse."

She instinctively put her hand to her head. It was easing the headache. Of course, it would. She was out of that room. "It's been a long day."

He smiled a bit, "It's only half over. "

She suddenly felt foolish. She wasn't used to having people watch her so closely. She sank down to sit on one of the steps she'd climbed down moments before, continuing to breathe as all vestiges of ill-feeling began to leave her. He didn't join her on the steps, just walked out a bit into the courtyard, then turned around as though he were studying her closely. "What?" she asked, annoyed, just annoyed by his quietness that seemed to speak more volume than some people who never stopped talking.

He shrugged, "You're odd."

She crossed her arms in front of her, feeling acutely like this boy, this strange, lanky boy, was seeing too much. "Gee, thanks."

"Not a criticism, believe me. You just don't fit, you know."

"Well, give me time. It's only the first day."

He looked away from her, evidently toward something that had caught his interest in the distance. She took that minute to take a closer inspection. He wore the regulation school uniform, dark pants, and a light button-down shirt, but Iain Shaw wore it differently. And it was interesting that she hadn't noticed before. He wore it, and the only way she

47

could describe it was resentfully. She hadn't noticed him earlier in the classroom and thought perhaps if he hadn't introduced himself, she might not have. But now that he'd brought himself to her attention, willingly or not, something about him was unmistakably apart. He turned back to her, green eyes looking vaguely curious but not so much that he couldn't claim indifference. "I doubt time will fix anything."

Her eyes widened. She felt sure he wasn't trying to hurt her. But it did hurt. She did want to fit, mostly, she supposed, because she was tired of not fitting. "Phone numbers," she stated flatly.

He smiled sharply, "Does that mean you're done with me?"

She stood up. "I'm supposed to meet someone for lunch. And I do think you're criticizing me."

He laughed with a manner that told her he really didn't care much what she thought. "Sorry, feeling better?"

She nodded, digging out a small assignment pad from her purse, on which she quickly scribbled her phone number. On a level, it did bother her. It didn't seem right having to give her phone number to some boy she wasn't at all sure she ever wanted to lay eyes on again. But she did, abruptly tearing it out and handing it to him. "Here's mine." He took it, folding it over and shoving it into his pocket, and in the next breath, smoothly reaching over, taking the pad and pen out of her hands. He glanced up from where he was scribbling something down, "Phone number," and then he handed her back the pad where the name Iain Shaw was boldly written under it. "Didn't want you to forget my name," he said with no emotion, walking right past her, pulling the door with a quick motion, then disappearing into the hallway.

She stood there for a moment, staring after him, stunned and wondering why it felt keenly that somehow the ground had shifted a few centimeters under her feet.

CHAPTER 7

THE DREAM

"So, tell me about the dream."

Corey turned around within the growing shadows in the room. Her heart began a slower, deeper beat, at once fueled by anxiety and the realization that a threshold was being crossed — a realization that she was not at all sure she was prepared or equipped to deal with. She crossed silently across the cool, wooden floor without answering Iain's question, switching on a standing brass lamp in a far corner to illuminate the dusky shadows. It was nearly six in the evening now, and all that stretched ahead was darkness. And there he was, just comfortably sipping his coffee, looking quite relaxed as though this room held no ugly past for them. Then again, maybe it was just her ugly past. His eyes were frequently cast down or away from her, examining details of the large parlor, as her father had been apt to call it. She hadn't considered this uneasiness that would be inherent if they worked together. At the time she'd reached out to him, she had only sought to quell the growing panic and desperation growing inside of her. Only that extreme would have propelled her to reach in his direction. Ten years apart had not softened the sharp edges of the pain between them. It was clear to her now at this late hour that wounds unacknowledged did not fade but only lay dormant until awakened again.

She moved back to the mantle of the fireplace, resting her hands on the back of a large, dark blue, winged-back chair that her father had grown accustomed to using toward the end of his life. She breathed in deeply, feeling strengthened, albeit ever so slightly, by the remnants of her father's energy there. "I suppose it was a dream, but it didn't feel that way."

She saw him nod, but his eyes were focused out one of the long-draped windows that were partially open. She didn't know if she should be offended or grateful that she did not have to endure his gaze during this. "How did it feel?" His voice was low but sounded hollow, devoid of anything except perhaps a pragmatic curiosity.

"It was early in the morning, and I was asleep in my room. But then it felt as though I had awoken to the sensation of a hand on mine." Now, she turned away, feeling an instinctive trembling pass through her at the memory. "It felt so real, and when I opened my eyes, I saw it was him."

"Your father?"

The memory wrapped around her firmly in a way that felt quite startling. It had been many years since she'd felt much more than an inkling of her old capabilities. But then again, she wondered distractedly if this was due in some measure to Iain's presence. "Yes, he was standing beside the bed with his hand on mine. But not like he was at the end, not frail — strong, as he'd been when I was younger."

"What did he say?" his voice continued to prompt her, but now felt as though it were from somewhere far away.

"Nothing at first, he just stood there touching my hand but not smiling. He looked worried." She breathed in deeply, feeling a slight dizziness sweep across her body, almost like a ripple. It was truly as though it would be so easy for the thin thread that held her to the present to snap, allowing her to simply sink completely into the memory.

"Did he speak at all?" The cold voice again felt like an intrusion upon the warm place where she was. It ripped across her mind, tearing the light gauze of sweetness the memory had afforded her.

"Yes, he spoke. But not out loud. I heard him in my mind. I knew it was him, the voice, the quiet strength. It was him. There could be no mistake."

"Exactly what did he say, Corey?" She knew now that Iain's voice had moved in the room, but she couldn't see where he was. She'd sunk so deep into the impression that all she could see now was her bedroom and her father's face. Clearly, she could hear Clayton Knight's words inside her mind.

"I know how you've suffered, Corey. I know how hard it has been, but you must be strong now. The room has been breached and the seal broken. All is unstable now. Balance must be restored, or all of you and many others will be in jeopardy." She grabbed his hand tightly, but this time, it melted away in hers. Then she slept again, dreaming of the chamber.

"How did you know it was the Triquetra?" such a shock, his voice next to hers. It yanked her back into the room, swirling in dizziness. She was back, completely now, staring into his eyes, his green eyes with no softness piercing her.

"When I dreamed again, I saw it was gone."

And then his gaze brushed over her face as though he were considering. "How can you be sure?"

This time, she met his eyes directly. "I can't be, but we must be."

He paused momentarily, then nodded, his face expressionless, simply echoing her words, "Yes, clearly we must be."

Iain did not go home immediately. He had left Corey's house sometime after seven. In the old days, they would have had dinner together and spent some time simply relaxing and enjoying each other's company. But they were on a different plateau now, stuck in a place of unfinished emotion, and he could see that if unchanged, this would be a problem. He stopped at a coffee shop on the perimeter of the French Quarter. He had to park at a distance, but the night air was reviving, helping him consider what was next.

Iain sipped his espresso, gazing out the window at the still continually active Royal Street just outside. It certainly didn't feel like the New Orleans of his youth. There had been so many subtle changes, and some not so subtle. But in essentials, he felt that it had not altered, though perhaps in essentials he had. Age, disappointment, and years traveled had a way of humbling even the most arrogant of youths. He smiled to himself, the memory of old Mr. Knight telling Iain of his own arrogance: "Life tends to beat it out of us, humbles us." He imagined the old man would have found it amusing that he, too, had come to the same realization, although at a much younger age. Then again, Mr. Clayton Knight might have felt compassion towards him. He had always been difficult to predict, a chameleon of sorts in Iain's mind.

The bitter coffee filled his mouth in the next sip. It was good. It reminded him of Europe, of years of defanging his personal demons. And now, he felt the need to slay them all over again.

He sighed deeply, reluctantly realizing that to accomplish this task, he would have to give up something. He grimaced, feeling an afterbite of bitterness from the coffee. Give up his righteous anger? Lord knows he'd earned it. He was entitled to it. But the negativity filled his body with poison, a poison that clouded the mind, inflamed the emotions, and distorted in a way that he couldn't afford.

Part of him wanted to blame Corey, to blame a woman that he'd freely given the power over to hurt him so deeply. But sadly, he realized that perhaps it wasn't her fault, wasn't her fault that she didn't love him with the same finality that he had loved her. It bothered him more, he supposed, to find out the truth after all these years, that although so much had changed, that had not.

After his coffee, he went for a walk, planning and strategizing how to cope with all the elusive truths that still haunted him.

CHAPTER 8

THE HIDDEN CLOSET

"So, where are you off to tonight?"

Her father was sitting in a chair by his window. She was pleased more than she could say. The last few weeks had brought remarkable improvement in him. She pulled on her short, navy blue jacket. The temperature had taken a dip outside unexpectedly, but then again, that was the beauty of the Crescent City. One had no clue what to expect. "I'm going to get something to eat with Iain."

His blue-gray eyes focused on her now, making her revert to that feeling of being interrogated she'd had as a teenager. "You've been spending a lot of time with him lately. Is there something going on?"

She frowned, first hating that at her age, the question was asked and, secondly, not knowing how to answer it. "I enjoy spending time with him. We have a lot in common."

He returned to gazing outside the bedroom window. "Hmm, aren't things casual and indefinite? In my day, you were either courting or not. There wasn't that gray area. And don't think I don't remember that young man. He always had his eyes on you, Corey, acknowledged or not."

She picked her purse up off the hospital bed that still took up a sizable acreage of his spacious room. She hoped against hope that they could rid themselves of it before too long. The bed she found depressing, as a symbol and a tangible object. "Okay, Dad, will you be okay tonight?"

"Yes, don't worry about me." She crossed to him, kissing him lightly on the cheek. And somewhat unexpectedly, he grabbed her hand, which caused her to meet the gaze of the wizened blue-gray eyes directly. "Corey, just be cautious. You're not like everyone else."

She sighed, straightening up. "I'm fine, Dad. I've been able to cope with everything thrown at me for a long time now."

"Yes, my dear, I know that. But this man, this man I fear in particular, may be more than a challenge for even you."

It bothered him or perhaps intrigued would be a fairer assessment. This Corey returned from her not too long but entirely significant absence. There had always been a quality about her, even when he'd first met Corey Knight so long ago — a removed, elusive quality as though her body was indeed in your presence, but her mind, her spirit, was off floating somewhere in some intangible realm, inaccessible to mere mortal men. And perhaps it was then, even back then, that this quality began to entrance him — that the notion of reaching her had occurred to him, of anchoring her somehow to where he was, or perhaps simply enticing her to let him come along to wherever she traveled.

Before she'd returned, life had settled into a quiet but busy predictability. There was a woman about his age that he'd met through teaching. She'd been a student of his in his sculpting class, an older student, but then they'd begun seeing each other. He couldn't remember how it started, only that it did. Once, sometimes twice a week, they would meet. She was busy with a career, and his life moved at a deafening pace, so there was no question of permanency at that time but rather an understanding of convenience. He had to admit he found the relationship pleasant but certainly not inspiring. But then Corey had returned and brought with her this indefinable aura of electricity that reminded him, not altogether pleasantly, that life was about so much more than convenience. He'd stopped calling the other woman a week after Sebastian's get-together. She called once, and he'd told her he was too busy with work and projects. Perhaps she'd sensed the difference. Perhaps she didn't care enough herself to pursue it. Nothing had been officially declared ended, but then again, nothing had ever been officially declared anything at all.

He sipped his coffee. They'd shared a largely quiet meal in the Quarter and then had walked down Chartres Street to a pastry shop. He hadn't pressed, but he knew somehow, somewhere, things were not copacetic in Corey's small, rather insulated world. "Dad, okay?" he asked casually.

Her eyes, which moments ago had been off blindly staring at some invisible anomaly in space, now returned to him. "He's doing better."

He took another sip of the strong, bitter coffee. It was something he'd accustomed himself to when he was up late at night burning the candle at both ends and literally quite out of existence. There didn't seem to be enough hours in the day for all the aspirations that he'd crowded into his life. "So, what is it?"

She shook her head, still blanketed with that cloak of protectiveness to which she clung so tightly — something else he'd dearly like to have the time to strip away. "I don't know. Just bothered, I suppose."

"Want to be more specific? Or shall I keep guessing?"

A slight smile at his bluntness — it had always been a technique that worked well with her, even in the old days. "Dad thinks I should go back to New York. He wants me to pick up my old life."

He stared at her a little blankly, at a basic level disliking the prospect that had suddenly been placed before him. "Is there a life to pick up back there?"

Another smile, but there was a pain in this one, "No, I mean, I'm not sure. Life there was more about living daily, with no long-range plans. It's sort of the survival game."

"Hmm, well, I'm not a long-range guy, but even that sounds a little barren."

Her dark eyes lit just a bit with some idea that pleased her. "I don't know. In some ways it appealed to me, being so unconnected to anything. It felt harder, yet simpler."

Again, he picked up the bitter drink and sipped, "Not empty?"

"Maybe, but numbing. That isn't always so bad."

He considered. "Hard to live on numbing forever. And why else would your father want to get you out of town?"

Her eyes widened, "I don't know."

He smiled teasingly, "Your eyes are just too big to lie, Corey. There's no place to hide there."

She frowned, and speaking, he thought, somewhat reluctantly, "He's worried."

"About?"

"About me, about you and me spending so much time together, but I told him he shouldn't be, just old friends getting reacquainted. He thinks you're unpredictable."

He assumed a bit of mock gravity, "He'd prefer more predictable for you."

She laughed, "Don't take offense. It has more to do with me than you. I used to be too much of a handful for him. He forgets I've had to cope on my own for a long time."

"And what do you want, other than being unconnected?"

Her brown eyes narrowed, "I didn't say that's what I wanted. I said it's simpler."

"So is kindergarten, but I'm not yearning to relive that," he quipped.

She frowned a bit, studying him suddenly with only what he could describe as frustration, "So, why are you still on your own? Sebastian's all but married. Brae has been through a number of great loves. And Quinn," she glanced away, "well, I think he's just not interested, but you, I would have expected you to be with someone."

He leaned back in his chair, intrigued by the very personal turn the conversation had taken. Evidently, the matter was on her mind. "Who says I'm not?"

He was pleased. The sparkle in her eyes only moments before dimmed a bit. She wasn't completely unreachable. "So, there is someone. Why aren't you with her then?"

"I'm where I want to be right now." He stated perhaps more flatly than he'd intended.

Her eyes were wide, brown, and with unending depth like he remembered them. "I don't understand."

"It wasn't like you're thinking. I suppose neither of us had anything better to do."

A slight smile, "Oh, now that sounds empty."

He sipped his coffee again, gazing out the window for a moment. "I don't know, maybe it was." Then he turned to her, asking pointedly, "And in New York? Was there anybody?"

Corey shook her head tentatively, a sore subject perhaps. "Not really. Like I said, everyone was busy surviving. There wasn't much time for anything like that."

"And that's what you'd like to return to?"

"I didn't say that. I just don't have a plan yet, not sure what I'm going to do, where I fit."

He laughed, "Where you fit? Now that sounds like a familiar theme."

The beautiful wide eyes narrowed sharply, "So, tell me. What do you think we're doing?"

He paused seriously, considering for a moment. "Biding our time," was his answer.

There was a closet on the third floor, at the end of the stairs. It was inconspicuously placed along a hallway. Invisible, if you weren't looking for it, quite hidden to the distracted mind. But her mind was distracted in a specific way tonight, so she focused acutely on it. As a child, it had intrigued her, beguiled her. It was part of the wall, part of a distinct paisley wall print that echoed a long-ago Victorian age. There was no doorknob but a thin impression inward that one had to wrap fingers just so precisely on to obtain that nearly silent click, springing open a magic door in the mind of a five-year-old.

At first, she had felt sure it was indeed her discovery, her secret garden in the vast mansion on Esplanade Avenue. To the mind of a child, the high ceilings and echoing wooden floors were the stuff of enchantment, be it sometimes dark enchantment as was the closet on the third floor.

It was empty the first time Corey found it, and so it was claimed, marked at least as far as she was concerned as her own. Fancifully, she even thought it lay in another sphere, another realm, like the wardrobe in the stories of C. S. Lewis. For some time, she came to believe such things until her brother, then her mother and father acknowledged the closet's existence. She remembered a sweet, distant smile from Abigail Knight. This memory had taken on the aspects of some self-created phantom, lovely by design but ephemeral and fleeting as was any imagination. "It's your special place, a place to hide your treasures, a place for your sweetest secrets." Within a week of that whispered declaration, Corey had an elegant copper key in her hands with which to lock away her secret place. As she looked backward, she was sure over the short time during her childhood that her mother was with her that there had been other gifts, but in recollection, this was the only one that stood out — a sacred gift, a promise, and in her innocence a covenant of sorts. For in her immature mind, it became their place, their secret place of communion.

Corey felt the weariness of the past few days weigh upon her heavily as she ascended the dark wooden staircase at the Esplanade mansion. Its banisters were broad and heavy, unlike the thin mahogany ones at the house on Henry Clay Avenue. Its remembrance cut through her heart area in an uncomfortable way. She'd spent five years there, five long years that now strangely felt like they'd belonged to another time, another life of someone she did not know or perhaps she did not care to know.

She wasn't sure what was driving her tonight — despair, weakness, or a strange, detached illumination, only that her hands itched, itched like they wanted to create, itched like they wanted to feel the past in her palms.

She climbed the stairs, remembering when she had done so as a child bounding, running to a secret destination; as a young teenager, arms filled with private writings, journals, thoughts to be locked away; a woman in her twenties with albums of photographs of places that resonated with her, with her being, all of it to be locked away, all of it kept apart from the life she'd chosen.

She stopped at the bend of the stairs and turned. The delicate turning leaves of paisley were beginning to fade, fade after all these years, but then again, it had been some time since she'd examined it. It wasn't as if she avoided this part of the house. It was much worse, more that she didn't acknowledge it. She tried to forget it was even here. And for that, she hated him.

She'd had no idea, no idea at all, that this would happen. That bringing Iain Shaw back into her life in any capacity would dig open all these old forgotten vaults, ones that she'd spent a decade burying.

Without thought, she took the key out of her skirt pocket and put it into the lock. It was without any consideration, without any control. Something unconscious drove her now, as a crazed person who pushed their hands onto the last burning embers of a fire, to remember at whatever cost what it feels like to be warm.

The door swung open into the darkness. There was a string that connected to a light at the top of the shallow closet, but it wasn't needed. She knew exactly where it was, what she sought.

"It's beautiful."

"It's horrible."

The whispers surrounded her, voices from a past that still did not feel like hers. But it must be because there was memory — thick, lucid memory.

Laughter, *"It seems harmless enough. It's all stories."*

She reached to one of the top shelves. It was a box on the second of three high shelves in the dark, thin closet, a cardboard box, brown, old, unlabeled. But even touching it sent a tremor through her fingertips — fingertips which had touched nothing of such energy for so long.

She pulled the box out, closing the door and locking it, out of habit more than any other consideration. There was no one, no one left to protect her secrets from now, no brother, no father, and the memory of her ephemeral phantom-like mother had left long ago.

She leaned against the far wall on the third landing of the Esplanade mansion and sunk to the floor, holding the box in her hands for some time like a lost child. She wondered fleetingly what her father would think of her now, his strong child, what he would think of what she'd made of her life. Corey inhaled sharply and began to rip the brown tape with her jagged, broken fingernails off of the past.

CHAPTER 9

THE MARGUILLERS

"What did you call them again?"

Sebastian Morris frowned, clearly rethinking the choice that had been decided upon approximately a half hour ago by the brotherhood of the secret organization of the Marguillers — the decision to open up their very secret society of three to two new members, members of the female persuasion.

He turned to his brother in arms, figuratively, of course, Iain Shaw (code name Jacques DeMolay), with a grimace that spoke of his concern for their future, concern for their survival, concern that they were about to be laughed at. And he was met with a look of cool amusement and merriment in the eyes of his blood brother. But Iain turned to the girls with a cool look of detachment as though their approval or disapproval meant less to him than the dust on his sneakers.

"Look," was how he began, "if you're not interested, it's no problem. Let's not waste each other's time. We just thought you seemed like the adventurous sort."

Corey shuddered at how quickly Brae took the bait. She, in many ways, was so innocent, dare she say gullible, unthinking, but then again, she hadn't experienced loss so early in life as had her far more reticent friend. "What's that, some sort of challenge?"

Sebastian furrowed a brow that seemed entirely too young to be furrowed. And deep down, Corey knew very well this had everything to do with Sebastian Morris, had to do with Brae Ryan's overactive young hormones and Sebastian Morris's already extremely cultured good looks. And Corey, like a good friend, was being dragged along for company.

It had started innocently enough, less than half an hour before, on the very same bench.

"So, are you sprung or not?"

Corey scowled lightly as the stern visage of her father floated through her mind. He was dug in, and no amount of pleading, throwing tantrums, or debating would get him to move. She sat on the cold cement, feeling the chill creep through her school uniform. An early spot of cool weather had crept into the ordinarily warm New Orleans September. She shook her head somewhat despondently at her new best friend, Brae Ryan. "No, he's immovable. He's convinced himself it's for my own good."

A short burst of laughter that sounded akin to a cackle came out of the redhead's mouth, "Oh, I love that one. It's for your own good! Sounds like my parents' litany." She tossed her long red locks, leaning her hands back on the cool cement bench as though she was unaffected by it. Corey wondered if she was anemic on top of everything else. The cold seemed to go right through her skin as if it were paper. "Well, at least you have your new lab partner to keep you company."

She frowned explicitly. She wished she'd never mentioned Iain Shaw to Brae. Now, she would never hear the end of it. "I wish you would lay off this."

The redhead smiled broadly. "Come on, Corey. He's cute — in that brooding, rebellious way. I remember him last year. I heard he took out three guys at once who tried to jump him outside the school grounds."

"Oh, how attractive."

She nudged her. "Come on, and he hangs out with that rich kid, Sebastian Morris."

Corey tried hard to look disinterested, "Richer than you?"

She nodded, "Yeah, hard to believe. His family has the money from way back." Then she leaned in closer to Corey, "And I think they're into some strange stuff."

Corey raised a studied eyebrow, "What does that mean?"

Again, Brae leaned in a bit closer, and she cloaked her youthful voice in a husky whisper. "I don't know. I heard rumors about voodoo."

Corey burst out laughing. "Are you kidding? What does one of them want to be Marie Laveau?"

Brae bristled a bit. Clearly, she wasn't too comfortable with being laughed at. "You know, some people in this city still take that religion very seriously."

She looked away, continuing to smile. Funny thought, two strapping young men interested in voodoo. "What? Are they concocting love spells?"

Brae tossed her reddish curls, "Well, maybe Iain is after meeting you."

"Iain Shaw is a jerk, and I imagine all his friends are jerks as well."

Brae laughed, "Yeah, Corey, I'm sure you're right." But the expression on her young face reflected something altogether different.

While just yards away, another conversation of a different nature was taking place.

"So, what do you think?"

The dark green eyes did not stir from their point of interest across the stone pavilion, where the students of Ecole Issoire took a brief respite after lunch before returning to a grueling school day. His gaze was not one that he would admit reflected interest but rather curiosity, like studying an interesting new species of bug he had dug up from some hidden place deep within the earth. And then a rather abrupt and aggressive nudge shattered his focus. "Hey, are you in the building?"

His disinterested stare shifted to the tall, brown-haired boy straddling the bench beside him. He frowned, "What?"

"Do you want to see this place I was talking about after school?"

He shrugged, "You mean that old house on Prytania Street."

Sebastian Morris looked somewhat annoyed. And it irritated Iain. He'd seen the expression before on the faces of snobs that his parents felt obliged to rub elbows with. It was one aspect of his friend that bothered him, but fortunately, the attitude rarely surfaced. "Hey, if you're not in, that's okay by me."

He smiled at Sebastian's bravado. How easily he ruffled. "And if I'm not, what are you going to do? Take Quinn with you?"

Again, the handsome boy frowned. How he hated admitting that he needed anyone. "Yeah, that would be a disaster. Quinn's a wimp, the first sign of weirdness at the place, and he'd bolt like an old lady."

Iain laughed at the image, "No, I don't think an old lady would run quite that fast. He leaned back against the stone pillar just behind him. "You're sure this will work."

Sebastian narrowed his dark brown eyes, leaning in a bit toward Iain with a determined expression. "I told you my key is reputed to work on any lock. It's a goldmine."

"And what if your Dad notices it missing from his collection?"

"He rarely looks at that stuff. He just collects it and then puts it in that room upstairs. Besides, I'll have it back there tonight."

Iain nodded. It was a crazy idea, but then again, the house was a famous one in the city, reputed to be haunted, and once it was sold, the opportunity would be gone. "Is Quinn coming, or is it just you and me?"

"He'll come. If you're going, he'll come."

Iain allowed his gaze briefly to return to the pair of girls sitting across the pavilion. He'd known Brae Ryan since grade school, albeit at a distance. But the other, the new girl, Corey Knight, was the curiosity. And then a tantalizing thought fluttered across his mind. This afternoon's exploration would be much more interesting if he could entice them along. Deep down, he felt their trio could use some new blood.

He turned to Sebastian with a genuine smile at the new thought. "Want a real challenge, Hugues?"

Sebastian's eyes narrowed at Iain's public use of his secret name. It was a promise, a covenant between the three that they would only use their secret names at times of the greatest solemnity or perhaps just when they really meant business. The expression had dropped from Sebastian's sharply boned face. "Always Jacques."

He turned his face to clearly indicate the two girls a half dozen yards away from them. "Get them to come along."

A look of puzzlement crossed his friend's face, and then it melded into something akin to amusement. "I guess that would liven things up, but why them?"

Iain shrugged, "Just a feeling, just a gut feeling."

Jacques DeMolay, Hugues de Payens, and Geoffrey de Charney — little did the halls of the Ecole Issoire School on St. Charles Avenue have any notion that such prestigious and perhaps notorious personages haunted their hallowed corridors. It was an idea born of restlessness, boredom, and, more deeply than any admitted, frustration. Quinn Murdoch was a history buff, not a robust youth, but instead one intermittingly plagued with ill health, so much down time left ample opportunity for mental exploration. And so, once the tentative plans were made for the order, Quinn became the Seneschal, the right-hand man of the grand master. The power behind the brawn as he liked to think of himself, and so he chose the name of Geoffrey Charney, a Knights Templar who followed his brother Jacques De Molay into martyrdom for the cause. Sebastian, who liked to be in charge, chose the personage of Hugues de Payens, the first Grand Master of the Templars. And Iain, being intrigued by the courage of perhaps one of the most famous knights who was tortured and burned at the stake for proclaiming his innocence against papal persecution, chose the name of Jacques DeMolay. The idea of standing firm and dying for a cause captured his imagination at the young age of thirteen. They were all thirteen, all three, when they first banded together to form the modern-day Marguillers. The Marguillers themselves were another secret organization that held great sway with the Roman Catholic parsonages of New Orleans in the eighteenth and nineteenth centuries. So, in their young minds and vivid imaginations, the two orders of the Templars and the Marguillers merged.

But as fate would have it, the modern-day Marguillers were relatively inactive during the first years of their existence, except for occasional meetings involving grand plans that never tended to bloom into full fruition. There were a few odd explorations, an old, abandoned cathedral down Magazine Street, the ruins of a Civil War fort down the banks of Bayou St. John, and time, much time, spent on the development of a code, a code of behavior not unlike the antiquated templars, a code of devotion, honor, and chastity — chastity that was until one of them found reason not to be chaste. But as it was, nothing had yet interfered with their oaths.

There were only three of them, and at some point in the future, they had vague, insubstantial thoughts of expanding. But it hadn't happened yet, not until this year, this day, this lark in the mind of one code-named Jacques DeMolay.

Corey turned away, smiling. It was her unfortunate fate that odd things would strike her funny at inopportune moments. She looked at the building connecting to the open outdoor pavilion where they stood, concentrating on the uneasy flow of students in and out of the swinging glass doors. But all she could see in her mind was lovely Brae's face and her wrinkled brow.

She glanced back, and it was a mistake. It was Sebastian Morris's face, an expression that was a cross between irritation and outrage as though moments before, he had left his most precious possessions at their feet, and they had deemed them ludicrous. His voice was low and stern, and it only made Corey want to giggle. "It doesn't matter about the name. The question is — do you and Corey want to go or not?"

Brae sort of cocked her head to the side. Clearly, she would have much preferred if he had asked her to go out. "So, what exactly would we be doing?"

Sebastian stepped back with a scowl, glancing rapidly at Iain, whose expression had not changed during the whole exchange, although Corey had met his cloaked stare several times in the last few very awkward minutes. "Look, just forget it," Sebastian expelled with an indignant huff.

Brae's lovely eyebrows furrowed again, "Forget what exactly?"

And then Iain stepped in with a flat but detectably deep voice for his age. "An exploration, sort of an adventure, if you will. A test, you could call it."

"What sort of test?" Corey asked. She had not intended to get into this, but something about his words compelled her. And his eyes again met her at the question.

"A test of your will, if you're up to it, that is."

Brae turned to Corey with a blank and irritated stare and then a shrug that simply stated it was up to her. Her senses were tingling madly, telling her that diving into anything was beyond a mistake, that it could, in her case, be quite detrimental. But something about her mood, something about the atmosphere that day, something about a cosmic alignment of stars, made her ignore warnings. "When?" was all she said. But it spoke volumes, and Iain's indiscernible expression melted ever so subtly into something that might be mistaken for triumph.

CHAPTER 10

OLD PHOTOGRAPHS

Corey picked up the tattered box and took the stairs back to the mansion's second floor. She had nearly opened it on the flight above, but something had made her hesitate, to stay the memories for just a little longer. Perhaps it was the shreds of self-preservation that she still possessed. Perhaps it was only that it was the end of an exceptionally long day, and fatigue was wrapping its iron grip securely about her. She entered her bedroom, placing the box on the dark burgundy satin coverlet that spread across her bed.

She allowed her fingertips to traipse across the top of the box.

"Are you sure it's all right?"

"Does it matter if it is? That's half the fun of it, knowing you're somewhere you shouldn't be."

The phone on her nightstand gave out a shrill ring, shattering her momentary reverie.

"Hello," she answered, not even bothering to check who it was first on the caller ID, as was her custom. "Hello," she said again after a moment's silence.

"Corey," the voice was soft and cultured but clearly recognizable. She purposely leaned back against the heavy oak headboard of her bed frame. The day was only getting stranger.

"Yes," she answered, still a bit overcome.

"It's Brae."

"Yes, I know."

A light laugh on the other end of the line stirred the memories from so long ago. "I'm sure you didn't expect to hear from me."

"No, no, you're right. I didn't."

"I can't believe it's up for sale again."

He laughed that deep, throaty laugh that always seemed to affect her. "I can't believe someone hasn't torn it down." She smiled, but even staring at the house from where she and Iain had parked across the street sent ripples through her. Some were remembrances perhaps, but then also something stronger, tentacles reaching out already. "Maybe we shouldn't have come here."

She shook her head. She was stronger now. Living in New York had empowered her, made her able to resist such things. "I'd like a picture, but not inside, from here."

She felt his hand on her back. She could nearly feel its warmth through the thin shirt she wore. Through the camera lens, she could see its beauty — curving walls nearly forming a turret of several levels on the western side of the house, its elegant lines, its screen porch wrapping gracefully around half the house. So lovely, but when she snapped the picture, her hands ached and shook. And she heard the voices, young, wise, but so reckless.

"*We shouldn't be here.*"

"*Does that matter?*"

"Odd, at how little it has changed." Iain's voice behind her, and then Iain's voice in her mind, "*After all, it's just a house. What could be in there to be afraid of?*"

She tried to resist, but the past seemed to wrap around her like threads, threads tenacious, binding her, pulling through the closed doors into a hallway filled with afternoon shadows.

Brae whispered into her ear, "*You're sure this is a good idea. It feels creepy.*"

And Iain, walking beside them, clearly eavesdropping, "*It's just a house. What could there be to be afraid of?*"

They stood on a stoop on the side of the house, an entrance not directly facing Prytania Street, a choice that told Corey that the members of the

Marguillers weren't quite as comfortable with this escapade as they let on. Corey was shielding herself mentally, a technique she'd developed with the aid of a counselor and several years of therapy. "You must develop your own mental armor and use it when you feel most vulnerable." She had stopped considering whether being here at all was a foolish decision on her part. It had taken several awkward steps to get them here: a call to her father explaining that she would be spending the afternoon studying at her new friend Brae Ryan's house, and then a call from Brae to her parents telling them a less concrete story about a study group gathering after school. She'd remarked glibly, "It doesn't matter. They probably wouldn't notice if I were home or not." Then, there was a hike of about five blocks from the Ecole Issoire grounds.

Next to the members of the Marguillers, she was aware of another who joined them that Corey had not met before — a gaunt, wiry boy with very bright blue eyes. He muttered to Sebastian nervously, "Are you sure you can get into this place?"

"Settle down squirrely," was his quick reply. Then, Corey saw him reach into a side pocket of his backpack, where he produced a rather odd-looking long piece of iron. Corey's eyes focused on it sharply because just that thin, off-looking piece of metal managed in one fell swoop to shatter her mental armor. "What is that thing?" She asked Sebastian directly, whose eyes met hers, she felt, for the first time since they had been introduced.

He looked at her with curiosity and then replied softly, "Well, princess, this is what is going to get us inside."

Beside him, Iain gave him a sharp nudge that went unnoticed by no one. "Get on with it."

Sebastian frowned, removing his focus from Corey and rather gingerly sticking the slender piece of metal into the lock. "What if it breaks?" the thin boy they called Quinn asked.

Sebastian muttered, "It won't. It's stronger than it looks." And then Corey saw him close his eyes for a moment and then give the strange key a quick twist. She heard the lock pop and the door creak as Sebastian swung it open.

Corey looked out of her bedroom window into the darkened Esplanade Avenue below. She held the phone in her hand, waiting still for Brae to explain, having neither desire nor inclination to make any of this any easier for her.

"I want to apologize for how I acted the last time you called."

Corey allowed her fingertips to gently push back the gauzy fabric of the window shears covering the bay window. "Well, I was a little surprised."

"You caught me off guard."

"Clearly." It was odd. In all these years, she hadn't truly thought about being angry with Brae. But the simmering resentments that now were bubbling to the surface spoke of old feelings that hadn't been reconciled but instead simply stored away in some forgotten scrapbook.

"You're not making this easier."

"Am I supposed to make it easier?" she replied softly.

Again, the laugh, that light unaffected laugh that seemed a signature element of this human being, "You have to understand Corey. My life now, my family, has nothing to do with the past."

Corey sat down on the edge of the bed. Her head was beginning to throb. "Well, if you're happy, Brae, then that's wonderful. I suppose if some of us have made a success of our lives, that's something. But in any case, I don't need your help."

There was hesitation that heartened Corey for some reason. "You don't?"

"No, you needn't concern yourself. Someone else is helping me."

"Someone else? You mean Quinn?"

"No, not Quinn. Iain had decided to help me."

And then a silence, a gulf of silence, "You're kidding, Iain?"

"Yes Brae, Iain, and frankly, I think he's just the person to help."

"Yes, yes, I remember the extraordinary things that Iain used to accomplish. But honestly, how can the two of you do anything together after everything that happened?"

"We're managing." was all she said. And then she added quickly. "Goodbye Brae," and hung up the phone. It was childish and uncalled for, but in some far-off segment of the universe it lifted the spirits of a very tired heart.

Her eyes returned to the box that she had so unceremoniously plopped down on the middle of the bed. It seemed right, all of it converging tonight— Iain, here in this house again, Brae just moments ago. She unconsciously allowed the phone to slip from her fingers and drop softly to the throw rug at the foot of her bed.

She sat next to it and continued what she had begun earlier, ripping off the brown masking tape, then pulling apart the top of the box that she had sealed nearly ten years before, just before she had sealed off this house — closing it up, covering the furniture and locking it away.

She reached inside, feeling the back of her hand roughly brushed by jagged envelopes, large envelopes, brown faceless unmarked. One by one she pulled them out and piled them on the bed. By the time, the box was empty, there was a pile of six, of seven. Of course, this wasn't all of them, not nearly. But this was the last of them, the last ones she had packed away.

She began to pull them open quickly, surveying the pictures within, so many of them, faces staring at her from another time. She hesitated on one picture, a rather stoic face staring back at her, brown eyes intense. It was taken the summer before her father died. Sebastian was still engaged at that point, engaged to someone whose face she could barely summon in her mind and whose name completely eluded her. She let the photo drop out of her fingers onto the bed, wondering how things would have changed if he had married that other woman and taken his life in another direction.

She picked up another envelope and pulled out its contents. This stack made her hands tingle in anticipation. She stopped at the first photo and let the others drop. Memory rushed forward like a warm blanket, its curves, its edges, the echo of its empty rooms, and reverberations of nervous laughter.

"*What is there to be afraid of? It's only an empty house?*"

And she smiled even though she was crying. There was so much, so very much to be afraid of there.

CHAPTER 11

THE FABACHER HOUSE

"I can't tell you why your mother was the way she was," Clayton Knight hesitated. And she felt quite certain that he was questioning the wisdom of continuing, or perhaps it was the wisdom of beginning at all. He turned away from her, staring out of the long guillotine window on the far wall of his study. He seldom talked of her mother. None of them did; neither she, Samuel, nor their father. In some skewed way, she believed they felt the silence, the unacknowledged absence, would make it less real, less a part of their lives. But even at her young age, she had begun to suspect that the unspoken could become a stronger presence than if it were acknowledged. There, after all, was no invisibility in avoidance.

"She," he began again, "well, in so many ways, she allowed the world to crush her." He frowned, turning to Corey with a stern expression, one that quite truly did not in any way suit the very delicate nature of his subject. "Some might say she was gifted by God. I'm quite sure most of her life she considered it a curse — a curse that, in the end, took its toll. You must choose, choose not to let what she has passed onto you destroy you as it did her."

A coldness wrapped around her, a fear that had no form, no substance, except what lies in abstract imagination. "But I'm not like her."

And then his cool, silvery blue eyes softened for a moment into only what she could interpret as pity. "No, my dearest, unfortunately, you are far too much like her."

It wrapped around her like a warm blanket as she crossed the threshold, a muffled warmth as though someone had thrown a heavy coat over her slight body. She breathed in deeply and breathed in the fragrance of faded flowers, roses that were just beginning to wilt.

"Are there any lights?" young Sebastian Morris's voice behind her.

"Do you think that's wise? If someone sees it, they'll know we're inside." Quinn Murdoch, she felt, just on one side of her. But his presence was muffled. There was something stronger here, pulling her.

"So, what are we going to do? Stumble around in the dark?" Brae was perhaps a step behind on the opposite side. She'd felt her breath in her hair, but she'd also felt other breaths and whispers surrounding her. Corey glanced around. The light from the fading afternoon could scarcely penetrate the heavy brocade drapes covering the long windows of this enormous room that they had stumbled into moments before. Her eyes carefully scanned its shadow-filled corners. But where she looked wasn't dark anymore. It was filled with light from the blazing fireplace. It warmed all the hidden corners of the room, and the plush velvets of the furniture weren't hidden now but exposed, luscious, rich colors that only a moment before had seemed covered in dusty white sheets. She breathed deeply but was hard-pressed to still the trembling of her knees.

A hand on her shoulder sent a jolt through her body, realigning her with where she was. "All right?" Iain asked in his direct, jarring manner.

She glanced around. All was steady now. No fire, no uncovered furniture. Even the scent of roses had been quickly replaced with the musty smell of a house that had been closed off for some time.

She turned around, staring into a youthful face that seemed even more guarded now than when they'd first entered the house. But in the eyes, the dark green eyes, there was something else, an understanding between them that existed on a level imperceptible to anyone surrounding them. She nodded quietly and then walked further into the center of the room. It was different in layout from her father's Esplanade house. But as her eyes followed the ceiling with its ornate molding, she recognized that the room was two large ones joined, a double parlor as it was once called.

"So, what are we doing? Taking a tour?" Quinn's voice, trying to be funny. But Corey felt the trepidation beneath.

Quinn walked past her to the direct center of the room, beneath the huge crystal chandelier. Corey glanced up, dazzled by its flickering lights, the reflections cascading across the finely polished floor. Then she squeezed her eyes shut and looked again. And it had disappeared, replaced by a heavy dark cloth that covered its former glory. She looked forward to Sebastian, who was talking, but strangely, she was only picking up his conversation in midsentence. "That's the best idea, so this won't be a complete waste. We pair off. Go exploring and meet back here in about fifteen minutes."

Brae's voice, "You guys really didn't plan this out so well, did you?" With exasperation, she continued, "We'll play a little longer than that's it. But pairs won't work. There are five."

"Yeah," began a disgruntled Sebastian. "Quinn, you—"

"Quinn, go with Brae and Sebastian upstairs," Iain broke in abruptly with a strong tone. "And Corey and I will look around down here."

A little stunned, Corey's eyes flew from Iain to Sebastian's face. There was a surprise, a hesitation on Sebastian's part, but then, in the end, he held back, "Yeah, come on."

Corey watched silently as Sebastian purposefully led his group up a grand curving staircase that she'd barely noted when they'd entered. On parting, Brae shot her a quick, perturbed glance, but it barely registered as she felt another curious tendril of warmth transverse her arm. It was pulling, drawing her. But she concentrated, anchoring herself onto the cold, dusty floor that was present.

She turned to Iain, who had crossed to a large marble fireplace, still grand in its neglect. "Well, what do you guys usually do on these expeditions?" He turned round to her, an odd, bemused expression on his face. "Dunno, this would be the first," and then a shrug. "The first like this anyway."

She was feeling acutely uncomfortable for a number of multiplying reasons. "So, what did the original Marguillers do?"

He frowned, "Tried to control the church behind the scenes."

Her turn to frown, "And the Templars?"

"Oh, fought the crusades, took control of quite a few things."

"That's not terribly helpful," she murmured.

He rested his elbow on the mantle of the black marble fireplace, and again, from the corner of her eye, she saw flames shooting out of its long-dead ashes. "Sorry," but he just stood there looking at her pointedly.

"What?" she asked, more than a bit bothered.

"I was just wondering when you were going to tell me what's going on here."

She crossed her arms in front of her in a mixture of discomfort and disdain, "What do you mean what's going on?"

He smiled, "You see things too. Don't you?"

Her eyes widened, "What do you mean too?"

And then he laughed, "I wasn't sure, but I am now. Can you hear the music?"

Slowly, she shook her head. "No, not music."

"But other things?"

"It feels warm."

He nodded, "Yes, feels that way, cozy and music. But it's all a trap. I knew it the first time I laid eyes on it. This is a really bad place."

"So, where should we start?"

He smiled at her directness — one thing that clearly had not changed about her. He'd noted when she'd arrived at the coffee shop that morning shadows under her eyes, a face slightly even more pale than usual, though her complexion had always tended to be fair. He sipped his strong blend of coffee. "You really should eat something. You don't look well."

She leaned back in the wooden chair, crossing her arms in front of her. "I thought we were going to work."

He picked up what remained of his croissant, taking another bite. "You have to be in the proper frame of mind to work."

Her eyes narrowed on him but then glanced away, picking up her own coffee mug and taking a sip. "I'm only tired. I had a bad night."

"Why?" he asked, finishing what little remained of his breakfast.

He sensed an understandable reticence. After all, confiding in him must feel a bit like baring your soul to an arch nemesis. "A lot of things, none of which I feel comfortable talking with you about."

He felt acutely as though she'd hit the nail on the head. "Well, I've been thinking about just that, Corey, about quite a few things, actually."

He paused momentarily, allowing her to absorb and hopefully anticipate where he was going. She stared at him blankly, "Am I supposed to guess what that means?"

"No need," he interjected abruptly. "I'm talking about trust. Something we two are sorely lacking and something integral if we hope to have any success."

Her eyes flickered across his face with skepticism that felt so hauntingly familiar. "Trust? That seems like a bit of a tall order at this point."

"Yes, but you were the one who brought me in, Corey, barring any ill feelings."

Her eyes narrowed again, and then she looked away, "I know. But I think the fact that I'm even here expresses a degree of trust on my part."

He laughed shortly, "No, that would be lovely, but unfortunately it expresses a degree of desperation."

"We can't help where we've come from, Iain," she softly replied.

He felt determined to keep this as rational as possible between them. "No, we can't, but if we are to go where is needed, we must rebuild some measure of trust between us. I'm sure you can see how it is necessary."

She sighed a little too deeply for his comfort. Something was happening with her that he was not at all comfortable with. "Yes, I suppose," she agreed with what appeared to be substantial fatigue. He wondered if it was possible for them to get anywhere today.

"So, let's start small. Tell me about last night."

"There were a number of things on my mind," she answered with no elaboration.

He felt more than a bit frustrated with her resistance. But how he loved a challenge, "Like?"

"I, uh, got a call from Brae last night," she said flatly.

"Really?" he found it hard to keep the surprise out of his voice.

She smiled fleetingly, and then it was gone so quickly he wondered if he'd seen it at all. "Yes, seems she had a change of heart about helping, about being so definitive with me when I called the last time."

"Was she definitive?" he asked, echoing her vague choice of words.

"Oh yes, she hung up on me."

"Hmm, seems extreme even for her."

Her eyes had focused on him in a speculative way that he found endearingly unnerving. "The past scares her, but evidently she reconsidered."

"And you said what exactly to her offer?"

"I told her that you were helping me." Then he felt her brown eyes lock on him as though intensely interested in his response. "She didn't think that was a good idea."

"Well, that sounds like Brae."

And then there was another smile, not unlike the first that he didn't understand but that prickled him beneath his skin, "Yes, doesn't it?"

He focused on her face, allowing himself to truly feel for the first time this morning, feel the odd energies that were swirling about her. "There's more."

"Not about that." She looked away, and then he deliberately put his hand over hers, trying to focus concretely on where this was going. And then she met his eyes. "It's the past."

He nodded, feeling that intently. "Yes, it certainly feels like the past, Corey."

"I took out old pictures, pictures of that house."

And then a familiar flood of sensation ran through his skin, a disturbing, disorienting sensation. "Why that house?"

She shook her head, "I don't know. It's like I couldn't stop myself from looking back there."

"Looking back can be a dangerous thing." He closed his eyes, feeling the strong draw of a long-ago curiosity. And then he opened them, focusing again on her delicate face framing the wide, compelling eyes. "But it seems as good a place as any to start."

She remembered that moment, one of those odd moments when reality seemed to shift, when the world that one can easily see becomes something different — of course not because it is different but because you see it differently. "What did you say?" she whispered in a tone that nearly crossed the outer boundaries of what qualified as a whisper.

His green eyes canvassed the stairway where the others had disappeared only moments before. "I don't think any of them get it." And then he was staring at her again, through her. "But you do."

She swallowed painfully, feeling as though nothing around her was quite solid. "So, why come here if you know what a bad place it is?"

He smiled a bit enticingly, "I guess because it is dangerous." And then a moment of consideration passed, "Why did you come, Corey?"

She hesitated, facing the question, realizing, unfortunately, that this was indicative of a significant pattern in her life — one of being swept along and not actually having made any conscious decision on her own. She was here ostensibly because Brae had decided. "I have no idea."

He whispered, "Yeah, I can see that." She breathed out deeply and closed her eyes, allowing the warm lights and the colors to pull her along. "It's not safe to do that, you know."

"I know," was the last words spoken by someone before she let go.

Corey, Corey, the sound came in a whisper, something tangential to where she was. The house was warm again with warm pink colors, the fireplace blazing amid the party. She breathed deeply, feeling a singe of smoke brush through her throat. But it didn't matter. It was all laughter, laughter coming from beautifully dressed people. The room was so filled with laughter and music, Iain's music. "This isn't safe, you know." She heard his voice behind her, felt him there, but turned around and didn't see him at all, just a man and a woman, a lovely couple standing by the long window across the room. The woman was dressed in a long, fitted, blue satin dress and he in a tuxedo. And there were more beautiful people — several others, three women, one in black lace, another red, the last pink, a long pink chiffon gown. Laughing, glasses of champagne, and music from the piano across the room — a man playing light, happy music. It was warm, so warm, it made her feel dizzy. The soft conversations felt like a muted building roar. But what could be wrong here? All was well.

"Can't you feel it, Corey? It doesn't fit." Her throat tightened. She glanced around, but there was no Iain, no Brae, or the others. And she was so tired.

She could feel it in her chest, everything just draining right out of her chest.

"Corey, Corey, *you have to leave.*" She spun around in the direction of the voice. It wasn't Iain, not at all— someone else who didn't belong here, not in this house. It was a woman she only knew through family photographs and distant memories. She stood in a pale yellow dress, not like the others at all. Not gay and bright, but soft and glowing. "Corey," she whispered in her mind. "*You must leave this place. They'll only drain you. If you let them, they'll take everything.*" She glanced around the room. All was silence now, and they were staring at her with wide, hungry eyes that sent horror through her young heart. "*Go!*" was the rush she felt, and then hands catching her as she fell into Iain's hands.

CHAPTER 12

CLOSING RANKS

She felt stunned at his last words. It hadn't occurred to her that he might want to take this tactic. "I don't understand."

His eyes, unreadable, now seemed to be studying her. It bothered her. She'd almost rather have his rage than this disinterested curiosity. "I'll explain, but not here, Corey. Tell me more about your conversation with Brae."

She felt distinctly uneasy about whatever was to come. "There's not much more to tell. It was a short conversation."

"So, I take it you two haven't stayed in touch."

"No," she glanced away at the disappearing breakfast crowd in the restaurant, at the outside street through the front window, at anything else at all.

"You two were close once."

And then she focused on him squarely, "Yes, well, we were close once too. But that was a long time ago."

He smiled, so prickly still. Evidently, her life choices hadn't set as well with her as she'd hoped. "Well, that's because you left me for another man. That is something that disrupts a relationship."

"And you became involved with Brae. That caused a disruption as well."

He sipped his coffee, wondering if this was at all constructive, but a morbid fascination compelled him on. "Yes, I always found that a bit strange. You had moved on. Why should you care who I was with?"

Her mouth seemed to thin a bit, "I didn't. Brae cared and never forgave me."

He frowned explicitly, "Forgave you for what?"

"Forgave me for the fact that you never really loved her."

An odd tangential realization swept in on him — collateral damage that he'd never taken a real interest in examining. "Well, that was between her and me."

She smiled in that odd, distant way. And suddenly, it dawned on him why he found it so troubling. It reminded him of a man he'd met once during his time in Europe — an old man, well versed in many methods of Eastern philosophy, quite a brilliant teacher, actually. But he was troubling. He'd asked him why he didn't practice and use his vast abilities. And he remembered that smile, that same smile. Then he'd simply answered, "This world has taken too much from me. I have no desire to give it any more of myself."

"Well, Iain, you weren't around to blame. So, I was a convenient target."

It hit him again oddly that Corey had somehow carried the burden of all their youthful mistakes — that she had born much more punishment than any of them. And in this odd retrospective moment, it really didn't seem fair to him. "I'm sorry."

She looked away with little reaction, again his words not truly seeming to pierce that strange, impenetrable veil that kept her separate from the world around her. "It doesn't matter. But I don't like looking back. I'd like to find another way."

"Well, we'll see. Are you ready to go?"

She answered, "Yes, I am."

"Not really, in and out."

The murmurs were loud, loud talking in her head, from both places, from her companions, and from the room filled with people, whispering, murmuring, like a low rumbling sound, a chant that made her skin crawl.

"Corey, wake up, Corey, try." The voice was low but strong, edged with urgency. Her eyes flickered open, and the light that filtered in wasn't from the house. It was brighter, though waning. She rubbed her eyes, her head throbbing.

"What's going on?" she whispered, trying to connect the collage of images tumbling in her mind. Hands pulled her into a sitting position. She looked around. It was the porch. That was why her skin was still prickling. She was still touching that house, touching its wood.

"Are you all right? Are you sick?" She heard Brae, then turned to her side to see her worried face.

"I don't know." Then she focused on another familiar figure standing before her, watching intently.

Iain spoke in a low voice, "You passed out."

She nodded, feeling a wave of nausea sweep through her. "I need to go home."

From beyond Iain, Sebastian interjected, "That might not be a bad idea. I think we're drawing attention. I've seen a few cars slow down in front of the house."

"I'm sorry I ruined things," Corey murmured, still feeling as though her head was swimming.

And then she saw a strange smile spread across Iain's face, "You didn't. We actually have a lot to talk about. Is there somewhere private where we won't be interrupted at your house?"

"Yeah, I guess, lots of somewheres."

He leaned over her. Then, extending her a hand that pulled her to her feet. Quinn Murdoch was suddenly beside them. "Where did you say you lived?"

"Um, Esplanade."

Then Brae said, "We'll have to take the streetcar."

On her heels, Sebastian added, "We can catch it on St. Charles."

The voices seemed to be swirling about her in a muddle. And then there were the other ones, still ringing in her head. Iain was beside her, hand on her back, as they began to move off the porch. "Can you make it?" he asked.

"I think so," she answered, but her mind was still crowded with the faces from the house, leering unnatural faces.

"Don't worry," he said. "It will pass."

"Can you still hear it?" she asked.

"It's fading," was his response.

They walked slowly down the streets of the French Quarter, largely in silence for the most part. He absently marked their direction, but at the moment, it had little importance. He focused himself entirely on the strange vibrations surrounding his companion. He had begun to pick up on it at the café, an odd circulation of energies in conflux around Corey. Clearly, something was out of balance. Perhaps it had to do with the missing Triquetra, but he was confused as to why that would be causing this disruption around her specifically. "Tell me about your memories."

They'd stopped at a cement bench near the cathedral in Jackson Square. "What memories?"

"The ones that come to mind most clearly." She brushed her long black hair off her shoulders. It flashed across his mind that since he'd first known her, she'd always kept her hair long, even as a girl. And then, in response, an image flashed across his mind of Corey dressed in a somber black dress at her father's funeral. Odd how he'd forgotten it. Corey's face was pale, and her hair was shorn, cut to just above her shoulders. It was only about a month after marrying Sebastian.

"How can that matter now?"

He reached beside him without looking at her and grabbed her hand. It felt cool, in fact nearly cold in his. "It does." He squeezed it tightly, disturbed, willing some of his warmth back into her. "What do you remember of being in the house?"

"I don't know. I remember faces, music, laughing. Why? Why would that matter now?"

"You're so vulnerable. It's strange. I can't figure out why."

"What do you mean?" she asked, her voice tired, distant.

"Those spirits in the house, they drained, you know."

"I think I remember something about that."

"A concentration of drainers," he reiterated.

"Yes, but they didn't really affect us then."

"No, we had a protection then. But I think they're draining you now through memory."

She turned to him with a look of incredulity. "What are you talking about?"

He laced his fingers in hers. "We need to go somewhere quiet."

They gathered in the sunroom of the Esplanade manor.

It was a comfortable room lined with light wicker furniture and white wooden tables, a place that Clayton Knight left largely to his children. However, Corey seldom found Samuel here, except occasionally to entertain his current girlfriend. Her brother had always moved easily in social circles that neither intrigued nor compelled her.

It was a quiet room, somewhat remote in the house, but not five minutes after the members of the modern-day Marguillers settled in. They were interrupted by her father. He appeared behind a set of closed French doors that he unceremoniously and abruptly swung open. "What's this?" he smiled in his most charming manner. "Corey, I didn't know you were bringing home friends today." His mouth smiled widely, but his eyes canvassed speculatively.

Still dizzy, she stood up from a white wicker rocker she'd gratefully settled into moments before. "Hi, Dad. Sorry, Brae's house was noisy, so we decided to come here. Hope it's okay."

He nodded, "Of course, this is your home. But I'm a bit surprised. I knew you were with Brae."

It clicked. That was right. She'd told him she was only with Brae. That was the downside of lying, keeping track of all the threads. Her cluttered mind whirled, quickly searching for an explanation. But before she could speak, Brae had jumped up, interjecting. "Didn't Corey tell you, Mr. Knight? It's a new club, a school club we've formed. It's our first meeting."

He smiled wider, taking in Brae's abrupt fabrication with evident skepticism. "Club? I didn't know you were involved in any clubs, Corey."

Brae gushed prettily, "It's sort of under wraps, probably why Corey never mentioned it."

His focus swept across Brae, settling squarely on Corey's shoulders. "What does that mean, under wraps?"

And then, to Corey's dismay, Sebastian stood up, taking a step in her father's direction and extending his hand. "Hello, Mr. Knight, my name is Sebastian Morris."

Corey saw an odd flicker of recognition cross her father's features. "Yes, I'm familiar with your family, young man."

Sebastian smiled in a way that seemed to rival her father's charm, "Yes sir, well, we certainly don't mean to intrude. The club, it's a bit of a lark. I suppose you could call us a sort of history club with a particular interest in the city."

"The city's history, in what respect Mr. Morris?" Clayton Knight responded smoothly.

Corey felt a wavering in Sebastian but saw none of it in his demeanor. He certainly kept his cool. "Well, in many respects, Mr. Knight, this city, as I'm sure you know, has such a colorful history as do so many of its houses, buildings. Why, I'm sure this house itself has many stories."

Her father eyed Sebastian with irritation and skepticism, an expression that Corey was more than a bit familiar with. It certainly wasn't the substance of what Sebastian had said but rather the way it was said. Clayton Knight had a barometer for insincerity that Corey had found nearly infallible. Feeling obliged to step in, she thought she should at least attempt to smooth the waters. "Is it all right if we stay, Dad? It's harmless, just something to do."

His eyes focused on her again, telling her with none too much subtly that this story was thin, "Of course. I'll see if Mrs. Vaughn has anything in the kitchen you young people might want to eat during your meeting." And then, with a quick step, he was gone.

Iain almost immediately slammed at Sebastian, "History club? Do you really think Corey's Dad is going to buy that bull?"

Sebastian pursed his lips in a manner of irritation that, in their relatively short acquaintance, Corey was becoming accustomed to, "Probably not. But it's all I could come up with on short notice." And then he directly shot her a pointed look, "What's his problem anyway? He looked like he wanted to toss us all out on our butts?"

She frowned, "He's protective. Ever since my Mom died, he's been very protective."

He nodded, seemingly accepting her explanation, and then he turned his focus on the thin, wiry boy who hadn't opened his mouth since they'd arrived. His back was to them, and he was staring at the several levels of white bookshelves built into the far wall of the sunroom. "Quinn, you still with us?" Sebastian prodded, his voice still laced with unrepressed aggravation.

Slowly, he turned around, his eyes rather larger than Corey remembered them being. "How long have you lived here?" he asked rather quietly.

She felt a quick wave of exhaustion pass over her as she sat back down in the rocker, trying to draw a calming breath. "For a while, I was young when we moved here. At least eleven years."

"Quite a place," he murmured, slowly sitting on a window seat. "Sebastian, you might want to tell them what happened upstairs in the Fabacher house."

Brae jumped in, "Yes, it was bizarre. I was really surprised, wasn't expecting to see much of anything."

"What happened?" Iain asked abruptly.

"Hang on," Sebastian jumped in. "What happened with you two first? With Corey?"

Corey opened her mouth to explain but was quickly cut off by Iain. "Not much. Corey got light-headed. That was all."

Sebastian came to his feet, staring down his friend. "That's all? That wasn't the impression I'd gotten when I came downstairs, not nearly."

"So, what happened with you guys?" Corey desperately wanted to diffuse this very odd situation. She didn't really understand why Iain wanted things kept private, but in her present state, she was willing to let it ride.

Brae began with enthusiasm. "It was the oddest thing. The three of us went upstairs and then decided to split up, each taking one of the rooms on the second floor. And there were many, more than just three. The place is enormous."

"I thought we were all supposed to stick together," Iain interjected.

"I decided we could cover more ground," Sebastian fired back curtly.

"What happened?" Corey whispered, already she was beginning to pick up images from Brae's words. She could see the bedroom as the door swept open. A huge room, but like the downstairs, with sheets covering the chairs and a bed, also draped.

"It was so odd, so cold, probably colder than the rest of the house." She could see Brae there at the center of the room, standing, her arms folded about her, rubbing her arms. "And then all of a sudden, I could smell something."

"What?" Iain asked with a note of distraction in his voice.

87

"You'll think it's strange, but something burning, like someone smoking. But of course, there was nothing around."

Iain's eyes passed over Corey, then back to Brae, "Anything else?"

She shook her head, "Not really, it was just creepy."

He stared across to Quinn, who just sat quietly listening, "What about you?"

He shrugged, "The room I went into was some sort of study, had a billiard table, though."

Corey, again in her mind, saw images floating in but strange split pictures of Quinn walking slowly through a room. It was like the others, furniture draped in sheets, but then another image layered on top of it with Quinn there but less substantial — men dressed in suits, smoking cigars, with drinks in their hands. They were from the party. The same one she'd seen downstairs. "Honestly, there wasn't much to note there, nothing like what happened to Sebastian."

Corey noticed that Iain's eyes flew to Sebastian with some surprise. "Holding back on us, Hugues?" he asked pointedly.

Sebastian shrugged, "No more than you two. I'm not an idiot. I know more happened than you're letting on, Jacques." He pronounced the Templar name with some exaggerated emphasis. "So, are we going to be candid, or should we just disband our new history club right now?"

Iain's response was interrupted just then by Mrs. Vaughn, their part-time housekeeper, entering the sunroom with a huge tray of lemonade and cookies.

"Hope this is all right for you young people. Next time, give me some warning, and I'll have something a bit more substantial ready for you."

CHAPTER 13

THE AFTERMATH

Corey was more than a bit surprised when Iain brought her to a small house just on the fringes of Audubon Park. It was a wood frame house, very pleasant, landscaped quite prettily with a small courtyard on the side. It was a lovely area, but finding that Iain had set up shop here, she found a bit astounding. And for a number of reasons, it felt oddly unreal being here at all, given that a few days earlier, he had essentially told her to go to hell. How that quaky ground had shifted so abruptly left her at the very least uneasy and at the most massively suspicious. At times, a lurking fear drifted in that this was some sort of massive revenge that he was weaving about her. But then again, surreptitious activity wasn't exactly Iain's style. The man she remembered preferred to punch you in the face rather than stab you in the back. But then again, she hadn't known Iain for many years. The man she once knew could ostensibly no longer exist. "How long have you been here?" she asked as he turned the light on for them in the den.

"A few months," he replied. "Not really all that long."

She remembered his last place, the last place of his that she'd seen before he'd left for Europe. It was more of a studio than a home at the end of City Park Avenue — a big, airy place with a loft. This house, however, was something different, somehow oddly more personal.

The inside was spacious, nice-sized rooms with large windows, although rather sparsely furnished. She breathed deeply. There was a pleasant atmosphere here, unlike her father's house, not thick with memory. "Do you want something to drink?" he asked her. She'd wandered into the center of the room, somewhat unconsciously.

"No," she answered. "I'm all right, though still puzzled by what you said."

She turned to him. He'd divested himself of his jacket and placed it on the armchair near the door. It made her smile. She remembered this. Iain would just throw clothes here and there indiscriminately. Back then, she'd always chalked his untidy nature to an artistic temperament.

"Well, I'm not surprised. To be perfectly honest, I'm not entirely sure what I meant."

"Well, don't you think we should be concentrating more on the Triquetra?"

He smiled in that distant way, one that she truly didn't remember from before. "Corey, don't you remember the way we found it? The winding path it took to get there?"

She glanced away, trying to sweep away the varied images that his words had brought to her mind. "I suppose."

"Yes, we must follow its path, not try to force ours upon it."

"So, have you decided?"

She looked up from the stack of photos that she'd just been rifling through. She'd found a dark room on Magazine Street where you could rent time to develop your pictures. Doing this, however, made her truly yearn to set up her dark room in the Esplanade mansion. But then again, a step like that would clearly denote a commitment to staying in New Orleans — something she was still hesitant about making. Brae sat across from her at the table, waiting expectantly. "Decided what?" she answered, still distracted. She was pleased. Some of the shots she'd taken in Algiers had really turned out to be exceptional.

Brae smiled broadly as though she'd found some circumstance amusing. "Decided to stay on, more permanently?" She glanced up, feeling unnerved at how Brae seemed to ferret out exactly what was on her mind.

She slipped the photos back into their oversized brown envelope, shaking her head. "Hard to say. That sort of depends on Dad." Their lunch meeting had been a bit impromptu. In fact, she'd tried getting out of it, feeling more than a bit reclusive today. But Brae had insisted, and they'd arranged to meet at a small bistro on Magazine Street.

Again, Brae smiled in that knowing way that suggested there was something specific on her mind. "Is that all it depends on?"

She looked up, suddenly recognizing the inferential tone. "What does that mean?" was her direct reply that probably came out a shade too stern.

The redhead easily picked up on it. She frowned, "No need to get testy. I was talking about Iain."

"What about Iain?"

She shrugged, "I don't know. I was talking to Quinn the other day, and he implied that you'd been seeing a lot of each other."

"Quinn? How does Quinn—"

"Um, let's see. I gather he'd called Iain the other day for something, and he was on his way out to see you."

"And from that, you put together that we've been seeing a lot of each other?"

Again, the elusive smile, "No, your reaction tells me that you've been seeing a lot of each other. Sorry, is it some kind of secret?"

"No," a sudden irritation at Brae's prying swept over her. Even in their old acquaintance, Corey liked to maintain boundaries, boundaries that she oddly felt were now being trampled upon.

"So, you have been seeing a lot of each other?"

An inexplicable uneasiness shifted around in her stomach. She didn't think much about what was going on between her and Iain, mostly because she couldn't define it or quite wrap her brain around it. And so, the idea of discussing something with someone else that she herself didn't get — well, that was too uncomfortable. "Some," she replied, siping her rather oversized glass of iced tea.

"Hmm," she smiled again. "Some, well, I think it's great. He's always had a thing for you, even in the old days."

"No, he didn't," she murmured.

"Well, then, you were the only one who didn't think so. I imagine he wants you to stick around."

"I don't really know. We haven't talked about it much."

Brae leaned back in her chair, running her hand through her short, curly bob of red hair. "You know, I don't get you. Iain's an amazing guy, very intense, and has always had an attachment to you. It's not like you're tied up with someone else. What is the problem?"

Corey felt an odd fluttering panic in her chest. And the only way to describe it was a premonition, a feeling of imminent turmoil binding her somehow. It was in that strange, awkward moment that she understood what the problem truly was — the odd elusive anxiety, feeling that something was approaching, day by day creeping closer, becoming inescapable. She had no idea what it was, only that it was coming and would hit like some sort of wave that would change everything. But she smiled pleasantly to Brae, for it wasn't something that she felt she could rationally voice or layout in any coherent way that could be understood.

"So, do we come clean, or is it time to disband?" It was odd as Corey watched the clash between the two friends, watching the bizarre dynamic of their relationship in play. Friendship, foes, and rivalry were all swirling in the mix, but then again, maybe it was just the brooding aura of the Fabacher house that still cloaked everything. Sebastian stood staring down Iain in his confrontational manner, and Iain stood just feet away from him, looking at Sebastian with that mask of his, that expressionless deadpan look as though they could be discussing the weather. And of course, Quinn and Brae were sitting on a long wicker bench watching with interest and still munching on Mrs. Vaughn's sugar cookies.

"What makes you so sure we haven't come clean, Hugues?" was Iain's very cool response.

She felt Sebastian's eyes slide over her briefly, making it clear at that moment that he felt her to be the author of this infringement somehow. "I don't know. I feel it. Like you two have become some sort of conspirators."

Iain laughed, "That's stupid."

"Oh good, now I'm stupid," Sebastian spat out.

Brae stood up, cookie still in hand, "Okay, guys, do you really want Corey's Dad back in here? Keep it down. This is not fun anymore."

"Brae's right," eyes turned to her. For a moment, she hadn't realized it had been her voice, but it had. And evidently, it would need to be the voice of reason. "Look, something did happen, but I haven't told Iain. I haven't told anybody. It shook me up too much."

Iain's eyes clashed with hers in response to her partial fabrication. But she didn't feel like coming between these two friends or whatever they were. So instead, she blindly plunged forward, "I saw something in the house. It was as though there were a party going on."

Brae was the first to interject, "What does that mean, a party? We were the only ones—"

"Let her finish," Sebastian cut her off abruptly. For the moment, he seemed wholly focused on what she was saying.

"Um, it was in that big room downstairs. I guess it was a parlor or den or something. But it started to change. I could hear people laughing and then see them dressed up in old-time clothes."

"Evening clothes?" Quinn piped in from his bench on the other side of the room.

Corey nodded, "Yes, but more old-fashioned."

"What do you mean, like hoop skirts?" Brae asked with evident confusion.

She shook her head, "No, not that old, I don't know."

"Thirties," again Quinn interjected.

She shrugged a bit, scrambled by the rapid interrogation. "Maybe."

"Makes sense," Sebastian added.

"Yes," echoed Iain, whose voice now seemed very measured, perhaps thoughtful.

"What else?" Sebastian prodded.

"Um, well, they were laughing and drinking and then seemed very strange. I don't know. I had a terrible feeling as though I was threatened."

Sebastian nodded, walking toward one of the long windows as though the young man was carefully considering everything she'd said. "Well, that does fit in."

Iain was standing beside him now, looking disgruntled. "What does that mean exactly? Your turn, Hugues."

Sebastian smiled, "Aren't you overusing that name a bit?"

Then Quinn stepped in, "You know it was in 1934 that they were all found in the house."

"What does that mean, found? Who was found?" Brae's voice had become slightly more shrill than usual.

Corey felt a creepiness wrap around her at the turn of the conversation. "What is the history of that place?" she asked, now recognizing acutely that this was the question that should've been asked before they went in.

Iain frowned, then looked to Sebastian as though permitting him to explain. "A whole group of people were found dead there."

Corey waited, more than a bit stunned, for elaboration, "What does that mean, some sort of mass murder?"

Sebastian shook his head in response to Corey's question. "No, from what Quinn gathered through newspaper clippings, it was a sort of ritual suicide. Seems they were some sort of Satanists."

Corey turned her glare directly on Iain, "Satanists? Are you serious? What are you guys, completely nuts? You couldn't have told us this ahead of time?"

He answered matter-of-factly, "We really didn't expect much, if anything, to happen. It hasn't before."

Brae jumped in, "You're saying you've gone in places like this before, and nothing has ever happened."

Quinn hesitantly answered, "Yeah, there was an old church down Rampart. It had a dark reputation as well, but there was nothing."

"And another house down Annunciation Street, reputed meeting place for an old Voodoo coven. But zip, we even took pictures. So, why would we expect this time to be different?" Sebastian's voice sounded incredibly distracted to her. Clearly, she and Brae weren't the only ones shaken.

"But it was different," Iain commented dryly. She glanced at him, and then it hit her abruptly. He'd told her about the music and told her he'd heard things before. So clearly, he was lying to the other two original Marguillers. Then abruptly, Iain turned to Sebastian, "You still haven't told us what you saw."

"I didn't see anything," was his curt reply, but then he stretched out his arm and slowly began to push up the long sleeve of his white button-down shirt. Within seconds of his pushing up the shirt sleeve, Corey gasped in shock at what she saw. There could be no mistake of what it was — a vivid, nearly scarlet claw scratch on his arm.

· CHAPTER 14 ·

MEDITATION

"I think we should attempt a meditation."

They were sitting on the moss-green sofa in Iain's den. She was drinking a cup of tea he'd brewed her only moments before. It was an odd flavor, laced with some delicate spice, but one that she found very relaxing. In fact, she was feeling very relaxed and unguarded, which the little voice in the back of her mind was reminding her was very foolish — foolish to let this man so close, this man who could so easily hurt her. No one else had ever possessed the array of weaponry in that respect that Iain seemed to wield. "A meditation?"

He sat down beside her but not too close, not as close as she had instinctively expected him to. "Yes," he responded rather quietly.

As he smoothly took the cup of tea out of her hand, she leaned back against the couch, relaxing. "I haven't tried meditation since I took a yoga class back in New York. And that wasn't what I considered a great success."

"I find it helps you to gain perspective," his voice was soft, lulling. And she wondered distantly if she should be alarmed.

"And this you discovered in Europe?"

"In France, actually Rouen, I spent some time there studying things other than sculpting."

Her eyes flickered open, and she glanced over at him watching her. She hadn't realized that they were closed. "And this will help us find the Triquetra?"

"I don't know," he replied. "It's a place to start."

95

"What do we do?"

"Just relax and close your eyes." As she did, she continued to hear his voice. "I'll lead you through Corey."

It began with light, dark colors that were being pierced by great shafts of white.

Distantly, she remembered that her first meditation had taken place many years before, many years before Ecole Issoire in the office of a psychologist. It had been nearly three years since her mother's death that the dreams began, then the odd visions and the maelstrom of inexplicable, disjointed emotions. Dr. Jeffreys, her pediatrician, had suggested horrible specters like schizophrenia and an array of other mental illnesses. But Clayton Knight seemed oddly unfazed and quietly took her to a specialist instead.

Marian Rochmore was an accredited psychologist on paper, but as Corey discovered through the years that she spent in her care she dabbled in many alternative treatments. Dr. Jeffreys had suggested a psychiatrist and had even recommended several noted ones. And her father had graciously accepted the names, even allowed an appointment to be scheduled, but then quietly cancelled and dropped Dr. Jeffreys as the children's primary physician.

Corey hadn't questioned her father's actions, just allowed her fears to be allayed by his reassurances. "It's all right, Corey. You're like your mother, touched by all sorts of gifts you must learn to master."

It was unexpected — the odd familiarity of it all. Though her conscious mind would say emphatically that this all was new, every other part of her whispered that she had been here before.

She breathed in deeply and felt the cool air permeate her lungs. It was an energy that surrounded her, touching her skin, her face, lightly, skimming it — making her feel as though she had a body when she did not.

She looked upward, the tall trees overhead arching over them, at least several stories high, still gently dropping cascading leaves down like a soft spring shower. "Where are we?"

"Somewhere peaceful," was all he said. But not spoken. She felt it in her mind. The blue sky overhead was barely perceptible through the branch cover above them, but she could see it was nearly nightfall.

And then, in a jarring, abrupt yank, they were back on Iain's sofa. She breathed in deeply, feeling a pain ripping at her chest. Her hand was still in his, clutching tightly. "It's all right," his voice had a breathless quality. "I didn't expect we'd get that far."

Slowly, she released his hand, recognizing for the first time that she'd been holding it. "You've been there before."

"Yes," he murmured just as an acute sweep of dizziness passed over her. She leaned her head back on the sofa, closing her eyes. She tried to regain some control while still struggling to retain the feeling of peacefulness she'd glimpsed in only those brief moments in the forest. "It was nearly night," she whispered.

"Yes," his voice seemed a bit more controlled now. Clearly, Iain had the capacity to recover more quickly than she did. "That leads some credence to the missing Triquetra."

She opened her eyes, looking at him with a bit of surprise. "You still doubt it's gone."

Abruptly, he stood up and walked across the room, briefly looking out a window, then turning back to her rather sternly. "Clearly, something is out of balance where it should not be Corey. But as of now, I'm not completely convinced the Triquetra has anything to do with it."

She straightened up, feeling a bit as though he had punched her. She had not sensed a glimmer at all that he possessed such doubts. "Well, what about Dad?"

"Yes, your father was an extraordinary man, but also, as I remember, not always completely straightforward in his motives." He frowned, "All I'm saying is that we should proceed with caution and look at everything. Not get too wrapped up in what we assume is happening."

She leaned back on the sofa again, feeling fatigue and nausea simultaneously take her over. "Fine, Iain, I'll go along with whatever you think is best."

In seconds, he was beside her, his cool hand on her forehead. "This really took a lot out of you."

She nodded, not speaking, just feeling a darkness reaching up around her, swallowing everything before she slipped into unconsciousness.

It was odd to her when the cycle began, not when she was a young girl or a teenager or when the Marguillers had their heyday. No, it was truly when the dreams returned, a point that was difficult upon reflection to pinpoint, but now, wandering in this disjointed place between time, it became clearer. Some weeks after she'd returned from New York to care for her father, even before she'd begun seeing Iain, they'd come back. But at first, as with all unpleasant things, it was easy to ignore them, disregard them, refuse them real access to her life until, of course, they refused to be denied.

It was caves, or so she believed, sometimes caves by the ocean, sometimes in the desert, and sometimes in the forest. And she walked, always walked into the caves wearing a long white nightgown, just ending below her knees, and no shoes. She was aware of this because invariably, before the end, her feet would bleed from the sharp rocks by the ocean, the hot sand, or the broken twigs on the forest floor. But today, it was the ocean because the soft spray from the waves filled her nostrils and mouth as she ventured into the shadowed cave. Today, there was only a distant light within — a soft glow, a hurricane lamp, and a figure seated beside it, waiting patiently for her.

And then she felt hands squeezing her tightly, almost painfully, yanking her back into a dark place. "Corey, Corey," her eyes snapped open, staring into Iain's worried face. Her head spun with dizziness.

"What happened?" she asked as he less than gently pulled her up into a sitting position on the sofa.

"You passed out," he snapped out. He abruptly placed his hand across her forehead, still looking at her with concern. He was shaken. Clearly, after all these years, she could reach him.

"I'm all right," she managed to get out. "I guess it was all a bit much."

He still stared at her with frantic sternness, but it had leveled out a bit. She glanced away from his gaze. Again, she could feel it. He was trying to read her, trying to feel her thoughts, and that made her vastly uncomfortable. Then he grasped her chin and softly turned her back to face him. "I thought there were to be no more secrets, Corey."

Slowly, she took his hand in hers, gently but deliberately removing it from her chin. "I said we would work together, but I don't remember promising anything else."

Speculatively, he slowly traced the bottom of her chin with his fingertips, sending a tendril of remembered sensation reverberating through her skin. It caused her to shiver visibly, which seemed to please him because he smiled. "Well then, you are going to promise it now. From here on out, no more secrets."

Very slightly, she nodded, "Yes, from here on out, no more secrets."

· CHAPTER 15 ·

SCARS

"When did that happen?" Corey asked with more than a bit of shock in her voice.

Sebastian glanced up, for the second time that day, directly engaging her gaze. It was odd the contact she felt from him — a mixture of emotions, the most prominent of which was triumph. He wore that brutal scratch as though it were a badge of courage. "Upstairs, at the end of the hallway, there was a double set of doors up there with huge brass knobs. I had just put my hand on one when I felt the tear at my arm." And then he lowered his voice clearly for effect, "It felt like some kind of animal."

Beside him, Iain inquired, a bit too sedately given the circumstances, "Did you see anything?"

Sebastian straightened up from the more conspiratorial pose he'd struck with Corey. "No."

"Hear anything?" Iain grilled with no emotion.

"No," he answered with irritation.

"Well," Iain replied, "that gives us a lot of information."

Again, Corey glanced down at the bright red scratch mark on Sebastian's forearm, "That's unbelievable, something so physical."

"Did anyone bother to look in that room?" Iain continued to grill.

"Are you kidding?" Brae exploded. "After that! No telling what would have happened to any of us if we'd tried."

With deliberateness, Sebastian began to roll down his sleeve. And then, rather calmly and unexpectedly, Quinn interjected, "It's odd. That this time we all experienced something, and the other times nothing at all."

"Maybe it was the house," Sebastian stated.

"Maybe," Iain replied, "or maybe it was us, all of us going in together that triggered something."

"Maybe," Quinn responded thoughtfully. "Maybe both."

"Enough for today." He pronounced rather abruptly.

She straightened up on his exceptionally soft, moss-green couch. "Are you sure? It doesn't really seem as though we've gotten anywhere."

He sat down in a thin, wicker, straight-backed chair on the other side of the room. She had no idea what time it was, how much time they'd spent together today. But with the blinds on the windows closed, the room was in shadows. Except for a few standing lamps, there wasn't much light. "Don't be impatient, Corey. I think we've laid a good foundation today. Tomorrow, we'll do more."

It was odd she'd been in his company all day, but it was only now that she remembered to be nervous. "I-I have a few appointments tomorrow with clients."

"Clients?"

She hesitated. Something in her was so reticent to give him too much access to her life. "I make jewelry, like—"

"Like your father did," he finished for her.

"Yes, a few years back, I took it up and began rebuilding his business."

He laughed softly, "Well, I'm sure you would have made Clayton proud. But I don't remember you showing any interest in it."

She cleared her throat, feeling uncomfortably on edge. He was probing. She could feel it on her skin. "No, I didn't back then, though he did show me the trade. My interest came later."

"And the photography?" he asked, rather hollowly she thought.

"I let it go."

There was silence for a few moments, then he responded, "That's too bad. You were good."

She stood up on wobbly legs but steeled herself to remain standing. "Well, if we're not going to do any more tonight, I should get home. I have some work to do before tomorrow." For a second, her vision blurred, and then she concentrated sharply, bringing everything back into focus with sheer will. She couldn't allow herself to be this weak.

And then he was standing in front of her in the dim light, looking at her speculatively. "You should get something to eat, Corey. You haven't eaten lunch. It might help."

"I'm all right," again, the dizziness swept through her, and he reached out, steadying her arm with his hand.

He smiled, seeing through her. "You know, you must reconcile that I'm your ally in this and allow your guard down."

"I still don't understand," she spoke so quietly that she wasn't sure if she had or if it remained a thought in her mind.

"Understand what?"

"Why? Why are you willing to do this at all?"

She saw something cross his face, and she knew she'd reached him somehow with her raw vulnerability. "I'm not entirely sure yet. I've learned, though, over the years that things that are unfinished never rest." And then he met her eyes directly, his green eyes as she remembered them. "I think it might be selfish. But it feels as though I have something to finish here."

She felt the truth of his words resonate in her. But she knew she was here simply because her father had asked—the idea of resolution she'd given up on long ago. Living now had become merely a matter of getting by. There was no continuity anywhere in her life. It was simply a mass of tangled, unwinding threads — none connected nor having any hope of being so. "Will you take me home?" she asked.

"Yes, but we'll stop and get something to eat first." She nodded, accepting, knowing quite well by his tone that it was useless to try to argue.

CHAPTER 16

ROUEN

She didn't see her father the rest of the afternoon, not until dinner, where the three of them ate largely in silence. It was an odd thing, their mealtimes. Clayton Knight insisted on a limited number of things, but on those, he was immovable — one of them being their presence at dinner. Having moved into a more social time of life, Samuel had tried to breach this particular barrier, often pleading special cases. But rarely, and Corey was surprised at her father's obstinance on this point, did he get out of this ritualistic family meal. And contrary to what one would expect, these dinners often occurred mostly in silence.

That evening, following the impromptu meeting of the Marguillers, Corey had expected to be grilled ad nauseam, but luckily, so far, nothing. Quietly, she ate, occasionally glancing up at her father's unreadable face that was either poised over his half-eaten meal or looking forward as though deep in thought. Next to her, Samuel was hurriedly eating. Clearly, he had other plans for the rest of the evening. Then, suddenly and jarringly, her father's deep voice breached the silence. "Have you told Sam about the club you've gotten involved with?"

Samuel's face pulled up from his plate, and he looked at her with mild confusion, "What club?"

A little shaken at the abruptness, she answered awkwardly, "Um, it's nothing. Just a group of kids getting together to form a history club."

Sam looked at her a bit blankly, "History? That sounds boring."

"One of the Morris boys is involved," her father coolly interjected.

And then Sam was eying her with a bit more interest. "I didn't know you knew any of the Morris family."

She swallowed, wondering distractedly what all the interest was in Sebastian. "I don't really, just met him today through another friend."

"Who?" Samuel asked her directly. She glanced over at her father, whose expression told her he was interested but content to let Samuel do the work for him.

"A boy in my chemistry class."

Samuel stared at her intently, clearly focused now. "Okay, kiddo, does the boy have a name?"

"Does it matter? We're in a club, not going steady."

And then her father stepped in with his low, rich voice that, for some odd reason at that moment, reminded her of caramel candy. It was undeniably a talent of his, supplying manipulative intonations with his speech—a talent he was completely in control of and used at will. "Corey, you're new to this school. We simply don't want you falling in with the wrong crowd."

His voice was so soothing, but all the same, making her feel like prey trapped by a charming hunter. "Hang on. You were the one that forced me to go to this wonderful school, nearly at gunpoint. So, I am and trying to make friends."

"Hey, kiddo, don't get so ruffled. What's the kid's name?" Sam interjected pointedly while gesturing at her with his fork, a potato strategically perched on its tip.

"His name is Iain Ssssh—something."

Samuel smiled broadly, "I don't know, Dad. I'm not familiar with any Ssssh something kids at Ecole Issoire."

"It's Shaw, all right." She delivered with way too much exasperation for this calculating crowd.

Sam grinned broadly while gulping his iced tea, "Wow, that was hard. Yeah, don't know much about the kid. Don't think he's incredibly rich."

"Oh then, he must be trouble," Corey mumbled with aggravation.

Sam shook his head, "Not that I know of. But the Morrises, damn, they think they own the world."

Her father, who'd watched the animated exchange with quiet interest, leaned back in his tall chair. "Well, be appraised, Corey, to keep an eye on that one. There are people in this world who have money. Then there are people who have money and think it gives them license to do anything."

"He's only fifteen, Dad."

He nodded, "Some start young, just be aware."

And that was the last time he brought up the subject for some time, in fact, for many years.

Once Iain returned Corey to her house, he spent some time roaming the city, feeling a turbulence of emotions swarming about him. He took the time more to regain his composure and reign in the feelings that threatened to drag him back into a place to which he had no desire to return. He'd studied for many years while he was away, studied to give himself a different sort of life. It began when he was on his own, his early years living in France — taking a small apartment in Rouen and focusing nearly exclusively on his sculpting.

While not particularly soothing, concentrating on those memories did lead him to a place of balance. By any generous description, he could have been called a hermit in those first years, only having direct contact with people when he was forced to for financial reasons. He managed to secure an instructorship at one of the smaller colleges in the city, teaching drawing, painting, and strangely enough pottery making — something that became useful as he filled his cupboards with cups and dishes of his own making. Of course, there was also the opportunity to teach sculpting, but he passed on it. At that time, sculpting had become more than an art to him. It had become an integral, personal lifeline that he was no longer willing to share in a classroom setting. Doing so would be like prying open a secret wound, so instead, he obtained raw materials for his art from the college and sculpted in the spare bedroom of his apartment.

He remembered clearly, two years after leaving New Orleans, he worked up the courage to bring several of his pieces to a local art gallery. The owner was a man in his early fifties, of a smaller stature than himself, brown-haired, bearded, and he remembered clearly from that first meeting, with piercing dark eyes. They were eyes that he'd found oddly familiar but, at that time, didn't know why.

That night lay firmly lodged in his memory. It was perhaps only half an hour before the gallery closed. Except for one or two straggling patrons, the place, which was rather spacious, was empty. The owner greeted him warmly in French, and Iain replied as fluently as he was able. Aside from work, he had put effort into learning the native tongue over the last several years. But the man smiled, catching quickly onto his awkwardness. "We can speak in English if you are more comfortable," he said, then he glanced down at the large tote bag that Iain carried. Quite kindly, he spoke, "That must be very heavy. Have you brought something to show me?"

It was odd. Even in English, he fumbled with speech that night, though it was his native tongue. He truly felt like a hermit stumbling out of his cave. Quite honestly, this meeting was ostensibly the only real human interaction he'd had since he'd arrived. His students, others working at the college he'd managed to hold at a disinterested distance, not allowing anyone to penetrate the solitude he'd deliberately woven about himself. But in only seconds, with a few words, this man had cut through those artificial defenses like a cool breeze sweeping over a desert. "Yes," he answered more shakily than he was comfortable with. "I'm a sculptor."

And then the man reached out his hand, taking Iain's in a firm grasp, replying lightly. "Good to meet you. My name is Andre Desmarais." Certainly, looking back now, he acknowledged that it was a meeting that changed the course of his life.

CHAPTER 17

THE POLITICS OF ADVENTURE

It was unsettling returning to school the next day after her first exposure to the adventures of the Marguillers. Corey ostensibly had no idea what to expect. And she was neither disappointed nor particularly encouraged. Pretty much nothing happened. She saw Sebastian in the hall between classes, and he nodded to her and then walked on. She saw Quinn muddling around during lunchtime. For a moment, she caught his eye, and he smiled awkwardly, then turned away quickly.

And then there was Iain, Iain, who met her eyes with a stony expression and a raised eyebrow. So, she just turned away, feeling more than a bit disgruntled. And so, it went on like this for a week. The only person who breathed a word about what happened to her was Brae. Brae, sitting on the cool cement bench that had become their haunt between classes, shook her long red hair and whispered with irritation, "I don't know what their problem is. It's like they're giving us the cold shoulder."

Corey frowned, "Really, you think so?"

She shrugged, "I don't know. I went up to talk to Sebastian after first period and asked him what's next. And he just sort of brushed me off. I mean, what is their problem? All this stupidness was their idea."

Corey shook her head as perplexed by the turn of events as Brae seemed to be. "I don't know. Maybe they had second thoughts about inviting us in."

Brae made some sort of unintelligible, exasperated hiss, "Yeah, well, who cares? It was so much fun the last time. Can't wait to do it again." And then, rather quickly, she derailed onto another train of thought, "So, do you want to go to the movies this weekend?" And so, it went on, although not so far away, but out of their earshot and vision, another conversation was going on.

Sebastian was pacing up and down while Quinn sat perched on the stoop of an outside building door. And calmly watching and unfazed by his friend's agitation was Iain, leaning against the outside brick wall. "So, what did you tell your Dad about the key?"

"I still can't believe he noticed it was gone. He never looks at that stuff. He collects and puts it in a glass case in his little museum upstairs, then never goes in there. He caught me completely off-guard when I came in. He just slammed me with his grilling."

Quinn muttered, "Well, there goes our skeleton key. That makes everything so much harder."

"Well, sorry to inconvenience you," Sebastian snapped out. "And on top of that, crazy Brae shanghaied me in the hall today, asking in front of other people what we were doing next. I guess the term secret society goes whoosh over her head."

"So, Sebastian, what did you tell your Dad?" Iain placidly repeated.

He turned, glaring at Iain. "Like I said, he caught me off guard. He rattles me when he gets in his accusatory mood. I hate it."

Iain frowned. Getting information here was like pulling teeth this morning. "Understood. What did you say?"

"I just said I wanted to show it to some friends. Something stupid like that."

"And he said?" Iain prodded.

"Let's see. He said how entirely irresponsible that was. How valuable that piece was, how much money he'd paid for it. What a disappointment I was to him. How I am banned from that room for the rest of my natural life and, oh yeah, grounded for two weeks. How'd that sound?"

"Sorry you had to take the heat like that, mate."

"Yeah, and now I have Miss Bubble Head spreading news of what we're doing all over the place. I told you it was a mistake having them along."

Iain retained his calm demeanor and said flatly, "If we hadn't invited them, I'm sure nothing would have happened."

Quinn glanced up at him with a bit of shock on his face. "Are you serious? You really think that?"

"Yeah, having them there somehow ignited things. And however much complication it caused, you have to admit it was a rush."

Sebastian eyed him a bit warily but, in the end, agreed. "Yeah, it was. But it's going to be blown to bits if she blabs."

"She won't," he cut him off. "I'll take care of it. Just mend things at home, and we'll just lay low for a bit."

He smiled, his thin face seeming genuinely pleased to see his old friend. But the odd pallor of Quinn's skin disturbed Iain. His old friend was not yet forty years old, but his face and his body spoke of someone who had waged a long battle, a battle that clearly, he was tiring of.

He reached out to shake Iain's hand, "I was surprised to hear from you," he said, still with a light in his eyes. "Last time we spoke, there seemed to be a fatalistic air about you. Thought you might be moving on."

Iain sat in one of the wrought iron chairs at the patio table. He'd called Quinn early that morning, arranging for this brunch in the Quarter. It was spontaneous but also born out of a need to immerse himself in places that he did not understand. It wasn't a particularly logical choice, but then again, this journey was beginning to unwind in a way that didn't feel particularly logical. Only after he'd been up some hours early in the morning did he remember the business card that Quinn had pressed in his hand at their last meeting. He smiled back at him grimly, "Well, at that point, I wasn't really sure what I'd be doing."

Quinn nodded, taking a menu from the waitress who'd just appeared near their somewhat secluded outside table. "Hot tea," he directed to her.

And Iain followed with, "Just coffee," and then they were alone again. The restaurant inside was busy enough, but fewer patrons seemed to frequent the establishment's outdoor section, which suited Iain well. At the moment, quiet seemed best, as he had no idea where this was going.

"So, you've changed your mind?"

He glanced up. Quinn's rather penetrative gaze was focused on him. That, he thought interesting, the body surrounding him might be showing signs of fading, but the eyes at moments were so intensely grounded in this world. He found it hard to imagine him ever not being a part of it. "For now."

Quinn seemed oddly amused by Iain's responses. "So, tell me, old friend, what are we doing here? Or have you finally decided to let me in on whatever brought you back in the first place?"

He shrugged, "Well, I don't know, maybe middle age. Maybe a desire to make peace with the past."

Quinn laughed sharply, a sound that even Iain found a bit startling. "Make peace with the past? Oh, my, then that would make you a vastly different man from the one I remember. When you first showed up on my doorstep, I thought perhaps you had finally come to settle things with Sebastian. Hmm, make peace? I always thought there would be no peace until you had his head on a platter. But then again, maybe that's why you're here."

But before he could respond, the waitress had appeared with their respective beverages, giving Iain a few spare moments to consider his old friend's comments.

CHAPTER 18

THE READER

She was running a bit late, and that was unusual for Corey. She was usually punctual, but then again, these past few days had been anything but usual. Seeing Iain, beginning to work with him to find the Triquetra, had left her, to say the least, a bit disoriented. Luckily, most of the work on Lucy Charbonnet's amulet had already been completed. It was a complicated but beautiful piece that she'd actually been fine-tuning for the last six months. Complicated was an apt description. Far from being simply decorative, the primary jewel, a high-grade piece of lapis lazuli, was a conductor of energy. Lucy Charbonnet, after all, was one of the best-kept secrets in the city. She was a tarot card reader, an extraordinarily talented, private reader obtainable by exclusive appointment only.

Corey was escorted through the rather extensive Carrollton Avenue estate by Lucy's housekeeper out onto a courtyard built on the very edge of an elaborately landscaped rose garden. It was a lovely little patio, nestled at the back of the house, completely secluded in privacy, as were the best of New Orleans' courtyards. As she walked through the double French doors to the outside, she fought back a chill that involuntarily traveled down her spine.

Lucy, who was at least a decade older than Corey, had only acquired this house a little over a year ago after her divorce. She'd bought it for its high degree of spiritual activity, and for that same reason, it made Corey uneasy. There were unsettling forces at work in its walls, something from which Lucy drew inspiration and something that Corey found taxing and draining.

The thin, wiry, blond woman stood up smiling with hands widely outstretched. She was dressed in a rather flamboyant indigo-colored silk robe. At that moment, she recalled that Lucy was a bit of a late riser. Taking Corey's hands in hers, Lucy remarked with exaggerated concern, "Oh my goodness, your hands feel absolutely chilled. How about some hot tea? I was just drinking a cup of chamomile mint."

Corey smiled, again feeling an odd sweep of dizziness that seemed clinging to her from yesterday. "I have the piece finished. But I want to see if you want any changes before I put the final touches on it."

Lucy's eyes were sweeping over Corey speculatively. Clearly, there were other things on her mind. "Yes, I'm looking forward to seeing it. But let's put off the business for a few moments at least. I'm all curious as to what is happening with you. There are so many conflicting energies swirling about you."

Corey smiled back at her but inwardly felt a mounting discomfort. The disturbing thing about Lucy, even with all her eccentricities, was that she was the genuine article. She was a bona fide seer, and just now, that was the last thing Corey needed to deal with.

"So, do you see much of him, Sebastian?"

Quinn seemed unruffled by the question as he continued to sip his tea. "Occasionally, I'm an odd bird. I try not to cut many ties. One never knows when they could be useful."

He nodded, taking in all the facets of that statement. "What is he up to?"

Quinn eyed him cryptically. "I thought you were here to make peace with the past."

"Actually, right now, I'm just gathering information."

Quinn sighed thoughtfully, "Sounds harmless, as long as you can assure me that it won't lead to bloodshed."

"It won't," he said flatly. "Although Sebastian and I will never break bread together, what happened was a long time ago."

Quinn sipped his tea, then continued, "Well, he has worked his way up to a senior partner position at the Morris firm. It seems once he and Corey, well, dissolved, he threw himself once again into his work. I thought that he might remarry, take up again with an old girlfriend from his college days but didn't happen."

Iain was listening carefully, seeing some scattered images in his mind of brief meetings between Quinn and Sebastian, arguing, an iciness. Clearly, there was more here than his affable friend was telling him. "After the divorce," he chose his words carefully, "do you know if Corey saw much of him?"

"After the divorce? I don't really know. I mean, from what Sebastian said, it wasn't contentious, just something they'd both decided on. You know, the civilized sort."

"Was it?" he asked calmly. But he saw something different, not anger but cold, calculating emotion. It was only a glimpse, gone as quickly as it had come. He was beginning to think this avenue was a waste of time, not getting him any closer to the Triquetra.

"Yes, as far as I know, though Corey didn't speak to me much about it. It was several years after the split before I saw her at all. She withdrew from just about everything. But then you've seen that change in her, I imagine."

"But you did see Sebastian while they were together."

"Yes, infrequently, but yes, it seems as though once they realized there would be no children from the union, then things began to unwind more rapidly."

He straightened up, the mention of children jarring him a bit. "Sebastian told you this?" he asked bluntly.

Quinn again shrugged as though he were uncomfortable under the sudden scrutiny. "Yes, in confidence, it seems he needed someone to talk to. And now, well, I suppose it doesn't matter. It's all over and done with. Apparently, something was wrong with Corey, couldn't have children. Seemed to be quite an issue."

Iain continued listening but felt within Quinn a tall, dark wall of emotion blocking him. "I had no idea," he murmured.

"Well, why should you? You were well out of it, weren't you?"

"Anything in particular bothering you just now?" Lucy Charbonnet inquired, shuffling an oversized deck of cards in her slim, bony hands while never taking her penetrating light, almost silvery looking, eyes off Corey's face. At the moment, this woman, who she did consider a well-meaning acquaintance, was making her skin crawl. As Corey had long ago determined, most people were a mixed bag: a little selflessness, a little ego, a little humbleness, a little good and a little bad. And Lucy fell within that inconstant swirl, gifted indeed but often tipping into the self-serving arena. And in all honesty, it didn't bother Corey. She accepted her as she was, with flaws and cracks. But she also knew always to keep her at arm's length in case the viper might get too close and strike. "You know, I doubt I'm in the best frame of mind for this now."

"I'd imagine not. From what I can see, you're an absolute mess." Lucy commented with distraction. She'd now moved her pointed gaze to the cards she'd fanned out on the table face down. "You don't have to shuffle if you'd rather not. I've already got you."

Corey raised an eyebrow at that and frowned. Got her? This woman, in all her many lifetimes, could not begin to get her. "That's fine. As I said, it's not a great time."

Then Lucy Charbonnet's gaze returned to her, and she smiled indulgently, "Well, let's see if we can help that, shall we." And in her studied, intense fashion, she began to silently spread the Tarot cards out on the table before Corey.

Iain breathed in deeply, with increased agitation, watching as Quinn ordered his breakfast from the waitress who had returned to their table. Each breath he took felt like a knife, and he was shaken and alarmed at the intensity of his reaction. It was ridiculous for him to experience such gripping emotion at something that happened years ago, not even to him, not even his life.

He forced himself to look down and study the menu, but, just now, the thought of food was intolerable.

"And for you, sir?" He glanced up at the young woman now waiting expectantly for his response.

"Just more coffee," he answered, catching Quinn's expression of curiosity.

"You're making me eat alone?" he laughed awkwardly.

He smiled surreptitiously, "Sorry, no appetite."

Then, Quinn nodded to the girl, who quickly made her exit back through the restaurant's patio doors. "Feeling all right?"

Again, he breathed in deeply, wishing to be anywhere else just now, to regain some composure. "So, tell me more." It was odd this morbid curiosity that had crept in on him. He didn't want to know about them, yet he craved details, as though somehow scraping the knife along the old wound was beneficial.

"More?" Quinn frowned. Although he had never been particularly gifted in the paranormal arena, he wasn't without his sensitivities and his subtleties. "About Sebastian and Corey? Sure you really want to go there, my friend? Perhaps it's better to let these things lie."

"Perhaps," he murmured. But then his instincts told him something else, told him there was something here. It might be important to what they were doing or might not, but it was a feeling that couldn't be ignored. "But I think it's time to hear it and then put it to rest."

Then Quinn smiled again broadly. He remembered now finding it odd, the places where this frail soul seemed to find humor. "Well, all right, since you're buying my breakfast, I suppose I can trip down memory lane with you. Although this idea of putting it to rest even now, I can't help but find it a bit absurd. After all, I'd determined a very long time ago that peace, real peace, wasn't in the cards for any of us."

"A lot of upheaval."

"Hmm," Corey responded with distraction. She checked her watch. She was really hoping to get out of here before eleven. She had one more appointment to meet with someone who, luckily, was a bit less self-indulgent, and then there was the afternoon. Who knew how she and Iain might be spending this afternoon. Lucy glanced up as though prompted by her thoughts.

"There's a man involved here."

Corey frowned. Damn, this was what she was afraid of. Unfortunately, the woman did have some talents. "Really?" she answered.

Lucy started tapping the card emphatically, which was right in the middle of the spread. "Yes, he's right there." Corey leaned in just slightly to feign some interest.

"You mean The Magician."

"Yes, yes, a powerful card, practically dominating everything."

"How lovely," she commented.

Lucy wrinkled a brow, "What was that?"

"Well, what does it mean?" she asked bluntly.

Lucy leaned back, staring at her in an enigmatic fashion. "Mean? Well, it means your whole life is changing, changing completely and dramatically."

"Sounds a bit unsettling," she responded dryly. "Just his presence does all of that."

"No, no, but clearly, he is the instigator." Her rather long, manicured nails swept across the Celtic Spread into another direction. You see here," she pointed dramatically. "The Tower."

Corey peered down at the card. She was familiar with the Tarot cards, but she'd avoided any prolonged contact with them during her life. Admittedly, there was an inexplicable aversion. Indeed, The Tower did look a bit disturbing — the building's top being blasted away by a bolt of lightning. "Hmm, does look bad," she responded with little emotion.

"Well, yes and no, my dear. Maybe just a big shake-up, clearing away the old. But here, this is interesting." And now she was pointing toward the end of the spread toward a card entitled The Moon.

Admittedly, Corey had no idea what that meant, "The Moon, more upheaval?" she asked blankly.

And then she glanced up, feeling Lucy Charbonnet's eyes boring into her. "No, not exactly. It just means all the hidden things, all the secrets will come out."

Her words hit her strangely, like a low blow in the solar plexus region. "I don't have secrets," she whispered rather slowly.

And then Lucy smiled with a look that told her pointedly she saw through this lie. "Of course you do. We all have secrets."

"Did you see anything of Corey?"

"Hmm, let's see. I stopped talking to Corey just before she eloped with Sebastian. It was odd, too, but then, when she made that decision, she seemed to cut everyone out of her life, except him, of course. Before that, we'd made it a habit to go to lunch or meet every couple of weeks. I always thought it was because she felt a little sorry for me. But she said that it was because I was easy to be around, accepting. And I guess that was true. I never really expected anything of anyone."

"So then, you never spent time alone with her after that?" Iain prompted.

"No, I wouldn't say that. After her Dad died, and you left, she called me. We met in the quarter down by the river one afternoon. It was a hot day, August, I think. I remember thinking how strange it seemed. She'd called me and then talked very little. I remember that she looked pale, but then again, she'd just been through the funeral and all that. But she really seemed so, well, hmm, what's the word?"

"Distant?" Iain offered.

"No, the word I was looking for, unfortunately enough, is buried. Considering what she'd been through, I know that's a horrible irony, but I think it was apt. The woman I'd known that we'd known for so long was just completely muffled away somewhere, if she was there at all. And then she left, and I didn't see her alone again until after she and Sebastian had divorced. We ran into each other downtown. I remember that, too, distinctly. I called out her name, and she turned round, sort of stunned. And then she walked up to me and put her arms around me. It was quite a surprise after all the distance we'd had between us. But then, I just felt fortunate to have my friend back again. You know, I was always a bit in love with her, but I knew she'd never feel that way about me. So, I never let it get out of hand."

His words took Iain by surprise. He'd never truly considered Quinn's feelings in this matter, perhaps to his failing. "I never knew that Quinn."

Then he laughed as though it were meaningless, "Course you didn't. I didn't want you to."

Iain breathed in deeply, looking away for a moment to gather his thoughts and master the impressions that were floating about his mind. And within, he shifted his focus to an old Master and a sunny day in Southern France.

"It is a gift," he'd said, "but one fraught with peril. Used for selfish ends, it could turn against you and exert quite a price."

But his quest now, he told himself, was not for selfish motives. The seal had been breached, and now he must find out how.

In the few moments he'd turned from Quinn, he focused his energies completely. Then, with purpose, he turned his gaze back on him. The surprise that lighted across his friend's face told him he felt the impact more strongly than Iain had intended. Iain very lightly placed his palms flat on the table, never losing eye contact with Quinn.

Now, he spoke, but directly into his mind. *"Tell me of Sebastian."*

A blankness of expression fell across Quinn's face as he answered. "I saw him during their marriage."

Quinn spoke aloud while Iain continued to direct his thoughts mentally. *"What of the items in the temple?"*

"You sealed the temple," he whispered.

"The blade, the chalice, the triquetra, the staff, did he go after them?"

Quinn's voice sounded hollow in his ears. And Iain knew he was speaking from another place, a distant place of the mind somehow disconnected from the world. "Did he. . ." he stumbled.

Iain could feel resistance in Quinn's mind. Clearly, bonds, promises, and obligations had been made. Ones that he would have to push to break, but he was wholly conscious of the delicate line he walked. Push too hard, and there could be real damage to the psyche. But he could push just a bit more. *"Did he try?"*

"Of course, of course he tried. He never stopped trying."

And then Iain dropped his gaze, feeling a sharp pain around his chest. That last effort had drained quite a bit out of him. He removed his hands from the table. Once again, he looked to Quinn, who was returning from that distant place that Iain had propelled him into. "That's odd," he commented a bit shakily. "I can't remember what we were talking about."

And then Iain answered, "It's all right. Nothing important."

· CHAPTER 19 ·

DIGGING INTO THE PAST

It was after one before Corey returned to the mansion. Her head throbbed from the morning's excursions. Once she'd finally gotten Lucy around to business, she'd deemed the jewel exquisite, with only minor alterations necessary. It was a high-grade piece of lapis lazuli flanked by very pure quartz crystals on four sides. Geometrically, it was a powerful construction. This was as Corey designed it. She knew when she held it in her hands as it sent delicate frissons of energy through her skin. As much as she'd abandoned some of her gifts, this one would not be denied— the sense of touch, the ability to textually feel powerful forces. But Lucy's new acquisition was undeniably a distinctly pure jewel, lapis lazuli.

"This one is a powerfully clarifying substance."

She remembered sitting near her father during his convalescence as his strong, capable hands passed over the unpolished chunk of mineral. As a teenager, she knew he'd dabbled in the art of jewelry-making which for some seemed to be an odd hobby for such a rugged, powerful figure as was her father. But she'd never questioned it. As she'd learned long ago, Clayton Knight always had distinct and usually very pragmatic reasons for everything he did.

"No doubt that was why the ancient Egyptians were so fond of using it. It is a substance that inspired and, yes, even demanded credulity and fortitude."

She wondered vaguely if this would be an aid or a hindrance to Lucy Charbonnet. It was possible she might find the possession of it somewhat uncomfortable in the end. Lucy, she'd sensed for some time, had

121

a way of straying from the true path, and possession of this particular jewel might make this tendency a bit less simple for her. But for Corey, it was only a passing thought. It was the stone her client had requested for her amulet, complexities and all.

Corey's last appointment had thankfully been much less problematic. It was a smaller piece, but in many ways, a more satisfying commission — a necklace of black onyx for a bookstore owner downtown. "The onyx is a grounding stone, particularly helpful in deflecting the negativity of others." The sale itself was not a particularly high profit one, but she'd known the elderly owner for much of her life. He was an old friend of her father's who'd always been good to them. She remembered Mr. Palphrey and his wife at her dad's funeral, even then assuring her if she ever needed anything, they would be glad to help. So, when he'd requested that she make this special gift for his lovely wife on their forty-seventh wedding anniversary, there was no question that she would do so at a manageable cost for them. Fortunately for Corey, some of her father's long-term investments had finally taken root a few years back, leaving her financially extremely comfortable even after splitting the profits with Samuel, who was congenially settled on the West Coast with a wife and three children. For her, jewelry making, as it had been for her father, had become a bit of a hobby, something to fill the time as she further entrenched herself in a quiet life.

It was just after two when she was awakened from a light sleep. After coming home, she'd only intended to sit for a few minutes in the sunroom. Clearly, the fatigue from the morning had insidiously slipped over her, causing her to fall into a heavy sleep. Only the sound of the doorbell jarred her back into consciousness, leaving her a bit dazed and disoriented when she discovered Iain waiting on her doorstep. He eyed her with a rather speculative glance. "How was your morning?" he asked as he followed her into the sunroom.

"Busy," she replied, settling in the old wicker rocker at one end of the room while trying to regroup her senses. It was essential, she'd found in dealing with him, always to have your wits about you. But as she glanced back up at him, she realized he was caught amid his thoughts. He was silently and intently surveying the room around them. And then she realized she'd nearly forgotten about that long-ago first meeting of the Marguillers here, after the Fabacher house.

He commented a bit distantly, "Hasn't changed much."

"No, I always liked this room the way it was, so I tried to keep it the same. It's always felt like a bit of a refuge."

And then his dark eyes were on her, "So, you needed a refuge living here?"

"Occasionally, things got a bit overwhelming at times."

He slowly sat down in one of the white wicker chairs on the other side of the light sofa, although the way his eyes bored into her made it feel as though he were directly in front of her. "You don't mind living here alone?" Why did that sound more like an observation than a question?

"No, I don't mind." He continued staring at her in a strange, unnerving way that she could now feel all over her skin. "What is it?" she asked pointedly.

And then he replied directly but very slowly, "Who did you see today?"

Her eyes widened a bit at the unexpected question, "Why?"

"Tell me." He said calmly.

"Just clients. I told you I had appointments."

"More specific, Corey, tell me," a bit more insistent.

She was beginning to feel irritated, not liking his demanding attitude. It felt entirely too much as though he was cavalierly breaking personal boundaries. "Let's see. I saw a little old man who owns a bookstore and wanted to give his wife a necklace for their anniversary."

His gaze was unflinching. Then he shook his head. "No, not it, who else?"

"I don't know what this—"

"Just tell me," his voice was controlled, but he cut her off abruptly.

"I saw an old friend. She's a reader, palmistry, Tarot Cards. I made her an amulet."

He nodded slowly, "She's a problem. It's all over you."

Then she stood up, "What's all over me?"

His voice was flat, as though he were a scientist observing some odd phenomena. "You're covered in yellow."

"Yellow? What the hell does that mean?" she demanded unsteadily.

He leaned back in his chair, "I see it on you, your neck, your chest, your waist. She's trying to exert some control over you. Probably drained you a bit. Did she do a reading for you?"

She felt stunned, completely knocked out of breath at his pronouncement. "Yes, sort of."

"Did she touch you?"

"Of course," she stammered, "she always hugs me when I get there. How can you—"

"I suggest you take a shower." He rudely cut her off again.

She stared at him blankly, wondering where he'd learned about all this. "When did you start reading auras?"

"We have a lot to talk about. Go shower and change your clothes. And I'd advise more limited contact with this woman. She's a problem."

She stood shakily, unsure if she should be grateful or angry at him. "I'm not comfortable with this, Iain."

He leaned back in his chair. "I'd imagine not. But comfort yourself in knowing it's only likely to get worse."

Iain freely wandered Clayton Knight's Esplanade mansion while Corey was upstairs. The sunroom, as he remembered, reverberated a nice healing energy coming through its long picture window — probably why Corey had been drawn here after being so drained by this woman. It concerned him how defenseless she'd become against such things, even to the point of not reading people correctly. As complicated as Corey was, he'd always known her to be tremendously gifted. She should have seen this woman as a problem from a mile away. But she didn't; instead, she allowed herself to be compromised.

He drifted into a closed-off room on the far end of the house. The dark oak doors were closed, but he opened them, allowing his memory to guide him. Inside, he noted, as was with most of the house, not much had changed. Her father's desk and his books were all kept as he remembered. He sat in the low chair in front of the long mahogany desk. No one was here. He could have easily sat in Clayton Knight's chair, but he did not out of reverence for the old man.

Theirs had been a problematic acquaintance from the start. And quite clearly, he was sure the crux of it had been Corey — Corey, the girl her father had tried to protect, and Iain, the young man determined to drag her into his world. Whatever their differences were, Iain had always felt there was mutual respect between the two men, especially at the end of Clayton's life. He closed his eyes, still feeling the old man's presence clinging to everything around him. He breathed deeply and wondered, not for the first time if her father's interference had pushed her in Sebastian's direction. If he'd been more accepting, then perhaps she'd have been less impulsive, less desperate. But it was a thought he quickly pushed aside. As he'd learned, the past was a place to learn from but not to dwell in for too long.

He felt her presence behind him before she spoke, "What are you doing in here?"

He stood up and turned around. She'd changed into blue jeans and a long blue silk shirt. She'd always liked the softness of silk on her skin — which he remembered well. Her long hair was still slightly damp. And it hung in long strands about her shoulders. That he remembered too, so clearly, the feel of it in his hands. "Just looking back a bit."

She nodded but still seemed uncomfortable and vulnerable, and then he let himself feel and smiled. She, too, was remembering what had been — not immune from the heavy pull of their past together. "I don't come in here much," she murmured. "But I never had the heart to put Dad's stuff away. Makes me feel like he's still around."

"He is," he replied, "and trying to tell us something."

"Yes, the Triquetra."

"Perhaps," he said, but now wasn't at all sure.

She finished dressing in her bedroom, intently feeling Iain's presence downstairs. She breathed deeply, staring at her reflection in her bedroom's long black, cheval mirror. Begrudgingly, she had to admit he was right. Her head was clearer, and the water had washed away the heavy fatigue she'd carried from Lucy Charbonnet's Carrollton Avenue residence. It was odd. Of course, she felt conflicting things about Lucy, but she'd always viewed her as rather harmless. She frowned at the pale, strained face staring back at her from her reflection. Then she begrudgingly recalled that her father had always said, "Some of the most dangerous people dress themselves up in clothes of benevolence. That is their secret weapon."

What was most troublesome was not that Iain had spotted the gravity of the problem but that she had not. She brushed out the long black hair she'd quickly blown dry moments before. It was sad to say how she had let her awareness of things dry up. Quietly, she sat on the end of her bed, gathering her thoughts for a moment before she went downstairs to face him again.

If she had not deliberately shut herself off so completely after the divorce, perhaps she wouldn't have needed Iain's help. If it had been a subtle choice, she could feel less responsible for the current situation. But it had not been. It had been deliberate, and in all honesty, it had begun long before she separated from Sebastian. It had begun because of Sebastian.

Her mind wandered again to the sensation of finding Iain downstairs a few moments ago in her father's study. Sitting in front of Clayton Knight's desk, seeing him there felt so familiar, as though she were flipped back into another time. There were several occasions when her father summoned Iain for one of their long talks. And then the heavy doors had closed off, and whatever was between them was closed away from her. Her father, to put it lightly, was an odd man, in some ways, she thought, a bit chauvinistic. There were lines embedded in him from long ago that a daughter was simply not meant to transverse. But Iain crossed them and was, in perhaps a very tangential way, more of a son to Clayton than his own. Undeniably, they could connect on a plateau that Samuel simply did not spend time on.

She pulled her hair back in a large metal barrette that Samuel had sent her from one of his trips overseas. Italy, she thought. Bless him, her brother did enjoy life — didn't contemplate it too much but took all there was to get out of it. In so many ways, she envied him. "Why make things complicated?" — he'd always said to her. And then, she would reply, "I don't make them complicated. They just are." He would laugh and shake his head as though she were nonsensical. And she would accept that she was misunderstood, misunderstood by most, but not all.

She didn't hear the quick step on the landing or the carpet leading to her room. In fact, she didn't realize he was there at all until he was standing in her doorway. It was a bit of a shock that she hadn't felt him approach. But then again, he hadn't wanted her to.

CHAPTER 20

THE WEB

Corey had left him still sitting in her father's study, leaving him awash with memories of the past. He'd felt her surprise and confusion at finding him there. And something else he'd felt, remorse — remorse flooding out of her like a caustic poison. Then, as quickly as he'd felt it, she'd buried it all over again. It caught him by surprise, like a punch, not unlike his conversation with Quinn today. He stood and then quietly paced the length of the long room. What bothered him immensely was getting caught off-guard, blindsided, so to speak. He needed to get a handle on it if he were to be effective at all here. Sooner or later, he and Corey would be doing some traveling, and he certainly didn't mean in the conventional way. And to do so, he needed complete control over himself; he couldn't afford to be hit by unknowns that could reach his emotions.

He closed his eyes, willing himself to that calm place of meditation. Initially, it had been difficult for him to reach and even more so to anchor himself there. But he'd done it; after years, he'd done it with the help of others, teachers. The first of which had been his old friend Andre Desmarais, who'd taken a lost young man under his wing, introducing him to one of the very well-kept secrets of French culture, a somewhat secret and currently thought extinct society called the Eleusians, where he'd begun to learn how to live again.

"*Vous devez avoir un endroit pour aller là où vous pouvez vous protéger contre les ravages du monde.*"

Andre only spoke to him of these matters in French. He told him that such studies required control and discipline of thought. Essentially,

he'd said, "You must have a place to go where you can protect yourself from the ravages of the world." It was a first step, one that took some time to achieve. But then again, Andre had also said: "Time is of no consequence."
— "*Quand vous avez maîtrisé cette une chose puis ce sera la bonne heure de passer.*"
— "When you have mastered this one thing, it will be the right time to move on."

Of course, looking back, he now realized that by accomplishing this task Andre had set before him, he was simultaneously learning another lesson, perhaps one that was even more challenging and important. He had learned patience— patience to allow things to unfold in their proper time. If you rush the natural process, as Andre had often told him, you might miss something, something significant.

In moments, he thought, or perhaps minutes, as the measure of time became non-essential, he'd re-mastered his thoughts, emotions, and energies. The room around him hummed with knowledge and pockets of significance. Completely centered, he now opened his awareness to follow the strongest pulls. Most, he saw clearly, had nothing to do with the present. It was so interesting that in this house, what was happening now seemed like the pale backdrop against what had been — like the faintest echo of a sound emitted long ago.

"What are you doing in here?" she asked, completely taken off guard by Iain's sudden appearance in her bedroom doorway.

He stared at her with an odd look of controlled inquiry, then answered. "I wanted to see if you were all right." And then he walked inside, carefully looking around, and she knew quite clearly that this wasn't his reason for coming here. "When did you start using this room?"

She stood up, feeling completely shaken and vulnerable at this intrusion. "When I moved back in."

He continued to move around the bedroom slowly and quietly, his hand absently brushing the beige drapery shears at the window. "This was Samuel's room."

"Yes, of course, he was long gone by then."

And then he turned to her, eying her with curiosity. "I thought you liked your room. You always said it was the best room in the house, overlooking the garden."

She glanced down at the carpet, feeling a tug of emotion in her throat. "I guess I changed. Didn't seem to suit me anymore."

And then he was remarkably close to her, but for some reason she didn't want to look at him. And she didn't until he gently lifted her chin with his hand. "I saw Quinn today."

"Really?" She caught her breath, a bit unhinged by his proximity. "I didn't know you were meeting with him."

He nodded, slowly moving his hand away but keeping her gaze. "He told me quite a few things about you and Sebastian."

It was a shock reverberating through her, jarring, unexpected. She had no idea why he'd go this direction at all. "Why? That doesn't have anything to do with what's happening now."

He spoke quietly but deliberately, "I wish that were true, but unfortunately, everything here seems connected like a web."

She swallowed painfully, feeling a disorientation passing over her at his intense gaze. His eyes, his dark green eyes, they were so insistent, and then she realized. "What are you doing?" she whispered.

And then she felt his fingertips brush the side of her face ever so lightly. "Trying, trying to get closer to the truth."

She tried to step back, but it was no good. Something strange was happening. She couldn't, couldn't move. All she could do was continue to stare into Iain's eyes. And she could feel him pushing more deeply into her mind, trying to push to places she shielded. "Stop it," she whispered.

"*Why?*" She heard him say, somewhere but not spoken. She tried to push him back, back outside, but something about him was so strong. "*It's all right.*"

"Just ask me what you want to know. Don't do it like this."

"I can't be sure of you. I can't be sure you'll tell me what I need to know."

"Let me try." She could feel tears beginning to fall down her cheeks. Then she felt him step back, step back from her physically and her mind. Her hands were shaking as she brought them up to her moist face. She was trembling, trembling with fear, with rage that he'd try something like this with her. "God, you're a bastard," she rasped.

And then he took her hands in his, in a grip that was just a hair's breadth from being painful. "And you are a liar. Now make good on your promise, Corey, or I'll drag it all out of you."

She pulled back from him, and with shaky legs that seemed unwilling to support her, she sunk back onto the bed — now for the first time with him feeling legitimate fear. What had she done bringing him into this, and now that she had, how could she stop it? He'd crossed the room and turned around to face her with a cold, expressionless face. "What did Quinn say to you?"

"Did you help him?"

"What?" she snapped out, feeling an insane surge of fury that eclipsed her fear.

Then he smiled, smiled in a way that reminded her of long ago, reminded her of Iain at his worst, at his vindictive worst when she'd left him and when all he lived for was lashing back. "Did you help Sebastian steal the Triquetra?"

His words felt like cold water splashing over her. "What? Did Quinn say he'd taken it? When? I haven't seen Sebastian in years."

"It might not have been taken recently — maybe years ago and is just now being realized."

She stood up, incredulous. "I don't know why you think this. Why would I have contacted you to find something I helped someone else steal? Doesn't make a whole lot of sense."

"Many things you've done over the years haven't made a whole lot of sense to me. Clearly, you have lied to me, Corey."

"How? How exactly have I lied to you?"

"You told me that Sebastian lost interest in the objects once you were married." She stared at him stonily, a bit surprised at this declaration. "Isn't that what you said?" he demanded coldly.

"Yes," she said calmly.

"Yes," he repeated, "but then less than two hours ago, Quinn told me that, in fact, Sebastian never stopped trying to break the seal, never stopped trying to get his hands on the items in the Temple. And I know he wasn't lying."

She blinked, feeling ever so slightly repulsed at the lengths Iain would go to get what he wanted. "Because you did to him just what you were trying to do to me."

He nodded, "Yes, I did and will again if I have to because all my fine, good old friends are all filled with deceit. Now, are you going to give me the truth, Corey, or are we going to do a repeat performance?"

"I wasn't trying to lie. I just knew he hadn't succeeded in anything."

"And how did you know this?" he asked with an iciness in his voice.

She paused momentarily, recognizing how dangerous opening this door might be. But there seemed no help for it now. No help at all. "Because I made sure he didn't."

CHAPTER 21

SEBASTIAN

This was a surprise. A week had passed since the Marguillers had led their somewhat semi-successful expedition into the Fabacher house on Prytania Street. Over the long week that followed, Corey had come to the opinion that all the hullabaloo would fizzle out in an unseemly demise. But as it was, she was wrong.

Just after Chemistry class, she felt a firm tap on her shoulder, which she responded to rather sluggishly as it had been another droll, uninspiring hour. She turned to find the author of the tap was the very stony-faced Iain Shaw. At that moment, a little disbelieving, she glanced around to ensure it had been no one else. But his frown told her that, indeed, it was he who wanted her attention.

With a bit of sharpness, she replied, "What?" It had been pretty much an entire week of being ignored by the founding members of the Marguillers, behavior that, given last Thursday's extraordinary events, seemed way beyond uncalled for. To put it plainly, she was in no mood to play nice.

"I need to talk to you."

She scowled, "Oh gosh, let me drop everything now and come running."

"This is serious," he remarked flatly.

"Yeah, well, so am I. Bug off."

And without another word, she picked up her backpack and stalked out the door of Freshman Chemistry. She had a fifteen-minute break between classes and would not spend it in any way, shape, or form with one Iain Shaw. For all she was concerned, he could jump, and before she could complete that thought, he was walking right next to her. "What are you so mad about?"

She stopped in the middle of the hall, allowing the masses of moving students behind her to jolt to a stop and then bend around her like a heavy stream of ants frantically on their way back to their hill. "I don't know genius. Why don't you figure it out?"

And then he smiled, which she found infuriating, "Got me, why don't you tell me?"

"I would if I wanted to talk to you, which I don't."

And then, quite unexpectedly, given their conversation, he grabbed her arm and began leading her toward an outside door. "Come on."

She thought to wrench away and make a scene. But part of her was curious and thought there might be more opportunity to give him a difficult time. He led her outside, down some steps, and around a corner of a building where, presently, there was no one in sight. "Are you sure we should be out here?" she instinctively asked as he finally released her arm.

"Do you really care?"

She frowned, "Yes, what is it? You've ignored me all week, you and your nutty friends."

He nodded, "So, that's why you're so hot." And then he grinned, "Mad, I mean."

She waited, now feeling perfectly awkward. What was it about him that was so destabilizing to her? "Are you going to talk because I do have another class in—"

"Ten minutes, American History," he finished for her.

He knew her schedule. And just now, she found that rather creepy. And then she leaned back against the building, folding her arms angrily. Time to put him on the spot. "So?" — was all she said.

"We decided we needed to lay low for a while."

"Nice of you to tell us."

"I thought you'd catch on."

"You were wrong."

And then he looked at her with a bit more interest. "Do you just want to be mad?"

She looked away, "Why, why lay low?"

"Sebastian got in trouble with his dad about the key."

Then she turned back to him with surprise. "He did? I thought he said it was no problem."

"Yeah, well, he says a lot of things. Some of which are true. Anyway, he got blasted, grounded, and life threatened. You know the drill."

"Is that the drill in his house? I can't say I've had my life threatened."

"Really? Your dad seems pretty tough."

She looked at him with a bit of surprise at the description. Yes, he was strong and stern at times, but he was not unreasonable. He was just protective. "He's not that bad. I can see why you'd think that. So, what does this mean? Are the Marguillers history?"

And then he smiled again with a sparkle in his green eyes. "No, no, just a bit underground for a time. Why disband when things are just getting interesting? But look, tell your pal Brae to quiet down. All this is supposed to be a secret. Does she understand the word secret?"

She couldn't help but smile at his quick estimation of Brae. "Yeah, well, she's a bit confused at everyone's coldness. You guys have been pretty chilly."

"Oh, sorry, we're not exactly the warm and fuzzy type."

"Really? That's news."

"So, are you still in Miss Corey Knight?"

She answered quietly, "We'll just have to see."

He stared at her, a bit stunned, "What did you say?"

He'd expected many possibilities of outcomes once he'd confronted Corey. In fact, all of this he'd considered downstairs before he'd decided to approach her. He truly didn't anticipate much success in reading her thoughts. Corey had a powerful mind, one whose defenses would take great effort to breach. But it was a bluff that he hoped would make her believe she was vulnerable to him, vulnerable enough to be forthcoming with the truth. There was no doubt in his mind. In fact, he'd known from the beginning that Corey was holding back much. The question had always been whether what she held back was truly important. It was his conversation with Quinn that had convinced him that it was indeed time to clear the air.

She walked across the room, away from him. Perhaps, he thought, as far away as she could get from him in this restricted space. And then she turned round slowly to face him, delicate face braced, stonily set, and brown eyes filled with shadows. "I didn't want to talk to you about Sebastian."

"Clearly," was all he said.

"He's part, a very painful part, of our past together."

"I'm not interested in your relationship with Sebastian, just his connection to the Triquetra."

Her eyes remained on him, unflinching but so unreadable, filled with some strange emotion that he felt deeply inept at identifying. "The problem is it's all bound up together. As you said, everything is tied and tangled like a web."

He instinctively began to walk forward at the sound of the pain in her voice but then stopped himself, instead just sitting on the edge of the bed. He wasn't here to comfort. He was here to ferret out the truth. That was what he'd been drafted for. This was why Clayton Knight had reached out from beyond the grave. The old man was not exceptionally sentimental when the stakes were high. And just now, it was becoming apparent to Iain that the stakes were getting increasingly high. "Why did you lie about Sebastian, about his continued interest in the paranormal?"

"It seemed simpler and didn't seem important."

"Didn't seem important?" he echoed her with a measure of disbelief.

"I don't think he's responsible."

He sighed, really wishing he didn't have to go this direction. It felt like a quagmire, a bog of quicksand to him. "Why Corey? You said you'd prevented his success. This, after all, was your husband, the man who incited you to disrupt so many lives. Why wouldn't you help him?"

She was still, just standing across the room from him in stillness. And then she answered quietly, "He wasn't the man I thought he was." It was like a cut in his chest, a physical cut. He should've said something but didn't — just sat there waiting, hoping that maybe she'd just stop. "I made a mistake with him. It wasn't easy. The years were very hard." Her voice was halting. He knew how difficult it was telling him this after what she'd done, after how she'd hurt him for Sebastian. "I stayed and tried. I stayed too long. But there were many times I knew he was trying to get back, back to where you'd sealed the temple. And I did everything I could to stop him. Again and again, I quit trying because I knew he'd become too weak to succeed. So, that's how I know it wasn't him. Whatever he had, he'd lost long ago."

"And you, Corey, what did you lose?" he asked, knowing he had no right to but was unable to stop himself from doing so. But her face remained in shadows to him, and she quietly left the room without answering.

"How is your dad doing?"

It was a windy day, a windy day in late November. That was as she remembered it, although the memory was incomplete, clouded over by layers of emotion, events, and times that shifted and twisted and turned one's very soul. But that day seemed and felt innocent, though as she was to come to know where he was concerned, there was no innocence, no matter even if he intended it so. Some dark karma, some baggage that he carried with him, inevitably seemed to taint the purity of whatever he touched.

For years, she'd questioned with some mixed conclusions whether he could be blamed, whether indeed some people were cursed, fated to live a life of shadows and lies. But then again, she supposed one always had the choice whether to help the curse along its ravaging path or try to impede it. And in all honesty, she could never remember Sebastian ever taking the time to struggle against his own nature.

She stood in an older section of the French Quarter, Conti Street, taking scenic pictures. She'd set off early on foot that morning with her camera determined to get some shots to try to sell to local publications. While there were places no doubt that had been seen before, they were not places that had been seen through her view. And it was that aspect of her work that she hoped imbued her photography with a personal quality that set it apart. At least, that was what she hoped.

And being so engrossed in her endeavor, she was quite stunned when she spun around to find Sebastian Morris walking up the sidewalk towards her. She stood there for a moment, speechless, not sure at all what to say. Since the party at his house several months earlier, she'd had virtually no contact with him except through scattered updates forwarded through the secondhand sources of Brae or Quinn. She lowered her camera, staring at him a bit befuddled.

"What are you doing here?" It could not be more than eight-thirty in the morning, an odd hour, she thought, for a chance meeting.

He smiled broadly, "Now that's a nice greeting for an old friend."

It was a chilly morning, and Sebastian was well-dressed, a light overcoat over a business suit. Next to him in her blue jeans and long-sleeved cotton sweater, she felt quite underdressed, but then again, he had sought her out. "I'm a bit surprised. A little early for you to be out roaming the French Quarter."

"And you as well," he laughed cordially. "Actually, I was looking for you. I called your house and managed to wheedle your whereabouts out of some Mrs. Peterson, housekeeper?"

She shook her head, "No, my dad's nurse. She's staying with us full-time."

And then his pleasant expression melded easily into concern, and she often wondered, looking back, how much was genuine and how much was crafted. "How is your dad doing?"

"Stable, not rebounding as strongly as I'd like. But then I always think of him as the vibrant, strong man who used to push me around when I was a kid."

He grinned at her comment, "Yes, he was intimidating."

She was feeling oddly relaxed with him, "I thought nothing intimidated you."

"Really? Well, then, I see my façade worked better than I thought."

"Why were you looking for me?" she glanced away, suddenly feeling a slight wave of impatience pass over her. After all, she'd come out to accomplish something, not stand in the street and hold a casual conversation.

He nodded, "Well, right to business, how about you let me buy you some coffee, and we'll talk before I have to go to work?"

She checked her watch. It was still early. She supposed she could stop for half an hour and then return to her shots. It was an overcast day, and the light she wanted would hopefully be good for some time yet.

Corey wasn't sure where she was going. Her heart was full, filled with tears unshed, and her eyes threatened to completely blur over with the emotion of what had occurred. His voice, his voice, the one that was always so controlled, so disguised, was raw with the pain of the past — not an old pain, not a dead embalmed pain, but a raw one, as raw as the day she cavalierly smashed their dreams to pieces.

Of course, she'd always known how she'd hurt him, but like so many other difficult things, she'd stored it away somewhere, like everything, in her secret closet at the top of the third floor. But this wasn't neat or controlled. It was like a wire zapping back to life and striking anything nearby.

By instinct, she drifted into the sunroom and sat in the old wicker rocker. She had no idea where he was. She couldn't feel him. Everything was too flooded now, too much pain. Her eyes blurred over with tears. There was no stopping it now. No one is here for her to tell her how to deal with all of this — no one is here to help. She was alone, completely alone now. Silently, she rocked as the pain and the tears cascaded down her cheeks and began to soak the front of her blouse. She thought grimly. Not neat, nothing neat here, just an unraveled, uncontrolled mess.

She felt the pressure of his hand on her shoulder. But she didn't look at him. She couldn't bear it, couldn't bear any more of it now.

But then he knelt before her and grasped her shoulders with his hands. But still, she didn't look at him. It was too hard. The façade of well-being had melted away, and there was no wall between them now, no protection for her. It would be so easy for him now; just kill her with a word, and then maybe it would be over. And part of her hoped he would, so it would finally be over, and she could rest in some quiet, dark place where nothing hurt any longer.

"Corey, Corey," his voice was a husky whisper. "Why didn't you come to me? You could have told me it was all a terrible mistake. Why?"

And then she looked up, looked up into his eyes. And she saw anguish there as well. Anguish now, but then later, the logic would set in, and this one moment of hope would fade, fade in the blinding reality of who they were and who they were not. "Because," and she was astonished at how stable her voice sounded. But then again, this was the moment of clarity, "Because you know, Iain, you would never have been able to forgive me."

It took a moment, perhaps, for her words to sink in, and then she felt his hands on her stiffen and the anguish in his eyes fade into something else that didn't wish to confront this particular truth. But she'd hit right on the mark. Because in only seconds, he'd removed his hands and straightened up. She didn't watch him leave but heard his footsteps as they retreated. She sat in the old wicker chair for some time before finally deciding to go upstairs and clean herself up.

CHAPTER 22

CROSSROADS

They sat in a small coffee shop on the edge of Decatur Street. For some odd reason, Sebastian seemed pleased with himself, although he hadn't said much about why he'd wanted this meeting. And she couldn't resist but shatter that quiet moment with some abruptness, "What is it?" she asked, nearly a bit perturbed.

He shook his head, smiling. "I was just thinking that the moment I saw you, you know, that night at my place, I knew I wanted to see you alone like this." He shrugged, "Not entirely sure as to why, just that I felt I'd like us to catch up without everyone else around."

She followed his awkward comment with a smile and an interjection of reality. "So, how's Amanda?"

He laughed out loud. "Well, you're direct. This isn't at all like that. Just as old friends without the others."

"Don't you mean the other Marguillers?"

Again, he grinned broadly, almost with an enthusiastic quality of excitement that she remembered in him when he was younger, although granted, she didn't see it often back then. "Now, that's a term I haven't heard for quite some time."

"Well, I was never completely sure it suited us."

"Probably not, but Iain and I did think it sounded cool."

At the mention of Iain's name, she suddenly felt a bit self-conscious, not really sure why because, as Sebastian said, this was only a meeting of old friends. She took a sip of her café au lait, which had a tinge of the burnt flavor of old coffee, but she ignored it. "It was an interesting time."

"Yes, it was a very interesting time, which oddly enough is part of what I wanted to talk to you about."

She slowly placed the heavy, white ceramic mug back on the small wooden table they shared. "I don't follow."

He stared out the plate glass window next to their table momentarily as though gathering his thoughts. And then his gaze was back on her. Sebastian had eyes of a peculiar shade, somewhere between the color of a dark whiskey and brandy. Warm at times but then in the next moment turning on a dime, more like the eyes of some huge predatory cat. "My life right now is complicated, intense, regimented, and, well, confining."

She found his disclosure a bit unsettling as she was beginning to find this whole meeting. "Well, if you're not happy, why don't you change things?" she asked matter-of-factly, still unable to feel out where this was going.

And then he looked at her with an expression that she could only describe as envy, "That must be nice to have that kind of freedom. If you don't like something, just change it." The whiskey-colored eyes narrowed. "Unfortunately, it's not so easy for me. I'm expected to follow a certain path. My family expects it, and if I don't, well, I'm out, out of being a Morris and all the perks that go with it." And then he shrugged as if that thought of escape was as flimsily disregarded as a paper napkin. "Frankly, too much to lose."

She grasped the heavy mug again and sipped her coffee, trying to buy a little thinking time as much as anything. "I don't really know what to say about that, Sebastian, except that maybe we make our own prisons."

He smiled again at her directness, curious response. And she was struck by his charm. He'd always been charming when he wanted, but over the years, he'd cultivated it, perfected it, until it was highly difficult to see now that it was an artificial construct. He laughed a bit, "Well placed dagger, Corey. That's what I've always liked about you: your unflinching honesty. But unfortunately, just now, I can't change much about my life. But I can inject some interest to balance its mundaneness."

"What kind of interest?" she asked blankly.

"What would you say about re-energizing our old group, bringing the Marguillers back into the land of the living?"

It was unexpected. She felt a bit of surprise and confusion, but then again, his enthusiasm made it hard not to be taken along. "Aren't we a little old for ghostly investigations?"

"Maybe, maybe not. I mean, think about it. No creeping around anymore. The only limit is our imaginations."

She could feel that her heart had picked up a beat at the suggestion. After all, if she were to be honest with herself, their escapades during the time at Ecole Issoire were some of the most exciting memories she'd had in her life. But something else was present too, something that she, at that moment, managed to effectively suppress. Upon reflection, there was no doubt that it was present, an apprehension, a faint cry in the back of her mind telling her to wait, to think. "I don't know Sebastian. You'd really have to run this by Iain."

And then he leaned back in his chair with the slightest and almost indiscernible glint of satisfaction in his eyes. "That's funny," he said lightly. "Iain said I needed to run it by you."

It wasn't quiet because, for some obscure reason, she did not find the quiet to be a thing of comfort. Ever since she was a child, she recalled her inclination to be suspicious of the silence, mistrustful, and view it plainly and clearly as a foreboding signal of what was to come.

But here, it wasn't foreboding as she sat quietly on the rocks outside the cave, watching the turbulence of the ocean splash upon the shore. Behind her, a light flickered clearly, compelling her to follow it to its source within. But the cave did not contain the wild hiss of the splashing and swirling ocean waves, the quiet roar all about her that soothed her chaffed and damaged senses. She didn't want to follow that light, not now. She only wanted to stay here out on the sharp rocks where she felt a comfort, a comfort in the knowledge that she was truly only a small insignificant piece in the vast scheme of things.

She breathed deeply inward and felt the cool seaside mists fill her lungs, purge her own life from her, and entice her to another beyond herself.

In fact, so absorbed was she in the natural turbulence around her that the pressure of his arm almost went unacknowledged until it went about her shoulders. It was strange that it felt so tangible here. She deliberately scraped her leg along the rough edge of the rock she was perched on. It helped reassure her that all this was real and that where she'd been before was the dream.

He pulled her closer to him, but she still wouldn't look. And then she heard his deep, rich voice, soft and smooth like caramel. "Come on, little one. It's time to pull yourself together."

And she shook her head in negation like a stubborn child, "No, not going back this time, Dad."

He whispered in her ear, and she barely heard it above the loud roar of the surf, "You don't have to, not yet. But it's calmer inside."

"Not for me. I like it out here. Where it's so loud I can't hear myself think."

And then he laughed softly, "I know it seems bad. But you've always chosen a rough road."

She felt a lump in her throat, left over from back there. "I've really made a mess of things."

"You know, that's what I thought too when I left. I looked back and told myself what a foolish man I'd been, what a mess I'd made of things. But then your mother was there to reassure me. Reassure me it's not so much what we do. It's what we learn from what we do."

She straightened up, shaking out her long black hair, now damp from the ocean splash. "No, I think it's definitely what we do. And since I can't fix anything, I'm not going back. You might as well get used to it."

And then her father bent over, kissed her on the cheek, and said in his warmest, most soothing tone. "Oh yes, you are. You're not finished. You and that boy still have a job to do."

And before she could reply, she found herself sitting up in the darkness of her bedroom. The clock on the nightstand reflected 3:00 A.M. Shakily, Corey's hand brushed her cheek where she could still feel the imprint of her father's goodbye kiss.

CHAPTER 23

ANNIE BESANT'S JOURNAL

Iain had begun to pack his things early in the morning. The night had little rest but much reflection, too much memory, and questioning — the kind that is circular and brings no resolution, no conclusions. He thought perhaps he should meditate. He should bring himself back aligned as he'd been taught. But for the moment, what he'd acquired over those years in France seemed just beyond his reach. Instead, all he could grasp onto was a sad, muffling regret that seemed determined to wrap around his heart.

It was so hard to be angry with someone who'd suffered so much. It was hard to blame someone he couldn't help but feel was so innocent. In all the years he'd known Corey, he never remembered her once striking out to genuinely hurt someone, not even when she stood in the great den of her house telling him she was leaving him. And in all its oddness, it had always struck him as something she believed could not be helped. It was not meant to hurt him, just something that could not be helped.

And then he'd thought about himself if he could claim the same innocence in his actions. If every step he took, every attack he launched, was indeed because it could not be helped. Her words haunted him in a way he could not begin to believe was possible, *"Because you never would have forgiven me."* Words he would not have expected. And the unacknowledged role he'd played in their demise. Would he? He asked himself, hoping that he could answer yes but wondering if it was truthful at all.

When he heard the soft knock on his front door, thoughts of why he'd come here were a million miles away. He'd only resigned himself to the fact that there was too much pain between them for him to be able to help — no matter how much he wished it was otherwise.

He hesitated at the door, breathing in deeply. It was Corey. He was sure, but even now, he felt utterly ill-equipped to deal with her. He opened the door, greeted by a lovely, quiet woman with eyes wide and dark, with the clear evidence marring her lovely face that last night had been no picnic for her as well. He stood leaning against the door, at a complete loss as to what to say. "You shouldn't be here," was all he could manage.

"Can I come in?" she asked softly.

"Corey, I don't think it would be a good idea."

"I know," but then she pushed past him and walked into the house. He closed the door behind her, and she turned around slowly, "Iain, I haven't been fair to you." Then she smiled weakly, "But that's not even the point. I had another dream last night, Dad."

His head had begun to throb beneath the weight of all that had occurred between them, and now, all he wanted to do was stop her from going on. "Look, Corey, this is just not going to work."

But she continued as though he hadn't spoken, "He said we couldn't leave this unfinished. We have to set things right, no matter how hard it is."

He couldn't seem to focus on what she was saying. It was clear to him that he needed more time. "I'm thinking of leaving. I just don't know how we can do this together."

She just stood there staring at him, but her eyes widened at his pronouncement, "You're leaving again?"

"I don't know what else to do," he stated flatly.

"Yes, I see that. But I don't have anyone else, Iain. What do you want me to do? Go back to Sebastian begging for his help? That would be great. As soon as he got his hands on the Triquetra, he'd use it for himself. Is that what you want?"

Just mentioning his name sent an impulsive rage through him that caused him to stiffen. "Honestly, I can't see how it's my problem."

She looked at him with an expression of complete astonishment, which then transformed into that cool, matter-of-fact demeanor — the one that he hated and admired all at once. The one that told him above all, above everything, Corey would do what she felt was right despite and above any cost. "It is your problem and my problem and all of our problems. But we're the only two who seem decent enough to do anything about it. Or are you? Are you decent enough to do anything, Iain?"

At her words, he felt a cold, sobering chill suddenly pass through him. Partially cold anger at her audacity to judge him for anything and partially just a nearly physical slap in the face that somehow managed to quench away all the wild, destructive emotions and passions governing all night. And in this unreal and obscure moment, he could see himself differently now through her eyes — not who he'd been but who he was now. He recognized it, the inevitability. The time to get off this moving train had passed. For better or worse, it seemed they were both buckled in on this determined quest of Corey's to do what she thought was right wherever it might lead. His voice sounded more controlled, even to his ears now. "I'll put on some coffee. Then we'll talk."

But it was exactly what she wanted to hear. Because for the first time that morning, he saw a slight smile pass across her lips.

"It's just a game." Corey's eyes scanned the dimly lit room with unease. "All this stuff, his collections, is just a game to him." She dimly heard Sebastian's voice in the background, but all her focus was drawn to what she was feeling around her. The room itself was daunting — huge shelves all built with dark, nearly black woods and a plush oriental carpet in tones of burgundy, crème, and deep forest green that stretched endlessly across its spaces. She assumed the desired effect was to impress with its richness, but for her, it went too far, toppling somewhere into the realm of garishness. "This was originally the library of the house. That was until Dad got his hands on it. It was crazy the way he ripped out bookshelves and closed in windows. Shame, too, it used to be my favorite room."

"How long ago was that?" Corey heard Iain's voice directly behind her.

"Not as long as you'd think, just three years. That's when the bug got him."

"Bug? What the creepy bug?" Brae had that disconcerting tone in her voice that told Corey clearly that she was not enjoying this expedition.

But then, as if on cue, Quinn silently moved around her, gravitating to the huge display cases running practically along all the walls. Even from where she was, she could see his features' intense, crazy-looking animation.

"Look at this stuff! You mean he collected all of this over the past three years."

Sebastian, who stood on the other side of the room staring a bit disinterestedly into one of the cases, murmured, "Oh, I don't know how long he's been collecting this stuff. It just didn't see the light of day until after the room was finished."

"I thought you were banned from here for the rest of your natural-born life," Iain interjected dryly.

"Yeah, well, Dad's out of town, and Mom doesn't really care about this."

"Sure, you won't get in trouble for this?" Corey felt oddly compelled to ask.

And then Sebastian smiled broadly at her, "You aren't really worried about me. Are you princess?"

She frowned explicitly, "No, worried about me."

And then he shrugged, "Well, life's no fun if you don't live on the edge."

Brae walked up beside Corey with her arms crossed in front of her. "So, what are we doing here? Just looking in glass cases? I could just go to the Cabildo and do that."

Sebastian shot a quick look over to Iain. "Told you this wouldn't be a great idea."

Iain shook his head, "No problem if they don't get it." And then, very softly, he put his hands on Corey's shoulder. "Why don't we use our resident psychic to ferret out what's really important here."

Struck by impulsive aggravation, she squirmed out of his grasp, stepping away. "What does that mean? I'm not a psychic."

"Okay, sensitive, whatever term you'd prefer, it's clear you have a nose for this kind of stuff."

"Clear to who?" It shook her, feeling somewhat like a betrayal from Iain. Somehow, she'd thought the details of what happened in the Fabacher house were just between them.

"Look, don't be so defensive. I'm just saying you might be able to pick out what's most powerful here."

She pushed her long black hair securely behind her ears. It bothered her immensely. He'd done what she hated most of all: put her in the spotlight. "Why don't you ask Quinn? He seems to know more about this occult stuff than any of us."

At the mention of his name, Quinn's head, which had been bent over one of Gabriel Morris's exhibit cases, pulled up. "Ask me what?"

Sebastian walked over to the slim, young boy, jovially slapping him on the back, "Ask you what you think of Dad's stuff. And if any of it, well, we'd find particularly interesting."

Quinn expelled what sounded like a short laugh. "All of it's interesting. But then some of it's probably junk, like the voodoo collection."

"I'm sure Dad would be thrilled to hear that. Um, anything that the Marguillers would want to look at?"

Quinn wrinkled his long, thin nose at the question, "Hmm, well, I'd like to take a look at that," pointing to something in the far corner of a nearby case.

Without thought or direction, Corey's feet began to walk toward where Quinn was pointing. She leaned over, peering through the reflective glass, only to see what seemed to be an old book with an ornate style of script writing on the cover. She could not make out all the words except the name written in an old-fashioned style of ornamental penmanship at the bottom. "Annie Besant," she whispered.

"Annie Besant?" echoed Brae. "Who is that?"

"A famous mystic, writer, Freemason," answered Quinn.

"I thought Freemasons were only men." Brae queried, drifting in a bit closer.

"Traditionally," Quinn responded, "but she formed a co-masonic lodge, amongst other things." Not for the first time Corey found the breadth of Quinn's random knowledge a bit bizarre.

"So, what is this?" Corey asked, now truly beginning to feel a strange magnetic pull to the book.

"A journal," Sebastian answered, looking down at it. "I remember my father saying it's a handwritten journal that he paid a bundle for."

"So, your dad had an interest in women's issues?" Brae asked kind of blankly.

He laughed, looking up at her as though she were insane. "Dad? Please. I think he'd prefer to return to the days when women didn't have the vote."

"Then why would he want Annie Besant's journal?" Corey asked with confusion.

"Dunno, maybe because there was something inside it that was of some value to him. He never does anything unless it's of some personal interest to him."

Iain moved next to Corey, and she felt his eyes on her in a tangible way, watching her much too closely. "So then, do we get a look at this journal?"

Sebastian shrugged, "Yeah, sure, if you want, I have all the keys."

As he began to sort through a mass of keys in his pocket, Corey again felt her eyes drawn to the old book. Most of the items in the room radiated strange, confusing energies, a good many of them bad. But the book was different. She had no idea why, but there was a purity to it, and behind that, a power, an undeniable power. Next to her, Iain whispered in her ear, "So, this is the one."

"I didn't say that," she murmured.

He answered softly, "You didn't have to. I saw it on your face."

· Chapter 24 ·

Old Alliances

"So clearly, the only way to go about this is to go back to the beginning."

Corey's eyes opened widely at that pronouncement. They were seated across from each other at the small dinette set in Iain's house just off the kitchen, a table with just two chairs. It had struck her on first seeing it that Iain intended a solitary purpose for this house and everything, every piece of furniture was selected with that goal in mind — no clutter, clean, nearly sparse, functional in some way. She breathed deeply and noted not for the first time how clear the air was, clear from contradictory vibrations, unlike the house on Esplanade, which was always absolutely exploding with layers from the past. Quite clearly, it was his goal to live in the here and now and not be embroiled by messengers from another time. "The beginning?" she questioned, sipping her coffee. The energy rush she'd experienced coming over here and confronting Iain had vacated now, leaving in its wake a quakiness that seemed to permeate all the way down to the fingertips holding the cup in her hand. She glanced up, finding his eyes on her, undoubtedly taking in her shakiness but saying nothing about it.

"Yes, I've been giving it some thought. Our inability to reconnect with—" he cleared his throat, "well, the way we used to be able to. It seems the fact that we are two now instead of five has created an imbalance. To put it bluntly, we have to start over."

"How, how could we possibly do that?"

"Well," he answered rather matter-of-factly, "I think it starts with the journal."

She swallowed painfully as a tumult of recollections accompanied that one pronouncement. "Annie Besant's journal?"

"Yes, I don't see a way around it. We may have to find a different way in this time."

She brought her cup rather unsteadily down to the table. She didn't know what she'd expected, only truly considering the end goal. But getting there, it had never occurred to her that he'd opt for this path. "Don't you remember, Iain, how long it took? We actually laid the foundations at least a decade before we could do anything about it."

"I know. But we were children then and didn't know what we were doing. Now we do." Then he added softly, "And we're not the same people. We have one goal. We won't be distracted by others."

She swallowed hard on a lump of fear that had formed somewhere in her chest. "Yes, that's true," she murmured in acquiescence.

"So, Corey, the first step is the journal. I know this might be difficult, but we must get our hands on it again. Do you have any idea where Sebastian would keep it now?" Her head swirled for a moment at the question. It was so bizarre, crazy that now so many things would converge, so many secrets brush so perilously close to others. She could feel his eyes on her, marking every nuance of her reactions, and his mind poised, ready for any breach in her defenses that he could glean something from. "What is it?" he asked with some degree of concern.

She closed her eyes briefly, steeling herself, and then reopened them, staring at him directly. "Sebastian doesn't have the journal," she calmly stated.

Although he greatly suppressed it, she noted an element of surprise on his face. "He doesn't?"

"No," momentarily, she looked away. "You must understand this is difficult Iain, my past with Sebastian, well—"

"I'm not interested in your past with him, Corey," he answered her, perhaps a beat too quickly. "We've moved well beyond owing each other explanations. All I'm interested in at present is the whereabouts of the journal."

She felt a definitive lack of breath in the amount that was needed for speech, "Before he died, Dad took it out of Sebastian's possession."

He straightened up in his chair, "Clayton took the journal? How was that possible?"

"He asked me to give it to him for safekeeping. That's why Sebastian found it so difficult," she hesitated, "well impossible—"

"To repossess the items." In a swoop, he'd completed the thought. "Like us, he couldn't without the five. What did your father do with it, Corey?"

She shook her head, "I don't know exactly. I gave it to him, and he promised to put it into safekeeping."

His eyes widened. He wasn't bothering to cover up his amazement now. "No idea?"

She shrugged uncomfortably, "I always felt it was in the house somewhere. I could feel it, but I've never found it."

"And you never bothered to look?"

She turned away from his gaze, her head pounding. The past was too present now, too much in this room. "I didn't, but Sebastian did. Several times, he went to the house and looked everywhere. At least, that's what he said."

He stood up and abruptly strode across the room, his back to her. She could feel his emotion, raw emotion churning in him. All of this tapped too deeply into things that should have stayed buried. And then, after a few moments, he turned back to her, his green eyes wide, focused, and demanding. "When did all this happen, Corey? When did Clayton ask for the journal?"

A tightness wrapped around her throat that told her if she lied now, he would know it, and it would be to both their detriment. "Just before we eloped."

His face looked as though her words had impact, but she couldn't interpret exactly what kind. "Before? Why, then, did he say why?"

She nodded slowly, "He said it was for my protection."

"Your protecti—" and then he stopped in mid-sentence. "The old man didn't trust Sebastian with the journal, felt like he had to protect you, and yet he let you go off and marry that man."

She bowed her head a bit, feeling now during this conversation that Clayton Knight was here, in this room, also demanding truth. "He didn't want me to, but he knew he couldn't stop me."

She looked away again. It was nearly unbearable. She could feel his eyes, his eyes probing on her skin. And then he spoke flatly, "So, you still think the journal is in the house?"

She looked up at him again but cautiously, "I don't know why Sebastian didn't find it, but yes, somehow, I feel it's there. I feel its energy in the house, although it's muffled somehow."

He spoke slowly, deliberately, "He didn't find it because Clayton didn't want him to. But clearly, he wants us to, don't you think?"

After a moment, she answered, "Yes, I think he does."

It was mid-morning when they entered the house on Esplanade. It was just ten-thirty, but she'd already felt as though an entire day had passed, perhaps many days, and her fatigue mirrored that feeling. As she and Iain crossed the threshold, the chill of the house hit them like a weight. Odd that in all the years since her father's death that she'd occupied the house alone, this weight it carried with it had never been as obvious to her as it was at this moment. Something about Iain's reemergence in her life was like a candle illuminating shadowed corners that she'd willfully allowed to go dark. His presence continued to awaken sensitivities that, over time, had formerly gone numb and dormant.

She walked into the darkened hallway, feeling his presence behind her as he closed the door. Softly, she spoke, "I don't know where to start."

And then she felt his hand, the unexpected contact on her shoulder. "You're exhausted."

Surprised, she turned around, smiling with acknowledgment of the weariness that she felt in every inch of her body. "Yes, but this is important."

He nodded, "I know, but it's no good like this. You should go upstairs and take a rest. It will give me some time to piece things together."

Her eyes widened a bit, feeling a nudge of nervousness. "What things?"

"Try to retrace old Clayton's thought patterns."

It made her uneasy, and if she weren't so tired, it should have made her panic — the idea of just letting Iain rummage around this house. But the fatigue that had overtaken her would brook no resistance. "Don't you think—"

She began, but her thoughts were blindsided by Iain gently grasping her shoulders and placing the gentlest of kisses on her forehead. "Time to stop fighting so much," he whispered. And then, just as unexpectedly, he tenderly murmured in her ear, "Go and rest. Let me take care of things."

It jolted her, this behavior, more so than if he'd slammed her to the ground with a blow—the gentleness, the long-forgotten tenderness that pierced that wall of iciness around her heart as surely as a burning arrow singeing through snow. She didn't say anything, just pulled away from the strange embrace and walked away, not stopping until she reached her room, and she was behind a closed door, not stopping to acknowledge the unforgiving tears that had begun to stream down her face.

CHAPTER 25

ECHOES OF ANGELS

"And you really think this is a problem?"

She frowned, "And clearly you don't?" Iain focused on the mound of gray clay on the well-worn art table before him. It wasn't her custom to drop in on him at his City Park Avenue apartment unannounced. Nor was it her custom to drop in at ten o'clock at night. But the conversation with Sebastian that morning had stayed with her, distracted her, and then took hold of her in a fashion that drove her to do what was unexpected. "What are you working on?"

He glanced up at her, eyes glazed, circles under them. Evidently, she wasn't the only one in this scenario who was driven. "Preliminaries, I need a clear idea of what I'm sculpting before I begin work in another medium."

"Thus, the clay."

He smiled broadly, "This is upsetting you."

"He said you told him to check with me."

"Yes, I did. I figured if anyone had a problem with any of this, it would be you," he stated rather bluntly.

Her eyes narrowed a bit. "Why? Because I'm a stick in the mud?"

He shook his head, laughing, refocusing on the clay before him, his hands melding strongly into a yet as unidentifiable creation. "No, no, because you're more cautious than Brae, or Quinn, or I suppose even me. I don't take nearly as much time considering what's being risked as you do."

She crossed her arms in front of her, feeling a bit vulnerable at that statement. "You haven't known me for a long time. You don't know if that's true anymore."

Again, he stopped, focusing on her while leaning against a doorframe across the room. "Yes, you've been gone a while. But I don't think people change all that much, not the essentials. They just build on what's already there."

"Or deteriorate?" she stated flatly.

His green eyes narrowed. "What's scaring you, Corey?"

She shook her head, "I don't know. I suppose just not knowing what's ahead."

He looked down, continuing to knead the clay before him, "That's a shame. That's exactly what interests me about all of this." She wondered where that fearlessness within him came from, the kind that allowed one to freely jump into unexplored waters without consideration of what may come or what one might lose. How his very essence seemed born without fear and hers — well, hers had been born surrounded by it. "What are you thinking?" he murmured, attention now diverted away from his creation and wholly on her.

"Actually, I was wondering what it's like to be you," she said quietly.

He shook his head, smiling a bit, but eyes darkened by thoughts she had yet to touch. "It's like being hungry all the time, but you can't figure out exactly what you're hungry for." He shrugged, "Just dissatisfied."

She crossed her arms in front of her again, jolted a bit by surprise. It wasn't the answer she'd expected nor perceived, but then again, had she really tried to perceive or simply project her own insecurities upon him? He'd left the table, wiping his hands off with a well-used cloth that he'd laid beside his work area for just that purpose. And then he made his way over to her, facing her now and casually letting the cloth drop to the floor as if it were of no consequence. She raised an eyebrow, "Are you expecting the maid to pick that up?"

He nodded slowly, "Sure, just as soon as I hire one." And then he was staring at her or rather scrutinizing her in that very intense manner of his as though trying to puzzle something out. "So, you didn't like my description of myself?"

"Don't know. I guess I didn't believe it."

"Really? Think I was lying, do you?" he said softly in a manner she felt disturbingly compelling.

She glanced away, not liking how intense this seemed to be getting, not sure if she liked how he was looking at her. After all, this late-night visit concerned Sebastian and his unstable schemes, not other things, not personal things. "I don't see how that's possible. You would be different if that were so, not so at ease, not so settled within yourself."

"Maybe I've just learned how to cope with dissatisfaction, make a place for it within my life."

"Maybe," she murmured as she felt the very lightest touch of his fingertips grazing her cheek. And then she raised her eyes to meet his gaze — an odd gaze, wondering, speculative. "I don't know. I wonder if you are really the kind of person who could make room for dissatisfaction in your life."

And then there was a slight smile, and his voice more of a heavy whisper. "I didn't say I've made a permanent place for it. I've just patiently allowed myself to tolerate it."

"Patient?" she echoed.

Then he added, "Within reason," just before he began to kiss her. She remembered the moment quite clearly. It wasn't their first kiss, but it was the one that sealed things for them, sealed the certainty of what they were always meant to become.

"What is it? What's in the book, Quinn?"

The boy glanced up from the old journal sprawled before him on Sebastian's bed. Zeroing in on the old journal as their current object of interest, Sebastian had led them around some twisting back staircase up to his rather cramped bedroom on the third floor. And when they entered, Corey had been markedly surprised. Even if she didn't know it as a fact, she could glean from the opulent furnishings and just the general size of the mansion that the Morris family was quite well-off, more so than her family, although they were quite comfortable in their own right. But all this you wouldn't know by the size of Sebastian's room, which in actual dimensions seemed about half the size of hers. It was puzzling, an odd contradiction in circumstance. "Have you looked at this before?" Quinn directed to Sebastian, who was hovering nervously near the doorway.

"That thing?" he asked with a mix of surprise and disdain. "No, it's just some old book. If you hadn't noticed, Dad has tons of them." And Corey quickly took his meaning. In terms of impressiveness, this artifact scored low in comparison to some of the other more intriguing acquisitions in Gabriel Morris's collection. On the surface, the nearly tattered journal was nothing to crow about. But the vibrations, the strange conflicting vibrations that even now Corey could feel tingling in her hands, were so confusing.

"But not all of his books ended up behind the glass case. Your Dad must think this is something unique," murmured Brae.

Sebastian impatiently answered, "Who knows what goes on in my father's mind. Anything special yet?" he directed to Quinn, who had returned to his intense examination of the book. For a few moments, he didn't respond, and Corey began to wonder if he had even heard the question.

And then, finally, he answered, shaking his head as he delicately turned some of the oversized pages. "Special? Hard to say. It would help to figure out what I'm looking at." And then his piercing dark eyes surfaced from the object of inquiry. "Nearly all of it seems to be some kind of code," and then he turned his attention directly to Sebastian, "Any idea where the key to the cipher is?"

Sebastian looked at him wide-eyed, "Yeah, sure, let me just go get my handy decoder book."

Iain interjected with a measure of irritation, "That's it! Everything's in code?"

Quinn mumbled, "Appears to be, except for some sketches." And then again back to Sebastian, "Your dad, do you know if he has anything else by this Annie Besant?"

Sebastian's eyes narrowed, "Look, Geoffrey, I don't have an inventory of what the old man has."

"That's too bad," Quinn muttered, slowly turning the old, yellowed pages. He seemed more than a bit deflated by Sebastian's stern response. From the little amount of observation time she'd amassed with the Marguillers, it had become clear to her that Quinn's great passion was in discovery, the unraveling of old mysteries which more often than not usually occurred within the pages of old books.

"What about the sketches?" Iain asked Quinn, evidently not so quick to throw in the towel on this recent find. "What are they?"

"Umm, much as I can make out tombs, old tombs."

"Old tombs?" Corey asked, feeling a strange fluttering somewhere around her solar plexus. It was that odd feeling she'd get every once in a while — the one in which she wasn't really learning something new but rather remembering something that had been forgotten.

Quinn looked up again after scrutinizing Annie Besant's journal, "Yeah, old tombs and statues."

"Statues of what?" Sebastian spat out with disgruntlement.

"Statues of angels," Quinn replied flatly.

He sat within the confines of Clayton Knight's study, darkened, because he had not bothered to light the lamps. He sat in the chair across from the old man's desk, feeling the pull of a long-ago lifetime.

"How could you allow her to do this?"

By then, the man was frail, his once broad shoulders now more stooped with age and the burden of ill health. "You're wrong, young man if you think I wield that much influence with my daughter."

"You can't think this is a good thing. You must know what Sebastian is. He'll only bring her pain."

Clayton had turned his back to him, his thin but still formidable hands resting on the back of his chair. He stared out the long, tall window to his left as though the conversation was entirely distasteful. "Is that your honest opinion of him or just the bitterness of a jilted lover speaking?"

And then Iain had stood before that great desk, long, heavy black wood he remembered. He'd stood up and slammed his hands down loudly on the desk with as much force as he could manage. And it did accomplish his goal, jolting fiercely the old man's head back in his direction. "Now that I have your attention."

Clayton frowned, his face stonily set and yet lined with fatigue. His voice came to Iain's ears as a harsh rasp, "It's pointless. What's done is done. All you can do is learn to live with it."

He remembered a laugh, perhaps his, emitting from some deep, cold place of disbelief at what he was hearing. "So, you throw your daughter to the wolves without looking back."

The old man had stepped forward and sunk into his chair with more of what seemed a collapse than any kind of deliberation. "Sebastian does care for Corey." His thin, bony fingers rifled through some loose papers on that great desk. "And it is what she wants. Let it go, boy. Go on with your life. That's all you can do now."

It was still sharp, the memory of standing there, being dismissed by the old man — a coldness just flowing over him as though some part of him, a limb somewhere, had been dismembered, and he was in that odd numb place before the real pain set in. "And this is what you want for her?"

And now he remembered clearly, although it had not penetrated that antiseptic, mindless fog. The old man's eyes had settled on him directly. "I would wish her peace, my friend, as I would wish it for all of you. One day, you'll realize that no price is too high to pay for such a treasure."

And then Iain had left, walked out, intending never to set foot in this accursed place again. But there was one more visit to an old man on his deathbed before he'd finally closed the door here on what had been.

Iain closed his eyes in this old, darkened room, opening himself to the past, to a past that had nearly destroyed him. And for the first time, he allowed his mind to hear the echoes of angels.

CHAPTER 26

THE LOCKED DOOR

She slept deep but not dreamless and not without purpose. Perhaps it was the journal that spurred mythology into reality, or perhaps it was the synthesis of their energies, an odd alchemical accident that merged something that should not have been merged, something that opened doors that again were never meant to be opened.

But she began to dream of the angels long before they took on a deeper meaning, long before she recognized them as markers.

"There are steps, you know, always steps."

Her mother's voice, or perhaps not, perhaps it was the woman from the journal, or perhaps both.

"I know," she whispered, sending the thought forward into the darkness of the dream, for it was darkness that she confronted now, fog, mist, and dusk.

"Why so hesitant?"

"You could move more quickly. This ground has been tread by you before."

"Yes," she answered, questioning herself as to why indeed. She felt the coldness sweep in. But her eyes focused around her, the chill of the chamber. And the reflection of the moon filtered through the stained-glass window, reflecting what little light there was onto the cold stone floor.

The angel, a cold marble angel, lay before her bent over in prostrate grief. The familiar hum began to reverberate in her ears, almost like a buzzing but at an elemental level, in her skin, across her forehead, circling her throat. Familiar but frightening now, then she had no idea, but now she knew. She knew precisely what it meant and where it could lead. Her eyes began to tear from the acidic smell in the air. It filled the room, burning her eyes, but she forced them to stay open. She watched painfully through blurred tears as the white head of the marble angel raised off its pedestal, staring into her tortured eyes with flat white orbs.

Corey jolted up in her bed. Her breathing was pained, as was the stabbing sensation in her chest. But the shock of coming awake so abruptly was magnified by seeing Iain standing directly on the side of her bed in the shadows.

His face was expressionless, calm, and he spoke softly with little inflection, "You shouldn't have tried this by yourself, Corey."

She straightened up further. She'd been lying atop the covers and had just rested briefly. "I didn't," her voice sounded raspy in her ears.

He sighed, "You didn't? Well, maybe not consciously, but something inside you is driving you to go it alone."

She shook her head, the dizziness grabbing her in its grip. "Iain, I mean it. I wasn't intending."

"You didn't let me finish," he interjected. "I won't let you, Corey. I won't let you do this alone for so many reasons. Even if I have to watch you every minute of every day."

She stilled herself, trying desperately to clear the heavy fog that seemed determined to cling with a death grip to every thought. But then his words penetrated and cut through to a cold realization. His face was calm but steeled, and she knew. He'd done it, pulled her back with some power that she had no idea he possessed. She grimaced, greatly disturbed by the realization. "What does that mean?"

His eyes narrowed, "Looks like until this is settled, we will be inseparable. So, tonight, your place or mine?"

So much about him had changed, and yet this tone, this implacable tone, was so strongly familiar. "I didn't agree to that," she retorted, albeit a bit shakily.

And then he smiled, "Of course you did, the minute you dragged me into this."

Iain did not dream of the past. In some formidable way, he had managed to seal off his mind, waking and sleeping from the scorched life he'd left behind in the States. It was a blessing to begin again, or so he believed, with a largely blank slate. The waking memories he drove from his mind with the single-mindedness of one leveling, stripping, and tilling the land in preparation for a new harvest. And what he planted in his new life, he chose with much more deliberation and more profound thought than he'd ever managed in his younger days. Once he began his tutelage with Andre and the society known as the Eleusians, he believed he was a changed man who, rather than having made peace with what had been, had amputated himself from it. That was what he believed.

But truth, if not insidious, was a persistent companion that held a silent vigil with him until he was ready to hear — and then it whispered gently in his ear.

"I'm having dreams."

Andre looked up from a stack of papers he was studying. They were in the gallery, after closing one night, another successful opening with Iain's second collection. The elderly man smiled, "Well, I would hope so." He had taken to speaking to Iain in English as of late, an odd occurrence as for the first four years of their acquaintance, the old man had insisted on French.

Iain smiled back. No matter the tension or gravity of their conversation, this man always had a way of putting him at ease. "I don't dream much, not vividly."

Andre replied with little emotion, "For an artist, that's odd. So many creative impulses are fueled by the unconscious."

"Well, it hasn't been so for me."

"But something's changed?" the older man asked perceptively.

He answered without hesitation. He'd learned long ago it was pointless being guarded with this individual. His mind was too powerful, "It's been three nights of the same thing, same dream. I thought," His voice drifted off.

"You thought it might be important."

"Yes," and then with a sigh, "but it's meaningless, at least to me."

The Frenchman replied lightly, "Well, I'm no Sigmund Freud, but I know something about symbolism. Why don't I give it a try?"

Iain sighed deeply, somewhat reluctant to go forward, although he had been the one to broach the subject. "All right, let's see. I'm walking outside, a bright day, blue sky, and then I come to a wall, an old-fashioned brick wall, not new, with ivy growing on it. And then I find the door, the door with no key. I try to climb over the wall but slip, and there is no footing. And I try to force it open, but it won't give. And I wake up."

"Feeling?" Andre asked.

"The first night feeling nothing, then the next bothered, and last night," he hesitated, "well, crazy with frustration. I've no idea what's beyond the door, but it seems I've become obsessed with finding out."

The older man smiled at him in a kind way — reminding him strangely of another old man from a different life that seemed like a million years ago. "Well, my friend, if it truly becomes an obsession with you, I would think that you'll find that key."

It bothered him. He didn't know what he expected, but the thought of pursuing this made him more than uncomfortable. The dream stayed with him for another month, unsolved, not progressing, and finally faded. The year before he returned from France, it made a reoccurrence that he would never forget.

CHAPTER 27

LIVING STATUES

"Let Corey have a look at it."

Quinn's head bobbed up from examining Annie Besant's journal with a look of surprise at Iain's proclamation. "Sure, if you want to."

She shook her head, suddenly feeling four sets of eyes glued to her every move. "That's all right. I don't know anything about ciphers."

From beside her, Iain continued to push as though he were now rigidly fixed on the point. "Come on, Corey, give it a look. Couldn't be any worse off than we are now."

"You know that's true, Corey. You were the one that thought this was important," Brae chirped in. Corey met Brae's eyes with frustration and was met with a quirky smile, then a shrug that said, essentially, what have we got to lose? This is a wash anyway.

Bracing herself while ignoring the odd swirling vibrations that even being in proximity of the journal seemed to elicit in her, she moved forward. Quinn deliberately stepped away from the book to give her room to do whatever they expected her to do. Rather gingerly, she sat on the edge of Sebastian's bed, feeling a restlessness creep into her skin but then pushing the feeling deliberately down. This was Sebastian. She was sure it had nothing to do with the journal. She glanced up, again seeing all eyes focused on her. "Could you all do something else? You're making me nervous."

Sebastian frowned, "Yeah, um, maybe Brae wants to see the balcony off this floor."

She looked up at him blankly, "Well, I guess. Is it nice?"

Iain grinned at the absurdity, "It's wonderful. Come on, guys." Corey watched with a bit of anxiousness as the last vestiges of the Marguillers closed the door behind them. Quinn had closed the book, leaving it on the bed for her. She hesitated to put her hands on it. For an instant, the image of her father loomed in her mind.

"You're going to have to live your life differently, Corey, more cautiously, more protective of yourself. Like your mother, you're vulnerable to the world, aware of things that most people will never know. You can't afford to be foolish."

She frowned, wondering what her father's take on this would be. Her fingertips brushed the surface of the old book, and she felt the slightest trembling of torment and then devotion. She wondered if he would see this as foolish or as her selected path. For that, too, was his diatribe: "You must find your reason in this world. Our presence here isn't random. We're all part of some great plan." So how do the two reconcile, she mused in that shadowed moment.

Placing her hand softly and solemnly on the cover of Annie Besant's journal, she said a silent prayer and asked for guidance before she opened the book.

Storms come in various disguises — the subtle rumbling of the sky, a quickening of the breeze that softly stirs the landscape, and that electric indefinable quality of the air that one feels in their very skin that they mistake for benign excitement. In recollection, Corey wondered if she had just returned to New York after her father's illness if she'd never become involved with Iain if she'd never agreed to reanimate the Marguillers. Perhaps all these steps had led down that unexpected spiraling path. There were so many places she might have diverted fate, but then again, she wondered if it were truly possible to divert fate. Or if that presumption was an illusion we held onto just to comfort ourselves. And sometimes, she thought of how shell-like her life would have felt upon recollection without those early days with Iain, even if the cost was what would come later. In quiet moments, she considered these things and then sometimes just remembered, remembered before the storms.

It was perplexing as she recalled the very moment that life began to eclipse her control.

"I'd like to see you today." Her fingertips delicately fingered the receiver of the phone as she silently considered what that meant exactly. "Still there?" Iain asked pleasantly from the other end of the line.

"Mmm yeah," she replied. She hadn't considered that he'd be calling so soon this morning and that she'd have to confront all those conflicting emotions from the night before so quickly. She had hoped to put it all on the back burner for a time, swept away with all that material that was too off-beat to deal with. She'd been spending a great deal of time with Iain since she'd come home to New Orleans, but all between them had remained close yet just cordial, nothing more. At first, she'd expected something, and then she'd stopped expecting it, just enjoying the particular rapport and, yes, intensity of their friendship. And then, last night in his studio, Iain changed the playing field. He'd kissed her, not once but many times, not chastely but passionately, so that she wasn't at all sure where things might lead. Everything inside her had seemed to spin into an entirely different sphere, and then, amid that windswept intensity, he'd decided to end it, sending her home with little explanation. She had no idea what to make of it, not then, and certainly not now. "I don't know," she whispered, truly having no idea what to say. Her mind succinctly told her this involvement, if they indeed were developing an involvement, would be something she wasn't prepared for. In fact, if she had ten lifetimes of experience, she wasn't sure she'd be prepared for it. Maybe it was better to back away now before, well, before, that wasn't an option.

"Corey," his voice sounded softer somehow, not its usual strong, direct tone. "I need to see you. Regardless of what you're thinking, we need to talk today. The question is when. I'm working until two, but I can meet you after that, my place?"

"No," it just flew out of her mouth, and she felt childish for sounding so immature at this point in her life.

"Okay," he murmured, seeming undaunted. "How about City Park, by the pavilion?"

She smiled. "By the pavilion?" she asked.

And then he murmured softly, "Yes, you know the place."

"So?" she glanced up into the discerning gaze of young Iain Shaw, that penetrating gaze that oddly, in this moment, reminded her of her father.

She turned away, now understanding with clarity why he'd accompanied her out the door of Mr. Andrews' Chemistry class. Several times during the hour, she'd caught his eyes on her with an expression that she could only describe as speculative, speculative in a way that made her very uncomfortable. They hadn't spoken much since the odd visit to Sebastian's house on the weekend. He hadn't mentioned the book again, but something in her skin told her the subject hadn't been dropped but rather shelved.

It had only been a few minutes that she'd spent alone with the book when Brae came flying back into the room holding those very odd keys in her hands that Corey had seen Sebastian open the glass cabinet with earlier. Brae was, to say the least, flustered but, more aptly put, panicked. Her long red hair was in more disarray than usual and her blue eyes wide with fear. "Come on," she exploded. "Sebastian's dad is back. The boys are trying to hold him off until we can get the book back into the cabinet."

Corey felt herself clutching the book to her strongly as the girls began to move in a whirlwind. Such a blur, she was following Brae, climbing the odd winding back stairs, the book so hot against her body, nearly burning into her light sweater. Brae, without hesitation, burst through the strange dark doors that led into the study, and then she halted, "Oh God, I can't remember which one."

Corey's eyes sped around the room, dizziness sweeping through her, trying to pull her back to a strange room with a cold floor and blue light flooding across the white. She pointed to one of the glass cabinets positioned against the back wall. Brae turned towards her, hands outstretched for the book, but instinctively Corey yanked it to her, closer against her body. "Open it," she rasped, "I'll put it back." Brae shot her an odd glance that she barely registered. It didn't matter. The other pulls were too strong. *Too soon*, it whispered. *Not yet*, but sluggishly, she followed Brae and gingerly returned the old book to its place among its other misunderstood companions.

Quietly, they slipped out of the room, hearing murmurings entering the third-floor hallways as they descended the winding staircase. When they reached Sebastian's room, the door was open, and all three Marguillers were there, somberly waiting for them. "I thought you were heading him off," Brae breathlessly inquired, nearly stumbling into the room.

"We were," Iain responded grimly.

"Yeah, until we were dismissed," Sebastian commented with a dryness in his voice that Corey found quite hollow and insincere.

Quinn rose from his seat on the bed, "So, I know you didn't have much time. But did you pick up anything from that book, Corey?"

She felt all their eyes upon her, waiting expectantly, but she'd known from the moment she'd opened the book that whatever she felt would remain in shadows. She shook her head slowly, "Sorry, just not enough time."

"Knew it was a wild goose chase," Sebastian offered cryptically.

Quinn shrugged, "Too bad," then turning to Sebastian, "Wonder what brought your dad back early."

"Don't know, don't really care. You guys want to play pool? We've got a table in the Billiard Room downstairs."

"You've got a Billiard Room?" Brae laughed impulsively, "Sounds a bit stuffy."

Sebastian nodded, grinning a bit, "Yes, well, stuffy is right up my parents' alley. Come on. I'll show you."

The group began to file after him, one by one slowly, but Iain caught her arm just as she was about to leave. She glanced up into those odd eyes of his, green just now. "Okay, Corey?" he asked. Seemed like a simple inquiry, but, in that odd moment, she wasn't really sure what he was asking.

"Yeah, okay," she answered. And he left things as they were for a bit.

"So?" she repeated his question a little blankly.

They were standing in the hallway, just outside the classroom where he'd intercepted her progress. "Are you going to make me drag it out of you? The book, tell what you thought of the book."

"I told you—"

"Sure, right, not enough time. Now, I want you to tell me the truth."

She started moving slowly down the crowded hall again, not at all sure where she was headed now. "I'm not sure what you mean. You want me to make up something?"

"No, how about the truth?"

"That's kind of insulting. What makes you so sure I haven't told you the truth?" she murmured.

He grabbed her arm, halting their meandering, rambling progress through the hallway. She looked pointedly at his hand, and he dropped it. "I don't know Corey. For some weird reason, you're easy for me to read."

She glanced away, trying to figure out exactly what she should say to him. "Look, it wouldn't help you. I mean nothing concrete enough that the Marguillers would be interested in."

He laughed, "Why, because we're so thick?"

She shook her head, "No, because I'm not sure if I really felt anything or just imagined it."

"So, just tell me anyway. Forget the Marguillers."

She frowned, "So loyal, fine, it was just impressions, lights, cold places, and the statues, like the drawings. I kept seeing the statues, but they were different."

"Different, how?" he asked.

"Well," she paused, thinking how she could even voice the words, "they were alive."

CHAPTER 28

CALCULATED RISKS

"Are you sure you don't know where it is?"

She glanced up at Iain from across the round breakfast table in her father's house. It lay in a warm, sunny room just off the large kitchen in the Esplanade mansion. Her father had acquired it at some point after Corey's mother had died. It was a lovely table, round, light-colored oak, but not very big. In fact, she'd often thought he'd wanted it that way, just to accommodate her, Samuel, and him. The dining room contained a massive dark oak table, large enough to accommodate many guests. But this one and this little sunny room with its lovely bay window had just belonged to the three of them.

Iain had spent the night in her former bedroom, making good on his declaration that they would be joined at the hip until all this was over. "What are you talking about?" she asked with a groggy mind. When she had arisen, he was out, always the early riser, as she remembered, particularly when something was driving him. She made coffee, trying to rid herself of a clinging headache that morning, when he reappeared just in time to join her for a cup.

"The journal Corey, it's essential."

She closed her eyes, trying to focus for a moment and clear out the cobwebs before she could address what he'd said. And then she reopened her eyes, confronted by his face, this older Iain, which at times felt like a stranger to her — not so accessible anymore, those places where she used to be able to reach him. Deliberately, he held himself separate from her, and she supposed it was for the best. But at times, admittedly, it didn't feel so. "No, I told you I didn't. Why are you asking again?"

He shook his head, "I don't know. It's something I feel that you know more than you realize. I've been thinking about it, Corey. If we have any hope of getting back there, it will be starting from scratch with that journal. It's essential we get our hands on it." She sighed deeply, turning away from him. She wished, acutely wished, that her father was here just now to advise. They were swimming in dangerous waters where she was sure she was most at risk, although exactly what she had left to lose was a bit intangible just now.

"Think Corey. Do you know?" he asked again, voice hard, determined. Yes, she did remember he was like that. Once he'd latched onto an idea, it would be impossible to pull him away from it. "Maybe Sebastian knows something. It might be worth looking into."

Her eyes flew up into his. He was goading her, trying to push her into a corner. He knew that bringing Sebastian into this was the last thing she wanted. If he didn't know anything else, he had to know this. "That would be pointless," she replied icily. "I told you he doesn't have it." Frustrated, she shook her head, "I never knew where it was, and frankly, I didn't want to know."

"*Calculated risks, my dear,*" her father would say. "*The risk must be warranted, and the alternative, not taking the risk, must in itself be more costly.*"

"But you did," Iain's voice stated rather hollowly.

She looked at him blankly, "You think I'm lying?" she asked softly.

"It's not exactly the same as lying, Corey," and then his hard stare softened into something she might almost call pity. "It's more like willful ignorance."

It was a curious gleam that she saw in his eyes. For a minute, she was convinced he would laugh at her, which made her angry and embarrassed for saying anything. But he had insisted, and here they were, penned in the crowded hallway of Ecole Issoire between classes discussing living statues. "They were alive?" his voice animated, a bit of an unusual occurrence for Iain.

"I have to get to class," she muttered.

"You have fifteen minutes. What exactly does that mean, they were alive?"

"Look, I knew you wouldn't understand."

"And you do?"

She hated it so much when he was right. "It was probably my imagination, a daydream."

He frowned, "Come on, Corey. I want to hear it all, no matter how nutty it sounds." She glanced around them, still noting students milling around, close enough in earshot to pick up this bizarre conversation. Picking up on her concern, Iain motioned for her to follow him down a side hall into an empty classroom, where he closed the door behind them. Turning to her abruptly, he spoke quickly, "Not much time, spill."

Wasn't this lovely? "Well, it was like I was walking in a graveyard with statues around me."

"Recognize it?"

"Not really, it was like other cemeteries except, I don't know, more so, the statues were really beautiful."

"And you were walking?"

"I think so. It was dark, night, and then I was inside a room, a small cold room."

"Mausoleum?"

"I don't know," she spat out. "It's not like I spend a lot of time in those places. But it was cold and blue. There was a strange blue light all over the floor. And there was a statue of an angel, leaning over something." Then she stopped, and he looked at her expectantly, waiting.

"Is that all?"

She shook her head slowly, "Then I saw her wings move, her white wings, and she straightened up and looked at me. Her eyes were blue, pure blue like that light."

"What did you do?"

She looked down at the floor, then back up at Iain cryptically, "I screamed. I screamed, and I was back in Sebastian's room."

He stood there staring at her momentarily, then commented a little too flatly after what she'd just told him, "Sounds like there's more to that book than meets the eye."

He couldn't remember when he'd developed the technique. He rather suspected it was one he'd always possessed but allowed to be dormant for a good part of his life. At times, he'd dismissed it, then repressed it, and then, of course, while he was in Rouen, he'd cultivated it. It wasn't exactly reading someone's mind but rather reading the vibrations and emotions that a person emitted. Andre had called it a psychic lie detector, laughingly, but had encouraged Iain to fine-tune this particular tool. It took a good degree of focus, but as soon as he'd mentioned Annie Besant's memoir that had been so critical to their success in the early time, something coming from Corey began to register on his radar — high levels of emotion that did not at all correspond to the subject. And then, he thought, perhaps it was the mention of Sebastian. But there was, even though masked now, just momentarily something here that could be classified as sheer panic.

He leaned back in the light wooden chair in the breakfast nook in Clayton Knight's Esplanade mansion. Oddly, all the time he'd spent here as a teenager and later when he and Corey were together, he couldn't remember ever having sat down for a meal or even a brief conversation in this room. It seemed to be one of the secrets of this old house, but, granted, not the only one. "You still feel it's here?" He echoed what he'd just heard her say at the very least to confirm it in his mind.

She nodded. Her face was deliberately blank of expression — how she was covering now. It was so clear to him, holding back and curiously engulfed in fear. "Yes, I'm relatively sure. Dad never took it out of the house."

He raised an eyebrow, "But where do you think he put it, Corey?"

She sipped her coffee quietly, not answering, but she was thinking about it, thinking about answering him, weighing, considering, debating — why and what exactly he had no idea. "He never told me. But he said he was putting it in safekeeping."

He straightened up a bit, "Safekeeping from who exactly?"

Rather gingerly, she placed the cup down on the table. There was a strain around her eyes, around her mouth. He could see a deliberate bearing down on her emotions. "Why does all of that matter? You said you needed the book, and I'm sure it's here."

"So, I see. You'll parcel out the information when and where it suits you. I thought I told you, no more secrets."

She looked into his face directly, dark eyes wide. "This has nothing to do with—"

And then he cut her off, exploding in determination, "With the missing Triquetra? How do we know that, Corey? Every little thing, every little thing you deem as separate and unimportant, can have something to do with this. You forget how all things are intertwined, and no action is so separate that it does not touch another."

Her eyes remained on him, but he noticed an odd cloudiness seem to pass over them. "I told you Sebastian couldn't be trusted. My father insisted that the book leave his hands."

"I don't understand. How could what Clayton wished carry any weight with Sebastian?"

She crossed her arms in front of her, her head bent a bit and then returned her eyes to him, not confrontational but matter of fact. "My father would not let the marriage go forward if he was not given the book."

Her words were so opaque — it took him more than a moment to assimilate what she was saying. "What does that mean? How could he have stopped it? You were married already."

She looked away. "My father was a powerful man, more than most realize. He could have—"

"So, he sold his daughter for an old book," he snapped harshly.

And then her eyes flashed in a way he remembered so well. "He was protecting me. He was protecting us all. He knew what Sebastian was capable of."

"And yet he let you stay with him."

"That was my choice," she retorted, hating so much that he would blame her father for anything.

"One I still can't understand. You didn't love him, Corey. I knew it then, and I know it now."

She rose from the table, turning her back to him and looking out the great bay window. "You're wrong."

He closed his eyes, forcing himself to master the surge of emotion that now threatened to take him over. There was no time to travel down these old paths. It was now that must be focused on. He stood, rounding the table and standing beside her. "I'm sorry," he said. "I went too far. All of this, as you said, doesn't matter now. We need the book. Do you have any ideas?"

She turned to him. His dark eyes were still filled with cloudy, indecipherable emotion. "Let me go upstairs and change, and then we can try something." Quietly, she left the room without once meeting his eyes again. He breathed deeply, mustering all his strength to dissipate the acute stab of pain that seemed mercilessly lodged in his chest.

CHAPTER 29

MAGIC

It was easier certainly to tell herself that there was feeling there. It became easier certainly once Iain left the country and, for a while, the powerful essence of what had once been left with him. Sebastian had encouraged the selling of the Esplanade mansion. She had even put it on the market twice, only each time to call the agent and cancel. It was no problem with Samuel. He was more than agreeable. He'd built a new life, and his roots had always been shallower than hers, so much easier to pull up and start to grow anew.

Herself, however, she'd found was indeed another creature.

"You've chosen Corey, so make the best of it. Try to build a life now. Cut your ties with the past. Forget what has been and start over."

Her father's advice, and then he'd shown her the way in all practicality. Two days later, he died, closing another door that led back to who she'd once been.

"You're stronger than he is. You can show Sebastian a different way. You are strong enough to change him. Make it your life's work."

But the house, the old house — she often wondered, if she'd let it go, would things have been different? But in those crystal, clarified moments when she no longer had the strength to lie to herself, she knew that it did boil down to the fact that she didn't love him. Iain had left her incapable of loving any other man, and all she had to offer were empty words and hollow gestures.

She moved through the old house, heavily cloaked in the dust of its memory. Her father's room was at the end of the hall on the second floor. For her, it had always been his room. The memory of her mother had faded long ago until it was now only a fleeting impression that showed itself as nuances here and there. This was her father's room, stamped and imprinted with the heavy hand of Clayton Knight.

She'd never really questioned if her father could be called a good man. He was a man who'd made choices, definitive choices and stood by them for good or bad. It had not been in his nature to live life indecisively. He was no bystander.

She quietly pushed open the heavy set of wooden doors that led inside. It was shadowed. What little light was creeping through the curtained windows seemed engulfed by the heavy, massive furniture — a black oak bedroom set that Clayton had acquired after his wife's death. Unlike Corey, Clayton Knight was one who wanted to get on with life and not dwell in places that were fruitless. Of course, he'd never remarried, though he was a successful and powerful widower upon his wife's death. What Corey had also gleaned about Clayton long ago was that he was a pragmatist. As was her case, he would only love once. His wife held an iron grip on his heart, one that it was a waste of time to try to dislodge. Aside from his children and some acquaintances, he'd lived the balance of his life alone. She drew open the heavy brocade drapes covering one of the long windows in the room, and light hesitantly filtered inside. There were still sheets untouched over some of the furniture, but much she'd uncovered when she'd moved back in.

So many times, she'd been back in this room, especially when she first came home, just sitting sometimes for hours, feeling, trying to be close to that strong spirit. Not knowing how to start over again or if she could. But not once, not once, had it occurred to her to look for it.

She sighed deeply, profoundly. It wasn't really as if she would have needed to look at all. Sebastian had been in here, rifled through bureaus, tables, and the massive wardrobe against the far wall, and she smiled in memory, even under Clayton's mattress, to no avail. And he'd looked in the chest at the foot of Clayton's bed. That too was fruitless. But she didn't think about it much, and that too she now had to admit was deliberate. Perhaps because of Sebastian, she'd buried the knowledge deep, although clearly, he'd never possessed Iain's talents for foraging through the mind. His gifts had lived in a more tangible realm, although his choices had managed to shred even that.

She sat on the edge of Clayton's bed for a moment, exhausted by the collage of memories. She was fairly certain that it hadn't been touched since her father had taken it from her. Without an actual confirmation of this, she was sure. Because she knew her father, he had no aspirations to power that he did not earn himself.

When the door behind her swung just a bit wider, she was unaware, so deeply buried in her own reflections. But as was the custom, Iain's low voice cut a clear, surgical slash right through the dense thicket of recollection she'd enmeshed herself in. "Corey, is this where it is?"

A chill ran up her spine of dread, fear of opening a book, fear of reopening those old, vaulted chambers. But as was everything these days, there was no help for it. "I think so. But he could have moved it, I suppose. I haven't seen it since I gave it to him."

"Did you ask him?" He was beside her, his fierce, sharp energy cutting through the shroud that seemed to cover this room.

"No," she shook her head. "I didn't really want to know." But slowly, she pointed to the rather large, ornate trunk at the foot of her father's bed — the one that Sebastian had searched but found empty. Clayton acquired it on a trip he'd taken out of the country a year after her mother's death. It was one of the few times she remembered him leaving her and Samuel with a family friend. As she remembered, he'd said it had come from India, and to her recollection, in all their childhood years, he had never locked it.

Iain shot her a curious glance and then moved toward the old iron trunk, whose length in proportion was just a little smaller than the end of Clayton's bed. As a child, she had tried to hide inside during a rambunctious game of hide and seek with Samuel, but her father had caught the back of her collar just before she'd closed the top. Effortlessly, he'd lifted her out, whispering in her ear, "Don't go in there, Corey. We might never find you again." He'd said it laughingly, but something about it chilled her, now marking the trunk as some odd and forbidden place. Iain knelt before it on his knees, and a smile came to her lips as she recalled his words.

"*Is it magic?*" she'd asked.

"*The best kind,*" he'd responded to her seven-year-old self. "*Real magic.*"

Iain gently lifted the trunk open, allowing the top to fall open noiselessly. For some moments, he stared at its interior before looking at Corey. His face looked puzzled, and she remembered the same reaction as a child. "It's empty," he murmured, still questioning in his low voice. And the smile inside her grew.

"*But there's nothing in here.*" Clayton Knight had grinned widely at his young daughter, and for a moment, the veil of grief parted.

"*Of course, there is, but you have to want to see it. Try again, Corey. Close the lid and close your eyes. This time, see with your mind what's really there.*"

Her eyes were closed the second time when she reopened the trunk, and she felt with only her hands, books, and boxes. And then her eyes opened when her fingers had met the texture of a velvety ribbon. It was a lovely satin box tied with a dark red bow. She laughed, "*Is it mine?*"

"*Of course, it's yours. After all, you found it when it wasn't there.*"

"You have to try again," her voice was nearly a whisper.

"What?" He looked at her with confusion that made her truly want to laugh, laugh for the first time in a long while. It was their secret now, she and her father's — their magic.

She crossed her arms, shrugging a bit. "It's how it works. Close your eyes and concentrate on seeing what's really there. And then open it again."

He frowned, "You're not serious."

And then she laughed a bit, a sound unaccustomed to even her own ears. "It's how it works, Iain."

He looked about the trunk for a moment, running his hands along its fabric interior. "What is it, a false bottom or something?"

She sighed, "You won't find anything. I tried a long time ago. It's just one of those things that you have to let be magic."

He looked at her again with narrowed eyes. Not the kind of man who liked to surrender to something that was just magic. Although, given their past experiences, one would think he'd learned to let go a bit. "Fine," he shook his head, "what do I do?"

"First, close the trunk. Then, close your eyes." She watched with an odd, elusive joy as he complied with her instructions with trust. When had he last truly trusted her? "Now, see clearly with your mind what is truly there." She saw his hands hesitate for a moment over the lid of the trunk, then they firmly grasped it, and he opened it again. Before Iain opened his eyes, she saw a stack of old books, but on top of it was the journal resting, looking just as it had the day that she put it into Clayton's safekeeping. Iain slowly opened his eyes and rested his hands on the old book, carefully taking it into his grasp and then coming to his feet. He glanced down at the trunk with a glitter of something in his green eyes akin to amazement. "How does this work?" he asked.

She murmured, "It's magic," was all she knew and all she could respond.

· CHAPTER 30 ·

DANGEROUS

"The dreams have returned."

Andre Desmarais seemed unfazed by the proclamation. And as intuitive as Iain had become under the older man's tutelage, he could not begin to read this reaction. He waited, but the Frenchman continued to rifle casually through some extraneous papers on his desk at the gallery. Then, he sat in his chair and casually took out a cigarette to smoke. Iain, in their years of acquaintance, had become used to the old man's peculiarities, but this blatant dismissal began to chafe him. "Did you hear me?" he asked explicitly.

Andre glanced up from the desk, exhaling from his cigarette, then flicking the ashes in a small shallow pottery bowl that he kept for just that purpose. "Yes, the dreams. Yes, I heard you."

Iain bristled a bit, "What do you make of it?"

He shrugged. "It really doesn't matter one whit what I make of it. They're your dreams, your undealt with karma. No, I'm not surprised. In fact, the only thing I'm surprised of is that it didn't happen earlier."

Iain's eyes widened, "Earlier?"

"You're powerful, my boy, but not powerful enough to escape what you are. It's time, you know, to set things right. I, well, I haven't the time to spend to nurse you through this anymore. The truth is I simply haven't the time any longer." With a deliberate motion, he put out the cigarette in the dish and stared directly but placidly at Iain. "We're all only allotted so much time here, not so much, hopefully, just to waste." He closed his eyes, sighed deeply, and then asked as though he were concentrating. "Tell me about it again, this dream."

He cleared his voice and knew from experience that Andre had put himself into a meditation and would see clearly whatever was in Iain's mind. "It is as before. In a forest, thick, the sky shielded by the branches, and then there is a wall, high, overgrown, in disrepair."

"What else?" his voice was direct, sharp.

"There's a door, an old door with a lock that I can't find the key for."

"Can't? Or won't?"

His words were harsh, but not his tone — just flat, pragmatic. And it was a question Iain had never asked himself before, not really.

"I don't know."

And the old man opened his weary eyes, and Iain could clearly feel that something had changed here. "It's important you know and then act, Iain. Life won't wait too long for you to decide."

Within a month, the old man had died of heart disease. And within two, Iain had returned to America.

The book burned in his hands. There was heat emanating from it — heat that he wouldn't have detected as a teenage boy or a young man, but only now. Now, he wondered with distraction how he could have missed it. And then he looked into Corey's face, her dark eyes quietly watching him, waiting for his next move, ready to follow his lead or intercept his progress depending on which occasion presented itself. But she had known, known as a young girl and as a young woman, and had protested when they'd moved forward. And perhaps, if he'd known the cost, perhaps he wouldn't have. But then that is the callousness of youth, the blindness that allows one to rush forward unthinkingly and without caution — the time that creates great achievement or great catastrophe, and more often both at once.

He'd laid it on the table in the mansion's breakfast room. It was true he'd had the oddest inclination to simply run with it, walk out the front door with it in his hands, as though it were some rare treasure to keep safe, apart. As his hands skimmed the cover, they prickled with the energy that, even now, after all these years, flowed from its cover, prickling energy, not necessarily all positive. "*Some things can be used for good or ill, which doesn't necessarily mark them as either. A tool, nothing more, but it does mark their existence as precarious."*

He'd also told Andre about the book and other things, although not right away — some years after he'd moved to Rouen. He was inclined for some time to bury the past, with sheer will, simply wipe away its existence. But undeniably, things never remain buried. They surface in odd benign places that spark a memory, women with long dark hair and sensitive brown eyes, and dreams of course, always. Dreams felt like the most insidious place, peaceful images that turned, and doors that refused to be unlocked yet refused to leave.

"What's the next step, Iain?"

He glanced up. She'd moved next to him soundlessly, or perhaps he'd been too enmeshed in thought to hear her. He leaned back in the chair again and thought momentarily about women he'd seen on the streets of Rouen with long black hair. The palm of his hand rested quietly on the surface of Annie Besant's journal. And the energy made him think about a walk long ago in the park. "Why don't you sit down, Corey, and we'll figure it out."

He couldn't help but smile at her uneasiness, at her determination to have control over, well, everything it seemed. "Why do you have to figure everything out, Corey? Life is random. It throws the unexpected your way."

They were wandering along the paths of City Park, not particularly heading in any direction. When she'd stepped out of her car, Iain could easily read her features — all nerves. She hadn't expected him to kiss her last night. They'd been spending time together at an accelerated level since she'd returned to New Orleans. Longer conversations, more confidences — he'd quietly stopped seeing Trish, but Corey didn't know about that, and Corey clearly hadn't seen this coming. Perceptive as she was, she was blindsided. "So, you're saying this is random?" she murmured.

He laughed at the absurdity of that statement. Random was something that he would never use to describe the two of them. In fact, he was sure they'd been moving to this moment ever since he'd first laid eyes on her at Ecole Issoire. It just had taken him a while to get here. "No, no,

I've had it in the plans for weeks, in fact, long before I ever knew you were coming home."

She pulled her red leather jacket a bit closer to her. For being so cautious at times, he found her choice of attire quite contradictory.

The color of the jacket wasn't calm or sedate but rather bold. She wore jewel tones, deep blues, and emerald greens, choices that were stimulating as well as inspiring to the artist's eye. And she was an artist. This he had always known, feeling that creative tenor in her soul. "You're making me feel silly. Is that your goal here, Iain?"

He shook his head, "I don't know. I think I want you to relax and not worry so much."

"I don't know if the time is right for things to get complicated, with Dad and my plans so up in the air. Things just feel unstable." This wasn't surprising. He'd expected her to say something similar, something to backtrack, as though that were even possible now.

"And you don't want me making things more unstable."

"I," she hesitated. "I don't know, Iain. You and I, how can I say this? It feels dangerous."

He stopped in his path, keenly struck by what she'd said. Putting his hands on her shoulders and turning her to face him, the word reverberated through him: dangerous. It traveled through his blood in a tantalizing way. As though someone had taken a bell and rang it abruptly in his ear, waking him from some deep slumber he'd fallen into. "Dangerous," he repeated as though it were a seductive caress.

Her eyes were wide, staring back at him like that intense and yet horribly insecure fifteen-year-old girl. "I'm serious," she whispered.

He nodded in agreement, "So am I." And then he reached in, pulling her closer, and began to kiss her. It was powerful, dizzying — a new awakening coursing through him. Perhaps it was wrong to jump in recklessly, but recklessness had been gone from his life for so long. Strongly, he pulled her into a closer embrace, feeling her acquiescence. She might fight it every step of the way, but deep down, she'd always been as reckless as he.

She settled in across from him at her father's breakfast table. "I'm still not sure how this can help us at all." She breathed in deeply, the sight of his hand resting almost possessively on the book making her progressively uneasy. She'd always had an elusive feeling that it was safer in the hands of a woman. Even while it was in her father's keeping, she had been inexplicably anxious, although she knew without question that he had no plans to use it. While she lived in this house alone after leaving Sebastian, she'd almost forgotten its existence. It had been such a deliberate move on her part to remove it from her conscious mind. And during that time, all was quiet, though admittedly not restful.

His eyes appraised her in that measuring, calculating way of his, soaking in and collecting some information that was significant to him but completely elusive to her. "So, you've said before."

"Well, the only time we succeeded was when we were five. Now there are—"

"Only two." He quietly finished her thought.

"Yes," she repeated, "only two."

And then lightly his hands moved, deliberately and efficiently flicking open the front cover in a manner she found surprising and jarring. "Yes, but so much has changed, Corey. And we are not at all who we used to be."

She hadn't decided to become involved with Iain. In fact, in retrospect, she believed that she had decided not to. But that didn't change what happened. And she, in later years, did come to believe that some things are ordained to be regardless of what insignificant influence we think we have upon the Universe.

Involvements she had always considered very carefully. In New York, there was more than enough opportunity, but something held her back. She'd always thought she was cautious because of her sensitivities, her gifts. But in the moment now, it seemed there was a timing to everything — timing that took great effort to escape.

The next days strangely meshed together in fluidity. What she remembered of it became fragmented. They were at the park, and then they'd left, taken his truck because he'd insisted, and gone to his apartment just at the end of City Park Avenue. If she'd made a decision, it had drowned somewhere in the rage of emotion, the feel of his lips, his hands, eyes that brimmed with a perceptible tinge of determination. Something in him had decided, and in the grand torrent of it all, she had accepted.

She remembered the echo of her footsteps on the cool wooden floors of his City Park Avenue apartment and again being drawn into his strong arms. She thought, perhaps more than once, to slow things down, but the thought was never uttered. By the time thoughts crystallized again, Iain was making love to her on his bed and had already taken her virginity. It was not something she'd thought about when they began. There was no thought — just desire, just necessity. And then it was done. He hesitated for a moment, whispering quietly in her ear. "All right?"

Did she answer? She couldn't remember. All she remembered was being swept along by the tidal wave of need and passion so deep it blotted away anything else.

· CHAPTER 31 ·

THE TREASURE HUNT

He stared at her with a curious expression, one that made her think perhaps that he thought she was crazed and one that only succeeded in making her angry. "You don't believe me," she spat out a bit too strongly.

"I didn't say that," Iain replied calmly. He glanced back toward the hallway, beginning to clear out of students. And then his cool green eyes were on her again, and she dearly wished she'd never opened her mouth about her impressions. "So," he murmured, leaning against the classroom door as though he really had all the time in the world. "What do you know about Annie Besant?"

She looked at him a little dumbfounded, wondering where this was going, wondering if she would make it to her next class. "Um, let's see. She wrote a journal, right?"

A slight smile, "Yeah, there's that. Let's see. She crusaded for women's rights in England, was an atheist and communist, and then claimed to be able to view the past and future by viewing the Akashic records."

"The what?"

He grinned a bit, "Yeah, exactly, and toward the end of her life, she went to India to study all their philosophy and died there."

"How do you know—"

"Quinn."

Of course, always the fount of information — she waited and then was propelled forward by the pressure of time. "So?"

"Yeah, well, the so of it is that far as we can tell, she never stepped foot in New Orleans. Sebastian's father got the journal from an antique dealer here in town."

"Here?" she repeated.

He nodded, "That's not all. The dealer had it for its local interest. Of course, the writing meant nothing. He couldn't break the code. But the drawings, the statues, were from local cemeteries, prominent statues, particular ones."

"Maybe she saw pictures," she offered.

"Sure, maybe, except some of them weren't made until after her death."

She opened her mouth to answer, then closed it again as the import of his words finally hit her.

"*You don't seem at all worried.*"

His blue-gray eyes refocused on her from that faraway place that, lately, they seemed settled in.

"No," he shook his head. "In so many ways, it feels like a relief."

The tears welled up fresh again in eyes that had become far too accustomed to their presence. "I don't know how I will get through things without you."

"Yes, that's the only thing I think now that's still holding me here." There was a faint attempt at a smile, and then it faded. Too much effort, she thought. She knew he was in pain, but he would only allow limited help with medication. Her father told her it would cloud him too much and blocked him from seeing and feeling the transition. "You know, I can hear your Mom talking to me again, whispering to me. She's worried about you, too. She thinks you'll regret it all too much and will lose yourself."

The tears came flooding again, and she bowed her head down, unable to entertain his pure blue gaze any longer. She felt his frail hand gently touch her hair. "But I don't think so, Corey. I think you're stronger than us all."

The day was cool. She dressed in her long black wool coat and brought gloves along as well. Although elsewhere in the city, the wardrobe might be too warm, the cemetery was well sheltered by trees, and she knew from experience that the cold breeze whipped around the towering family crypts. Iain parked near the northernmost corner of the grounds. Once they exited his car, they began to walk silently.

They didn't move one after another. They moved side by side, both familiar with where they were going, although she knew with certainty this time that they well might need to take a different path.

"It's quite extraordinary. She practically plots the whole cemetery, markers in great description, specific tombs. But these markers, I think, should be of particular interest."

"How on earth did you find the cipher after all these years?"

It had been late one evening in the den of Sebastian's Nashville Avenue townhouse. She remembered clearly that he'd lit a fire in the fireplace because it was the middle of February, one of the colder months in New Orleans.

Sebastian smiled and placed his brandy glass on the mantelpiece. More than anything, Corey felt he was enjoying making a show of this. Clearly, a fire was burning in more than the fireplace that evening. Again, it was in his eyes that spark of adventure that she remembered clearly from long ago.

"Well, I suppose you might say it was the thing that always nagged at me, that unfinished task of the Marguillers or the one that got away. All these years, it's been in the back of my mind."

"Are you going to get to the point, or are you going to dramatize much more?" Iain was sitting next to her on the sofa, and for a moment, with his old boyhood friend's jab, she saw the light dim ever so slightly in Sebastian's eyes.

Across from them in a wingback chair, Brae interjected, "Oh, come on. Don't spoil it. I'm enjoying this. Any moment, I'm waiting for Sebastian to announce who killed Mr. Body."

Sebastian frowned, seeming even more dispirited by Brae's remark. "Well, the short of it is I didn't discover the cipher, just the source of it. Quinn here completed the task."

Quinn nodded, his eyes that night also taking on a strange feverish quality. "Yes, Sebastian pointed me in the direction, and I ran with it, Sanskrit, actually."

"Sanskrit?" Corey asked with curiosity.

Quinn nodded, "Exactly, I always knew about Annie Besant's connection to India. She spent so much of her later life there. Mistakenly, I'd always thought the cipher must be related to Theosophy, a philosophy she was heavily involved with, but it was older than that and simpler in a way. A modern variation of Sanskrit, kind of simple once you figure it out, which is fortunate because I don't claim to be a language expert, just have some excellent computer software."

Corey straightened up, feeling an odd chill passing over her — a mixture of trepidation and excitement. "But what does it mean?"

Sebastian smiled with genuine enthusiasm, then, with a flourish, rolled out an extensive map filled with markings onto the coffee table in front of them. "It's a treasure hunt, you see, of sorts, right through the heart of the Metairie Cemetery."

Chapter 32

The Weeping Angel

Iain stopped in front of the tomb of the weeping angel. The doors were ajar, but he hesitated at the outer steps. Beside him, Corey's eyes were completely fixed forward, almost as if in a kind of trance. It still hummed. After all these years, after all this time, it still hummed with that strange energy that he remembered. "I don't think it will work," she murmured. "The balance."

"Yes, I remember," he said. "We all brought something with us that made it work."

She nodded, "Brae's primal energy."

"Quinn's intellect," he added.

She sighed deeply, "Sebastian's force of will."

"Your intuitiveness," he murmured.

And then she looked at him, dark eyes filled with wisdom, "And your refusal to accept limitation."

He met her gaze, "I already marked it."

Her eyes widened, "Why?"

"Because I knew where we'd end up."

"So, where does this door lead, the one you can't open?"

It was late one night, late one night in early April in Rouen. He and Andre had stopped at a café not far from the gallery. The older man was in an odd mood that night, and so when he broached this subject, Iain was more than a bit surprised. It wasn't something they'd talked about much. In fact, Iain, for some reason, had seen fit to steer clear of the topic. He strived to keep life here simple and himself, in odd ways, disconnected. It was undeniable that he'd learned much. Much more than he'd ever entertained as possible when living back in the States. By keeping himself unconnected, he'd glimpsed a complexity of living that he'd never conceived. It was all genuinely like a web, one massive, intricate, pulsating web of life's energies. One had no idea how one distant action set off a chain of reaction that could not remotely be anticipated. Only by separating himself from his own life had he learned all of this.

"Why bring this up now?"

The man across from him smiled, sipping a glass of red wine that he'd ordered. "Well, time is a funny commodity. And tonight, it feels like the time for this."

"I've told you I don't really know what it means."

Andre strummed his thick fingertips on the red tablecloth. "The question, my friend, is why you don't know. Why you don't want to know?"

Iain turned away, looking out of a nearby window into the night outside. The street was nearly abandoned except for a few stray pedestrians taking a stroll. "I suppose it's the past."

"Well, that would make sense."

"I've turned my back on it, finished with it."

And then he heard his friend chuckling, and he turned back, feeling a bit puzzled, "Finished with it, are you? Well, clearly, it's not finished with you just yet."

He blinked his eyes and then saw again what was before him. The door to the vault of the Weeping Angel was closed, but only moments ago, it had not been. It had been open. He breathed in deeply, the cool air surrounding him. But the understanding, the realization, that came like a blow straight to his chest — two possibilities, two outcomes.

"What's the matter, Iain?" she whispered beside him.

He swallowed on a dry throat and then stated flatly, "I'm not sure. But things, for some reason, aren't stable."

It was agreed that they would meet next Sunday on the grounds of the Metairie Cemetery. Historically, the Metairie Cemetery was a young institution dating only to the latter part of the eighteenth century. It certainly wasn't the oldest burial institution. That privilege was given to the St. Louis Cemeteries, closer to the French Quarter, but its grounds were unique and unusual. In many ways, Corey had always thought it resembled more of a museum than a graveyard.

She and Iain were the first there. It was a chilly day, almost too cold to be out. They would begin at the Montleone tomb. This had been agreed upon because it was the most obtrusive monument on the grounds, a massive white obelisk shooting up into the sky, not so much unlike the Washington monument itself. Except this one was surrounded by the statues of four women leaning against its base, each holding an object representing faith, hope, charity, and memory. Corey pulled her short, red leather jacket more tightly around her as the chill of a passing breeze seemed to cut right into her. "Too cold?" Iain asked beside her.

She answered with distraction, "Yes, what do you think of all this?"

He wrapped his arm around her, "What do I think of Sebastian's scavenger hunt through the graveyard?"

She turned to him, grimacing, "Yes, when you boil it down, it kind of comes to that."

"I don't know. I think our friend needs to find something better to do with his time."

She smiled at him, "You're really not interested in this kind of stuff anymore."

He sighed, "Well, I guess, as the good book says, everything has its season, and it feels like our season for this has passed."

She nodded in agreement, "Maybe we should go then."

"Maybe we should." He echoed, kissing her lightly just on her forehead. But then, all plans of retreat were jettisoned as she heard more cars arriving.

Her gloved hand lightly brushed along the surface of the closed doors. "Did you see it?" He asked, placing his leather-gloved hand directly on her shoulder.

Her dark eyes widened, "See what?"

He turned away, his eyes carefully and completely sweeping their entire surroundings. Everything else appeared in order. His gaze returned to the vault, heavy iron doors still closed securely, although they had not been only a moment before. And it was certain that Corey had not seen what he had witnessed. "What do you mean things aren't stable?"

He shook his head, "I don't know, but I want you to stay here. Stay here and wait. I'm going for a walk."

He ignored the look of confusion that marred her face and descended the few short granite steps back to the ground. Without thought, he began to head in a specific direction. His feet instinctively knew the familiar path.

"It's possible, you see, under certain circumstances, to pierce that veil that separates what we perceive as now and what we perceive as past. The key is in recognizing what is perception and what is truth."

He felt a dizziness swirl somewhere inside his head.

"What are you saying?" he'd asked his friend.

"That time is not at all what we think and not nearly as final as we would like to believe."

He saw the tall monolith in the sky before its base became in any way visible.

"You see, my friend," the older Frenchman explained, *"it's not impossible to change the past, to change it and therefore change the present."*

He rounded a corner and then stopped abruptly. It transfixed him, what he was seeing. It took him some moments to recognize that the group gathered about the base of the Montleone tomb could not see him — the group standing there that Iain was a part of, Brae, Quinn, Sebastian, Corey, and yes, his younger self.

He breathed in deeply, feeling a sudden pain cut right through his chest, just beneath his ribs. He bent over with its intensity, feeling a cold wind accompanying it, tearing into his lungs. It was impossible. He felt there was no air, and at any moment, he would slip into blackness. And then, from nowhere, arms went around him, and he felt her warm breath on his face. For a moment in delusion, he wondered which Corey this was, the woman he'd come here with or the one he'd just seen standing next to his younger self. "What's wrong, Iain? What's wrong?" Her voice was frantic with fear.

When he finally straightened up again with Corey's aid, he saw quickly that the gathering had dissipated, dissipated as if it all had been a mirage.

Chapter 33

Rosslyn and Joan

Brae leaned into Corey as she gathered her books from last period's Algebra class. "The Marguillers are meeting after school today."

Corey raised an eyebrow, feeling more than a bit irritated by this sudden pronouncement. "I can't. My dad is keeping me on a short leash right now." She flung her book sack over her shoulder and started heading toward the door as Brae trailed closely behind her.

"Why?" she whispered harshly, sweeping her red hair behind her ears.

She continued walking, making it out into the hallway and wondering how long Brae would be following her. "Don't know, something about last weekend at Sebastian's. He has a sense of things, and he thinks something is up. Look, Sam is driving today. I have to be out in the parking lot, or he'll likely forget and leave me."

Suddenly, Brae grabbed her arm and said, "Hey, I have an idea. We'll all go to your house, you know, another meeting. Your dad shouldn't be suspicious about that."

Corey looked at her blankly, "You mean just spring the whole Marguillers group on him."

Brae smiled broadly, "Yeah, you think Sam can fit us all in the car."

She frowned, "Tightly."

And then Brae was beaming, "That's okay. I was hoping to get a little closer to Sebastian." And then she flew enthusiastically in the opposite direction down the still-crowded hall. "Just stall him," she called behind her. "It may take me a few minutes to sell this."

It was awkward, and for some reason, Corey was in no temper for uncomfortable scenarios. Again, they all sat in the back sunroom of Clayton Knight's Esplanade mansion. Mrs. Vaughn had supplied them with lemonade and cookies that tasted suspiciously lemony. And largely, they were silent. "Do you think this is private enough?" Quinn whispered, leaning over the large, white coffee table that separated the day sofa from everything else.

Corey responded blankly, "It's the best we've got," taking a bite of one of Mrs. Vaughn's lemon cookies. "What are we going to discuss, state secrets?"

She noted Sebastian rolling his eyes in exasperation and a curious quirk of Iain's mouth that looked suspiciously like a smile wanting to break through. But she couldn't help it. The whole way home, she was literally smushed against Brae in the front seat with Sam, who periodically was shooting her suspicious and perturbed glances. At the same time, the boys in the back whispered continually, worse than a group of old spinster gossips. Quinn frowned, "No, but they are Marguillers' secrets, and although you girls might not take this seriously, we have taken oaths."

Again, not for the first time today, Corey felt a tickling of irritation explode right up her spine. "You know, that's right. Brae and I aren't officially part of anything."

Brae chipped in with huge blue eyes, "Yeah, we don't even have secret names."

Iain laughed, "That's true. Who would you like to be Brae, Godfrey or Guilliame?"

Brae frowned, "That's all they had, men?"

Corey added, "Yes, it was the age of the damsels in distress and repressed."

Sebastian laughed at the quip. "Well, look on the bright side. At least you have the vote now."

Corey glared at him, "What are you, some kind of chauvinist?"

"You know, actually. There are some women connected with the Templars," Quinn interjected diplomatically.

Corey crossed her arms, leaning back in her chair, still glaring with irritation at Sebastian. "Like who?" Brae took the bait. She was just way too eager as far as Corey was concerned.

Quinn cleared his throat, "Well, some theorize that Joan of Arc had some sort of connection to a reorganized group of Templars, and then, of course, there is Rosslyn Chapel in Scotland."

Sebastian asked, "That's that chapel that has all the Templar symbolism?"

Quinn nodded, but then Brae asked. "That's pretty, Rosslyn. Who is it named after?"

Quinn responded hesitantly, "Um, just the Roslin area."

"Well, that's thin," Corey spat out.

Iain laughed, "You just can't be pleased today."

Brae smiled, "Well, I like Rosslyn. You can have Joan, Corey."

"Let's see. Warrior, martyr to the French cause, Saint. Yeah," Iain nodded, "suits you."

"Fine, it's settled. Our two new members codename Joan and," Sebastian hesitated, seeming to choke a bit on the word, "Rosslyn, only to be used at high priority moments."

"High priority?" Brae questioned.

"Yes, we'll hammer out the details later. Can we move on now to the important stuff?"

"By all means, we wouldn't want to slow you up." For some reason, Sebastian was getting on her nerves today more than usual.

But her last barb seemed to hit home more deeply, "Look, Ms. Knight, this was our group first, our invention. If you don't like how we do things, you can hit the road."

Corey stood up. Something broke inside her. "Yes, well, maybe that's preferable to having to do homage to a bunch of egos."

And then Iain cut in, his voice low but steely. "No, Sebastian, the girls stay. We can't afford to lose Corey now if we intend to really do anything."

Sebastian glared at him a bit, taken aback by his interference. "Really? Can't afford to lose her, you say, Jacques?"

Iain's green eyes narrowed at the challenge, and Corey felt a peculiar vibe between the two in which she was placed directly in the crossfire. "High priority Hugues, or is it just at the whim of your temper?"

Quinn sighed deeply, "Okay, guys, enough. Can we talk about what we've decided to do?"

Corey slowly sat back down in the large wicker rocker chair. She tried to calm herself. It was so odd. Something was pushing her buttons like crazy today, and it had started with all of Iain's proclamations about—

And then, Quinn completed her thoughts, "the journal."

"Annie Besant's journal," Corey murmured.

"Yes, we've talked at length."

Then Brae's eyes widened, "We've talked?"

Quinn looked a little uncomfortable, considering the most recent exchange. "Well, the three of us," indicating the original Marguillers "have talked about it, and well, maybe we should get your input."

He turned his focus on Brae, "What do you think?"

She looked a little perturbed, "About?"

Corey interjected, "The journal." She leaned back in her chair and then asked quietly, "Why don't you tell us what you think, and then we'll let you know how we feel about it."

"We think we should shelve the whole thing. At this point, we don't have what we need to do anything with it." Iain's voice was very flat and matter-of-fact. But she felt quite surprised at his proclamation, given what they'd discussed earlier in the day.

Her eyes canvassed the other two boys, and she asked, "And you agree?"

Quinn nodded, and Sebastian added, "It would be difficult to even get at the thing right now. My Father has become suspicious. Might be best to let it go and move on."

Again, her eyes met Iain's, but there was no flicker of anything there, just masked. "Well, that's fine by me. It really doesn't matter to me." Brae added.

"So, you're the only one left, Corey. What's your take?" Iain asked directly.

She met his green eyes with a coolness that matched his, "Fine, shelve it." She stated with no emotion.

"Well, this is a surprise," Clayton Knight had entered the room silently and stood on the threshold. "I didn't know you were having guests today, Corey." She stood up, feeling a bit winded by his sudden appearance and the intensity of what had just occurred.

She walked over to him, kissing him lightly on the cheek, "It was spur of the moment. Hope it's all right."

He nodded with a casual smile as he speculatively canvassed the room. He'd been out when they arrived, so she had no idea he'd returned. "Well, since everyone's here, I'd like to invite all of you to dinner. I'm sure Sam wouldn't mind getting everyone home later."

Corey smiled up at her dad and then turned back to the surprised faces of the Marguillers.

He breathed in deeply, and another sharp pain raced through him in the heart area this time, causing him to fall to his knees. Corey went down beside him, her arms still wrapping around his back and under his arms in support. "Oh God, what's wrong?" Her voice rasped in panic.

Iain kept his eyes squinted closed as another vibration of pain ripped through him. It was clear that he had gone somewhere he was not yet equipped to travel into. "It's energy," he muttered, "lost a lot."

He bowed his head, trying to center himself and fend off the onslaught. And then he felt her hand that she'd removed from its glove slowly move to his chest to directly over his heart area. Even in his weakened state, he could feel the warm rush of energy she was sending to him. "No," he gasped, still in pain.

"Be quiet," was her reply, and then she instinctively put her hand beneath his coat, roughly pushing inside the neckline of his sweater until she reached direct contact with skin. Her palm felt absolutely and incredibly warm to him, almost feverish. And the moment that she again began to pour energy into him, it was nothing short of an electric charge. He heard her breathing deeply, concentrating, and he knew she was depleting herself. But his mind was dizzy with sensation as he remembered sharply the power that they created together. Operating without coherent thought, he instinctively reached up, pulling, nearly yanking, her face towards his until lips met, kissing her with sheer determination. He felt her initial shock, an attempt to pull away in surprise, but his hand was like steel and would not allow any retreat. Then it changed, and there was no resistance, as it had been, kissing her, connecting again in a way that both had always been powerless to deny.

Corey waited on the steps of the tomb of the Weeping Angel. As she watched Iain disappear into the cemetery, the coldness of the day swept around her and penetrated her heart. She pulled her coat closer, recognizing intently that he was hiding things from her. She could feel it on her skin, see it in his eyes — probing, speculations, loose ends that simply did not connect.

She'd been foolish, thinking somehow this would be simple, that she could keep everything separate — that it would be simple, neat, finding what was lost, and then going back to what was. But on this cold day, standing on granite steps in this City of the Dead, she wondered what she would return to — a hollow life, marking time until its conclusion. It had once been a retreat from pain, but now, oddly, with Iain's return, it felt like a self-made prison.

She closed her eyes, breathing in deeply, and then, hearing the whispers behind her, she turned. The heavy iron doors were still closed, but her leather-gloved hand brushed lightly along the handle. She took the pull fully into her grasp just as it whispered to her that it would give way for her again. She pulled ever so slightly, and the heavy latch moved, but then she dropped her hand and stepped back. *Not yet.* Something inside told her. You can't confront yourself with lies on your lips. She stepped down the four steps backward, stumbling a bit. *Not with lies*, it echoed again. Then she turned back toward the cemetery, trying to follow the path that she'd seen Iain take.

CHAPTER 34

RETREADING OLD GROUND

He felt stronger as he managed to walk back to the car with Corey. She didn't say anything. She didn't say anything when he stopped kissing her. Just silently helped him to his feet and continued supporting him on their trek back. Once they were in his sedan, she asked pointedly, "Do you need a hospital?"

He shook his head. "No," he murmured, "just some rest."

She started the engine, "Where?" she asked.

"My house, it's cleaner," he answered. Of course, he didn't mean actually cleaner but cleaner with energy. But she seemed unaffected by the strange comment, and now that they were moving closer, he could feel in her emotions that she understood exactly what he meant.

She was concerned because he still seemed very pale. But once they arrived at his house, Iain insisted he could walk unaided to the door. He sat on the couch, leaning back with his eyes closed. "What can I get you?"

And after a few moments, his eyes opened slowly and focused on her. An indefinable sensation shot through her as their gazes locked. "Something to drink," he said quietly.

She headed to the kitchen. As she reached up to open a cabinet, she noticed for the first time that her hands were shaking. Leaning against the sink, she tried to get hold of herself. It was insane. He hated her. She knew it. She remembered on that first meeting, the way he looked at her, the cruelty in his tone. But then he'd softened. She grimaced. He'd softened at times when it suited him. This was as she remembered him, the sleeping lion — never quite knowing when he would be roused to fury, but once he was, he was relentless in his determination to draw blood.

She forced her hands to still as she reached into the cabinet for a box of tea. She found a mug that she filled with water and a tea bag, placing it into the small microwave that he had situated at the back of a counter. The kitchen wasn't too large, but it was bright and sunny, with a bit of an alcove attached for the breakfast table. It was sparse, minimalistic in furnishings. He hadn't planned to stay here very long, so he hadn't made this place a home, just a stopgap.

Taking the hot mug out of the microwave, she waited as the tea steeped. And her mind impulsively recounted how he'd grabbed her, almost roughly, and kissed her, not disinterested, not carefully, but with need. Her heart felt as though it was slamming in her chest at the memory. It hurt because it reminded her how it felt to be awake again. She put a teaspoon of sugar from the white bowl that he had near the sink. This was how he used to like his tea, only one more thing that she had no earthly idea if it had changed.

"I made you some tea," she said as she handed the steaming mug to him. He looked a little better. Color was returning to his face. "I made it, well, the way you used to like it." She stumbled across the words, suddenly realizing it might not be the smartest thing to say now.

His eyes met her face, and then he sipped the steaming beverage. "It's fine," he answered.

She stood there, mutely staring at him, feeling more on eggshells than when he first returned. "What happened out there? What made you sick?" she clarified quickly.

"I think it was an energy drain of sorts. I tapped into something, not sure why."

"What? Do you know what it was?"

He shook his head. His eyes focused on her face, "Not exactly, but you helped. Your being there helped pull me out of it."

"Well," she felt her face absolutely going flushed. It felt ridiculous at this point in their lives. "It seemed serious."

He smiled a bit, "It was."

"What?" She asked in response to the smile. She shouldn't have asked, but it was instinctive.

"Why are you so uncomfortable?" he asked directly.

Still maintaining his gaze, she sank into a chair across from the sofa, "Am I supposed to pretend that it didn't happen?"

"Is that what you want to do?" he replied smoothly.

"Just like you to answer a question with a question."

"No, how about I just answer what you want to know."

She nodded, "Fine, why? Why did—" Then she stopped. Perhaps it was not something that needed examination at this point.

"Why did I kiss you?"

She sighed deeply, "I feel like I'm fifteen again. Maybe we should just drop this."

"Maybe," he replied a little distantly. "I suppose all I can say is that I needed to. That there is a power between us, and I'm realizing, maybe for the first time, that our being together was the reason that we were successful in the past."

She stared into his green eyes, feeling as though she were caught again in something that was beyond her. "I don't think I understand, Iain."

He answered quietly, "I'm not sure that I do either. But rest assured, I will figure it out."

He closed his eyes but could still hear the murmurings in his mind; the past, but not as he'd always remembered it, the past with a newfound clarity and crystallized perspective.

The wind whistled above him, and he could feel his body leaning against her — the warmth of her body through her lightweight coat, his arm around her. But nervousness, which he had not been aware of before, permeated her skin. From the beginning, there had been an unease in her.

He heard his own voice, "We were getting ready to leave. Thought you all had given up on Sebastian's wild goose chase." Back then, he'd laughed and had not taken any of it seriously. He was too wrapped up in the newfound joy that Corey had brought to his life. It was intoxicating, the beginning of their relationship. For a boy who had lived such an emotionally barren life, for it suddenly to be full, the cup brimming over. It made him reckless and unguarded and painfully unaware.

Sebastian walked toward them, his face smiling but eyes not, eyes cold and steady. He hadn't noticed it back then. He hadn't noticed the change in his friend. In fact, for years, through college and after, he'd disregarded him as inconsequential. He could see now the mistake, arrogance on his part.

His friend pointed at the monument behind them, "According to her instruction, this is where we begin."

Iain turned round and stared straight at the obelisk behind them, capped with a cross and the four female figures guarding it. The sun behind it shone painfully into his eyes.

Then he opened them. She was standing in the darkened doorway of his bedroom. "I'm sorry. I didn't mean to wake you." She didn't move from her spot, so still, so cautious of him. "I thought I heard you call out."

He sat up in the bed, rubbing his head. After his weak spell or whatever one might call it at the cemetery, he'd felt totally drained and opted to lie down as soon as they reached the house. Corey insisted on waiting up front. At least, she'd said, until she was sure he was recovered. "I was dreaming," he answered.

She nodded, "All right."

Then, closing his eyes and leaning back on his pillow, he murmured, "Goodnight, Joan." There was no response, just a hesitation, then the sound of her footsteps retreating. He cleared his mind, determined this time to have a restful sleep.

Chapter 35

Clayton Knight

Clayton Knight was overly protective of his children. This he admitted freely, although it was clear to him early on that his son Samuel was a free soul undaunted by his attempts to restrain him. If he set boundaries, Sam either blithely leaped past them or acquiesced temporarily, just long enough to get the old man off his back so he could return to his own interests. Clayton knew without much second-guessing that Sam would lead a happy and reasonably productive life. Because the truth was the boy didn't ask much of himself or others and was in a natural state of peace and acceptance. Where exactly he got those qualities, Clayton could not begin to guess. He'd decided it must be a throwback to former generations, for Sam and Corey's mother could never have been described as undemanding of life, nor dare he deem it superficial in any respect. Abigail felt too much, read too much into everything, and clearly saw too much of the truth. In dark moments, he believed firmly that this is what killed her, took her out of their lives too soon. And it chilled him at times how hauntingly like her his daughter seemed to be.

And so, while the idea of his daughter coming out of her shell and finally making some social connections seemed as though it were something any parent would be pleased about, in their case, in his case, it cheered and disturbed him at the same time. For Corey created a dual nature in him, a dual attitude — one part forcing himself to push her out into the world regardless of the cuts and abrasions that she would likely encounter and another part — one that he held at bay and bridled — that wanted to protect her, shelter her, even at the expense of her living her own life.

But what didn't help was the turbulent selection of personalities she'd chosen to associate with. Mrs. Vaughn had shifted gears this evening and dumped their regular itinerary for Thursday evening, which, as he recalled, was usually some well-prepared chicken entrée. She had made pizza, square pizza on cookie sheets because, as she'd informed her employer in animated terms, there wasn't a pizza pan in the house. This fact, she'd grumbled out but then reluctantly complied with his request. And he'd yielded as well, moving their early dinner out to several wrought iron tables on the patio. Sam had wandered into the kitchen sometime during Mrs. Vaughn's frantic preparations with question in his eyes.

Clayton had answered gruffly once it was broached. "We're entertaining Corey's friends."

"With pizza?" his son smirked.

"Yes, isn't that the normal diet of choice for you teenagers?"

He shrugged, "Sure, but I've never seen it around here before. And we're having pizza on your mahogany dining table?"

"No," now the kid was irritating him. "We're, or rather they are, eating on the patio."

He nodded, "And you, Dad?"

"I'll eat in my study."

Another smirk, "Mind if I go out with some friends?"

Clayton considered it, quickly though, difficult to hold the boy to his rules if he was breaking them for his sister. "Fine, don't be late."

"Thanks, Dad, you're cool." And then he was gone, clearly not wanting to wait around to see if the old man changed his mind. He wondered, and not for the first time at that moment, what Abigail would think of the parenting job he was doing. At times, he felt quite successful, patting himself on the back for his tight wire act between sternness and compassion, but at other times, and oddly in this instance, he felt as though everything was moving well out of his capable control.

"So, how was everything?" Clayton smiled broadly, appearing on the patio for the first time in over an hour. He glanced around. From the look of things, Corey's friends had pretty much polished off Mrs. Vaughn's square pizzas. Thankfully, the exasperated housekeeper had mercifully made him a sandwich from last night's leftover meatloaf and gruffly placed it on his desk without a word — emotional yes, but dependable always.

Corey looked up from her table where she and the other girl, what was her name again, were sitting. The three boys were seated at the other table, which given everything, suited him just fine. Corey smiled, looking happy, "It was great, Dad."

The other girl echoed, "Thank you, Mr. Knight. I love pizza, even though I've never had square pizza before." And then she reddened a bit. "But it was great."

At the other table, the boys looked up at him, nodding in agreement. And then the Morris boy, "Thank you, sir. We do appreciate the invitation." The green-eyed boy was watching him with an odd expression, which, if Clayton was not mistaken, told him that he thought his friend was a bit full of it, but he said nothing. And the other one, the skinny lad, was watching him with wide eyes, intimidated. Well, that was good. A little intimidation never hurt anyone. But the green-eyed kid wasn't intimidated. He could feel that on his skin, not intimidation but curiosity.

Corey stood up and walked over to him. "Thanks, Dad, this was nice." And she hugged him smiling, and his eyes momentarily caught those of the green-eyed boy — surprisingly, what he gleaned now was unmistakably sadness.

Corey watched her Dad exit their patio. She'd been surprised that he'd suggested this. It had broken all the routines of their house. But he'd done it to please her, and it did more than she was sure he could imagine.

"So, Corey, do you all ever drink anything other than lemonade?" Quinn asked from the other table.

She whirled around, a little surprised at the comment. "Iced Tea, too. Dad doesn't like sodas in the house."

Iain smiled, but it seemed more like a smirk, "Thinks they're evil?"

"Unhealthy," she frowned.

And then Sebastian, clearly needing to get in on the needling, "And what's with the square pizza?"

Brae laughed, "I know. How weird is that?"

Corey felt her momentary elation beginning to drain out of her with all the criticism. "We didn't have any pizza pans. I didn't realize the shape of the pizza changed its taste."

"The pizza was good," Iain answered. "Better than any dinner I'd have gotten at home."

His comment startled her but did help to soften things a bit. "Your Dad seems cool, Corey," Brae added.

She nodded, "He is protective since Mom died. "

"Well," Iain interjected rather dryly, "At least he's around. I can barely remember what mine looks like. He's gone so much."

It was night. He could clearly see the darkness outside the closed blinds of his bedroom window. When he awoke for a moment, Iain wasn't at all sure of where he was. The heaviness of his sleep and his fatigue made him disoriented, and for just an instant, although only an instant, he thought he was awaking in his childhood bedroom in the house on Carrollton Avenue where he'd grown up. But this room was too large, not like the small bedroom in that house. And the structure here felt quiet, not agitated by the negativity that had always seeped through the walls back then. He remembered after high school when he was finally able to raise enough money to move out, what a deep sigh of relief had permeated him at finally leaving that chapter of his life behind. His home life had always been an odd dichotomy. His parents were determined that he attend Ecole Issoire, such a well-respected private school, and yet their outright neglect in so many other areas of his life. He'd recognized from early on the skewed nature of the household that revolved around a tumultuous and unhealthy relationship. As a defense, he had developed a shell of protectiveness to keep him sane. It was clear from his very young years that there was little he could do for his parents. They were caught in an eternal dance of upset, anger, and sadness that neither had the will nor courage to break. He'd learned fairly quickly that it was nearly impossible to help someone who refused to change — better to save yourself than allow them to destroy you as well.

Cool air wrapped around him as he sat up in the darkened room. He could see a soft light coming from the den, which he slowly moved toward, still feeling a cloak of disorientation clinging to him.

He ran his hand through his hair, trying to wake himself further. In the den, there was one floor lamp lit across the room. And on the sofa was Corey, curled up, quietly sleeping. It was coming back now, the cemetery, the past, and pain in his chest and then — their kiss. And she'd stayed, worried about him, he was certain, because it was in her nature, a powerful thread of protectiveness for those she cared about. He shook his head, wondering how she could care about him after all he'd said, after all his anger, how she could. But he knew, as much and as clearly as he knew anything, that she still did.

"*Are you sure?*"

"No"

"*Why not?*"

There were questions and answers and cool blue light again reflecting off the walls and chilling her skin.

"*I shouldn't be here.*"

"*But you are*" — they answered.

She breathed deeply in the cold air of death.

"*It isn't time.*"

"*Are you sure?*" — they whispered.

"No," she voiced reluctantly.

Then it questioned, "*What do you want?*"

"*Peace,*" it slipped out. For here, it seemed impossible to lie.

"*Peace with no truth. Peace with lies?*"

The angel's wings fluttered, and cold marble came to life.

Corey opened her eyes into semi-darkness but enough light to see that Iain was sitting in the armchair across the room, silently watching her. She slowly pulled herself up to a sitting position on the sofa as her eyes adjusted to the dim light. She was certain she'd left on a lamp in the room, but the only thing on now was the glow emanating from the kitchen.

"I thought you were asleep," she murmured.

"I was," he answered with no inflection.

Swinging her feet to the floor, she straightened up, then glanced around on the walls for a clock, not remembering if she'd seen one before. But again, who could tell in this dusky semi-light? "Are you feeling any better?" she asked.

"I think so," he answered, not wanting to elaborate.

"Well," she pushed her thick dark hair behind her shoulders, hoping it wasn't the tangled mess she envisioned. "Maybe I should go home so you can rest some more. I can call a cab."

"At three in the morning?" She looked around, surprised, but still no clock to be seen.

"Is it really that late? I was just going to close my eyes for a few minutes."

"Best laid plans," he nearly whispered.

His odd mood was beginning to irritate her a bit now. "Is something wrong?"

"Well, I've been sitting here thinking for a while. And I think I've figured out how to get what we want."

"You mean the Triquetra?"

"It's a roundabout method, of course, but this afternoon in the cemetery, I realized, well, I touched its feasibility."

"This afternoon?" She'd suspected something had happened, "What exactly do you mean, Iain?"

"The way in is through the past."

"You mean to follow what we did before?"

He shook his head, "Not exactly. I mean, actually, go with them or rather us. I believe it's possible."

She sat there for a moment, trying to absorb what he was saying, traveling in the past. And then the amazement at his words faded as the enormity of what he was suggesting hit her — that past, their past, impossible, anywhere but there.

CHAPTER 36

GHOSTS

"So," Quinn, holding his second glass of lemonade, looked sheepishly at the girls. His eyes darted furtively from them to Iain to Sebastian and then back to them again like a mouse, not sure if it would get the cheese or get murdered.

They had left the patio and somewhat loosely reconvened in the sunroom, Sebastian commenting that they might need to wrap up a few loose ends. Corey had sunk back down into her favorite rocker, not feeling the need to say much of anything. It was obvious to her, even if it had eluded Brae that the founding members of the Marguillers were keeping secrets again from their newest inductees.

Brae, whose patience ran about as long as Mrs. Vaughn's these days, jumped at it. "What? So, what's going on?"

Sebastian, putting a cup of untouched lemonade that Mrs. Vaughn had nearly forced on everyone on the glass coffee table, started, "Well, Iain and I and Quinn, we felt we should let you girls know what we've decided to do next. Even though you probably wouldn't want to go along on this one."

Corey frowned. Worse than being left out of the loop, she hated when people decided something for her without asking. "Decided what exactly?"

Sebastian continued, although seemingly carefully selecting his words, "Well, Quinn, although we did decide to let go of the journal, well, Quinn was reluctant to let it entirely go."

Corey's eyes shot over to Quinn, meeting his soft brown ones head-on. "How come?"

"The drawings, all the drawings of statues and landmarks. I'm quite sure it's that cemetery near City Park."

Brae glanced up, "Greenwood?"

He shook his head, "No, the big one, with all the Civil War stuff."

"He's talking about the Metairie Cemetery," Iain stated flatly.

"But that's odd," Corey muttered. "I mean, it's certainly not the oldest cemetery in the city. St. Louis number one and two are much older."

"That's true," Sebastian agreed. "But it is one of the most historic."

"And it is the one in Annie Besant's journal," Quinn stated emphatically. "We might not be able to break her cipher, but I recognize some of those drawings. My great-grandfather's family has a tomb there, not one of the grandiose ones. But I've walked around the place with my family. I'm sure that's the one."

"Why would Annie Besant—"

Corey began but was abruptly cut off by Sebastian, "We can't know why. That's clear. Without the cipher, we can't know why. But we can go there."

"You mean visit there?" Brae asked.

"Not exactly," Iain interjected.

"Iain, Quinn, and I are going there this weekend after nightfall to spend most of the night," Sebastian said definitively, as though he were delivering a well-rehearsed speech.

Corey's eyes widened, and then she laughed impulsively, "Why? Do you think the ghouls are going to come out at night?"

Iain looked at her, and then he smiled, "Yeah, we do."

"There's no need."

"Then I'll call you a cab."

She shook her head, long black hair, which she unconsciously swept behind her ears. "No, I'll walk. You're not far from the streetcar. I'll walk there. It will clear my head."

He smiled oddly, with concern, she thought. "Don't be ridiculous. That will only take you so far. Not up to Esplanade."

"It's all right," she murmured. "I'll figure it out."

"Sit down," he said softly but with that authoritative tone as though all matters had been settled. "I'll get you some coffee, then I'll take you home. There's no point in an unaccompanied, beautiful woman wandering the streets of New Orleans with no one to protect her."

She sat at his small kitchen table, feeling too disoriented to mount much of an argument this morning. "I've been wandering around unprotected for some time now, Iain."

He was in the kitchen, by the sink, filling the coffee pot with water. "Why are you in such a hurry to leave? It's early, not even seven yet."

She looked down at her hands. The night hadn't been bad. Once, Iain returned to bed after providing her with a pillow and blankets. He'd even offered her the bed, opting to sleep on the sofa himself, but she'd refused adamantly. For some reason, it seemed unthinkable to her. This was his house, and although she slept soundly and undisturbed, it felt as though she were an intruder here. Whatever rights she'd had with him, she'd given up long ago. She heard the coffee pot begin its percolation and looked up to see him watching her. "What's the matter, Corey?"

She stared at him, wondering how to answer. When the answer itself was ephemeral, intangible, but simultaneously so present that it wrapped around her chest impeding breath, life. She smiled sadly, "Ghosts, I suppose."

He stared at her so quietly for a moment that she thought he might not acknowledge what she'd said. "Yes, it doesn't seem right that we should be here, unearthing the painful past this way. But an old friend told me once that this is how life works. Wherever you're bleeding, the vultures will circle until you figure out a way to heal the wound."

"Did he really say that?"

He smiled, "Yes, he wasn't one to beat around the bush. But at the time, I didn't know what he meant." He turned back to the coffee pot. "Are you hungry?" he asked.

"No," she answered, "I usually don't eat breakfast."

He brought a steaming cup to her, "I remember."

It was intricate. Lying had its inherent problems. Lying to this magnitude had hidden traps that could ruin one's life, but it had to be done. Why exactly did it have to be done? Corey had no idea except that her ego had been bruised, her courage challenged, and her resourcefulness questioned. And she was simply, to wrap it up, ticked off.

"All right, do you have this straight?"

Brae looked up at her dubiously, not unlike the stare of a condemned man who knew he was going down, even though he had yet to commit the crime. "Um, let's see. Sam is dropping you off at my house after school with your stuff. Then we are both going to Sara Morsten's," she shook her long red hair. "God, I don't even like Sara Morsten," she flailed her hands out in front of her for dramatic effect. And it occurred to Corey that this was exactly what concerned her about Brae, the intense drama factor. For an operation of this magnitude, one needed a cool head. "Okay, okay," she continued. "So, since Sara Morsten lives down the street from me, we convince my mother that we'll walk." She frowned, "As if it will take convincing. She'll be delighted to get me out of her hair."

"The plan," Corey murmured, trying to pull the young redhead back on track.

Brae grimaced, "You know, I don't know why you're so keen on doing this. They weren't planning on having us along in the first place."

"That's not the point."

"Really? What is the point exactly?"

Corey frowned, "Either we're Marguillers, or we're not. We can do this, and I want to prove it."

Brae shrugged with a keen lack of enthusiasm. "Fine, it's not like I have anything else going on."

"The plan," Corey repeated. Her intended technique was to beat the plan into Brae's head until it became instinct, like the alphabet.

"All right, we walk from my house to the St. Charles Streetcar."

"And you bring?"

Brae's eyes narrowed a bit. "Exact change," she stated icily.

Corey smiled, realizing she might have strong-armed a bit too much, "Good, then what?"

"We take the streetcar down to Canal Street. Then catch the Canal bus to the cemeteries."

Corey nodded, "Super."

"Then we walk to Quinn's house. Call our parents, lying about where we are, then all of us walk down to the cemetery and spend the night, hoping to be scared out of our wits. That's about it, right?"

Corey's smile faded, realizing how truly bizarre all of this sounded. It was a lot to risk to comfort a bruised ego. "And we do the reverse the next morning."

Brae nodded, "Yes, we do the reverse, provided we don't end up in jail or worse."

"Right," Corey murmured, feeling an attack of cold feet swallowing her up.

"So, do you really think this will work?"

Corey answered with little conviction, "Maybe."

Brae leaned back on the stone bench. "You know, I'm not sure I like Sebastian anymore. He's really a snob."

Corey was sitting on the other side of the bench with legs crossed, Indian fashion. Flattening out her plaid Ecole Issoire uniform skirt over her knees, she commented. "He's not really a snob, just real confused and insecure."

Brae eyed her strangely, "You think so?"

She nodded, "His family is so messed up. Did you see how everything in that house was so palatial, and he had this tiny little room? It was like his dad was trying to punish him or toughen him up so—" and then she drifted off.

"So, he becomes a carbon copy of him," Brae added.

"Maybe, but whatever the case, Sebastian's trying to fight it or trying to fight himself, hard to say. It's a mess."

Brae smiled cryptically, "Wish my parents cared enough to try to mold me into something. They're too busy living life to the fullest. So full, there's no room left for me."

"Sorry," Corey said, wondering what she should say.

Again, she tossed her long red curls as if to chase away more somber thoughts. "So, plan's in place, just one thing Corey."

"What's that?"

"Do you really think you will get this past your dad? He's a bloodhound."

A deep sigh escaped her. This was true. Something she'd tried hard not to consider. "I don't know, but I'm going to try."

She worked diligently to be calm because if she didn't, he would sense something. She'd packed a small backpack with a change of clothes, although she had no idea when exactly she would have the opportunity to change. As she waited in the long hallway of the Esplanade mansion, these random, nervous thoughts raced through her mind until an unexpected hand descended on her left shoulder, causing her to jump back and emit a startled squeal. Her father looked at her with curiosity and concern. She hadn't even heard his approach. She put her hand impulsively on her pounding heart. "You scared me."

He reached out, lightly touching her cheek. "You're sure you're up to going out. You look pale."

She smiled enthusiastically, "I'm fine. I'm looking forward to spending some time with Brae."

He nodded, "All right, call me."

"I will, don't worry," she said as she reached up, kissing him lightly on the cheek. As if on cue, Sam appeared just behind them.

"Okay, kiddo, let's get going. I've got things to do."

She quickly threw her backpack over her shoulder and headed to the door. "Corey," her father called. She spun around abruptly just before she walked outside. "Be careful," he said solemnly. But his eyes told her more than that. That, somehow, he knew. He knew that she was heading somewhere precarious. She felt it in her skin, but he did not attempt to stop her — just turned around and quietly headed back into the house.

· CHAPTER 37 ·

ENERGY DOORS

Her head throbbed, not from a restless night but from one which had passed too easily. She'd slept soundlessly and without dreams, something she was unaccustomed to. It was difficult to pinpoint when sleep had become no longer a place of rest but a frustrating domain filled with anxieties, trivialities, and cluttered images.

It hadn't been like this when she was young, of that, she was sure. As complicated as she'd felt, it hadn't flooded into the nighttime. She laughed softly to herself. How much simpler things would be if she only had the problems that had seemed insurmountable from her youth.

She walked somberly through her father's house, running her fingers along the banister of the dark wooden staircase. She closed her eyes, hearing clearly the sounds of girlish whispers,

"Can you believe this worked?"

"Look, we're only halfway there. Don't get too cocky."

Laughter, unconscious laughter from a girl who didn't allow shadows to touch her, "Come on. This is supposed to be the fun part. What's the matter with you?"

"He sounded funny on the phone, my dad. I don't know. I think he suspects."

"Did he say anything?"

"No, I just felt it, and he was so serious."

"Don't worry, it's all fine."

Corey let her head sink onto the banister, and she thought about Iain — Iain this morning, so relaxed, unruffled, cordial. And she felt as though she were walking around like a woman in a daze, arising from a drug-filled, heavy slumber. She'd slept on his couch better than she remembered sleeping for years in this house.

At times, she had to shake herself and remember clearly why they were doing this. Why? A dream of her father, one of the few coherent dreams she could remember having for some time. Oh yes, but the other ones were not so coherent: swirling heavy images, cold marble, living wings fluttering, brushing, echoes of cold voices in the long chambers.

She opened her eyes and swore she saw a young girl standing at the top of the stairs, watching her with long dark hair and dark eyes, then in a wisp fluttering away. So much she'd forgotten.

"Did anybody bring any food?"

"I have two bags of chips," Quinn said. He was sitting in the shadow of a huge white mausoleum that resembled a small chapel.

"I brought some Cheetos," Brae added.

"I have a box of granola bars," Corey reported.

"Oh yeah, more healthy snacks from the girl with no pizza pans." Iain jibed.

"Fine, you can make your dinner of potato chips and Cheetos while I eat something that might actually help me think," Corey retorted.

"Look, I brought some beef jerky." Everyone turned to look at Sebastian as though he were out of his mind. "It's protein. And did everyone bring a drink?"

Everyone held up a small bottle of soda except Corey, who held up a bottle of lemonade. She'd tried, but there wasn't a soda in her house.

Iain smirked, "Granola bars and lemonade, a meal to be envied."

"Shut up," she rasped, feeling more than a little agitated by the whole experience thus far. The telephone call from her dad had unnerved her. She'd put on her most jubilant voice. "Hey, Dad, wanted you to know I'm here. Everything's good."

"Glad to hear it," then silence.

"Well, things are going to get busy, so I'll probably talk to you tomorrow." She waited, hoping desperately he wouldn't demand another phone call later. But again, silence, then creepy silence, "Are you there, Dad?"

"I'm here." No elaboration.

"Um, okay then. Guess I'll go."

Then, finally, "Corey."

"Yes, Dad."

"Just be careful." And then he'd hung up. She couldn't believe it. It was sort of like he'd hung up on her. When she put down the receiver, her heart was slamming in her chest. She had no idea what to do, whether to push forward or abandon everything. And then Brae had come in, ushering her along, and the decision was made.

"All right, so here's the plan. It's ten minutes until five-thirty, when the cemetery officially closes. I have no idea what the procedure is around here. If workers or night security guards patrol to make sure everyone is out, this will be the tricky part. I suggest we all find separate places to hide until, say, six. Then we meet again at the Montleone tomb."

"The what?" Brae asked.

He gestured behind him. "The tall one with the monolith. It's hard to miss. Just make sure it's safe before you head in that direction." He held up his wrist dramatically, pointing to his watch. "It's exactly five twenty-two. Are we synchronized?"

Brae leaned over from her sitting position to whisper in Corey's ear, "He thinks he's James Bond."

Corey smiled, adjusting her watch. And then she asked as she stood up, "Do we all have to split up?"

Sebastian nodded, "It's safer that way. Come on. The original Marguillers would have handled things this way."

Brae looked a little cross, pulling on her light pink backpack, "How would you know?"

"Come on. Let's get going," Quinn interrupted. "It's almost time." And then, modern-day Marguillers began to disperse amongst the long aisles of tombs.

He had to go home again to get the journal. He'd thought of bringing it with them when he went to take Corey home, even thought about wrapping it up and putting it in the back seat. But he was sure she would have known. She would have felt it as surely as if it were in her own hands. The fact that Corey had deep sensitivities was not news to him. That she was somehow on a deep, fundamental, and yet imperceptible level tied to the journal was something that he had always suspected.

So, he told her nothing of his plans, just took her home, and then retrieved the journal. It crossed his mind that he was breaking his own rules. No secrets between us, he'd insisted, as well as no doing this alone. But the reality was that there were forces at play here, forces that he didn't understand, as well as things she was keeping from him despite her promises. All that, in conjunction with a growing frustration within him, spurred him to break his own rules and, quite hopefully, level the playing field.

He parked his car off a familiar road at the front of the cemetery. He breathed in deeply, the cool fall air around him, and, with book in hand, slowly began to walk back toward the Montleone monument.

She and Brae walked away from the group for a few moments but, feeling disapproving eyes on their backs, soon split up, going their separate ways. She wandered a good distance away from the original meeting place but every now and then glanced back over her shoulder to make sure she could still see the monolith. If she could spot it, she felt rather secure in drifting a bit.

And it was helping, calming her, as she walked more deeply into the cemetery. A cold breeze blew through her clothes, brushing her face, but she pulled the short wool coat she wore more tightly about her. For a moment, as she walked, she forgot her purpose there — her purpose in finding a hiding spot. She began to feel the pull of strong energies, calming energies. Her feet moved in one direction, then turned unconsciously as though they were following their own course. Her mind began to cloud over with images of glowing light and faces carved in white stone. She breathed in deeply as her feet planted themselves and, of their own volition, refused to move further. Slowly, she turned to the tomb she'd stopped in front of.

"Some markers are obvious. Others are deliberately hidden deeply in the cemetery."

It was Sebastian's voice that he heard in his mind. Iain stopped for a moment outside of his car. The book, he held securely in his hands. It was odd. He realized then that he'd never handled the journal before. It had always been Sebastian or Quinn or Corey at times.

"*I thought you said you and Quinn had made a map of all the important markers,*" Corey had stated.

They were at the cemetery on a day not unlike this one. All were standing near the Montleone monolith, a tall, imposing structure towering over the cemetery. The monolith itself was capped with a cross and flanked with four female statues holding in their hands a wreath, a cross, a cornucopia, and an anchor. It had always seemed a focal point but surely only a beginning. He remembered Sebastian back then, how he had thrived on being the captain of the ship. Sebastian had almost imperceptibly bristled at the inquiry. There was more polish, a subtle confidence that had been absent in his youth. "*Most of them, but the journal indicated that some, well other than the plotted ones, are hidden.*"

"Why?" Brae had asked. Her eyes were covered by a pair of sunglasses, but she still had her hand up to block the glare.

Quinn stepped up, answering before Sebastian could. Iain could see them now so clearly in his mind. Not as yesterday but now in heightened memory. He hadn't noticed it then. He was watching more closely now, from a different perspective. There was something between the two men, an alliance and comradeship of an unusual kind that evidently had been forged when he wasn't aware. "*From what I could decipher, Annie Besant calls them energy, well as I can translate, doors.*"

"*Energy doors?*" the Iain of then had asked. "*What exactly does that mean?*"

"*Clear as I can understand, they lead to a place of ritualized testing.*"

Brae had declared, "*I don't like the sound of that. Seems like some African tribal rite.*"

Sebastian laughed, "*Sounds bad, but from what Quinn and I have figured out, it's not a physical type of thing. Annie discusses over and over in this and other writings the spirit's evolvement as well as mentioning keys of power and keys of knowledge.*"

He remembered now how that struck him as odd. How easily Sebastian would use this woman's first name, casually and without respect. If there was one thing Andre had taught him, it was always to show the proper respect for everything and everyone that was clearly more evolved than yourself.

"*What about the hidden ones?*" Corey had asked. She had asked, and he hadn't noted it then. He'd chalked it up to general curiosity without any particular motive. But not now, now he thought differently.

Quinn had been the one to answer this time: "*It seems some of these doors she deliberately omitted in case the truly deserving had need of them.*"

She stopped and turned to the tomb, staring at it for a time, feeling its pull, the strong pull, even before she ascended the steps. There was a name on it, but her eyes were pulled to the iron bars guarding the center of the mausoleum. It must have been the autumn breeze she heard humming loudly in her ears, a soft, low sound that felt as though it truly reverberated through her chest.

There were things to remember here. Who she was? Where she came from, and why and why again. But it all fell away as she slipped her delicate pale hands through tall, black iron bars and peered closely at the cold marble face staring back at her from the darkness.

A man carved in white, an old man, a father—long beard, a cloak draped around him as clothing and over the top of his head as a hood. And a wreath of flowers wrapping across his forehead. She breathed deeply, pulled, mesmerized, his hand reaching up, one finger in front of his lips — gesturing silence. The sound intensified, and she felt as though it sung with its pitch. Answers, answers, whispers, whispers, silence it cajoled. Time passed, but clearly, she had stepped somewhere outside of it.

CHAPTER 38

THE FIRST THRESHOLD

Iain opened the journal. The words were still indecipherable. He hadn't bothered to obtain a translation. Every marker that Annie Besant had documented in it, he knew by heart, although it was the first time it had been in his sole possession. He almost deliberately walked past the weeping angel. But then he stopped in front of the tomb, not venturing closer, simply seeing it in his mind and the aura surrounding it. It radiated a strange energy, one that had changed over the years, bluish, blue the color of the sea, fluid, reverberating in its opaqueness. It was odd. He felt a weakness pass over him, then sound, voices rounding the bend. Instinctively, he stepped away from the tomb on the far side of a nearby tree, but then the dizziness swirled in his head. And he knew quite clearly that, willing or not, he'd begun to cycle through again.

Laughter filled the air, *"It won't work."*

"Do you care?"

"No, I don't care at all."

Corey's long dark hair was tousled down her shoulders, and Sebastian smiled as though he truly had obtained the world. He recognized the clothes they wore. It was the same day, same day they'd all been about in the cemetery. His mind became muddied. Had he left her? Even for a moment? Had she slipped away from Iain's side to be with Sebastian?

She laughed, face alight, beaming in a way that was alien to her. *"We don't have any time?"*

"*We'll have time later.*" He spoke softly but loud enough for Iain to hear. And then his friend, his old friend was leaning in, holding her, kissing her passionately. And rage, old rage, flooded through — rage that blinded him, rage that flushed through to his fingertips. He wanted to crush him, with the strength in his hands, physically crush the traitor with everything inside him. It was dizzying, intoxicating, poisoning.

But he forcibly closed his eyes, stopping it. It was so strong, tantalizingly torturous. "*It's your right, your righteous anger!*" — the voices spoke to him, tempted him. "*They're deserving of your wrath and more.*" They whispered, trying to tangle around his senses, clouding his mind with the heat and the madness.

It was a battle, so easy to take that route of madness as he had before. But he placed himself against it. Digging in, digging deep, forcibly propelling the mad, rampant emotions away — standing, just standing his ground for a length of time that felt ageless, immeasurable until the whispers died away in defeat, left with no emotion to fuel them.

He forced control to return and then, with the power of his mind, willed the unreal to peel away. His body trembled from the exertion. The falseness had been so reluctant to release him. It had felt such power in his hate. It almost seemed as if it had clawed his body in fury at the end but had finally relinquished. In time, Iain finally released the steely control over his emotions and dropped to his knees. A soft breeze and gentler whispers brushed through his hair, affirming that he'd passed through the first door.

It was ten after six by the time Corey returned to the Montleone monument. In fact, it was only moments before that she had found herself standing on the steps of that curious tomb. Her hands felt cold and ached. She felt sure she had been gripping the iron bars on the door of its small mausoleum. But she didn't remember stepping away. Once she realized the time, she ran quickly back toward the meeting place, unaware of cemetery guards, night security guards, or whoever else might be lurking about — just simply panicked to get back. "Where have you been?" Iain asked immediately as she flew into view. "I lost track of time," she muttered, her heart still beating frantically from the wild sprint she'd just taken.

He'd moved in front of her, and she could see plainly that he wasn't irritated with her but genuinely worried. "You're not supposed to be sightseeing, just finding a place to hold up in."

She turned to the others, "Did anyone see anybody?" trying to remove the focus from herself.

Quinn shook his head, "No, it seems like they don't care much once the place is closed. I mean, what are we going to do, steal one of their massive statues?"

Brae drifted up to her, brushing dirt off her blue jeans from where she'd been seated seconds before. "So, what now? We're here. Anybody have a plan?"

She glanced expectantly from Quinn to Iain to Sebastian, waiting for several moments, then went back and sat down. "That's what I thought."

Sebastian said, "This wasn't supposed to have a specific goal, just spend the night here and see if we can pick up why Annie Besant was so interested in this place. Anyone got any impressions?"

He looked around but was met with heads shaking in all directions. Deliberately, Corey said nothing. She didn't know if she had any impressions. She had no idea what had happened except that she'd gotten spooked. So, why bring it up and probably be laughed at? She sat down next to Brae, pulling her knees up against her and not turning to meet Iain's eyes that she felt certain were on her.

She'd taken pictures of all of them, all of Annie Besant's guardians of knowledge. When exactly she'd done so, she couldn't recall. But it was when she was alone, not with Iain, and certainly not with Sebastian. It was after their first rendezvous at the cemetery and before the last — before they were all identified as important by Quinn's map. She'd left her father's bedside early one morning. The day was a foggy one, so she'd driven slowly but was inexorably drawn back to that place.

Carefully, Corey opened the folder containing the pictures she'd taken.

They were in the bottom of the box she'd retrieved some time ago from her secret closet. She spread them carefully out on her bed, side by side, in the order they were taken, feeling rather than remembering. The first was the angel, the weeping angel.

It chilled her to look at it. She'd always known it. There was a dual nature here, the yin and yang of existence, good and dark potential within everyone's heart. She could feel it clearly again as though she stood in its antechamber, the coldness wrapping around her and the stained-glass window reflecting an eerie blue light across the floor.

"*This is the beginning,*" Quinn had said.

"*Are you sure,*" she asked, feeling keenly that something was off here.

"*Clear as we can tell,*" Sebastian replied. But she remembered the warmth of Iain's hand upon her back.

"*What do we do now?*" the sound of Brae's voice behind them.

"*We wait,*" Sebastian said calmly.

And that was what they did that first time, waited. And absolutely nothing happened.

Iain returned to his house, feeling somewhat drained and confused by what had happened at the cemetery. It was clear to him that he was making slow and poor progress toward reclaiming the Triquetra. Somewhere along the way, it felt clearly as though he had lost sight of the goal. He and Corey were taking a long, twisted path toward their aim. As he pulled into the driveway on the side of his Chestnut Street address, he noted a small blue Honda parked just in the street. Its door opened, and Quinn stepped out of the car.

It was certainly not a welcome intrusion at this moment. He was exhausted and not at all up to concealing the fact. "How did you know where I lived?"

Quinn smiled congenially as he walked up to him, "What a greeting for an old friend. You weren't hard to track. I have a friend in the real estate business. I had a sneaking suspicion you were just renting, not looking for anything permanent just now."

Iain felt another wave of fatigue pass through him. "It's not a great time."

"I can see that. You look worse than I do right now. But I'm sure you'd be willing to offer your old friend a cup of tea."

Iain acquiesced, motioning to the door. He had consciously decided to leave the journal behind in his car. As he put his key in the front door, he asked pointedly, "What exactly is it that brings you by?"

Quinn laughed, "Still direct, frankly curiosity."

CHAPTER 39

THE PYRAMID

The sun had begun to set, and it was becoming clear to Corey that it would be a chilly, uncomfortable night. They all sat curled up, leaning against the base of the chapel-like mausoleum facing the Montleone monument.

"So, why do you think Annie Besant focused so much attention on this tomb?" Quinn asked.

"I have no idea," Sebastian answered. "There isn't much history of it except some guy built it for his dead wife."

"What about the statues?" Corey asked impulsively. "What do they mean?"

Quinn cleared his voice, "Well, each one holds a symbol representing the virtues. You know, faith, hope, and charity."

"There are four," Iain said, with just a tinge of irritation.

Quinn answered quietly, "Yeah, it's not certain, but the consensus is the fourth represents memory."

"Mmmm, that's interesting," Brae stated unconvincingly.

"So, why does this woman from England who spent so much time in India care about a monument in New Orleans?" Sebastian asked. Corey detected a bit of shakiness in his voice. Clearly, he hadn't anticipated how chilly the cemetery would be tonight. It was strange. The day had been tolerable, nearly warm, but now, here, it was getting downright cold.

"Good question," Iain responded flatly. Corey smiled. It was clear the Marguillers' strategy for the evening had been poorly planned.

"So, what are we going to do now?" Brae's question fell dismally on the group, as Corey knew no one had an answer. Some adventures evidently were just doomed not to pan out.

"Well, we could go exploring this place," Quinn interjected with feigned enthusiasm.

"It's cold and dark," Sebastian spat out.

"Flashlights," Iain said stonily.

"Fine," Sebastian stood up, "who's up for this?" Corey and Brae looked at each other and then quickly got to their feet. What was worse than roaming around a dark cemetery was being left alone in a dark cemetery while everyone else was roaming.

Iain sat across from Quinn, who was quietly looking around the den while gingerly sipping his cup of what Iain was sure was scalding hot tea. "Very Spartanish, my friend. I could bring some things from the shop to warm the place up if you like."

"No, that's all right. I find your taste borders a bit too much on the flourishy side."

Quinn frowned. Evidently, he'd wounded his vanity. But he wasn't much in the mood to be tactful, "Getting any work done here? I'd love to see what you're up to."

He shook his head, which was still pounding from the morning's events, "Not much. I've been occupied elsewhere."

Quinn looked at him speculatively, and Iain felt a strong wave of suspicion fire toward him. Ah, now it became clear. He should have realized that this could happen. He and Corey were stirring things up. It should have come as no surprise that Quinn would be feeling this, no doubt, as well as the other former members of the Marguillers. Quinn's soft brown eyes sharpened a bit. "What things?" his voice lightened, but his intent was purposefully direct.

Iain considered carefully in that strained moment if he should involve Quinn or any of the others in their activities. Rather speedily, he mentally weighed the consequences, the benefits versus the obvious deficits. But the most striking drawback stared him quite boldly in the face now: trust. Could he really trust the man before him, whose mind now felt as though it were filled with shadowed places? He had enough issues of trust with Corey. To bring others into this would stretch his control too thinly. But Quinn was no fool. Clearly, he knew something was happening. He had to throw him a bone, something that would shake him enough to throw him off the track.

He leaned back against the couch, calculating carefully. "Well, I have to say with mostly personal matters."

Quinn raised an eyebrow. Clearly, it wasn't exactly what he was looking for, "Personal?" he asked.

Iain nodded, knowing full well that this ambiguousness would not satisfy but also recognizing that something might be gained in the way of information. "Yes," he looked away, clearing his throat, "ordinarily, this isn't something I'd discuss with anyone. But I think you might actually be able to help me."

Quinn looked confused, sipping his tea but keeping his eyes affixed to Iain. They looked almost black now in the dim light, a fact that, at the moment, he found a bit disconcerting. "You think so?" It was more of an echo in response to Iain's words than a question.

"Yes, you see, I've been spending a lot of time with Corey, and I've come to a decision."

Quinn waited for him to elaborate but then, evidently overtaken by nerves, felt compelled to prod him. "What decision?"

He looked at him directly, trying to couch this in some way that didn't sound too juvenile, "I've decided I want her back."

Quinn stared at him blankly, then an explicit look of astonishment crept into his eyes. Perfect, he thought. He had thrown him completely off guard.

The night fell black and wrapped around them securely. Only the dim illumination of five small flashlights guided their way. In the darkness, Corey questioned the evils of knee-jerk reactions and the poor judgment of bruised egos. She wondered distractedly what Mrs. Vaughn was serving for dinner tonight. Surely not an entrée of granola bars and lemonade, nor the dessert of the few scraggly Cheetos that Brae had gifted her.

She pulled her coat about her more tightly and pointed her slim silver flashlight along the broken stone pathway that she traveled upon. She kept it down, having along the way been struck by the creeping fear that some nocturnal creatures, large or small, had eased out of the cracked granite once the sun had set.

Brae whispered in her ear, "You're not looking around at all, Corey."

"I'm trying not to step on anything horrible," she murmured to her friend.

Suddenly, the group, which had been traveling in single file ever since they'd embarked on this exploration mission, came to a halt. "Look at this one," Quinn's voice rang out excitedly. One by one, flashlights followed the direction of his onto a rather striking pyramid-shaped tomb. The night was cloudy, so not even the moonlight lit its slanted luminescent sides. "Amazing," Quinn exclaimed.

Corey did feel something, even in the darkness. Her flashlight swept across its guardian figures, a woman on one side and a sphinx on the other. A breeze whipped around her, and a rush of awareness traveled through her chest. And for a split second, it was daylight, and her fingers outstretched and touching the third eye on the woman's forehead, sending a bolt of energy right into her.

"What does it mean?" she heard Sebastian's voice, deeper, older, but then the youth again dragging her back to the darkness.

"Rosicrucian, probably," Quinn replied. "They love that Egyptian stuff."

And then behind her, Iain's voice, "All right, Corey?" And she felt a strange chill as though he'd spoken the same words many, many times.

Quinn continued to look at him with confusion. Good, whatever agenda he'd come here with, Iain had managed to reroute his focus, "You want her back?" he asked a bit incredulously.

"Yes," Iain replied flatly. "Look, we're not kids anymore. A lot has happened in all our lives. But I think I've gained enough clearness of vision through the years to see what has worked in my life and what hasn't."

The slight man sitting in his den across from him seemed completely befuddled, as though that was the last thing in the world he'd expected to hear today. "And you think Corey was one of those things that worked?"

He responded carefully, "For a time, I recognize now and admire what a remarkable woman she is."

Quinn was still staring at him with disbelief and bewilderment. He was pleased. It was exactly the reaction he was looking for. "Umm, well, what does Corey have to say about this?"

He calmly took a lingering sip of his tea, giving him time to strategize an answer. "I haven't told her yet. I'm trying to move cautiously. What do you think?"

"What, what do I think?" he nearly stuttered, causing Iain to suppress a smile. "I have to say I'm a bit astonished that you'd even consider such a thing. I do remember, although maybe you've forgotten, how enraged you were when, well, when—"

"When she eloped with Sebastian?" He finished his thought with no emotion.

His friend looked uncomfortable, seriously uncomfortable. Clearly, directness wasn't an attribute that Quinn had cultivated in the last ten years. "Yes, I'm amazed that you could get past that. I mean, it was a lot, and then Brae. You know, you might just want to leave it all alone, so much baggage."

He swallowed on a dry throat, a mixture of curiosity at Quinn's complete rejection of the idea and irritation at the same. Carefully, he replied, "Corey tells me that her marriage to Sebastian was a mistake. It seems as though she's had a difficult time."

"But the betrayal—" Quinn drifted off, unable or unwilling to comment on any specifics.

"Well, time has passed. What if I was able to forgive that?"

The frail man sighed deeply, "I don't know. Corey is, well, different than she used to be."

"Aren't we all?"

Quinn looked away, still seeming intensely bothered that the idea had been broached at all. It interested Iain why Quinn would take such a negative stance, as though he had a personal stake in this. "I suppose," he murmured.

"So, I do have a question for you that might help the situation."

Quinn's face looked a bit startled, and it was gratifying. He did want to keep him off-balance. That was how the truth seeped out from under deception. "Really?"

"Yes, I wondered about this and have for some time. I'd like to know what you think."

"I'll try to answer," he said a bit hesitantly.

And then he asked with little emotion, "How early do you think they were involved?"

Quinn looked at him a little blankly, "Involved?"

"Yes, Corey and Sebastian, their relationship didn't come out of nowhere. They must have been involved while she and I were together." He watched the slight man intently and felt his indecision, deep troubled indecision. It was clear he was torn about what to say. "Let me be more exact then." The image of them together at the cemetery passed through his mind. "Were they together when we began the path set out by the journal?"

Quinn's eyes looked at him directly, and what he saw was deep fear in them. The mention of that time frightened him acutely for some reason. But purposely, he did not break his gaze. He wanted the truth and, in that moment, demanded it. "No," Quinn said, affirming what Iain already knew.

"Then, when did it begin?" he asked softly.

Quinn's eyes widened, but then something in his mind closed. There was something there, something that he feared more than Iain's powers to surmount it. "That's something I imagine you'll have to ask Corey," he said quietly, then looked away and continued to sip his tea.

CHAPTER 40

ILLUSIONS

She'd left the pictures strewn across her bed upstairs and decided to devote the balance of the afternoon to catching up on unfinished projects. Working with jewelry was meditative for her. This was why she supposed she had cultivated this craft rather than pursued photography. Photography had become a frustration, always seeing something beyond the photographs she'd taken. While that had been invigorating initially, during her marriage to Sebastian, it had become downright torturous — always ghosts, phantoms of old feelings, another life, the life that could have been. Within six months of their union, she'd stopped taking pictures altogether, although she did not cultivate the jewelry-making until the marriage ended.

It was a piece of hematite that she held in her hand, calming. She gripped it tightly. Indeed, this was what she needed, something to soothe her nerves. Images floated in her mind, dancing about the fringes of her consciousness, images that she'd suppressed. Over the years, they'd lost some of their toxicity, their ability to wound, just leaving her now with a dulling sadness.

She thought to push them away out of reflex, as she'd always done, but hesitated, considering that perhaps she should look at them once more before closing them away.

She'd often wondered what it felt like to go down the wrong path, to twist away from what you were meant to become. Her father had told her that even mistakes were to be learned from, but he never told her how to learn to live with them.

"I'm in this to make it work. I've always loved you."

Sebastian always said what she needed to hear, but then she often thought he'd only said it for that reason, not because it was true. Truth began to elude them as they spiraled into that dulling sphere of falseness.

Images floated in — somber, intimate, and yet disconnected.

She thought she'd known what to expect, but nothing had prepared her for the hollowness and vacuousness of being intimate with him. And she realized that what they shared did not even qualify for that term. At first, there was the shock, then the repulsion, and then merciful numbness. In the final two years, they'd stopped altogether the semblance of trying to emulate any kind of relationship. She wasn't sure why they hadn't ended it sooner, except that they'd both lost themselves in this bargain, lost their strength. He, as well, whatever potential he'd had was dulled, edges softened, mind clouded. He couldn't understand how she could affect him so. She'd represented a kind of promise to him, but like any illusion, all that dissipated in the coldness of choice.

She breathed in deeply. She was wrong. The memories still held their poison, still able to cut — the sharp image of lying in her husband's arms while she forced the memory of her true lover away. She had to, or else she wouldn't be able to breathe.

And somewhere in their fifth year, one morning after a dream that couldn't be remembered, she'd packed her things and returned to her father's house. There was no resistance from Sebastian. She imagined he was relieved. It was ironic how two people could truly be the undoing of each other if put together. Upon recollection, she'd often thought this was one of life's elusive mysteries that her father had often spoken of — one that, rather than being taught, had to be lived. Sebastian filed for divorce rather quickly. In a relatively convenient space of time, it was all over, just a memory — a memory that had shredded the edges of her soul.

The sound of the doorbell dragged her away from the past, and the piece of hematite slowly tumbled out of her grasp onto the table.

She still felt disoriented as she opened the door. Iain stood there as she'd expected. She'd felt his presence before answering. It was becoming that way with them now. His eyes passed over her speculatively, and she looked away, trying to clear her mind before meeting his gaze again. "We need to talk," he said a bit sharply.

She nodded without saying anything but stepped back to allow him to enter.

She supposed it was close to midnight when they gave up their exploration. They passed by many tombs, some of particular interest, but none which had forged as strong a reaction in her as the pyramid. By the time they returned to the monolith, which she now considered the heart of the Metairie cemetery, Corey's feet ached from the tense and prolonged jaunt through the darkness, and her stomach churned riotously with hunger. Regardless of how anyone else might evaluate it, she personally categorized this expedition of the Marguillers as a complete bust.

She settled in against the wall of the mausoleum a few yards away from Brae this time, feeling for the moment a need of solitude.

And it was during that realization that Iain came and sat himself down directly next to her. "Are you all right?" he asked directly.

"My feet hurt, and I'm hungry. How about you?"

"You've been acting strange. I just wanted to see if you're okay."

"Strange? How exactly is one supposed to act in pitch darkness in the middle of a deserted cemetery?"

She thought he turned to look at her directly but couldn't quite tell, given the lack of light. "You know, you are very sarcastic," he noted.

"Really, you think so?" she stated, rummaging again in her red backpack, hoping for another wayward granola bar. "I don't know about you, but I think this whole thing has been a waste."

She thought she heard him laugh but couldn't be sure. "Yeah, kind of uneventful. So, I take it you haven't picked up any vibes."

"Nope, just darkness and hunger."

There was silence for a moment, and then he said rather coolly, "I wonder if you're ever going to stop lying to me, Corey."

CHAPTER 41

THE DEAD DON'T SLEEP

"Were you busy?" he asked.

She shook her head as she led him into the den. "I was trying to catch up on some work. I have a hematite pendant to design, but I'm not making much headway. Can I get you anything?" she murmured distractedly. She hadn't shaken the images she had been entertaining just before Iain arrived. It had been a mistake to travel there, but lately, she had found herself more and more compelled to toy with dangerous impulses.

"No, actually, I just had tea with an old friend of yours." For a moment, her heart clutched a bit, but then the image of Sebastian swirled away. Iain wouldn't be so calm now if it had been him.

She stopped at the far end of the room, turning to face him. He looked tired, not as well-rested as he had seemed this morning. "Who was it?" she asked with little energy.

He stood behind the sofa, hand on the back of it, watching her closely. "It was Quinn," he stated.

"Quinn, really?" she asked with the slightest hint of surprise.

"Yes, he just showed up on my doorstep. I think what we're doing is stirring things up. I wouldn't be surprised if the others were feeling things as well, Brae," and then he hesitated, "Sebastian."

She sunk down in the dark blue, wing-backed chair next to the fireplace. "You think so," she said weakly.

"I do. I know Quinn came looking for answers, wanting to know what we're up to."

She sighed a bit too deeply for his comfort. "I didn't say anything to him about the Triquetra."

He nodded, "I know. What about Brae? Did you tell her anything?"

"Not much. She was not particularly receptive to my call. I did say I needed her help, but she shut me down rather abruptly."

He smiled a bit, "Sounds like Brae."

"What did you say to Quinn?" It prickled a bit even now, hearing Brae's name on his lips. She'd always thought his involvement with Brae was just a knee-jerk ploy to get back at her. And she supposed it had succeeded to a degree, although she would never let him know that.

"I needed to throw him off guard. I don't want his involvement now or any of the others. I don't know if they can be trusted."

She smiled, "And you're sure I can be."

"Well, I've invested my trust in you. I'll put it that way."

She looked away, suddenly slightly uncomfortable with his direct gaze, "That's very opaque. So, how exactly did you throw him off?"

He paused for a moment, then spoke rather flatly, just like the Iain of old. "I told him I'd decided I wanted you back."

She waited for a moment, trying to absorb what she'd heard, then slowly turned her eyes back to him, "You told him what?" she said with disbelief.

He smiled with a hint of satisfaction, "Yes, that was about his reaction as well."

"Of all the things you could have said, why that Iain?"

"Because it was the most shocking and unexpected thing I could think of," he responded with deliberation. "He left quite distracted and confused."

"I bet," she said aloud but nearly to herself.

"But also had no further questions of what we were up to. Unfortunately, this fabrication might require some acting on your part if you run into him or the others."

She stared at him incredulously. The man who vowed not to help her until hell froze over wanted to play-act like lovebirds now. "Why?"

"It's important they stay out of our way. I think the tumultuous looming presence of a reconciliation on our part might do the trick."

"I can't imagine he believed you. He remembered how—" she stopped in awkwardness. "Well, how unlikely that would be."

Her words were tame, but her eyes evoked images of fierce and hateful emotions. She did remember his rage. He felt it on her skin, remembered it, and had been branded by it. "Well, however unlikely, he did buy it and oddly seemed afraid of it. Do you have any idea why?"

She continued to look at him while memories flooded through her mind unguarded. "No," she said. But quite clearly, she knew he saw through her.

She stood up, feeling a weariness permeating every inch of her. "I need some air," she said impulsively. "Are you up for a walk through the quarter?"

"Yes," he answered, but his eyes still rested on her speculatively. "I think I'd like that."

She'd made a pillow of her backpack and tried to close her eyes, but sleep only came in distant patches, disturbing swirling images of white marble wings cascading down over her head. When she awoke, she noticed Quinn and Sebastian standing by the monument's base, quietly talking while Iain was nowhere in sight. Beside her, Brae still lay crumpled over in sleep on the ground. She stood up with some difficulty. Her contorted position during the night had caused peculiar aches. Aggressively dusting herself off, she checked the time: nearly six hours before the gates opened at eight.

Looking around beyond Quinn and Sebastian, she noted that Iain stood at the end of a long road of mausoleum-like tombs. Without disturbing Brae, she began to move in his direction. He stood in front of a large tomb, where several steps led to a heavy set of iron doors that were now opened. "That's unusual," she whispered as she reached his side. "Most of these are closed."

"Yeah, I know," he said, not even looking at her. "This one kept making noise last night." She looked at him oddly, then remembered the Fabacher house. He'd heard the piano playing there.

"What did you hear?" she asked.

"Wings, like birds' wings, fluttering loudly."

Her throat went dry as she remembered the broken dreams of the night before. "Is this in Annie Besant's journal?"

"I don't know. I never really got a look at it. Do you remember?"

247

She shook her head. "No, I don't remember, but I'm sure it was." Even from where she was, she could see blue light cascading across the floor. Had she seen it in dreams or dreams that were yet to be?

He looked at her with curiosity. "What else was in there?" he asked.

"The Montleone tomb."

He nodded, "Yeah, I was sure of that one."

"And the—"

"Pyramid," he finished for her.

"Did that make noise too?"

He shook his head, "No, just obvious. Anything else?"

She breathed in deeply, trying to clear her mind. But what rushed in was a collage of images, one overlapping another, too fragmented to identify. "I thought there was another, but I can't remember it now."

"Maybe it will come back," he said.

She looked again forward into the tomb and saw the long white angel bent down, prostrate in grief. "Are you going in?" she asked.

"Not yet," he answered. And they never did on that particular trip.

It was one of the great marvels of living on Esplanade Avenue. Just a few blocks walk, turn a corner, and you are on the edge of New Orleans' historic French Quarter. Corey walked silently beside him. He wondered if she was even aware of his presence, not merely lost in thought but somewhere else entirely. She'd pulled her long black hair back artlessly in a soft ponytail at the base of her neck, reminding him so much of the girl he'd known long ago. Very unconscious of, and he might even say resentful of externals, she'd never cared much about how she looked but was always in tune with how she felt. Today, she wore a light emerald green top over blue jeans. Certainly not dressed up and simply concerned with comfort, he still couldn't help being struck from an artistic viewpoint of how devastating she was. Even now, he was impacted by the powerful aura she emanated. Perhaps colored by the lenses of his own experience, or perhaps it had simply always been her essence — the imperfections, her idiosyncrasies, her ethereal kind of beauty pooled into one haunting image.

She turned to him unexpectedly as though she'd felt the acute pressure of his thoughts. "Anywhere in particular you wanted to go?" she asked.

"Let's walk by the cathedral. I haven't been there in some time," he answered.

She smiled elusively, just momentarily, then turned away. It was late into the afternoon. The more they made their way toward the heart of the Quarter, the more people began to appear.

As they continued to walk, he felt the presence of Andre cross his mind and the soft sound of a door unlocking somewhere. It bothered him, all the loose ends, the secrets, and the work yet to be done. But he understood now, and the realization of that truth felt more chilling than the road that lay ahead. That nothing, absolutely nothing, he had told Quinn was a lie.

A door shuts, a window opens, and a great swirl continuously fluttered through her mind. She visited there a lot in the beginning. Her father was buried in a family plot in the Greenwood cemetery that he'd purchased when her mother died. Corey hadn't expected him to die. Not after she'd decided to marry Sebastian. Then, more than ever, she needed his strength, but in one instant, it was simply gone. And it felt as though her life were plunged into the madness and paralysis of grief. So, she would spend time sitting next to their tomb, her mother and father's, knowing full well that neither of them was present. But feeling comfort in the solitude.

And it was there that he'd found her, one morning in late April.

People were milling around in Jackson Square, some artists lined up along the tall black iron fence showing off their wares, although not as many as would be on the weekend. The air was cool, and Corey breathed in deeply, trying to let go of what continued to cling to her.

"What's bothering you so much?" he asked. And she looked at him with curiosity, wondering what would happen now if she began to tell the truth.

"I knew I'd find you here," he'd said.

She'd been a bit stunned to see Iain's truck pulling up on the road, stunned and then rather quickly the fear set in. She couldn't take it now, couldn't take his anger, while her whole world stood in ruins. She was just silent, unable to come up with anything to say.

He stood across from her on the other side of the Knight's tomb. It was one that lay flat on the ground like a large cement slab with two headstones perched on either side.

"I never got a chance to tell you how sorry I was about your father." She nodded, feeling her throat constrict with tears. "And I wanted you to know I'm leaving the country, Corey."

She looked up at him, feeling something in her chest akin to a punch.

She stared up at the tall steeple of the cathedral, feeling a power emanating from the structure. "I don't know, just old things being stirred up."

"I had a friend who told me once. The dead don't sleep unless you acknowledge them. Otherwise, they find ways to haunt you."

She turned to him, instinctively laughing a bit, "Sounds like a lovely friend."

His eyes softened, "He was."

She nodded, "I see." Not knowing what to say.

He looked away for a moment, considering, weighing. And then his dark green eyes were on her again, "I want you to come with me, Corey."

It wasn't what she'd expected to hear. It was what she dreamed of hearing in those moments when she allowed truth to sneak in under her guard. She looked down, "What about Brae?" her eyes had begun to swim with tears.

"That's over," he said. "It shouldn't have started. It wasn't fair to her."

She forced her gaze away, her mind reminding her of the course she'd set for herself, the course which now couldn't be altered. Her throat was constricted, but she steeled herself. "I hope you find something to make you happy, Iain. But I can't, I'm sorry."

And then she'd turned away from him on legs that were weak and knees that were shaking. She didn't look back but knew he hadn't moved from the spot. She felt his eyes on her back and his presence behind her. Something she wouldn't feel again for ten long years.

Iain could sense emotions passing through Corey — pain, regret, intense sadness. It concerned him that she continued to be trapped in such places. Instinctively, he wrapped his hand in hers and pulled her abruptly toward one of the benches in front of the cathedral. She looked surprised at the unexpectedness of this gesture. But he didn't release her, just continued to hold her hand, fingers interlaced with his. He pulled both of her hands atop his knee as though he were examining them with curiosity. "All right, tell me what has you so sad?" She looked at him with a mixture of surprise and irritation, trying to retrieve her hand, but he would have none of it. "No, you're captured until you tell me." He kept his voice light, trying to dispel the gloominess of her mood.

"You're out of your mind," she said under her breath.

"Yes, quite possibly, but I'm tired of all this secrecy."

"I'm just a little depressed," she said hotly.

"Really? Now there's a revelation." He continued to maintain a grasp on her hands, although she tried to wriggle out of it.

"You know, this is ridiculous, Iain," she muttered.

"Completely. Go ahead, spill."

"I don't want to," she snapped out.

"Ah, likes being depressed, does she? Sounds like you."

"You're a bastard."

He smiled, laughing softly, "Never denied it, but I also know everyone has limits." He looked at her intently. "You deserve to be happy, Corey."

She turned away from his gaze, "Let my hands go."

He smiled, "Certainly," he said. And dropping her hand, he quickly turned her face to his and leaned in to kiss her. She put her hand against his chest, trying to push away, but he pulled her closer until she allowed it. Not because he needed to this time but because it was what he wanted because she was undeniably what he'd always wanted.

CHAPTER 42

UNRESOLVED

Corey spent a good deal of the mid-morning at Brae's house, in fact, stayed until after lunch when she finally called home for Sam to pick her up. She'd managed to freshen up enough so that she hopefully didn't look as though she'd spent the night in a graveyard. The trip back to Brae's house on the bus and the streetcar was uneventful, both girls largely silent except for Brae's occasional complaints of "What a waste!"; "How stupid!"; and those of the like.

Corey had little to offer herself, exhausted and plagued with a strange headache. The boys, as well, had emerged from the Marguillers' latest adventure a bit somber. Quinn had noted on the walk back to his house, "Well, we did spend the entire night in a cemetery," and was greeted by a deafening silence.

"I think we can officially put Annie Besant's journal to rest," Sebastian had muttered.

And Iain had shot Corey a curious glance, which told her distinctly that he didn't believe this was true. Although it would be many years later before it was revisited, she often wondered what would have happened to them all if they had let it rest, simply and completely, just let it rest.

Corey pulled away from Iain, her head still reeling from his unexpected kiss. "What are you doing?" she asked a bit too breathlessly.

Her hand was still on his chest, her palm just pressed where his heart was located.

"Isn't it obvious?" And he held the hand in place with his own.

She shook her head, "Why are you playing these games? Is this some sort of revenge on your part?"

He took the hand in his and kissed it softly. "I don't have time for games of that sort, Corey. I don't have the time to waste anymore. Do you?" he asked intently.

She pulled away abruptly, completely — standing up and walking away from him, moving in any direction, any direction, because she couldn't possibly begin to absorb what was happening. What was he saying? It was so far afield from what she'd ever expected of him. She walked until she reached the tall iron fence on the edge of Jackson Square, grabbing its long black bars for support. She felt him beside her, touching her shoulders, bending close, and whispering softly. "Don't run, Corey."

"You can't be serious," she said. She had closed her mind to this possibility too long ago. She'd hurt him too deeply and herself. He could never forgive her. "I remember, Iain, how much you hated me. When you came back, how you reacted, how begrudgingly you decided to help."

"I know," he said quietly. "I was angry, furious, and I didn't expect this. I didn't expect to feel what I'm feeling." His fingertips brushed her cheek, touching her hand lightly as though he were trying to soothe her. "I don't pretend to understand it. Only that what's between us is still here. It's simply still here."

She breathed in deeply and turned around to face him, steeling herself. "You don't understand, Iain. I decided a long time ago. I decided after Sebastian that this part of my life was over — that I would be alone."

He looked at her solemnly for a moment and then smiled, "And I decided a great many things as well, my dearest. But as I've come to understand, something else clearly had other plans for us."

She stared at him, deliberately holding back the emotion that threatened to overwhelm her. She had to think, and she couldn't think, not with him here, not with him touching her. It was too much like the past, too much. She straightened up. "There's so much still to be done."

His eyes hardened a bit. She'd brought him back, back to their reality and all that faced them. "I know, and we should do it as quickly as possible because I think it's in the way."

She looked at him, crossing her arms in front of her. And he felt the shadows that she continued to let come between them. "I can't see past that right now," she murmured, bowing her head.

He wasn't sure what to expect, but this would be difficult. He could feel that there was a lot he had to struggle against. "Just promise me something," he said very softly, lifting her chin with his hand. Eyes dark and filled with fear, met his. "Promise me you won't close the door."

She hesitated for an instant that felt like an eternity, then nodded quietly. And he kissed her again, not asking permission, just taking what he felt was always his.

The night proceeded in a way that she found beyond unexpected and nearly unfathomable. They wandered around the quarter, sometimes sitting and talking, sometimes just walking until late in the evening. Stopping at a small restaurant on Decatur Street, they had dinner on its balcony. She felt it important to hold him at arm's length, to maintain some sort of distance until she could assimilate what was happening. There were too many traps here, traps from the past. She'd always felt, even after she'd left Sebastian, that it was safer if she and Iain were apart. But now, roaming the streets of New Orleans with him, talking of nothing consequential, just being in the moment, she realized that she'd made all these decisions with her mind, failing completely to consult her heart.

But he hadn't pushed, hadn't pushed for any decisions, hadn't pushed for any explanations, but seemed content to be with her and accept whatever she offered. His mood was light, although she felt some tremor of calculation somewhere. He hoped to gain something, but it was a fleeting impression that she couldn't quite get hold of. Or perhaps it was the mood he'd put her in — one that she remembered so well — one that to try to explain to anyone seemed impossible.

It was as if being near him, around him, caused a strange hypnotic haziness to settle on her nerves — a feeling that dulled sharp edges and buffered painful corners. And then, when he touched her, even for an instant — his arm brushing hers, going about her waist, his hand grasping hers as she ascended the rickety, metal spiral staircase inside the restaurant. That feeling, that languorous hypnotic feeling just magnified, spreading throughout her skin, making all the things her mind had prudently decided drift off somewhere else, far away.

As they dined on the small balcony overlooking Decatur Street, dusk was just beginning to drape across the French Quarter. The waiter had already brought them two glasses of red wine. It bordered on dry, nearly leaving a bitter taste in her mouth, an edge that felt in an odd way to epitomize where they were — somewhere poised near the edge of bitterness but numb and dull to it at the moment.

Her eyes passed over the street beneath them, sensing the familiar old energy of the city course through her. She turned back to him, feeling his hand brush hers lightly. "So lost in thought, Corey."

She smiled with a bit of weariness, "Sorry, just feeling contemplative."

"Don't worry. It's fine with me." He said a little matter-of-factly. "Silence with you is more relaxing than conversation with most people."

She smiled with amusement. "Well, I guess that might be a compliment."

He laughed, running his hand through his hair. She remembered that gesture as well. But she remembered it in a younger man, not one who seemed so tested by life.

"So, tell me. Do you ever get tired of living here?"

She sighed a bit, "Not really, I love the city," taking another sip of the semi-bitter wine.

"So, you'd never consider leaving?"

She reflected for a moment, "I don't know. I wouldn't say that. Dad always said never to say anything definitively. It will probably come back to bite you."

"He said that?" he laughed, visualizing the imposing figure of Clayton Knight sharply in his mind.

She looked away, liking the warmth she felt coming from him, perhaps liking it too much. "Well, maybe not in those words."

"I miss old Clayton. Despite our occasional differences, I think he was more of an influence on me than my father."

For some reason, his saying that greatly cheered her. "He liked you and respected you. He always said that."

There seemed to be the slightest trace of a smile on his face. But he covered it, as he'd always covered so many things.

It was after ten when they began the trek back to the house on Esplanade. Conversation had died off, although they had talked during the evening of many things — of France and his travels, the things he'd seen, of the city, its changes, but not of their past together. It was something they circumvented. But now, as they headed back to her home in the semi-darkness, all conversation had evaporated.

Her eyes settled on her father's house in the next block, and she wondered what would happen now at the end of such a strange evening. The evening had changed things for them in some yet unidentifiable way. It had cocooned and drawn them closely together. And as they drew nearer to her childhood home, she remembered things she'd forgotten about Iain. So many attributes and strengths ran through his personality, but as she well remembered at this moment, patience wasn't one of them. When they were together, their relationship had escalated into intimacy very quickly. But of course, as she recalled, it was simply their dynamic, a need rather than simply a desire to be close that had a life of its own.

Her mind felt strange and expansive as they walked slowly onward in silence. It felt clear of things that had been, clear of pressures perceived. What she felt seemed to stretch onward, around them, and above them like a three-dimensional canvas.

They stepped off the street and crossed the final road leading to her house, and her heart picked up its beat. Picked up a beat that she did not recognize because it belonged to a younger heart. It was one filled with possibility, one filled with hope and, yes, passion of the kind and intensity that walks in dreams and the imagination but never on earth, never in reality.

She tried to think about what she was supposed to say, what she should do, but it was all slipping away, tearing away like a thin tissue paper of no substance.

Once they began the slow walk up to the entrance of Clayton Knight's home, she paused abruptly, just in front of the great double doors of the house, and turned to Iain. His expression was masked in the semi-darkness of the night. "What do you want to do tomorrow?" she asked, trying to project into the concreteness of another day.

"We should start early, I imagine," he replied slowly.

"All right. I have some projects to work on, but I can put them off for a little while." Her voice sounded hollow and rambling in her ears. Saying things, saying things that didn't even begin to touch what she was feeling. "How early did you say—"

And then her voice had stopped because he'd put his hands on her arms and then pulled her toward him, holding her against him in an embrace.

Her arms slipped around him, and she held him more tightly, just holding so tightly. And then she pulled back a bit, her voice trembling, following the rest of her. "Iain, we shouldn't rush into anything. There's too much to think about."

He answered, "So much unresolved, I know. But I think I'd like to start resolving it now." And then he'd pulled her close again, kissing her not like before, not with restraint. But in a flood, the way she knew things would be with them, knew when he kissed her in the cemetery, knew even when she saw him in Audubon Park. Even knew, when she took her wedding vows with Sebastian, that some things could not be changed.

CHAPTER 43

THE DIFFICULT PATH

For a short space of time, she forgot, allowing herself to be caught up in the moment, to be swept away to that place where thought was absent. She pulled out the keys to the front door but found her fingers trembling — unable to properly grasp. But not even in the span of a heartbeat, Iain so smoothly pulled the keys from her hands, fluidly accomplishing what she seemed unable to do. The heavy door swung open into a darkened hallway, and she moved inside, still feeling his hands poised possessively on her shoulders, so close she still felt his breath on her neck.

But in that quick instant, the chill of the house swept around her in a sobering way, reminding her of all she'd thought to forget. Much as she'd like to pretend, she wasn't that young woman anymore who first embraced this passion. She had been touched by age, by hard experience, and by sorrow.

Iain closed the door behind him, but she moved forward, separating from his contact — drifting toward the dim light deeper into the house.

She stopped on the threshold of the great den in the mansion. There were so many echoes here, reminding her insistently of how she had stood there, not so many yards away from where she stood now, abruptly delivering the news to this unsuspecting man behind her — the news that she'd eloped with Sebastian. It was so cruel, delivering a sure swift blow with no hint of preparation with a sledgehammer. She'd been a coward, having no idea how else to do it. She could still see his face so clearly etched in her mind, but no one would have known, looking at him, how deftly and completely she'd shattered his trust. There was no hint of anything, nearly none, except a peculiar feverishness in his eyes and an almost imperceptible blanching of his face. And then just a soft whisper, "What did you say?" he asked quietly, no note of disbelief, no note of emotion.

She felt Iain's hands go on her shoulders from behind. "Don't do this," he whispered as if he could tangibly feel her thoughts.

"I can't help it. I'm not that same girl you used to know." There were heavy tears in her voice.

He pulled her against him, wrapping his arms around her torso. "Neither of us is the same, Corey. But that doesn't change what's between us."

She shut her eyes tightly, trying to desperately block out the painful images that seemed to want to ravage her. And then he spun her with a deliberate movement round in his arms. "Iain," she whispered as she momentarily met his gaze.

But he shook his head in negation as he softly pulled her long hair, which had come loose, sweeping it behind her shoulders, then bent his head to softly kiss the exposed skin near her throat. It felt as though her breathing stopped. "Iain," she whispered huskily again. She didn't know exactly if she wanted to stop him or just reach him.

"Sssshhh," was his response, and it was clear that there would be no more discussions now. His hands had moved up to the buttons on her long silk shirt that he was fluidly undoing one at a time.

She tried to gently pull his face, his mouth, away from her skin. "I can't," she whispered, but he resisted now, gently pushing her up against the doorframe and the entrance of the room, then pulling the shirt completely off her shoulders.

His mouth roamed and was hot on her skin, spreading sensations throughout her. "It's all right," he murmured as his mouth finally traveled back up to hers, reconnecting, plundering, and reminding her where all this would soon be leading. Everything was in dizziness.

They moved, or he swept her along, carrying her over to the sofa. She watched in the dim light as he divested himself of his shirt, letting it fall without concern onto the polished wooden floor.

"You're not listening to me," she spoke, and at this, he hesitated for a moment.

"Of course I am," he responded, pausing only long enough to tug her blue jeans off her long legs. "So beautiful, as always, Corey," was the last thing she heard him say before his body moved over hers.

It was a dream. It was a vision, and he knew now this time, he was taking the journey alone. Behind him, there was a turbulent dark sky filled with voices, whispering ramblings from planes of time that were converging.

"Are you sure you aren't making a mistake?"

He heard this whisper most clearly of all. He stood on the pedestal next to the woman, the Lady with the Scepter. He remembered this one clearly. There was deterioration, streaks of discoloration running down the bronze metal sides of her face. But still, she sat stately, elegant, beautiful despite circumstance, serene.

"You always choose the difficult path."

It chilled him. It was clearer now. The murmurings had coalesced into that one voice.

"Happiness could be easy, rather than tortured."

Just behind him now, and he knew it, recognized the inflection.

He felt her hand firmly touch his shoulder. But it did not feel warm. It was cold and inflexible. Slowly, he turned around, completely expecting what he saw but feeling jolted nonetheless. He had to admit even now, she was beautiful.

Brae stood there in the fading, dusky light around them. Not as she would be now, but in her youth, when they were together. She wore a long white dress flowing around her shapely figure. Her red hair tousled in the light breeze that blew across them both.

She smiled the smile of beckoning, welcoming, "Why do you make it so difficult when happiness is just within your reach?"

He breathed in deeply, feeling regret travel around his heart. He'd had no right.

"I loved you. Life with me would be easy. Why didn't you see that?"

"I'm sorry," he said.

"She won't make you happy. She doesn't have it in her."

He looked away, his eyes momentarily resting again on the serene statue — serene and calm and indifferent to her circumstance.

"It wasn't right between us." He said without looking back at her.

"You're a coward," she rasped. And he remembered the anger now, the apathy in him and the anger in her. That was their gift to each other.

"Go and be at peace in your life."

"Why do you choose what's difficult?" The voice behind him was fading.

"Because it's my path," was what he answered.

Iain's eyes opened, and he looked around the darkness of the room. It was Corey's room, Corey's bed. And as the memories flooded him, he looked at the empty spot beside him, realizing that she'd gone.

It wasn't difficult to find her, although there were many places in the large house where she could be. He could feel her presence now acutely. After last night, they'd become linked again, and there were many things he'd felt, deep, tangled impressions that would have to be sorted out. He'd dressed and slowly made his way downstairs through the shadowed rooms of Clayton Knight's mansion. The grandfather clock in the hallway told him it was just after two in the morning.

It had been a strange road to where he was now, in Corey's house, her lover again. As he made his way through the dusky, long hallway, Iain again felt the tugging trepidations reach up, wrapping themselves around his heart, his mind. The last time had nearly ruined his life. The man who had fled overseas had been hollow, damaged by a turn of events he hadn't seen coming or had ever in his wildest dreams anticipated. In France, he had learned discipline of the mind and spirit, yet that old cut, that old wound, had always remained, quiet at times, but flaring up in the most unexpected ways.

A face floated through his consciousness: a young blonde woman, French, a teacher at the University where he worked, Anna. She was the one involvement there had been for him. A brilliant smile and devotion — all the things that should make him happy.

"But why, why do you make things difficult for yourself? When life can be simple?"

He remembered her words now, strangely echoing Brae's. And he had no answer then, when he walked away, but somewhere during the last few days, perhaps weeks that he'd spent with Corey, it became clear to him why. Because it was her, always her, and complicated and difficult as that was, there was no help from it or peace for that matter. Something about her bound him to her. It was something he'd never really understood, but that didn't seem to matter either. Running away from it was no solution. He'd seen that. So, there was nothing else to do but fight through it now, fight through to whatever lie on the other side.

He followed the staircase down and then headed to the back of the house, where the sunroom was located. Corey was there as he knew she would be, sitting in the rocking chair, dressed in a white nightgown and a long, burgundy-colored robe, having fallen asleep. For a moment, he sat on the wicker sofa beside her chair, just watching her, remembering her sitting there as a teenager, dark eyes lively, wide, and beautiful. He smiled. Even as a young man, he'd recognized that he had always been drawn to her from the very first day, and now he was certain to his very last.

He stood up, reaching over to her, lightly brushing her cheek with his hand. Her eyes fluttered, then opened, taking a moment to focus on him. "Are you all right?" he asked softly.

She straightened up in the chair, still looking a little disoriented. "I couldn't sleep," she said.

"You could have woken me."

"I'm sorry. I just needed—"

Lightly, he put his fingertips over her lips. "It's all right," he said, squatting down next to the chair. "Let's just give it time."

Eyes so wide, "Iain, I'm so worried."

"I know," he smiled, feeling the panic inside her. He reached out, touching her face. "You'll see," he said. "It will be all right."

And then he stood up, pulling her up with him and kissing her again, not allowing thoughts and fear to interfere. He laid Corey down on the sofa in the sunroom, kissing her again and remembering all the times he'd thought to make love to her here in this room. And that tonight, it would be a reality.

CHAPTER 44

ENDURANCE

"What does it say exactly?"

"It's hard to interpret. It's almost as if prayers accompany the sketches, maybe Hindu prayers. I'm not sure."

Her eyes flickered open for a moment. The room surrounding her was white, white, and sterile, with no colors except sedate greens. Her head throbbed, and she closed her eyes again.

A cool breeze swelled around her, the soft chill of late winter in the cemetery.

Again, her eyes flickered open, and she was in the narrow bed, tubes in her arm, but silence around her. She was alone, alone in the hospital room, and she breathed in deep, wondering what she should feel — relief or devastation. But instead, there was numbness.

"What does this one say?"

"I don't know. It's sort of cryptic."

It was odd what comes to you in such moments. She remembered the statue of the woman kneeling on the grave, flowers in her arms, and shoulders bent in weariness.

"The traveler cheerfully bears all and resents nothing. The rocky pathway that ascends the mountain straight is not as easy on the feet as the well-traveled winding road."

Brae smiled widely, turning away from the granite figure, "What does it mean?"

"*Endurance*," Quinn had whispered — one stop on Annie Besant's scavenger hunt. And this one, they had left largely untouched, not really understood. Well, perhaps understood but not lived.

Her eyes flickered open again. The room seemed so narrow to her, so claustrophobic. Not like the one her father had died in months before. That one had felt filled. She'd felt so many coming to retrieve him from the other side. And sadly, at that moment, she'd felt envious, considering that she too would like to be retrieved.

She felt strange that she felt no pain, of course being certain it was the medicine they'd given her, masking everything. She turned on her side, still feeling profound guilt that losing a child at five months had not cost her more. But then again, upon reflection, it had cost her everything.

Sebastian had been at her side initially, but then, of course, his words to her after it was over were that maybe it was for the best.

And she realized then that he knew. When Iain left, she didn't know she was carrying his child any more than she had known when she married Sebastian. She realized then, when he found out she was pregnant, that he'd actually hoped for a normal, happy life for them. How he could imagine something pure being born out of something deviant was beyond her. But as her father always said, "People can truly convince themselves of anything. That's just how powerful the mind is."

She breathed in deep the peculiar medicinal odor of hospitals and understood that she was now walking through this particular test — *Endurance*.

For a moment after she'd learned of the baby, she'd fanaticized about finding Iain and telling him, but of course, that, too, was an illusion because the bargain had already been struck.

When she opened her eyes again, it was in her room's darkness, and Iain lay beside her asleep. She looked at him, remembering the intense closeness they'd shared that night and how hope now opened up in her life once more. But then the dream had brought back the reality of what lay between them. How much forgiveness could one person expect from another?

Again, when he'd awoken, she was gone, but it was morning, and he heard her in the shower. He dressed and went downstairs, putting on a pot of coffee in the huge kitchen of the mansion. The house with only the two of them felt so desolate to him. He wondered how she had managed to live here alone for so long. But then again, he knew there was an element of Corey's personality that was content to be hard on herself rather than make changes. Once the coffee was done, he moved into the small breakfast room where he'd left the journal and began strategizing for the rest of the day. He didn't think about their future or what tomorrow might bring, only of today and how they would move forward.

When she walked into the room, she was already dressed, but her long black hair still slightly damp. Her eyes immediately focused on the old book that lay across the table. "What are you doing?" she asked, her voice laced with a strange concern. He noted the dark circles under her eyes.

He smiled, "Making plans. Do you want some coffee?" Her eyes met his with notable trepidation. Clearly, she was disturbed. "What's the matter?" he asked.

She sat across from him, taking the old, tattered edges of the book in her hands and softly closing it. "Let's not do this, Iain." And then she rested her long, slender hand on the cover. "Let's just leave all of this behind."

He leaned back in the chair, feeling an odd throbbing in his head. "What about your father?"

She hesitated momentarily, then said with a measure of resolve, "I can't help that. I just want to leave all this behind us and not look back."

He nodded, feeling that old familiar sadness welling up in him. "I know you do, Corey. But the problem is it won't stay behind." And very deliberately, he put his hand over hers. "So, why don't you just start telling me everything you've been keeping from me?"

The dark eyes widened in fear and then weariness, a weariness he wanted to wipe away from her completely. She looked down, "I'm so tired."

"I know, but don't you think it's time?"

She looked up again, this time her eyes filling with tears. "There's so much, and I'm afraid that—"

"That I won't be able to handle it?"

She shook her head slowly, reminding him a bit of a lost child, "That you'll hate me."

He frowned, "Well, I wanted to for a long time. But that just doesn't seem possible."

She pulled her hand back, now a strange look in her eyes. "I know now I can't go on like this." And then she stood up, "So, let's go back to the cemetery, and this time maybe you'll see everything."

A coldness swept around him, and the image of a locked door fled through his mind. But he stood up beside her, taking her hand. "Yes, it seems it's time."

CHAPTER 45

THE JOURNEY

All was stillness, and yet she felt a great roar rising in her ears, like the stormy waves against the eroding shoreline. It was insane, suicide to even be contemplating this, but there was a pressure building up inside her, inside her head, that threatened to overtake everything. Iain had pulled to the side of the road. She felt his eyes on her, on her skin, as tangibly as she'd felt his hands touching her the night before. Then she'd allowed the roar to be drowned out in the moment, allowing herself to forget why this would never happen. But now, in the serenity of this city of the dead, self-deception didn't seem possible anymore. Its toll was too high.

"Where are we going?" he asked quietly. She didn't answer him, didn't look at him, just stepped out of the car.

The beginning felt like only visions, personal visions meant for some sort of self-illumination, or at least that was what Corey initially believed. Life was kind in that respect, not allowing you to see far enough ahead to comprehend the approaching peril. Otherwise, you would never take another step forward.

It was only the second day of the Marguillers' pursuit of Annie Besant's path. Upon reflection, she'd wondered why they tried at all. But then again, she could chalk it up to Sebastian's unyielding determination and Quinn's uncanny resourcefulness.

It had been a week since they were last at the cemetery, but schedules being what they were, this was the first day they were all available to resume their trek.

It was quiet, and the air was cool but dry, unusual in all respects for the area. Quinn, of his own accord, had decided to try something different at the first tomb, the one they'd coined as *The Weeping Angel*. Without a word to anyone, he put a symbol he'd found in Annie Besant's writing at the base of the statue, so light that it would be imperceptible to anyone not looking for it. It hadn't actively crossed Corey's mind then that his action was reckless, that he and they had no idea what sort of effect this might have. Then again, in retrospect, they were all diving in blindly.

"The first door concerns *the discrimination between the real and unreal.*" Quinn held up the journal as they all stood on the tomb's threshold. There were loose papers stuffed in the pages that Corey was certain were his translations from Annie Besant's original text.

"What exactly does that tell us?" Iain had voiced it, but his words had fallen on deaf ears because things were already in motion.

Brae had silently drifted away from the group. This had been almost unnoticeable, but then she'd abruptly taken several quick steps inside the mausoleum. Instinctively, Corey had tried to move forward to join her, but it felt oddly as though her feet were cemented to the granite upon which they stood. The remaining three around her were also motionless. She had no idea how long they all stood there, strangely rooted to the spot as the breeze seemed to swirl frantically around them and then an odd high-pitched whistle in her ears. It was dizzying and, at the same time, disorienting, not unlike the sensation when you're in a stationary car but are convinced you're moving because the car next to you is.

And in what seemed to be the next moment, Brae stepped out of the tomb and quickly walked away from them. Sebastian followed her — his head bent, whispering and then suddenly holding her in his arms. She was surprised to see him so comforting. Her eyes flew to Iain's in question, but he was staring back at *The Weeping Angel*. The whole event was disorienting and confusing. To observers, it would be perfectly plausible to conclude that nothing had happened. And she herself questioned indeed if it had. But Brae still stood in the circle of Sebastian's arms, visibly shaken and crying.

As they began to walk away from the tomb, they were left with nothing conclusive. The other three felt the dizziness, a moment of disorientation, and, according to their watches, a brief loss of time. Brae claimed that she felt upset, but nothing had really happened. This, however, Corey had always believed was a lie.

Corey remembered clearly counseling that it was time to stop and re-evaluate. But it had been Quinn who overrode her, "Are you kidding? We're finally getting somewhere. We should push on." His face shone with a strange triumph, and his eyes with that obsessive quality that Corey remembered from the early days.

And then Iain interjected rather quietly for him, "Maybe we should leave this up to Brae. She seems the one who was most affected."

Corey's eyes met hers only momentarily as Brae quickly looked away as if at something in the distance. Sebastian's arm was still around her, and she was leaning against him. "What do you want to do, Brae?" he asked comfortingly as she slowly met his eyes.

She smiled, wiping a few stray tears off her face. "We can go on," she spoke with false bravado.

Corey's gaze flew to Iain's with upset, but he only met her with an indifferent shrug that told her keenly that he wasn't taking any of this too seriously.

"Is this where we should be?" Iain asked Corey. The two of them stood alone in the present, and she hesitated on the platform's steps where the Lady sat perched on what Corey had always envisioned as some kind of throne. In one hand, the Lady held a scepter of fern, in the other a rose, with a second rose on her lap. The entire statue seemed to be molded out of some dark bronze metal that had become deeply tarnished during her residence there.

"This was Quinn," she murmured.

"I remember," he answered, standing just beside her.

In a very opaque and odd way, what was happening became clearer. The tombs and the statuary accompanying them were somehow linked to powerful energy points, energy points that, when approached by one gifted enough to tap into them, stimulated some sort of self-revealing vision. Like a sensor, it focused in on whoever was concerned.

Quinn's reaction to his vision had been entirely different, almost opposite from Brae's. He, the translator of the journal, had abruptly put it into Sebastian's hands and then walked up the steps to the bronze queen. He'd placed his hands on hers for some moments, eyes closed. This time wasn't nearly as dramatic, with no wild breeze and no dizziness. It was as though Quinn absorbed the entire experience into himself, greedily Corey thought with distraction, though exactly why she wasn't sure. And then he pulled away laughing. "Amazing," he'd laughed again.

"What happened?" Brae asked, a bit confused by his reaction.

"This one had to do with *indifference to external things*, just like the journal said. I saw myself in a lifetime filled with wealth and health as well. But not as I am, not with my mind intact. It seemed to be presented as some sort of choice."

Again, he laughed in an irreverent way that Corey found disturbing, "As though that were truly a choice."

It was then that Corey was beginning to see glimpses into the nature of the journey. And in the beginning, though disconcerting, it did seem rather harmless.

CHAPTER 46

CONTROL OVER THE PANIC

Corey led Iain away from the *Lady with the Scepter*. She knew where they were headed but was so hesitant to arrive there. He seemed deep in thought or perhaps feeling and content to follow her. She intended in some respect to recreate the journey — to do that would give the rest coherence. They paused beneath an effigy and stood in the shadow of two angels in agony.

"It's horrible. It's so sad."

Corey's eyes were locked on the statues above, holding onto each other. Strangely, they seemed as though they were dragging each other down.

"It's supposed to be a mother and daughter drowning at sea," Quinn commented.

"They almost seem as though they're fighting each other," Iain spoke from just behind her.

"Don't we do that, scramble, and pull each other apart in a panic?" Sebastian observed a little too dry, a little too detached.

"What did Annie Besant say about it?" Brae asked.

Quinn was holding the book, "It's hard to decipher. Something about *gaining control over one's thoughts.*"

Brae looked at him with disbelief, "What can that have to do with this?"

Quinn rambled, "*The restless, unruly mind, hard to curb as the wind.*"

Corey stepped forward, hearing the roar of the waves and the water around her, "It makes sense, control over your thoughts."

"Control over the panic."

"Control over the panic," Iain repeated. They stood in the same spot beneath the two angels, just as they'd done over a decade before.

And the memory was so close, so strong, as though it were right beside them where they could tangibly touch it. He moved closer to Corey, whose eyes were fixed on the pair. He could hear the deep breaths she was taking. "What did you see then? You never told me." The voices were in his head from long ago, but he could not see them yet.

"I saw the water," her voice sounded hollow, as though she were in a trance.

"But this one wasn't yours. It was Sebastian who stepped through this initiation."

So strong, with such clarity, she could see him clearly in her mind as though he were here now, stepping forward. Sebastian had fearlessly walked toward them and placed his hands right on the tomb's base, tempting fate to strike. But now, as then, she could see clearly what he was seeing.

"He saw himself on a vessel, a sea vessel that was sinking. There were so many, throwing their arms over him as they hit the water, pulling him down, scrambling in panic," her voice sounded hollow in her ears, as though she were indeed speaking from another place.

He whispered to her, "But you were with him."

She shook her head, "No, he was alone. That was the point of this. He was completely alone."

She looked back at Sebastian, going under the water, even now surprised at his determination. "But he stopped everything. He controlled his panic and allowed himself to sink without a fight into the water."

Iain murmured, "It is his strength, his willpower, gaining control over himself."

She shook her head, "It should be. But it isn't his strength. It's a curse." She whispered. Iain felt a dizziness sweep over him. And then, he realized in that strange, stretched moment that he'd forgotten something, something that now nagged at him. "Why did you return here?"

Then she looked at him, into his eyes. "So, you could begin to understand."

He stared in complete confusion momentarily at the desperate statues before him. The perspective changed the more you looked at them. At first, it had seemed they were blinded by panic, but now, in the vacillating light of this overcast day, he could see desperation and panic coupled with something else. One angel had its arms draped over the other as if hanging on for dear life, and the other hand on its temple but eyes cast to the heavens in desperation, in faith, in surrender. His head throbbed as he began to feel the energies converge around him again, positive and the other. Both, as was always with the world — pain, happiness laced with bitterness.

"I don't exactly follow your point, Corey?" His voice sounded thick and raspy in his ears as images began to converge on him, smothering him like the waves relentlessly creeping up on those desperate creatures.

"We're always being tested, my boy. At our best and worst, almost being hammered, fired into something much stronger than we ever imagined we could be." He'd thought Andre was speaking of himself. The man was dying, fighting his demons in the process. But he should have remembered that he never spoke without a goal, sometimes one that operated at many levels.

He turned to her. She was simply staring ahead, also lost in her thoughts, her own demons. "Let's move on," she said quietly.

They had started late that day that long ago day, and the first signs of dusk had already begun to settle around them. Corey imagined they had only perhaps half an hour until the cemetery gates were closed.

The adult Marguillers had already visited three monuments, all of which had yielded strange and oddly personal visions to members of their group — Brae, Quinn, and Sebastian. Brae still had said nothing about her experience, but Corey could feel it keenly in her very skin that something quite upsetting had happened to her. Quinn seemed largely untouched by the experience, and oddly enough, it seemed as though Sebastian had gained something, become more empowered. His step was quicker, his voice more vibrant. She didn't understand it. What she'd seen of what had happened to him was horrifying, disturbing. But with little effort, he'd been able to separate himself from the experience.

She whispered to Iain, "I don't know if we should continue."

It was odd. His eyes seemed glazed to her, and it felt as though he were being drawn elsewhere, affected on a wholly different level.

Sebastian eagerly began to ascend the steps of the next tomb. Her heart clutched at his boldness. There was something wrong here, some respect, deference to what they were doing that he lacked — too much recklessness in his manner. Iain stepped forward, "Sebastian, why don't we stop for the day?"

Sebastian had ascended the polished steps, standing directly next to the Lady. He turned back toward the rest of them but directed his comments to Iain in a laughing voice. "Why, old friend? Are you afraid it's your turn next?"

An irritation swept through Corey at his cavalier attitude. "We're moving too fast. We still don't know what we're dealing with."

And then her eyes, which had been focused on Sebastian, were drawn involuntarily to the statue of the woman that he stood beside. A low hum began to rise in her ears. The woman was dressed in a flowing Grecian gown, a statue that looked as though it were crafted out of some dark metal, darker even than the *Lady with the Scepter*. Her hand outstretched to the tomb but not touching it. As the hum grew louder, Corey felt rooted to the spot, rooted and alone. The others had disappeared or just been blocked from her vision, and she knew quite clearly that it was too late. Something had been triggered, and it was all too late. The metal fingers began to stretch and hook into the round brass holders that opened the door. One long hand in each as she pulled it open.

Corey heard a panicked gasp escape from her mouth when the blackness from inside the tomb began to rush toward her.

CHAPTER 47

THE CORNER OFFICE

She stood quietly in front of the tomb, wondering how she could move forward on this path that she'd chosen. And then she felt Iain move beside her. "You never really told me what happened here."

Swallowing on a dry throat, "At first, I couldn't because I didn't understand it. And then my mind forgot it."

She turned to him, feeling sobs brought on by turbulent emotion catching in her throat. How could she make him understand? "Do you understand how this worked?"

His face was grave, thoughtful. He was beginning to feel it now. How could he not, being here, so close to all the power? "I don't know. I've always thought I remembered exactly what happened here, everything, every detail. But now, it doesn't feel that way. It's almost as if—"

"Your mind has filled in pieces, the ones that were missing so that it would make sense. But now you can see all the places that are missing."

She turned back to the statue, which chilled her even now. She realized it, realized why she hadn't returned here. "I can remember now clearly what happened, but at the time, it didn't make sense because it hadn't happened yet. *Control that rules speech and actions.*" And then she hesitated. "I walked through those doors and was back at the park that day."

His eyes widened as he turned to her, "That day?" It felt more like an accusation than a question.

"Before it ever happened, I was seeing it. I was there telling you I was leaving you, trying to make you accept it, desperate to."

"I remember," he said with a bit of sharpness at the memory, "but I don't understand Corey."

Even as they spoke, she could feel herself there again, feel the acute pain in her stomach, the panic in her heart. She had to, had to make him believe her. "You see. I didn't understand either until it was time. That I had to play a part, that I had to convince you even though everything was a lie."

Iain's head was throbbing unmercifully. Control — he had to remember the control he'd learned overseas — the mastery of himself. But the remembered rage was flowing through his blood again. He hadn't believed her until she'd left with Sebastian, and they'd turned up married. "What are you saying? How can all that be a lie? You said you'd fallen in love with another man, with my friend. And you were leaving me. As you did?" He tried, but he couldn't stop from grabbing her arms and whirling her to face him.

"It was a lie," she whispered. "Don't you see? I did it to protect you?"

His eyes widened, his heart hammering. "What are you talking about? Protect me from what?"

Her voice came out in a whisper, a hushed sound so quiet she wasn't sure if she'd spoken. "From being destroyed."

That day long ago, when life began to unravel, she'd awoken to feel Iain's arms about her, but still, it felt as though she couldn't breathe. She looked into his eyes. They were with her now, focused. "What happened?" he asked. She was lying across the steps of the tomb, and he was kneeling beside her, holding her in his arms. The vision came back to her in bits and pieces but made no sense, leaving her with only the stabs of pain she felt in her heart.

"I'm not sure." She sat up, dizziness taking her over.

"I think it's time to stop for the day," she heard Sebastian's voice come from the bottom of the stairs. She looked into his face, and all she could feel was a rush of panic, then an inexplicable revulsion filling her.

But as quickly as it had come, in the descending light of the day all around them, it disappeared like a phantom.

The trappings were the same: dark, massive, imposing furniture. In fact, it had been hardly touched since his father's occupation of the corner and, for that matter, the largest office of the law firm of Morris, Delaney, and Bates.

As a boy, he'd always thought when — and back then, there was still quite an "if" in play — he occupied this office, he would change everything. He didn't want the intimidating and antiquated feel of the décor. He wanted everything to be different.

He picked up the last remnants of an expensive cigar and breathed it in deeply. It was a recent gift from a client, an old man in his early eighties who was more than pleased with his efforts to clean up some civil litigation for him. As he smoked the old man's expensive cigar, a habit he'd acquired just in the last three years, he could see him on the other side of his father's expansive mahogany desk, smiling at him from a face well-gnarled and convoluted by age. He remembered wondering oddly in that moment if your life's deeds do eventually manifest themselves on your face but then swept the uncomfortable thought away.

The old man had gleefully flung the cigars on the desk, then, laughing, had thrown something else at him that he had not found quite so palatable. "You know Morris, I've got to say you're truly your father's son."

After that, they had chatted for a few more moments, and then he'd walked the old man to the door, watching him leave. The thought crossed his mind how frail he seemed, as he made his way down to the elevators, and he wondered vaguely if the old man died today what sort of accountability he would face. What, indeed, would he have to answer for in that place where secrets and actions are laid bare and not covered by self-deception? It was a question that, of late, had begun to bother him.

Sebastian Morris returned the cigar back to the ashtray. It was the end of the day. There were no more meetings, no more appointments, nothing left to do but leave. He breathed in deeply, the burnt taste of the cigar still in his mouth. It would be convenient to tell oneself that what you see is what you get, and life begins and ends with that empty finality. He found it ironic that the thought of a finite life with no spiritual infusion seemed comforting. He imagined the old man who'd given him the cigars might opt for such an interpretation as well. They both seemed to belong to that segment of the population who had lived in such a way that the thought of any afterlife was intolerable at best. It was that pool of people that might include criminals, both low and high and the worse sort — the criminals who never admit what they are and consider themselves entitled.

He smiled grimly. For moments like this came few and far between. It was all he managed to tolerate — an occasional respite of reflection. But the old man spurred all this on, "You're truly your father's son." It rankled for a moment, then slowly sunk in. His father he remembered his father — a selfish, morally ambivalent, ruthless man whom he had despised most of his life. A man that, as a young teenager, he'd vowed to be as different from as night and day. And now, he was his father's son, and he felt a tightness wrap around his heart. He extinguished the cigar and walked out of the cold room his father had bequeathed to him.

CHAPTER 48

BE CAREFUL WHAT YOU WISH FOR

"Well, I suppose it's something you have to decide, whether you live in a world of monsters or flawed people."

"What do you mean?"

"I mean, from time to time, we all become the monster," and then Andre had laughed a bit at the thought. "Don't look so horrified. We always learn more by falling down than by walking perfectly. It's the thing that makes us try harder that humbles us."

The air around them felt thick and muffled, and he wondered for more than a single moment whether he had heard her correctly. "What did you say?"

Corey's face was pale, her dark eyes wide. He knew the look, fear, perhaps mere breaths away from terror. "I'm sorry," she whispered.

His hands that, he now couldn't remember putting on her arms tightened, "What are you saying?"

She looked down, but reflexively and perhaps too harshly, he shook her. Her eyes met his again, filled with pain. "Iain, it's so complicated. That's why I wanted to come here because I thought it would make sense of things and that you might remember."

He dropped his hands. A coldness swept through him as he felt the clamminess of a chilled chamber. "What do you think I've forgotten?" As that strange nagging set in.

She breathed deeply, and her soft, pained face seemed to set in determination. "I'm trying to tell you the truth now. Don't you see, I'm risking everything?"

The whispers around him nearly drowned out her words. Whispers surrounding him, those he hadn't heard for over a decade.

They almost hadn't returned. She'd often thought if only they had gone the other way and left all of this behind them, how things would be different. Perhaps Iain would have never left or maybe taken her with him. They would have lived their lives overseas, and the baby she lost would have lived. But none of that happened, and in quiet moments somewhere beyond the roar of pain and emotion, she accepted that it was all meant to be.

It was the following Sunday morning. She and Iain drove nearly in silence back to the cemetery. He seemed more than willing to forget everything. She remembered the look of concern in his eyes and the, for lack of a better word, pureness of his devotion to her. It was odd. Even as a teenager, she had not found this aspect of his personality so pronounced, this sort of innocence. In the early days of the Marguillers, there was a guardedness about him. She knew he had a difficult home life and imagined it was a shell he needed for protection. But now, there was something unvarnished and vulnerable about him. It was something she could only attribute to the newness of their relationship and perhaps the first time he'd ever felt truly loved.

He pulled his truck over to the side of the road, not at all where they were supposed to rendezvous that morning. And she looked at him with puzzlement. He stopped the engine, staring forward for some strange, long, extended moments, then looking at her intently. "How about we not?"

She smiled. It seemed the hundredth time that morning that he'd brought up this possibility. And more than once, she'd been tempted to acquiesce. "Now, where's that adventurous spirit of Jacques DeMolay?"

He frowned, "I imagine it had fled him just about the time he was being tortured and then burned at the stake." Quietly, he took her hand, "I'm just beginning to realize I have much more to risk these days." Those intense green eyes were staring into hers, and she didn't realize this would be one of the last times she would ever see him looking at her again in such an unguarded way, "A lot more to lose."

So many times, she would go back to this moment wishing she had it to do again, not recognizing that it wasn't just any moment but a crossroads that would decide all their fates for so many years. But something had taken hold of her, some distraction, some curiosity that beckoned her — born, she thought perhaps, in that dark chamber that had shown her unwilling mind things that could yet come to pass. And although she still felt now that there was a choice, something whispered to her just as strongly that the choice had already been made.

And so, she had smiled in much the same way that Eve had entreated Adam and said, "Come on. Let's see what happens."

Fear had taken hold, had gripped her stomach tightly as they moved on, to another place. The irony of it hit her strongly as they approached. How benign it seemed — that it had seemed and still did now.

It was the Sainet tomb, not the most striking but quiet and harmonious. The statue that graced its steps was a young woman, wreath in her hair, holding a harp in one hand and book in the other, head bowed in reverence. All was serenity. All was harmless and soothing. But Corey stopped a few yards away from the steps as she had already felt the peculiar power that emanated from this spot. Beside her, Iain stopped as well but then drifted a bit closer.

She heard his voice beside her, "What is this?"

She looked at him with confusion, "What do you mean?"

His eyes were wide, and his face set in something akin to irritation, "We don't have time to go off the beaten track."

She opened herself to him. Was he playing a game with her? But there was no trace of anything but confusion. "Don't you remember this one, Iain?"

He looked at her blankly, "Remember what? I've never been here."

He still held the journal in his hands, and she unceremoniously took it from him and began to flip the pages to where she knew the Sainet tomb lay. As the realization slowly hit, her breath caught in her throat. Again, she flipped through. Perhaps it was at a different point, but once more nothing, although she could clearly see Annie Besant's sketch in her mind. She swallowed on a dry throat, feeling a dizziness overtake her. "It used to be here," she whispered, looking up at him with confusion.

And then his face looked stern, set, as though he weren't certain whether or not he believed her. She knew there was some memory loss on his part, but not of this magnitude, as though it had never happened. "What do you remember?" he said firmly.

And then she looked back at the serene statue poised before them, feeling completely overtaken by dread.

"She's not for you."

He'd looked at his mother with surprise. He'd expected many reactions, but oddly enough, not this one. He'd smiled, still feeling a residue of stress that seemed to accompany the quick pace of events still clinging to him, "Well, seeing as how we've just eloped, Mother, it seems a little late for such an observation."

His father had died just three years ago, heart disease, and since then, his mother had drifted about the house on Henry Clay Avenue, sometimes, he thought, as a kind of phantom. It wasn't at all as if she was pining for her dead spouse. She'd taken to the role of being window dressing for his father some time ago. There was just an odd, absent quality to Lilith Morris, even when her corporeal self was present, except when she made an occasional unexpected appearance as she had today upon the news of her son's sudden nuptials. They were sitting out in the rose garden of his father's house, she across from him in a white wrought iron chair on the intensely manicured patio. Lilith was in her late sixties now and, aside from the servants, was living in the mansion alone. He'd noted, however, that whenever he was searching for her these days, the rose garden was where she usually turned up.

His mother's eyes were a strange shade of blue, blue mixed with other colors that at times gave them an almost disturbing shade of violet as they now appeared in the declining afternoon sun. But she placed a thin, fragile hand atop his, a gesture of warmth that was about as uncommon in his upbringing as hugs had been from his father. "No," she said in her voice that in age had mutated into a throaty whisper. "It's not too late, Sebastian. You could annul it."

He pulled his hand away in distaste from the woman he'd always viewed as more akin to a cold effigy than a maternal figure. "Why would I do that? She's exactly what I want."

And then she'd leaned back in her chair in their lovely but unmistakably cold garden, beautiful but lifeless, like so much else of their lives. "What you want?" and then she smiled in that way he remembered, which had always made his skin crawl a bit. She looked away again, drifting to that distant, self-created world that had so little to do with real life. But her last whisper stayed with him, "Be careful what you wish for," a soft, throaty laugh that just drifted off into silence.

Within a year after his marriage, his mother had slipped into dementia. He still visited her in the expensive facility where she resided, although she didn't recognize him now. He did wonder, often, though, how life would've been different if, just that once, he'd taken her advice.

She was telling the truth. He felt it with as much certainty as he'd felt anything. Again, he stared at the tomb before them and cleared his mind to find some hint of recognition. But all that came back to him was a feeling of something solid, like a tangible, implacable wall or — and then an image drifted through his mind — a door, a certain locked door.

"What happened here?" he repeated. He reached out and grabbed her bare arm. Her skin felt hot, almost feverish.

He touched her forehead, the same but maybe more so, so hot. "I can't," she whispered. He felt it acutely as she began to give way. His arms went around her as she began to collapse down onto the granite beneath her. Without another thought, Iain scooped her into his arms and carried her back to the car.

CHAPTER 49

A GENTLE TRUCE

"Was beginning to think you wouldn't show."

Sebastian said nothing, just pulled out the chair across from Quinn. The coffee shop was a hole in the wall not far from his law firm, furnished in dark woods with dim lighting. He couldn't help but wonder why this particular old acquaintance had chosen it. He assumed it was Quinn's taste for the dramatic. His own jadedness forbid him to use the word friend in connection with any of the members of the now-extinct Marguillers. Friendship implied some degree of trust, and as things stood and had for some time, he couldn't begin to imagine placing his trust to any degree with any of them.

"So, what's this about?" To the point was the best way to deal with Quinn, though admittedly, it had been three years since they'd last spoken.

"I see time hasn't improved your disposition or your health. You're beginning to look as bad as I do. You've aged, old friend."

He glanced down at his watch. He didn't have time for this, not that anything pressing was waiting for him anywhere. After Corey, he'd lost his taste for female companionship, barring anything deeper than the most superficial liaisons. All his friendships were business-related. His life was simply and unequivocally a shell, and that seemed to be all he could tolerate. He frowned, "Look, Quinn, get to the point. I don't have the stomach for talking about the good old times, tripping down memory lane, or any sort of small talk in general."

The frail ghost of a man before him smiled, and it unnerved him. It was a cold smile, not the Quinn that used to be.

It was palpable how life had hammered them all into such different beings. "How about for things not so small?"

He leaned back in the wooden chair, now bracing himself for it — for just what he had no idea. But for something. It was in the air, had been for weeks, a restlessness, a whisper of things to come or things to come apart. "Exactly?" was all he said.

The smile slowly dissolved with his lack of reaction. Drama needed something to feed off, and he was offering nothing. "Did you know Iain is back?"

He took a breath, took it in deeply, expecting some sort of response from himself, but there was none. The emotion of it all had dried up within him long ago. "Really?"

He nodded emphatically, "Oh yes, I've seen him a few times actually."

Sebastian reached for something to drink but realized he hadn't ordered anything. "Well, I imagined he'd come back someday."

A glimmer of that smile continued to play across Quinn's thin mouth. "You know, he told me he's going to get Corey back. Isn't that funny, after all this time? I wouldn't have expected that of him to be so forgiving."

And at that, there was a stirring, a slight stab of remembered feeling. Interesting that something could still reach him, "Why are you telling me this?"

"I thought you'd be able to put it together. If that happens, it all comes out, and it all tumbles down. What do you think he'll do when it finally comes out?"

He hesitated at what he saw in Quinn's face — a strange hopefulness, a wish that it was so. "Well, you've obviously thought about this a lot. What do you think he'll do?"

He shrugged his emaciated shoulders. "I don't know. I guess he'll probably kill you," he said just before he brought his steaming beverage to his thin lips. And then he added, "Don't you think?"

Sebastian waited, waited to feel an impact of Quinn's words on his insides, but he didn't and that in itself was disappointing. So, in response, he said, "Oh, I think he'll kill us both, my old friend."

Quinn brought the cup back down to the tabletop, a bit paler, if that was possible for him, Sebastian thought. "Do you ever miss it?" Quinn asked, his voice a tad less empty than before. "The old days?"

Sebastian gave this question a moment's thought before answering, then quietly saying, "I try not to remember them at all."

They descended like a cloud of feverish chaos upon her mind — visions, a splattering of feverish images that should make sense and come together somehow but did not. And then she felt his hands on her, rubbing her temples, a pressure that became nearly painful, but not quite, and then sleep, a heavy blanket of sleep that covered her mind, releasing everything.

Iain sat beside the bed and quietly watched as Corey finally settled into a slumber. He'd applied an acupressure technique he'd learned from another friend of Andre's while he was in Rouen, another member of the Eleusians. They all had their skills, not so unlike the Marguillers of long ago.

After Corey's collapse at the cemetery, he'd brought her back to his house. Touching her arm, it felt much cooler. Evidently, the fever was self-generated in some way, perhaps a response to the intense pressure she was under.

He leaned back in the wooden chair that he'd placed beside the bed. Closing his eyes, he forced himself to calm, to clear his mind. He'd learned long ago that trying to sort through things when one was in any heightened emotional state was futile. Everything became tainted by subjectivity. This was a time to understand, understand, and then later, there would be ample time to act.

His mind returned to the cemetery. He could see himself and Corey again on the steps of the Sainet tomb. But there was something around it, a haziness that he hadn't seen with his eyes, a sort of fog blocking him from receiving any impressions of it.

He cleared his mind again, now returning at a different angle, the time Corey said they were there last. He could see the group, all of them — Brae, Quinn, Sebastian, Corey, and he, walking toward the same tomb, and then, he smiled to himself, here again, the fog but a wider perimeter now. In his perception, it seemed as though they walked right past it, never stopping. He found it curious, truly curious. So again, he cleared his mind, returning to another time long ago, the night they spent in the cemetery as teenagers. He could see them. All of them were huddled up against the mausoleum across from the Montleone tomb. He remembered that night and did not remember the *Lady with the Harp*. But he did something that Andre told him could be dangerous. He entered the memory and found himself awakening again as a young man.

Corey didn't know how it was possible, but she had fallen asleep on the cold ground of the Metairie Cemetery. She knew this because she was now being awoken by a hard nudge. Her eyes flickered open. There was still darkness all around, but Iain crouched beside her. She sat up, feeling achy and disgruntled. "What are you doing?" she spat out. "I thought we were going to wait until daybreak."

She focused on his face, which became clearer in the darkness. His eyes seemed wider to her. "I need your help," he said in a heavy whisper.

She looked around, noting the still sleeping forms of the remaining three Marguillers. "What about the others?" she asked.

He stood up beside her, replying softly, "Just you." Then he outstretched his hand to her. Once she took it, he quickly pulled her to her feet. For a moment, they stood staring at each other, and she felt an odd jolt of energy pass through his hand right into her. "Come on," he whispered and then turned, walking away. Without thought, she followed just behind him.

They traveled through the darkness, although he held a small flashlight in one hand, and the other held Corey's hand — Corey at fifteen. He was guiding her through the darkness. She whispered once, "Where are we going?" But he hadn't answered, and now she seemed somewhat accepting of wherever he was leading her.

They were winding back, deeper into the cemetery, not taking familiar roads. It was a strange dichotomy of thought that was occurring within young Iain Shaw. It was almost like sleepwalking for him as the adult Iain of the present guided him. It was quite stressful for him to retain a balance. It would be perfectly natural for him to sink entirely into the thoughts and emotions of the past — although the past was fluid now, connected by gossamer threads to the present, and now unfolding in a new, unsuspected way.

He felt it when they were close. The fog around it had become nearly impenetrable in the present, yet in this time, it wasn't there, hadn't been created yet by whatever had occurred. He stopped a few feet away from the tomb. He felt the young Corey gently pull her hand out of his. It surprised him. He was concentrating so hard he hadn't realized that he was still holding onto her. He shone the flashlight onto the effigy before them. It was odd. Now, he could see it clearly for possibly the first time — the statue in the darkness. It was the woman holding the harp and the book in the other hand — the Book of Life, wherein your names will be written.

"Be careful. Sometimes, the most powerful things will be placed in innocuous places." It was something Andre had said.

"*Something's wrong here. It's not the same.*" It was Corey's voice. He could hear it clearly, but it was from that other time.

"*This one's a trap. I think we were supposed to avoid it.*"

"No," Quinn had said, "*A test.*" And he'd heard the roar around him, the sweeping roar, and something pulling, literally being ripped out of his chest.

It swirled around him like a tornado, the voices.

He felt his hands on his throat closing, choking out the life — and the red, all the red seeping out of his hands.

There was a slight pressure, a touch on his shoulder. "Please, let's leave. I don't like this place." He turned and was yanked away from it all by that young voice. Even in the darkness, he could see the concern in her eyes.

"I'm not finished," he said, his voice shaky.

"Please, Iain, please let's leave."

He reached up and covered the hand that still lay on his shoulder. And then he opened his eyes. Corey was sitting up in the bed, staring at him in the semi-darkness of his room. "Where were you?" she asked quietly, the same eyes from before, wide and filled with concern. And then, without thought, he reached over to her and pulled her against him. He sought oblivion as he kissed her, not at all sure how long their gentle truce could last.

· CHAPTER 50 ·

CHOICES

It's an odd thing when someone makes a choice. Could what is thought unthinkable at one point, then become possible, and then in some implausible way acceptable?

Sebastian sat in his father's study, the one downstairs. He never ventured upstairs in that room where they'd found Annie Besant's journal so many years before. The year Corey left, he had the whole bundle of his father's treasures packed up and donated to a museum up North. He'd thought about giving it to the New Orleans Historic Collection but realized that he didn't want it anywhere near him — nowhere near him. Quinn seemed quite surprised when he told him what he'd done. After all, Sebastian had been the one who wanted to get back into the chamber where Iain had sealed the objects. In fact, it had become an obsession for a time, like Corey.

He quietly sipped a glass of Scotch that he had poured for himself. He remembered Quinn's face. Yes, there was a sense of betrayal there. "You could have given that stuff to me." He'd said, "I could have sold it for a fortune, could have been set for life."

So, Sebastian did what he usually did these days when someone began to be a problem. He took out his checkbook and eased the sting of the betrayal. That was one of the last times he'd seen Quinn until tonight.

It bothered him more than he let on about Iain and Corey, but not for obvious reasons. He had gotten into a habit of sweeping away things that were distasteful to him, errors. There was a court case a few years back that he had thoroughly botched up. It was an embarrassment to the firm. But he

293

had enough pull and enough name power that the other partners were willing to overlook it. And now, it was never mentioned by anyone in the office, almost as if it hadn't happened. And that suited him.

He tried to treat his time with Corey in much the same way. He wasn't a man who liked to examine his feelings too closely. But he understood several things now that he hadn't then.

One was the enormous fallacy inherent in being raised with privilege. Even though he was a miserable child, he was instilled with a sense of entitlement. If you're told often enough that you deserve more consideration than anyone else, then you begin to believe it. And you start to want things you simply aren't meant to have. That poison of wanting and convincing yourself that you are entitled leads to a kind of madness. And, of course, the power given to one in the grips of self-induced madness is— Then he stopped and quietly sipped his Scotch. It was no justification, but it helped him to live with — well, it helped him live with the things that he'd done.

Corey awoke with a quiet feeling of contentment that lasted in forgetfulness for some moments. Light streamed in through the curtains of Iain's bedroom, and she wondered absently how it would feel if she spent the rest of her life waking up in such a way. She sat up and looked around — noting that she was alone as the gentle tugging of reality slowly encroached on the lightness in her heart. There was so much, so much ahead of them, and a familiar heaviness coupled with a dread set in.

She ran her fingers through her long black hair as she dressed. She allowed it to suffice. Iain had no mirrors in the bedroom. He'd deliberately kept the house quite sparse and utilitarian. She found him sitting at the small kitchen table with the journal in front of him. The sight of it caused a jolt in her heart. He looked up at her arrival with an expression that told her he had been deep in concentration. There was no greeting, just focus in his dark eyes this morning, "Why do you think it's gone, Corey, the Sainet tomb?"

She breathed in deeply. She wasn't quite ready to be hit with all this again. "I don't know," she said quietly, sitting in the chair across from him. "It was important."

"But you still retain memories of us being there."

Her eyes widened, and she tried to bring them to the surface of her mind. It was so odd to do so since she'd spent much of her life trying to erase them. "I do," but there was a hesitation in her voice because they were faded now. She might even say a bit garbled in her memory.

He caught it through the nuances of her expression, "What's the matter?"

She swallowed. How to go into this without explaining everything? "It's jumbled now, what I remember. I don't understand it. It's never been that way before."

He looked down at the pages before him. "It seems something is shifting, changing. I've been thinking about how we should proceed. I think we need to move on."

"Move on? But Iain, there's so much you don't know."

He looked back up at her, his expression unchanging, "I am aware of that now. But something larger is happening here. There's a particular path we're supposed to take this time." And then he reached out, covering her hand with his. "We shouldn't try to force anything else, not yet."

She sighed deeply, "I don't understand what's happening or how we got here. We seem so far away from where we started finding the Triquetra. Is that even a part of this?"

He smiled slightly, and just that encouraged her a bit. "It might be. It very well might be, just not in the way we think." He stood up and walked across the diameter of the small room. "I've been thinking about this. Perhaps, we've been going about this the wrong way." And then he crossed back to the table, lightly placing his hand back on the pages of the journal. "Maybe we should think about Annie Besant, her intent with this whole thing."

She breathed in deeply, trying to forcibly quell the upset that was threatening to overtake her. "Well, I have read some of her published works. Much of it concerns the nature of existence, different planes of existence, and the soul's evolution. I always believed that this path the journal set out represented that journey."

He nodded in agreement, "Yes, yes, that's clear. But, of course, it goes beyond that. In France, I became involved in an order. I suppose you could call it a secret society and took part in initiations."

She listened intently. Although she had suspected as much, given the changes in Iain, this was the first time he'd actually opened up to her about it. "The idea is that the initiation prepares you for the receipt of knowledge, prepares the spirit. The spirit must be in a special state to absorb what is given. And though the initiation, a ceremony if you will, might not seem terribly significant to the person."

"It does affect the spirit," she finished his thought.

"Yes."

She leaned in closer, looking more intently at the book. "So, you think this ties in with Annie Besant's journal."

He nodded, "I do. Somehow, these sites, these structures in this cemetery, are thresholds of initiation."

"And you think we underwent these initiations without realizing it?"

He shrugged, "What was clear was that we all were changed and that something was completed."

"Yes," she murmured, "the objects." But her mind was elsewhere, on her fading memories of the Sainet tomb. It was strange. She held memories of what happened there, but they felt altered now, transparent, making her question what if anything had truly occurred. "Iain, there's still much I haven't told you. But I don't understand it. It's becoming confusing to me now."

He was looking at her intently, feeling the distortion. "I think we should wait on all of this until we can sift out the truth."

Her eyes were wide and dark, "Are you sure?"

He nodded.

She wanted to speak. He could feel it acutely on his skin. But she waited. He wasn't convinced that he was following the best course, but there seemed no help for it — none at all.

CHAPTER 51

THE ACCOMPLICE

The darkness felt expansive, different than when she'd fallen asleep. As she followed Iain's lead through the cemetery, Corey felt acutely disoriented. It wasn't like him to take her hand as he did. Yes, it made sense to help her to her feet. But then, as they continued to meander further away from the others when she slowed down again, he would take her hand in his to guide her as though it were the most natural thing.

He was aiming his flashlight to the ground to illuminate their way. But she sensed acutely that he had no need of it. He knew exactly, even in the blackness all around them, where they were headed. She looked overhead as they walked on. It was a cloudy night, but it did not entirely shroud the sky. She could make out dim stars through the shifting clouds and even the slight crescent that was the moon.

And then they stopped abruptly. She followed the beam of Iain's flashlight that shone on a statue at the front of a tomb. He still held her hand in his but seemed completely focused on the eerily white carved woman before them. So strange, so perfect in proportions, Corey almost expected her to walk toward them.

"What is this?" she whispered to Iain.

But he made no attempt to answer her or any movement forward. She could feel something different through his hand, something that she couldn't begin to understand. A dizziness and complete disorientation swept through her. "We shouldn't stay here. Something's wrong," she whispered.

Again, there was no response, but now a feeling of sadness crept through his fingertips into hers. And her vision began to blur.

She could see him now, Iain in his house, sitting on his bed, hearing the house around him — anger, fighting. She breathed in deeply as she saw physically what he was hearing — the ugly red glow seeping through the walls of his room. And then she felt it inside him, anger like a physical pain eating at him.

She squeezed her eyes tightly to drive away the image. It was too painful, too personal. She yanked the hand that she was holding violently. "Iain," she rasped. "We have to get out of here."

And then he spoke finally in a noticeably quiet voice, "She seems so calm, so serene. Why would she elicit such violent things?" His voice sounded strange in her ears, not the Iain she knew, not the sarcastic, brash young man.

"We need to get out."

He breathed deeply and then answered. "What is it you see here Corey? I think it's something different," and then he stared intently at her, not releasing her hand but holding it more tightly.

Her head throbbed as violent images began to flow through her mind, images that didn't make sense, images that frightened her. "Please, let's go."

And then he did something strange, something she would later look back on and wonder if she had dreamed the whole interlude. He dropped her hand, then gently reached down and kissed her. It must have been a dream. It wasn't something that the Iain she knew would do. But he did, and if it were true, it was her very first kiss — first kiss in the middle of a cemetery on a cloudy night in October.

Perhaps she wouldn't have to tell him. She stared at the reflection in her bedroom mirror — a long, oval mirror matching the rest of the cherry wood furniture. Her dark eyes, wide, stared back at her, trying to make impossibility plausible, palatable. She hadn't expected the way the whole encounter would be simply wiped out. And she felt that if she just let herself, it would be wiped away from her as well. Corey breathed in deeply, and she felt a familiar pain, heaviness, wrap around her chest — the one that had disappeared for a short while when she had decided to tell Iain everything. It had come with fear and panic as its companions but with the promise of freedom as well. She thought, perhaps, she would lose him, that he would be unable to accept her again, knowing what had transpired. But the thought, the hope of finally being free, was nearly intoxicating.

She walked away from the mirror and sat quietly on her bed. Iain would be back this afternoon, and again, they would head out to the cemetery. So strange once she had finally decided, once feeling his heart open to her again, she knew she couldn't keep the truth buried any longer. But just when she was on the threshold, everything changed, became muddied again. "There are always signs in things," her father had told her. "But you must learn how to read them."

She breathed in deeply. It was painful. Vaguely, she wondered if there was something physically wrong with her. But she knew herself too well to believe it. She was like the criminal with a conscience, so guilt-ridden at their crime that she punished herself in secret and tortured herself. No doubt a more damnable sentence than if she'd confessed her crime, as she had almost done.

She closed her eyes and cleared her mind, reaching out to the only one who had ever truly understood what had occurred.

She remembered this clearly, the long rainy afternoon she'd spent in her father's study when, after a much torturous discussion, he'd become her accomplice.

"You can't do this." Clayton Knight's voice was as emphatic and determined as she'd ever found him to be. The man had lost so much weight from his long illness, but his eyes were as brilliant as she remembered them as a child and as terrifying.

She was sitting in the chair in front of his desk — head bent from the intense weight of emotion she now carried. "I told you if I don't do what he wants, Iain will be destroyed. What happened in the tomb is irrevocable."

The old man was pacing on the other side of his desk, highly agitated. It had been over an hour since she first walked in on him, feeling no less than like a drowning person desperately reaching out for someone to save them. "Why didn't you come to me about this journal? Damn it, Corey, you all have no idea what you're dealing with."

"I know," she whispered. "But now, after what happened, I gave my word. I have no choice."

He stopped. His face suddenly stonily set. "Let me talk to him. This parasite."

She looked up, "Dad, I can't let him destroy Iain. I'll just do what he wants."

He glared at her, "Even if what he wants is you. Why doesn't the bastard go out and hire a prostitute?"

"He says he's always loved me," she whispered. "That he needs me."

He laughed, "Funny way to treat someone you love, forcing them into a carnal relationship."

She looked at him with a feeling of shame covering her. She had no idea what to say. She'd never expected it of Sebastian, never expected the enmity he exhibited toward Iain. He was determined to rip her away from him. And then she spoke, her voice ravaged in her own ears, "I think it has more to do with his jealousy of Iain than me. I can't see how he cares at all for me. He's just using me to strike out."

He nodded, "And you all gave him his instrument of vengeance, this woman's journal."

"I didn't think it would become so dangerous."

"But you felt it, didn't you?" She looked down again, covering her face with her hands. She couldn't deny it. She had felt it on more than one occasion — how deeply over their heads they were, children, playing with a loaded gun. And now, this was what had come of it. He placed his hands on the desk, staring at her intently. "Are you sure he can't be reached?"

"Sebastian?" He nodded. "There's a coldness in him that I've never seen before. It's taken him over."

Then, slowly, he sank into his chair. "And you are determined?"

"I can't let him destroy Iain, even if it takes me away from him."

And then, she'd seen an odd expression across his face of such weariness, sadness, and resignation. "Then, my dearest, we will work to protect you as much as possible. I will speak to this arrogant boy and force him into concessions."

"What concessions?" she asked with puzzlement.

He sighed deeply as though filled with infinite fatigue. "He will have you if he marries you."

She looked at her father with confusion. "I don't want to marry him. I don't want to be tied to this creature in any way."

He stared at her unflinchingly. "I know. But it is the best way I know to protect you. The marriage ceremony is an old one, ancient. It protects the spirit from damage in such a union, even when your partner is so alien to your essence. Otherwise, the damage done to you would be possibly insurmountable."

The gravity of her father's words cascaded over her like a million shards of glass. Marriage to Sebastian? It was inconceivable. "I don't know if he'll agree," she murmured.

The old man nodded, "He will. If he is as determined as he appears to be, he will. And he must turn over that journal to me."

She thought to ask why but didn't. It was clear to her in her father's wizened blue eyes that such a powerful thing must be placed in safekeeping.

CHAPTER 52

THE PRICE

Iain had showered and then took a long walk, which culminated somewhere in the midst of Audubon Park. It was a Sunday, and the park was filled with commotion — families, children on bicycles, people walking their pets, all manner of activity about him. It was something that he found that he yearned for, that he had separated himself from at least emotionally while he was away — connection.

He settled on a bench that was not far, in fact, from where he'd first seen Corey again. He could still clearly remember the maelstrom of emotions he'd felt at their encounter, so unexpected. Arrogantly, he honestly thought he had completely extracted himself from his past. But in just moments, she'd destroyed all those misconceptions and humbled him truly, as though time had bent back upon itself bringing them right back to where they had started, where the truth lies undeniable.

He breathed in deeply, considering for not the first time that day the option of simply taking Corey away with him now and starting over, leaving all of it behind, all the ghosts, all the pain, where it would simply become the two of them. It was a plan that had become increasingly attractive to him over the last few days. But then again, that would mean forgoing their mission of finding the Triquetra and the mystery of the Sainet tomb with all its secrets.

He stood up, beginning to slowly head back toward his house. He was convinced he could live without knowing, but Corey was another matter. Could she live without him knowing everything? His pace picked up, and he broke into a slow jog back towards his home.

He dreamed of it, sometimes, as though it were close enough to touch. Sometimes, it seemed to glow as he remembered from long ago. Other times, it was simply there, just sitting on the mantle in the den of his Magazine Street shotgun house. Just lying there, next to Iain's sculpture — an odd piece, larger than a broach, brass in color, with the three interlocking ovals — harmless looking and at times less valuable than something you might find in an old antique shop in the French Quarter. He wasn't at all sure why it had lost its brilliance, but he didn't really care. For him, its value lay in another realm, another venue.

He could still remember the sensation of it in his hands, almost like a buzzing, holding some live insect that at any moment might strike. When he'd put it down, his hands were red, not blistered, but red as if all the blood had rushed into them.

It's powered from the earth.

He supposed that was why this was the only object they could handle. The rest felt less tangible, more like etheric visions — truly things he wasn't interested in. He lived in the world and could only make use of that which lived there as well.

Last night, he had dreamed of it again. But when he got up, he saw it was not here. He could feel it nearby. His hands felt that prickling feeling as though he had held it. Quinn was slowly drawing the Triquetra to him. It was no longer in the chamber. Of that, he was certain. It was between, in some other dimension, slowly making its way into his possession.

She walked, almost noiselessly, into her father's bedroom, quietly sitting down on the four-poster, black oak bed. She breathed deeply, feeling a familiar swirl of sadness cascade over her. It was true, although Clayton Knight had been the rock, the mountain of support in her life, he had always carried an air of despair about him — so slight, so disguised that it was not detectable to most of the population. For he was a proud man and did not wear his personal pain out for public display. But she had always felt it, even before she could put a name to it, the heaviness, the weariness, the quality of someone only marking time until they got to the place they really belonged, where their heart was. As a young child, she had not perceived the sense of loss her father lived with, the depth of his connection to her mother. But as she grew, she began to feel this invisible chord that tied her father to another place, that place where his wife resided.

She closed her eyes with purpose, trying hard to clear away all these memories, sweeping away the veils of impressions that crowded this room. Her mind then reached out for answers, for sense, for guidance within this dilemma she now found herself in. For some reason, the journal had changed, and Iain's memories were further corrupted. She had to restore things, restore the balance.

Suddenly, her mind expanded in a powerful rush. And she felt herself propelled back, back in the past, to a tomb she had seen long ago. She breathed in deeply and found her young fingers wrapping around the wrought iron bars in front of its antechamber. The energy around rushed through her head. So odd, it wasn't a memory, or rather, it was a living memory. The statue staring back at her was an old man. It was that night they'd all spent in the cemetery, and they'd separated. She'd stumbled upon this tomb and then had felt its power as she did now.

Dizziness swirled around her, and the face in her imagination became mobile, eyes opening, beckoning — her father's eyes.

It had been hers, though at the time, the significance seemed lost. And she'd wondered if anything had happened at all. A decade before, she'd walked away from the Sainet tomb as though in a strange trance. Only seconds they had been inside, the three of them together, she, Iain, and Sebastian. Although for them, while everything was happening, it seemed to go on forever, time stretching on endlessly. Once outside, however, Brae and Quinn reacted as though nothing had occurred. No one had been gone, just silence.

Her head spun with dizziness.

"Strange," muttered Quinn. "I guess this one was a bust."

Her eyes flew across to Iain, but he simply stared forward, trance-like. And she wondered if it had indeed happened at all. If it had been just a strange delusion on her part, and then her eyes met Sebastian's, and her heart sank. They glittered in the afternoon light, feral, darker, and she wondered if it showed on one's face when they took a step toward evil.

"My price," he'd whispered. "Anything I ask."

His words had wrapped like a coldness around her heart.

And she'd agreed. She moved beside Iain, wondering, wondering if the bargain had helped or if, indeed, his soul had been lost somewhere back in that coldness. But his eyes, blank and expressionless, finally focused on her, and she felt him returning from the edge of disaster. Finally, he connected with her, asking quietly so she was the only one who could hear, "What happened?" It stunned her and cheered her as she, who was slipping into an abyss in this moment, felt one of the last vestiges of warmth caress her face. Her mind opened to his, and she felt calmness there. It was clear he remembered nothing, nothing at all of the disaster that had just struck them.

CHAPTER 53

A BRIDGE TO MEMORY

"Did you forget something?" she asked. Her mind was pulled out of its preoccupation as Iain pulled into the driveway of his house on Chestnut Street.

He turned off the car's engine, then turned to her, and said "No," rather quietly.

He had been in an odd mood when he picked her up at the house after lunch. There hadn't been much conversation, except he'd told her to dress in something comfortable. She'd thought to tell him about the forgotten tomb in the cemetery she'd seen in the vision. But given the odd mood of his that she was sensing, she waited. There would be time once they again began their exploration. But now this, "Why are we here?" she asked. "I thought you wanted to continue retreading Annie Besant's path." She looked around in the car and realized for the first time he hadn't brought the journal with him.

He nodded, "I do. But this time, we will try something a little different." And then he leaned over and lightly kissed her. "Come on. Let's go inside," he whispered.

It was strange that he hadn't thought of this before, but then again, the possibility of it had not been present. It wasn't at all the same as the first meditation they'd attempted. There had to be a degree of trust and openness that had not existed between him and Corey before to accomplish what he had in mind. After all, just a day ago, he was convinced that she had betrayed him. Now, that scenario had changed. Something had happened indeed, something that he sensed in Corey as catastrophic, but for himself, he had no memory of anything, no memory that was reachable — so he had concluded he must reach through hers.

She stood in the center of his den, watching mutely as he spread out on the floor a long straw mat that he'd acquired during a day trip to a small town in the Languedoc province of France. He'd changed into a loose white cotton shirt, leaving some of the upper buttons undone. "*There must be energy in your heart area.*" Andre had told him. He had guided him in his first real meditation. "*You have to be careful. Much energy can be gained through your heart, but exposing your heart area can also leave you very vulnerable and open to draining and all sorts of spiritual attacks.*"

"What sort of attacks?" he'd asked.

"*The world is filled with multitudes seen and unseen, existing next to us and in other dimensions. Some are very good, and others feed off our energy like parasites. The world is so much vaster than most comprehend.*"

"What are we doing?" she asked quietly.

"It's all right," he murmured as he continued to prepare the space around them. On either side of the room, he'd placed two large white candles opposite them, two large pieces of crystal that he had also brought back with him from France.

"That doesn't exactly answer my question."

He lit the final candle and turned back to her. She was standing near one of the windows that moments before he had drawn the blinds down on. The room was dusky except for the illumination of the candles. She was so sensitive. He could feel her nervousness on his own skin. "Corey, there's nothing to be afraid of."

"Easy for you to say," she whispered.

"I want to conduct a meditation, somewhat different from what we did before."

"Why?" she asked furtively. She reminded him of a caged bird poised to flee at any moment.

Calmly, he answered, "It's clear there are things I've forgotten. You hold the memories, together we can—"

"We can what?" she interrupted, her voice shaking. "Iain, not like this, I can't."

"Pick and choose what you tell me," he stated flatly.

Her hand flew up to her forehead. He could feel the pressure in her head, migraines. Migraines brought on by stress. He could see them in her mind, one of the gifts bestowed because of all that had happened. The body was always the thing that paid the price for emotional disturbance. He cleared his mind. He had to convince her to do this. That much was clear. He stepped closer to her. "Corey," taking one of her hands in his. "Don't be afraid."

She looked up at him, eyes that had begun to brim with tears. "I am afraid, Iain."

He touched her face with his palm, feeling the fear, the fear that was choking her. "Of what?" he asked.

"Losing you again," she whispered.

Again? The word ripped at him. She'd lost him. He'd always believed she sent him away, but not her. That's not what she felt. She'd lost him, and he could feel the truth of it in her very essence.

"What are you doing?"

It was early, and he was on his way to a meeting downtown. Brae had just pulled up in her car outside his Nashville Avenue townhouse, and his heart sank. He didn't have time for this now. There were too many loose ends to tie up before he and Corey left town. He headed to his car, opened the front door, and threw his briefcase inside. "I don't have time for this now, Brae."

She circled his car, eyes bright with determination. "Of course not. You're not answering my calls. What the hell is going on, Sebastian?"

"It doesn't concern you, Brae. Just stay out of it."

He reached for the car door again, but she slammed it shut in front of him. "Iain came to see me. He says you and Corey are—"

"Together now, yes," he finished. And then he paused, looking at her oddly. "So, Iain's confiding in you, is he?"

"He's trying to figure out what the hell is happening."

And then he smiled, feeling something, an intuition that had been brought on somewhat by their recent experiences at the cemetery. It was as though something had expanded within, some power that, at times, he found intoxicating. He patted her arm, "It's good he has you. He needs someone to lean on now."

Her eyes widened, but then he saw a gleam of understanding — a gleam he thought indulgently that he might have placed there.

He considered for a moment. What was going on now was risky. But perhaps it was more important to clear the decks and get to the other side than continuing to try to navigate in unknown waters.

Again, he softly brushed her cheek with his fingertips, murmuring, "It will be all right, Corey," deliberately sending soothing energy to her.

"It would be easier—" she began, but he placed his fingertips gently over her lips.

"Since when have we ever done anything easily?"

He felt a deep sigh of weariness pass through her, and she replied with little inflection. "What do I do?"

He smiled, although he didn't feel cheered at all by her acquiescence, or should he rather call it surrender? "We need to sit on the mat, facing each other and holding hands."

She slowly sunk down, crossing her legs in Indian fashion. He sat across from her, positioned in the same way. For a moment, he reached out, lifting her chin upwards and saying quickly, "No worries."

"Easy for you to say," she answered. He clasped her hands in his, resting them on his knees.

"Close your eyes and clear your mind," he murmured. Almost on the instant of their contact, he'd begun to feel the energy flow. "It's important you let go, Corey, and allow me to lead you."

And then, the last thing he heard before they began was her voice, "Yes, that sounds like you."

CHAPTER 54

THE LADY WITH THE HARP

It's an odd sensation traveling as your astral self. Initially, it's easy to believe you still have your body. But it's essential to be cognizant that the body's limitations no longer exist.

He breathed in deeply, trying to remember Andre's instruction.

"Let go of emotion. Simply be."

It began with energy that he could see in his mind — massive bands of energy radiating in different color vibrations but largely white and blue-green about the room. It was gratifying. He'd worked hard to keep the house pure and uncluttered by disruptive frequencies. And then, the blinding sheets of whiteness began to clear, and he could see more clearly within the room. From the ceiling, he could see the figures below him, himself and Corey, and the auras emanating from their bodies. His was spread wide, clearly pouring energy into this endeavor, white, blue, green, and gold, and Corey's was also powerful. But he saw turbulence there — white, swirling pink denoting confusion, orange, linked with others, and dark red on the fringe, which startled him. Something was taking its toll on her, dragging her into a dangerous area.

He focused on her, seeing the aura around her widen with the influx of energy. He worked then to link himself empathically with her.

The scene began to shift and solidify. Energy was still everywhere, but they were somewhere now. At least, he was. It was often this way in meditation when two people were involved — one functioning as an anchor, remaining more earthbound, while the other traveling into the spiritual spheres. Iain began to move on as Corey remained behind.

He found himself on a threshold, several huge, oversized, luminescent steps leading him to a doorway. And a woman waited for him there, standing at the top of the steps — a woman in long shredded clothing, long tangled matted hair, and a pale, gaunt face with streaks of black running from her eyes. Something powerful stabbed through his chest. He struggled to regain control and let it pass through him. Emotions too strong and out of control would break the meditation.

It was disturbing, unexpected, but something he couldn't fail to recognize. Slowly, he moved forward toward the tormented shadow of Corey.

Whispers, voices reverberated all throughout him. He worked hard to focus. It would have been so easy to be drawn away, so many places to drift and vibrations, but he held onto the thread and Corey. The dark figure walked silently beside him through a long, distorted hallway, flickering in its concreteness, often simply composed of vacillating shadow and light and then walls that, at times, would simply dissipate. It was clear to him that he was traveling through the levels of Corey's reality.

And then, unexpectedly, a door flew open, and they were outside. He was himself again, and beside him was Corey — not now, but as she had been a decade before. They stood on the flat granite slab leading up to the Sainet tomb. But that was all that remained the same. The cemetery surrounding them, and everywhere else within their vision, was desert, flat, barren sand. He understood. This was her reality — barren emptiness created by wild, painful emotion.

"Why are you doing this?" she'd spoken to him, the young woman beside him.

"To free you," was his answer.

Her face remained expressionless, and then she gestured back to the tomb. And the maiden statue holding the harp, whose head was bowed, lifted her chin and opened her eyes, staring into his with blinding knives of white.

He hadn't expected it. In fact, he wondered, in retrospect, what would have happened if he'd never answered the door that day if he had simply had some sort of brief affair with Corey. That would have satisfied his obsession and his pride.

But when he opened the door of his Nashville Avenue townhouse, the old man, Clayton Knight, was standing there. Sebastian was more than surprised. From what Corey had indicated, her father was confined to the house because of his failing health. But outside the street behind him, he saw a cab. A million questions passed through his mind in that moment. He couldn't imagine that Corey had brought her father in on this.

"We need to talk, Morris," he said, and Sebastian stepped back— the realization flooding through him that she had indeed secured her father's aid in this matter.

Something clicked inside him, perhaps the key to a lock, perhaps the shift in a long-ago dormant fault line. Something moved, resulting in buried, forgotten events opened in his mind again. He felt Corey's fear wrap around him for a moment like a thin gossamer shroud but then melt away as he moved forward across the threshold.

He'd known, of course, that it was his turn the first time he saw her. The Sainet statue was so innocuous, her harp in one hand—the powerful spirit of creativity, and the book in the other—the arbiter of wisdom and perhaps fate. An inevitability had hit him then, that he was doomed to failure, and perhaps therein was the lesson.

"*We strengthen in our successes but become defined in our failure.*" Something else that Andre had taught him and only now had resonance.

He walked slowly within the cavern of the tomb, and every step became a young boy's steps, hitting a stone floor and then the deteriorating cracked floor across the kitchen of his parent's home.

He'd never known for sure. They'd kept it a mystery to the children, but here, in this place of shadows, he felt it. He felt the heat before he reached their bedroom, the heat of the anger, of the fear, the red seeping under the door, then heard the shouts, screaming. It had never happened except in dreams. He opened the door and saw his father bent over the bed, his hands around his mother's throat. And even in memory, the rage rushed up through him, filling him as a fifteen-year-old boy pulled the man off his mother, striking him with a wild blow across the face. His father, a man in his late forties, fell sprawling across the floor, bloody mouth.

He heard his mother's scream. The man was coughing. But it didn't stop. Something wild wrapped around his mind, and he fell on top of him, shoving him down with glee. His own hands wrapped around his father's throat with the wild rush of rage flowing through him — feeding him, as he began to crush away his life in justified imitation of what he'd done to his mother. And then it shifted, and it was no longer his father but Sebastian — Sebastian now who he was choking the life out of.

"Why are you doing this?" The old man wouldn't sit. He just stood on the far side of his den near the fireplace, leaning on his cane.

"It's complicated," he answered, feeling a wild mixture of emotions. He hadn't expected this, hadn't expected to face such an inquisition. He'd pondered this carefully and was convinced there was a connection between him and Corey, an elusive connection that was not within his grasp until now. But in this odd moment, he was split, part of him distantly wondering if he should drop the whole thing, but then the other, tenacious, convincing himself that this was his right.

"Corey has told me everything."

He sat quietly in a dark blue lounge chair that his mother had helped him pick out for this place. "Then you must understand that she and I made a bargain. She entered into it freely."

"What kind of man—" he muttered.

"The kind that loves your daughter and saw an opportunity." He resented this, resented the audacity of this old man to interfere.

"You honestly call this love," he accused.

He stood up, outrage now flowing through him at the old man's impudence. He couldn't see it. The time in the tomb had given him something, given him power. "I do, and I'll have Corey."

The old man paused, evidently taken aback at Sebastian's resolve. He spoke quietly, "Then marry her."

His words slammed unexpectedly into him. "What?" he asked in confusion.

"I said marry her."

It took a moment. It was a strange and oddly unnatural idea, but one he had pondered and considered at different times — the first time long ago, in the early days, when they were sitting in Clayton Knight's home, in his sunroom. The warmth of the old house had struck him oddly, profoundly in a way. And he'd wondered then what it would feel like to be part of such a house, one where people actually connected. "I would," he paused, as though speaking to himself, "if I thought she—" he said shakily.

"She will," said the old man flatly. "If you are determined on this course, then you will marry my daughter." And then he turned and started walking toward the door as though the matter were settled.

"What about Iain?" Sebastian called after him a little weakly.

And then the old man turned to him with a final look of disdain, "I can't help that. So, he'll be your problem to deal with."

CHAPTER 55

THE SHADOW

His mind was clouded with rage, but he forced it to clear. The pieces were here now. There was a test, a test for him, but a test that he seemed doomed to fail.

He could feel himself in the aftermath, surrounded by coldness, grayness, trapped.

And he heard their voices around him.

"What's happened to him?"

"He failed. He's lost."

Voices echoed around him in a chamber, but he couldn't see them anywhere. He was blind, lost. He had created his own damnation.

"That's not fair. How could he not fail?" Corey's voice echoed, so near him, but he couldn't reach her, couldn't touch her, only the gray, cold fog. "Didn't you see what happened?"

"I did," he answered, a voice, a familiar one. "Maybe he shouldn't have helped. Maybe he shouldn't have attacked him. Maybe it wasn't his battle."

"How can you say that? It was his mother. It's not fair. We have to reach him." He could feel her near, like a fluttering, brushing his shoulder, but not enough to cling to, not enough to hold to.

And he felt himself drifting, disconnected, further apart. It was as though he were separating from himself, his spirit disconnecting painfully from his earthly body. He couldn't articulate it then, but it was the price being exacted for a crime on this spiritual plane. The echoes were leaving him, distant, now part of someone else's life. "Help him," just a whisper now.

"Why should I?"

"*Please*," drifting away.

"*Then promise me——*"

Even where he was, a chill ran through him, a dread. And then, "*Anything*" was the answer. And something terrible dragged him out of the coldness.

There were flashes of light, sparks of light in his eyes, swirling numbness in his mind. Even in his astral state, he felt as though he'd been punched in the chest painfully. It would be hard to explain to anyone the gravity of the bargain that had been struck. Perhaps, if it had happened anywhere else, on the street, in old Clayton's house, absolutely anywhere, they could have all walked away. But Annie Besant's journal had pulled them into a sacred realm of initiation, where pure vows were exacted and lives were broken.

"Go back," she whispered. "Enough."

He struggled to center himself, separate from the emotion of that tumultuous memory. Swirls of uncanny energies and light all about him, but she was beside him now, the shadow of Corey, the face marked by self-torture and suffering. "Go back," she whispered huskily. "You've seen enough. You understand."

But he still saw the colors surrounding her, swirls of orange, yellow, and red. He shook his head and moved on.

It was the Monsignac tomb beyond them — the woman kneeling with flowers on the grave. He remembered this one after the Sainet tomb. His mind had been confused, muddied, but they'd gone there. And it seemed as though nothing had happened, then they moved on. He could feel rasping behind him. It was her breathing, deep rasping, rattling.

"What is this?" he whispered to someone, to anything.

"Mine," it rasped in a tortured breath. "*Endurance*."

His mind rushed suddenly forward into hers, and yet another lock turned and opened.

He could see Corey lying alone in a hospital room and then a doctor and a nurse beside him. "I'm afraid we'll have to do a DNC. The baby is dead."

He could feel a coldness wrap around the room. And then he saw the creature that was Corey drape itself across her bed, and he knew. This was where that tortured creature was born. It sobbed and wailed across the woman in the bed who lay there placidly accepting the devastating news.

When he returned from the meditation, the first thing he felt was Corey's hands gripping his tightly. He opened his eyes, which initially were blurry and unfocused. It took him some moments to recognize that he had come out of it and was not experiencing some sort of extended distorted vision. As his eyesight began to clear, a swirl of nausea coiled in his stomach, which convinced him that he had indeed returned to Earth. He released his grip on Corey's hands, and her eyelids fluttered. Her face was pale, and he immediately saw confusion in her gaze.

He breathed in deeply, trying to center himself, but was hit with another cramp of nausea. Some meditations were highly positive experiences, and others could be enormously draining. Slowly he stood up on shaky legs, feeling pain running up and down his skin. On so many levels, this had taken a lot out of him. He looked down at Corey, who was looking at him with a deep measure of confusion. It was clear that what she'd experienced had been quite fragmented, while he had just succeeded in putting together nearly all the pieces of the puzzle.

He put out his hand to her, which she took, and he unceremoniously pulled her to her feet. "What happened?" she asked.

More nausea accompanied by a maelstrom of emotion that just very well could tear him apart if he allowed it. With steely control, he responded, "We need to regroup a bit, then we'll talk."

CHAPTER 56

WHAT IS OFFERED

"Corey."

She was upstairs in her room. It was a Saturday, off school, a cool November day. And then she heard her name being called again, "Corey," — her father's voice. She finished brushing her long dark hair, pulling it up again in a ponytail off her neck, and then headed down the stairs. She heard his voice coming from outside, so she followed it through the sunroom and to the outside patio. Somewhere in her mind, she noted the roses blooming on the periphery of the courtyard. Her father was sitting on a wrought iron bench, just sitting quietly, as though he'd been waiting for her. Her mind fogged over for a moment, as she remembered a room with candles and holding someone's hands.

He smiled, "It's all right. I called you." Her father was as she remembered him when she was a teenager but oddly more robust, more vital.

She sat down next to him. She was dressed in a pair of blue jeans and a white cotton, long-sleeved shirt. "What is it?" she asked.

Again, feeling an unidentified tug, pulling her mind and sensation somewhere else, he patted her hand. "Stay here with me for a while Corey."

She turned away from him for a moment, as though magnetized. The garden seemed serene but just beyond it, just beyond it. And then gently he turned her face around to him again. "You know, sometimes fear creates more monsters than there should be."

"I should be somewhere else," she whispered.

He shook his head, "It's all for the best Corey. Everything in its time, and now it's time."

A panic began to flood through her, but he gently patted her arm. "Don't worry. You're safe. We'll wait here."

"Here, until what?"

He smiled warmly, "Until it's over, my dearest one."

Her head was spinning, and she watched curiously as Iain moved about the room. "Was it all a waste?" she asked.

He stopped as he was rolling up the straw mat and turned to her. His eyes seemed dark and turbulent. "What do you remember?" he asked with no emotion.

"I just remember being in a garden with my father."

"The entire time?" he said a little distantly.

"Yes, he said we were waiting."

"For what?" he asked quietly.

"For it to be over," she answered.

He nodded, as though in understanding, and then he sat down wearily in a chair across from where she was on the sofa. "Well, then, maybe we should finish it."

He cleared his mind completely. So many things to discuss, but everything must unfold in its specific way. "Do you remember the objects?"

Confusion passed across her face, and then slowly she replied, "I think so, but it's not entirely clear now." He recognized how events had shifted and memories had become opaque and confused. "It was after we'd finished with the journey." Her voice became distant. He could feel her trying to visualize what had occurred. "The last two went quickly. The Villere tomb, I wasn't entirely sure who it was for, seemed as though nothing happened."

He remembered, Andre had told him once, "*Some initiations may seem small to the recipient, almost passing without acknowledgement. But what you must understand is that things are greatly significant to the spirit that may go virtually unnoticed in the material world.*"

He leaned forward, an image coming to mind of a girl standing, holding onto a cross. "It was Brae," he murmured. "She told me later.

Clearly, it represented Faith, her experience." He didn't elaborate, didn't feel the need. For some reason, they were all tested at different levels and as far as he could gather, no one had gone through anything of the magnitude he had.

"And the last one was the Manuel tomb," she said. "The girl sitting, flowers on her lap, her head bent."

"Quinn again," Iain responded.

"Yes, yes I think so, but I wasn't sure." He shook his head, in his mind visualizing what had eluded him before. Quinn lost in thought, but determined, steeled. She continued, "I had no idea what it meant, what the representation was."

"No," he echoed, "seemed anticlimactic."

"Yes, and then the last was the pyramid, the Allegre tomb. But it was different. It wasn't a test." And then she hesitated, "Was it?"

The exterior of the Allegre tomb was extraordinary, in fact one of the more startling effigies in the entire Metairie cemetery. The outside was a miniature representation of a pyramid whose bronze entrance gate was flanked on one side by a marble sphinx and the other by a female figure on whose forehead was placed the radiant symbol of the all-seeing eye.

Even though still possessed by the clinging dizziness and disorientation from the Sainet tomb Iain well remembered this one, although they had seen it less clearly in the darkness for the first time during the Marguillers initial expedition so long ago.

"*Look at this one.*" Quinn's voice rang out.

"*What does it mean?*" Sebastian's young voice in the darkness.

He remembered their flashlights bouncing off its white, luminescent surface.

"*Rosicrucian probably,*" Quinn had answered. But it felt older, so much older than even that.

"I'm not sure what happened," Corey's voice in the present, next to him in his den, piercing the veil of the vision.

"We all crossed over together," he murmured. He could see them all in one moment. All the Marguillers were grown now, standing in the harsh afternoon sun at the threshold of the Allegre vault and in the next breath within.

"There was light, a strange powerful glow inside," Corey's voice sounded distant, as though she too were reliving the experience.

So strange, two places at once — here in his den, in the small house on Chestnut Street and there too, more than a memory, standing in that chamber. His head was still clouded, but the light, the energy was reviving him from the dark fog. "We all crossed over together," he murmured aloud. He could see them — Quinn, Brae, Sebastian, and Corey, all beside him, all bewildered by what they were seeing.

The walls within felt nothing of the tomb but rather of a sacred place, a temple he was certain.

"Is this really happening?" He heard Brae's voice beside him, and that connected him with the others because the moment felt like his own, his own personal vision, separate yet oddly connected to everything.

"They were all there." Corey's voice from the distant present.

It was true. It was as though the four statues, four marble women in long flowing gowns had stepped off their pedestals from the Montleone tomb. They now stood before them, not rigid like stone, but living marble, fluid, white fire.

He breathed in deeply, feeling the energy that they emitted seeping into his lungs. The light nearly burned his eyes, but he forced himself to keep them open.

"One held a blade," Corey's voice. He felt his vision drawn to it, the symbol in her hands oddly shifting, so he could see the truth of the disguise.

"It had been the cross before, when she stood on the monument," his voice sounded odd to him, thick, so enmeshed was he in the past. He couldn't remember if he understood the connection then, but now in the living memory, he could see it clearly. "Faith it seemed, but not fire. The sword is fire." The power of the recollection seemed to surge through him. He could see the blade, glowing in the pure white of the keeper's hand, and shining, flickering, as though it were a living thing in her grasp. He held his ground, feeling its power from a distance, intense power that molded and reshaped lives, worlds. He turned, expecting to see Corey at his side, but it wasn't. It was Sebastian who had moved forward when he wasn't looking.

"There was the chalice," he heard her, and now could see her clearly in his mind moving toward another figure. Something here drew her strongly. His eyes moved to the woman holding the cup, arms moving, hands holding out the chalice reverently in an offering. Corey stood in front of her, and he didn't remember that from before— standing with eyes wide, tears running down her face. Her voice was soft in his ears. It came from the present. "It had been the cornucopia on the outside. Charity, but here it's the cup, water." And he could feel its power rush through the temple all around them, cooling, healing, calming. Strange, the others — Quinn, Sebastian, and Brae — it was as though they flickered in and out of his vision. At times, they were present and at others strangely excluded.

From the side, he could see movement, but it was blurry — a figure moving in his direction, causing everything else around him, even Corey to recede. A fear rose in his heart, clutching at him, for the figure did not come peacefully but with purpose. He remembered and experienced his feet rooted to the spot, although he wanted to flee but could not. The woman held a staff, gnarled, as though from a tree in her long fingers. The marble face was still, serene. He swallowed deeply, feeling a pain in his heart. She extended the branch, and he was reminded as though it were something tucked away that he'd forgotten. The statue outside had held a wreath, a symbol of peace, but here she held the staff, connecting to the Air, the spirit, now a symbol of truth. He breathed deeply, her hands still extending the gift, and he stood frozen in hesitation.

"It was Quinn, remember?" again Corey's voice penetrated the veil of the vision. And his attention shifted from the keeper of the staff. This one, the last figure from the Montleone tomb, held it in her hand. Here, in its presence, he felt them all together, all of them were able to connect on this plateau. It gleamed solidly, continuously, while the other objects flickered in and out of reality. And he recognized its disguise without even seeing it. It had been the woman holding the anchor, the anchor touching the ground, rooting its connection with the earth.

How he'd forgotten, and now was reminded so clearly. Where he had hesitated, Quinn had reached out boldly, reached out his hand to touch the pentacle, the ancient symbol of the Triquetra. And for a moment, he had made contact, grasping it for only a few seconds, then releasing it.

"Why did you do that?" someone had spoken. It was a breach, for the cup had been offered to Corey and the staff to him, but Quinn had simply seized the object without invitation.

Quinn turned round in response, tears streaming down his thin face. "I don't know," he answered. "For a moment, just a moment, I felt it would heal me."

Time began to shift, and the vision was fading, pulling him concretely back to the present. But an instant before the walls of the temple melted around him, he chose. He turned to the figure beside him and placed his hand firmly on the gnarled wood of the staff. It was irrevocable now. A choice had been made, wherever that would lead.

The furniture around him began to appear and solidify now. He was there in the den with Corey, a place he'd never left. She sat there, kneeling back on her knees, her eyes seemingly focused elsewhere as though she too had been drawn along in the vision of the Allegre temple.

"I'm trying to remember what happened next," her voice was distant.

He sunk down onto his sofa. "I can't really remember, not leaving, not much of anything."

"It was all so dizzying, all the energy there. I remember feeling such hope, as though anything was possible."

"There was," he said. "It was purifying but it wasn't meant to last."

He could see her face, which had seemed illuminated only moments before, now cast in shadows. She looked down, "I suppose it wasn't."

"I suppose we weren't worthy," he said.

"Do you think it was that?" she asked quietly.

"I don't know. It was the last time we were meant to see them."

"Is that something you decided?" she asked.

He shook his head, "No, something your father asked me to do on his deathbed. I used to think it was his decision, but I don't any longer. I think we're used as instruments from time to time, as your father was and as he used me." He could see a few tears coming down her face now. "Don't be sad about it. I think he was wiser than any of us." And then he breathed deeply before he crossed the next threshold, because he knew without a shadow of a doubt that once crossed, it would change things forever. "So, tell me something Corey. When you were standing in that inner sanctum, that sanctuary at the end of Annie Besant's path, did you know you were carrying my child?" It was as though the moment was frozen there in the den of his rented house on Chestnut Street. But finally, there was acknowledgement, as she slowly raised her eyes to meet his. They were eyes stamped with raw, agonized emotion —the eyes of that tortured creature that had accompanied him during their meditation.

CHAPTER 57

WHAT IS LOST

It was a strange meeting. Corey remembered distantly, as though what had happened with her and Sebastian had unraveled all their relationships. Several months after Iain's departure, Brae visited her at the Morris mansion on Henry Clay Avenue. Sebastian's mother, whose health had been rapidly deteriorating, was living in a specialized care facility, so it was just her and Sebastian who occupied the house now.

Once Iain had gone overseas, Brae had also virtually disappeared from their lives, except on this day. They sat out in the garden. The city was approaching winter, so Corey spent as much time as she could in the cool air outside. The house itself she found extremely oppressive. And she spent her days solely pouring her energy into and concentrating on the birth of the child that she was carrying.

"I was surprised to hear from you," she commented as she led Brae out onto the private courtyard that was Lilith Morris's favorite spot.

"I imagine," she'd said.

Brae seemed uncomfortable. And why should she be surprised? Something had been broken between them, whether because of Iain or Sebastian or just the simple unwinding of everything. Whatever confidences and trust the two women shared had been shredded in the tumultuousness of what had occurred. She sat down in one of the white wrought iron chairs at a small table and Brae across from her. "So, what's going on?" she asked quietly. It was strange how she was living now, almost muffled, outside of reality, in a cocoon — willfully not allowing anything to touch or reach her. Brae looked at her a little oddly, a little quizzically, like the Brae of old, but she held herself distant from it, distant from caring. The only thing that mattered in her world now was the child. "You look different," her old friend commented. "Pale, different."

"Life does that."

Brae glanced around briefly, and then her sharp blue eyes returned. "This all doesn't seem to suit you. Are you taking pictures?"

She shook her head, "No time." She felt an irritation passing over her skin. She truly wished she would leave. Her presence was disrupting the world she was weaving around herself.

"Have you heard from Iain?"

And then she looked back at Brae sharply, "No, Iain hates me. I don't expect ever to see him again."

A strange look fluttered across her friend's face. It was perhaps envy but more sadness now, she thought. Brae did love Iain, loved him as Sebastian loved her, with no substance, without truly knowing, like someone loves a wish, a dream, or an image they've created. "I doubt he could hate you, especially if he knew about the baby," Brae said softly.

Her eyes widened as a specifically aimed arrow now pierced the gossamer safety of her self-created cocoon. "What are you talking about?"

She was not quite four months into her pregnancy and wasn't even showing yet. She hadn't told Brae. It had to be Sebastian or—

"Quinn told me."

"I see," she whispered. "Why should Iain care about this?"

And then Brae tilted her head and gave that odd little smile she remembered — the one she could never quite place as to its meaning. "Because it's his, of course."

She felt a coldness wrap around her, as though reality had finally penetrated all her defenses. "Why would you say that?"

And then again, the smile and the shrug, "Maybe I'm not as psychic as the rest of you, but I can read people. I ran into Sebastian and congratulated him, not exactly the response of a happy, beaming father. Although he smiled as he always does these days, his eyes couldn't hide it. It's Iain's all right. Don't you think he has a right to know he has a baby on the way?"

"It's my baby."

And then she sighed deeply and turned away, standing up and lightly touching one of the few remaining roses blooming in Lilith's garden.

"Well, it's your mess, Corey. Good luck with it. I'm off to England on a buying trip. And I have a feeling I may make it an extended stay."

Corey rose to her feet, her head swimming a bit with dizziness. "I see," she said.

She smiled again, that dazzling smile of Brae's. "I'd like to wish you luck. But I haven't got it in me. I think you've had more than your share for your lifetime." And then she turned around without looking back, leaving Corey entirely alone in the silence of the moment.

"Oh God," she whispered, slowly rising to her feet. But he just continued to sit there, waiting, perhaps waiting for an answer that would help it all make sense, an answer that would exonerate her from all the wrong choices. And then she thought about her father in the garden, holding her hand, keeping her there until it was over until he'd found out everything. A sharp pain hit her chest, directly affecting her breathing.

"Just stay with me, Corey."

She breathed in deeply, and it hurt, years of bottled-up emotion exploding in on her internally. "Iain," she whispered.

"Just the truth now."

The uncontrollable flow of tears spilled down her face, "No, I didn't know then. I didn't know until you were gone."

He nodded, calmly, too calmly, frighteningly calm. "And Sebastian, had he approached you then?"

Her mind tried to wrap around it. How much, how much did he know? "Approached?" she repeated what he'd said.

"Yes, approached you about the promise you'd made to him in the Sainet tomb."

"No," it came out in a rasp. "Not then. I really thought once we'd come to the end of the path, he would have forgotten, or at least."

"Let it go?"

She nodded, "Yes, there was so much good there, positive energy. I couldn't see how he wouldn't be affected by it."

"Like you were."

"Like we all were," she put her hands over her face, frantically trying to clear away some of the wetness from her tears. "But it was different for him."

"I think it was different for all of us, Corey. I don't really think the others could even see all of the keys, not like we did. There were limitations, especially for him."

She looked up with confusion, "He saw the Triquetra."

"He saw something, perhaps, something to use that incited his desire for conquest. We can only see as much as our perceptions allow us to."

She breathed with an almost uncontrollable panting. The sobs were threatening to come.

"Iain," she whispered, "you were lost, and I couldn't."

He stood and walked across the room, turning his back on her. He was trying to maintain some semblance of control, but his head was pounding, and the image of her alone in that hospital bed was feeding a growing fury inside him. "Do you really think I wanted you to sacrifice yourself for me that way, to be with that animal?"

She stood up but couldn't move closer to him. She was afraid of what she felt emanating from him. "It wasn't your choice. It was mine. I couldn't let you slip away like that, and I knew, I knew that whatever forces were at work, they would hold me to that promise, even if it meant your destruction."

He straightened up and turned around to face her. His eyes, too, were red, and she saw the slightest vestiges of tears streaming down his face. "And what about our baby Corey? Was that to be a sacrifice, too?"

She shook her head, tears rushing down her face. "I would have taken care of the baby."

"Without me?" His voice sounded raw, savage in her ears.

"I don't know. I couldn't see past it. I was just trying, trying to bring it safely into the world and then—" In the moment, her knees gave way, and she sank down to the floor. "And it slipped away," her voice disintegrated into painful sobs that would be held at bay no longer, "just like you, just like everything, just slipped away."

Corey lay huddled in devastation, a heap on the floor. Instinctively, he began to reach out his hand for her but then stopped and withdrew it. Instead, he headed out the front door and started walking, walking away from the house, trying to outrun the thoughts and ravaging emotions that threatened to overtake him.

CHAPTER 58

FUTURE GLORY

"I don't really get it. Why you'd pick him, DeMolay?"

"Why not?" he'd responded.

It was an afternoon, the end of a sweltering New Orleans summer. Quinn had left early that day, and Sebastian was lingering for some reason, not anxious to return to the cold rooms of his father's Henry Clay Avenue mansion. So instead, he and Iain were lying down on their backs in the backyard at Carrollton Avenue, watching the last storm clouds be chased away by the glare of the afternoon sun. It was before their fifteenth birthdays, before Corey, before Brae, but not before their dreams of the Templars and the Marguillers and lives filled with some sort of future glory. "Because he failed."

"What do you mean he failed?"

"Burned at the stake, doesn't wreak of success."

Iain sighed, even knowing then that the truth and purity of honor eluded his boyhood friend. "Sometimes success is only marked by remaining true to yourself and what you believe. He died for his own truth, gave everything. I can't imagine a greater mark of success. I wonder if either of us could ever have that much courage."

"Yeah, I wonder."

Sebastian returned home early from the law firm that day. There was no reason except that something was in the air, anticipation. He'd lost most of his early sensibilities over the years but still had a peculiar intuition — like the sensation of when a storm was coming and how destructive it would be. When the big hurricane hit a few years back, he'd felt it ahead of time, felt its inevitability. Of course, he said nothing to those around him. They weren't the sort that would acknowledge such a premonition. But it did happen, and most were caught unaware.

It was much that same feeling as he left his father's old law firm that day. It was that impending sense of destruction, but it felt more personal. Perhaps he wouldn't walk away as he had from Katrina virtually unscathed. It succinctly felt as though a clock that had been ticking virtually his entire life just ran out.

But being as he was, it didn't frighten him. It intrigued him. He longed for the chaos, the disruption, and in a way, he longed for an end to it all.

He gave the maid and the cook the rest of the day off and poured himself a brandy. It was nearly three when the doorbell rang. He'd divested himself of the coat and tie he'd had on earlier in the day and had undone several top buttons on his white starched shirt.

He didn't bother to check who was at the door when he opened it. He already knew. Something distant told him he should be afraid, but he couldn't even muster enough emotion for that.

"There are two men inside you. One from long ago, driven by emotion, pain, and rage, and another born here through learning, then wisdom and understanding. Both will always be part of you, but you have to decide which you give reign to and which will come to rule your destiny."

It blotted out everything else, the rage — blotted out love, sorrow, loss, and any gentle emotion that dared to cross its path. He didn't know consciously where he was heading, but of course, his heart knew, and his blood knew.

All the faces of his lifetime shadowed his steps and dogged his progress: his friend, Andre, in Rouen, who had shown him a different sort of life; Clayton Knight, who'd been more of a father figure to him than his own; his sad, bewildered mother, whose passivity had brought her so much suffering. And Corey, always Corey, whose absence had left him with that overwhelming reality of incompleteness. They were bound, bound together regardless of their desires, choices, and wishes — always and forever.

He'd taken the streetcar as far as he could. Mistakenly, he thought it would allow him time to gain perspective. But each moment, each step, each cursed memory that brought him closer to his destination only served to fuel that slow fire that was steadily increasing in intensity, that was beginning to blot out all thought and manner of higher thinking.

He walked half a dozen blocks until he reached his old friend's childhood home. It was the place he'd first laid eyes on Annie Besant's journal so long ago.

Sebastian opened the door to his father's house wide and stepped back. He'd expected to see Iain standing there, but it still came as a shock. There was a wildness about him — his hair, his clothing disheveled, and frankly, a darkness emanating from him that he had not expected to feel. It was clear that whatever this was to be, it would not be a civilized meeting.

"Come in," he smiled widely and gestured inward dramatically. "I've been expecting you. Granted, ten years earlier, but now will do just as well." He walked into the house and momentarily had a flash of Iain clubbing him over the head from behind. But he continued to walk forward. Long ago, he'd realized that what he lacked in real courage, he made up for in feral bravery.

He heard Iain follow him in and slam the door behind him, "Do you know why I'm here?"

Sebastian had stopped on the staircase, then spun around slowly, "Well, by the looks of you, I can only think of one reason. And since this has been a long time coming, how about we adjourn upstairs to Dad's old museum? Seems fitting to me, where it all began." He turned again and began to ascend the stairs, not hearing him, but more than confident Iain was right behind him.

He'd expected something, or rather someone else. He'd expected a rival, a nemesis, an incarnate of evil, someone who was a deserved object for his rage. But what he found didn't surprise him; rather, it stunned him. The man, his young friend, had become brittle and hollow. There was a weariness that cloaked him and had aged him well beyond his years. All the spark and vitality he had possessed was a distant echo now of what he saw before him.

Silently, he followed him up the stairway as Sebastian moved to the end of the hall on the third floor and pushed open the double doors leading into his father's museum. The room was dark, but Sebastian pulled back a set of dark brocade drapes that cascaded a filtered light across his father's prized oriental rug.

Iain's eyes scanned the shelves and the glass cases, all of which were empty. "Sorry, I'm sure you must be disappointed. I got rid of the stuff long ago. Since I could do nothing with it, it became useless to me. You see, as much as you might have coveted my time with Corey. Frankly, it didn't do a hell of a lot for me. Sort of left me barren, barren like she is, barren like this room. All the anticipated hoopla of Annie Besant's journal left us to inherit this, nothing but dust."

"You can't blame it on the journal," his voice sounded like something akin to a low rasp in his ears.

Sebastian smiled broadly, an empty animation, and practically flung himself down into the one remaining chair on the far side of the long, dark room. He laughed without emotion, a caricature of the young man he'd seen before leaving the country. "No, I suppose not. And you're here to tell me I've brought it all on myself. Well, my friend, I tell you I'd gladly give it all back to you if I could, with a lovely bow on top. Give you back all those years I stole from you, gladly, with interest."

"But you can't," he said slowly and with deliberation.

He nodded in feigned agreement, "No, no second chances. This is where we are, where the train stops. Right here."

"I could kill you," Iain said quietly, still in the middle of the room, yards away from Sebastian. There was only the stillness engulfing them in silent anticipation.

The words passed over Sebastian with no impact whatsoever. "Yes, if I were you, I think I would, but then again, maybe not. There's always been an element of self-preservation to me that I think you lacked. Isn't that right, Jacques? Martyr to his eternal cause." And then he stood up and crossed closer to Iain, baiting him, clearly wanting something. "What's the cause today, injustice? Well, get in line. It's what makes the world go round."

Without thought, words fell away, and he struck the first hit in a punch across Sebastian's jaw.

CHAPTER 59

IN THIS MOMENT

She was trembling as she heard the door close behind him, but she couldn't draw herself away from the floor. It took some time for her shaking to stop and even longer to pull herself to her feet. It was impossible to tell now if there was any relief here. It was as if she had been through a calamitous shipwreck and was now dragging her battered body from the wreckage.

She didn't wait long before calling a cab to take her home. She was certain where he was headed. There was an inevitability there. But it didn't feel as though it had much to do with her anymore. Her part was finished. What was left was now between them.

Sebastian staggered back from the punch, grabbing his face, then broke into an oddly contrived smile. "Best you can do? Not really holding up the reputation of the Marguillers are you, old friend?" Then he swung back, hitting Iain somewhere near the solar plexus. He bent over but then leaped again toward Sebastian, violently smashing him across the chest and plummeting them both to the floor. There was blood, blood that Iain felt on his hands, in his mouth, and all it did was incite the madness that flowed through him. Again, he hit and was hit back, but then he managed to propel himself on top and grab Sebastian's throat. A throat he relentlessly began to crush the life out of.

Sebastian had walked out of the Sainet tomb empowered. The strange energy he'd gained coursed through him wildly, more intensely than any kind of rush he'd ever experienced. He'd laughed to himself, even eclipsing the first time he'd taken a marijuana cigarette in his first year of college. Drugs were something he'd deliberately avoided, just for the simple reason that he'd always wanted to be in complete control of his faculties. But he had to admit, it had been a bit of a life-altering experience, not to be in control, to let emotions and desires fly rampantly — only one of a handful of times he'd ever allowed himself this sensation.

But now, the rush he felt from the Sainet tomb was not uncontrolled but one of total control. It was heady and seductive, the power of having someone else entirely at your mercy. However, this power that surrounded him did not take form or fully manifest until he crossed the threshold of the Allegre pyramid.

He had no idea what the other four experienced there, but in his skin, he purely recognized what they did not glean. In front of him, beckoning and serving him, was the keeper standing with the blade in her cold marble hands. Outside on the Montleone monolith, it had been disguised as a cross, a symbol that most would never recognize as an instrument of power. Here, it became a sword — the truth stripped away as she offered him the gift of dominance. Here was the power to remake one's destiny, to mold the world around you. Not good, not evil, simply a tool meant to be used by those ambitious enough to wield it. He'd reached out in that moment, taken it, and allowed his secret desires to take root in the outside world, becoming the creator of his life as he envisioned it.

The familiarity flooded over Iain like a crashing wave from a tumultuous ocean. Again, he was in the darkness of the Sainet tomb, crushing his father's throat and then Sebastian's as he was doing now. He stilled on the spot as the realization and shock swept over him. It wasn't finished, not quite finished, the test — the test that had gone on for over a decade. Here, in this moment, there was still choice. His hands shook with the recognition that there was still a chance. His hands trembled as he saw Sebastian's eyes clouding over. But he forced himself to release the grip and felt the tremors pass through his body. He stepped backward, standing up, and slowly but with definitiveness, the grayness began to lift.

Sebastian sluggishly pulled himself up into a sitting position, coughing. Iain continued to stare at him, just standing over him. But then, without thinking, Iain reached out a hand and pulled him to his feet.

Sebastian continued coughing a bit as he wiped the blood from his mouth. "Well, I'm awake now," he laughed sarcastically, rubbing his painful ribs.

"You don't deserve to be," Iain said in a low, distracted voice as he helped him to the chair. With some painful difficulty, Sebastian sat down.

Sebastian had begun rubbing his temples. His head was still spinning dizzily from oxygen deprivation. "Just tell me why?" Iain said in a low voice, still laced with repressed rage.

He looked up into his old friend's face, blood dripping, bruises forming. At least he'd made some impact. "Why?" Sebastian repeated.

"Why Corey?" he asked again. "You knew what she meant to me."

Sebastian let out a depleted sigh, then responded slowly, "I've answered this question a thousand times in my mind. But now," he choked a bit, clearing his throat, which was still clearly ravaged from Iain's attack. "I can say that I loved her. I think maybe I did love what she was, what she represented to me, what I saw between the two of you. I think she became a sort of symbol of what I felt I deserved to have even while she was away. Back then, I could rationalize it easily." The coughing started again, but Iain didn't stir, didn't move to help or leave, just waited. "Time makes all that harder," he laughed dryly, "all that rationalizing tends to wear down in the light of real living. But sadly, I think it was the power, just the power that place gave me. Made me feel like I deserved it, made me feel like I had a right to use it, just because I could. I was sure I could make her love me, have the life I envisioned. So sure, until I couldn't."

Iain stared at him with little expression, "Nothing positive can be created out of something destructive."

"Maybe," And then Sebastian leaned back in the chair in exhaustion, still wrestling with pain that seemed to be seeping in from many areas. "That tomb," he said quietly, "where it all happened. Did you ever figure out what it meant?"

Iain nodded solemnly, clearly lost in thought, "Tolerance, and I failed."

And then Sebastian laughed softly, "The one thing that I've come to realize after all these years was that it wasn't you who failed. It was me."

Iain stared at him for a moment, an elusive expression crossing his face, and then he silently left the room. Sebastian sat in his father's empty museum for a while, then finally left, closing the door behind him.

CHAPTER 60

WHAT IS SAVED

The solemnity of her father's house surrounded Corey as she entered the mansion on Esplanade. She felt exhausted, gutted utterly, emotionally, physically, in every way that a very tired mind could register. She wandered aimlessly and found herself in her father's study. It was usually comforting, but she was in a place beyond comfort now. She sank into the chair in front of his desk, remembering doing the same so many times when she was troubled or simply needed his strong presence to guide her. That was her last thought as she dozed into an exhausted sleep.

It was somewhere between a dream and a memory. That night, they'd spent in the Metairie cemetery, and they all separated, looking for a place to hide until it closed. Again, she was fifteen, forgetting her goal but being drawn by the vibrations about her.

She stood in front of the Nicolas tomb looking into the face of a statue, the wise sage, his fingertips indicating silence across his lips.

She spoke, she thought perhaps to herself, but heard her voice aloud, "What does it mean?"

"*Just a guide,*" the voices whispered around her. "A friendly helping hand," the voice beside her. She turned to see the figure of her father eying her with kindness. She smiled, "What are you doing here?" she asked with surprise.

"I'd never let you go alone on this mad adventure."

She looked back before her, and the statue of the wise old man had disappeared. And then the flood of future memory swept across her. She held onto the iron bars, whispering, "I've made so many mistakes."

His hand touched hers and covered it. "There aren't mistakes, dearest one, only learning."

The deepest pain washed over her, "The baby," she whispered.

"Time and miracles may help heal that one as well. Don't assume you know what the future can bring. It is a wide-open canvas." And then he looked into her eyes with great comfort and whispered. "Now go back."

Corey opened her eyes to the sound of the front doorbell ringing continuously. The comforting energy still clung to her as she made her way through the rooms of the silent house to the front hallway. Her hands hesitated on the lock of the door. She had no idea what was coming, what to expect at all. It was completely unknown now; the aftermath of a storm that had passed over them, through them, stripping down the terrain, leaving only the barest essentials behind — breath, life, and possibility.

She swung open the door and quickly took in the image of the man before her. One hand leaning against the door frame, shoulders bent a bit, and face bruised and beaten.

And in that moment recognition of what had passed between them flew out of her mind as she reached out to take his arm in support. "You look terrible," she whispered as they walked inside, and she closed the door behind them.

He emitted a low chuckle, groaning a bit, "Nothing compared to how I feel."

He put his arm around her for support as they walked into the den, where she helped him sit on the sofa. "Can I get you anything?" she asked.

He shook his head but grasped her hand as she began to move away from him. "Stay here with me," he murmured. And she sank down beside him on the sofa.

There was silence for a few moments, but he continued to hold her hand, seeming unwilling to relinquish it. And then she spoke, "I'm almost afraid to ask you what happened."

"I saw Sebastian," he said quietly.

She nodded, "Yes, yes, I gathered that."

He smirked a bit, "Well, you'd be proud of me. I left him alive."

She sighed deeply, and a few tears she had felt were no longer possible slipped down her face. "I'm glad for you. I would hate for you to have anything else terrible to live with."

He squeezed her hand and brought it softly to his lips, kissing it. "I want to say how sorry I am."

More tears, just when she was certain the well had run dry. "I made my own choices."

"I think you thought you didn't have a choice."

"I couldn't stand the thought of you just slipping away where I couldn't find you. I always knew wherever you were after that, you were all right." She still felt the old pain lodged deep in her heart. "So now we can both be free and maybe heal."

And then he'd released her hand and ever so softly grasped her chin and turned it to face him. "Let me be very clear with you, Corey," he said, his eyes that deep green hue, the color of Baltic Amber. "I need you with me. I can't begin to fathom a life without you, whatever that looks like, whatever that means."

Her eyes continued to tear over, "So much has happened, so much pain."

"Then we'll find a way to heal together, help each other, and forgive ourselves. But I can't do it without you, and I won't."

She nodded slowly, "You're so stubborn."

And then a smile, one that she remembered from long ago. And she thought to herself that wherever Jacques DeMolay was now, he must feel a sense of pride that this man had chosen to honor his name. She leaned against Iain as he put his arm around her and pulled her close. "I'm so tired," she whispered.

"Let's rest awhile," he said. "We have a lot of plans to make later."

And then, before the drowsiness overtook her, a thought lightly filtered through, "The Triquetra," she murmured.

"Don't worry," he answered. "It's almost settled."

EPILOGUE

Quinn didn't dream much these days, not vividly, at any rate. Most of the time, he went to bed so fatigued that the sleep was heavy and often colored by the pain medications he took. But this night was different. He dreamed in a way that felt more like the return to an old memory.

They were together again, all standing outside the Allegre tomb, the pyramid, at the end of Annie Besant's journey. He remembered that day well. It was a cloudy day, great black clouds hovering precariously over the grounds of the Metairie cemetery. It was a humid, oppressive feeling as though, at any given moment, the storm clouds would open and unleash their wrath upon them all. But as it was, they didn't, not until all was done.

He was in many ways astonished that they were all together that day, given that Sebastian and Corey had so recently eloped and the antagonism between them and Iain, with Brae siding so vocally against them. It went far beyond astonishing. It was impossible, and yet here they were. Later, Sebastian would explain that Corey's father had interceded, insisting they attend. And, of course, a word from Iain would bring Brae to his side these days.

It was an odd feeling, the way in which he was part of the memory and yet separate. The expanse of time gave him an odd, disconnected view of the whole event. Of course, at the time, he hadn't known that this would literally be the last time the Marguillers were ever all together. None of them had realized the full significance, and mercifully, he thought. That knowledge would have made what occurred even more momentous.

What he had hoped then as he wandered toward the entrance to the tomb was that they would all go in again. He realized that what he'd seen within was different from the others. He hadn't actually seen the keys as Iain had described them. To him, the staff, the chalice, and the blade were only blinding blots of whiteness, like liquid white fire that he couldn't even stare at directly for more than a moment. But the other was different — the pentacle, what they called the Triquetra because of its interlacing pattern. He did see it, and knowing that it was meant for him, he touched it, forming a link that, in time, would bring it closer to him. All these thoughts, even then, had crossed his mind. He'd felt its power and knew that if it was his, there would be no limits. Healing him would be the least it would do. It was tied to earth, as was the body, and continued exposure would re-energize his failing shell.

And then the unthinkable happened. Iain insisted the other four of them join hands in a semicircle around the entrance to the tomb. He was quiet and direct, and Quinn felt sure the others were humoring him. After all, given the stunt Sebastian had pulled off with Corey, it was the least they could do.

And once they did, he took out a piece of chalk, sketched strange symbols right on the door, and spoke words that sounded curiously like Latin to Quinn. As this went on, Iain then raised his hands, waving them in a deliberate, calculated fashion. Quinn understood before the others what was happening. But the words died in his throat as sparks flew and a pop like a small firecracker explosion went off. When the light cloud of smoke cleared, the symbols he'd drawn had completely vanished. Quinn's heart was hammering uncontrollably in his chest. There was nothing visible, but he knew. He knew that Iain had locked that mystical door away from them all.

Quinn's head reeled from the remembered outrage, but then Iain turned away from the others and walked right up to him. He smiled, and Quinn knew now this wasn't the memory at all but something entirely different. "It's time to let go, old friend," Iain said. "This door is closed again."

His head was swimming, "But you don't understand. You haven't led my life."

He smiled at him a little sadly, "I know. But this way is not your path. Our lives and what we endure are chosen for a reason. You must rise above the trials and not be consumed by them." And then he reached out, touching his shoulder lightly, and Quinn felt a jolt of energy passing into his weary body. "Peace to you, my old friend."

Quinn's eyes opened in the darkness of his room. But rather than despair, the lightest fluttering of hope passed into his weary heart.

Finis

Gravier's Bookshop

A New Orleans Paranormal Mystery (#1)

6 x 9 Softcover 190 pages

ISBN 978-1-61342-288-5

Max Gravier had no intention of becoming a recluse, but after his wife's death it seems his life is heading in that direction. He spends his time running Gravier's Bookshop on Magazine Street and occasionally on the quiet helps the police solve a crime with his psychic sensitivities. That is until he answers Caroline's call, a cry for help, out of his dreams that draws him into a fierce battle for a young woman's soul.

In this first installment of The New Orleans Paranormal Mystery series, Caroline Breslin, an amazingly gifted empath, is determined to strike out on her own and has moved out from the protection of her family home. All is going extremely well until of course she comes under siege from a devastating supernatural attack. The last thing Caroline wants is to run back to her family for help, even though she is painfully in over her head. What she really needs is a knight in shining armor or maybe just that guy that keeps haunting her dreams.

The Hotel Mandolin (#2)

A New Orleans Paranormal Mystery

6 x 9 Softcover 138 pages

ISBN 978-1-61342-290-8

Peril is wrapped up in the most enticing of disguises, in *The Hotel Mandolin*, the second installment of The New Orleans Paranormal Mystery series. It's opulent, it's classic, and it's one of the most renowned hotels nestled deep in New Orleans' famous business district, but something is amiss at The Hotel Mandolin. PI Peter Norfleet is calling out the big guns to help him investigate a recent suicide at the famous establishment — his good friend Max Gravier, a formidable psychic, and his girlfriend Caroline Breslin, a talented empath. But none of them can seem to scratch the surface of this puzzle, no one except Cassie Breslin, Caroline's clairvoyant mother, who has somehow tapped into an unexpected connection with a tragic ghost from the turn of the century. And the more she uncovers the more dangerous and malevolent the mystery becomes.

The House at Pritchard Place (#3)

A New Orleans Paranormal Mystery

6 x 9 Softcover 170 pages

ISBN 978-1-61342-292-2

Nothing is really wrong with the old Warrick House on Dante St. except that there most certainly is. Nothing is exactly wrong with its new mysterious owner except that Elise is sure that something doesn't add up. In the third installment of The New Orleans Paranormal Mystery series, with the help of the very psychic Breslin clan, Elise is about to embark on a wild rescue mission into another dimension that will land her squarely somewhere she doesn't expect, right back into her past. Right back to a childhood home whose memory still haunts her to this day -- *The House at Pritchard Place.*

Dragonflies - Journeys into the Paranormal

6 x 9 Softcover 120 pages

ISBN 978-1-88756-072-6

A powerful wizard, love-crossed ghosts, a mysterious dark warrior, and an enigmatic time traveler -- a mystical wordsmith entices you into the world of the paranormal with a collection of inspired stories. Each tale takes the journey of the dragonfly imbued with the momentum and energy of change, following a winding path that ultimately will lead you to find the truth buried beneath perception.

Treading on Borrowed Time

6 x 9 Softcover 198 pages

ISBN 978-1-61342-214-4

For Julia Moreau life seems complicated. Emerging from a failed marriage and managing a lifetime of diabetes, she lives alone in her childhood home where she communicates with the spirit of her Great Aunt Lilia. But Julia doesn't have a clue what complicated is until she is thrust into being the key chess piece in a match between two powerful men of extraordinary abilities on the wild hunt for a mystical creature hidden in the heart of New Orleans' French Quarter. Will Julia lose her soul to the karma of a devastating past life or her heart to the love of a man driven by dark forces? What is clear is that whichever way she turns she is *Treading on Borrowed Time*.

Appointment With the Unknown:

The Hotel Stories

6 x 9 Softcover 151 pages

ISBN 978-1613423608

A hotel for most represents a normal place, a predictable realm of commonality. One might even go as far to say a safe space, the reliable, where nothing particularly unusual is expected to happen. Or is it? Dimensional traveling, spirit guides, mystical storms, and soul mates separated by time are only a few of the elements dotting this supernatural landscape. Drop into a collection of romantic paranormal stories where that place of commonality is only the threshold, the jumping off point, for extraordinary adventures into the unknown.

A Quiet Moment

6 x 9 Softcover 295 pages

ISBN 978-1-61342-326-4

Jacob Wyss is caught in a rut, in fact on the verge of being engulfed by it. After an excruciating and disillusioning divorce, his life as an artist in a sleepy-college town at the foot of the Appalachian Mountains has become quiet, routine, and maddening in its predictability. One wintry day, his deep restlessness drives him out in precarious conditions to a largely empty bookstore nearly devoid of another living soul, nearly.

Aimee Marston isn't like everyone else. On the surface, she lives a sedate life working as a feature writer for a small local newspaper in addition to several other editorial jobs to help make ends meet. But just beneath, her existence is largely not her own. She is a sensitive, an empathetic psychic, guided by her calling to use her gifts to help others. Unfortunately, as a result, her secretiveness has made her defensive, protective of herself, and prevented her from having much of a life of her own.

A psychic call for help sends Aimee out on a freezing January morning where her destiny and Jacob's collide sending both their lives spiraling onto an unexpected and often disturbing track. Two lonely souls connect, not by accident, but by design. Theirs is the intersection of two spiritual paths, two lovers who must struggle to overcome the phantoms of a past life, as well as the challenges of their own inner demons to carve out an extraordinary future together.

Travels into the Breach - Accounts of a Reclusive Mystic

6 x 9 Softcover 176 pages

ISBN 978-1-61342-323-3

At first glance, his life seems quiet, serene, and even uneventful. Malachi McKellan, a 65 five-year-old widower and author of esoteric books, lives largely as a recluse in a house situated just off the banks of Bayou St. John in New Orleans. But unbeknownst to most, he is also a bit of a detective, a specific kind of detective whose specialty is psychic attacks. Alongside his lifelong companion and spirit guide Simon Tull, a nineteenth century, twenty something English gent, Malachi battles the unseen, and is an unacknowledged hero to the most vulnerable - most of the population who have no idea what is really happening beneath the surface of the world in which they live.

In this collection of adventures, Malachi McKellan and Simon Tull wage war against the most insidious elements of the paranormal. In "The Three," Malachi and Simon come to the aid of a young woman being victimized by a group of dark witches. An old apartment building is the scene of an unimaginable battle against monstrous forces in "The Lost Soul." Malachi and Simon find themselves strategizing against a psychic vampire in "Obsession," and "The Hotel" turns back time to the 1980's where Malachi confronts a demonic spirit. In "Between," a past life is revisited as Malachi attempts to rescue a beloved sister from committing her existence to vengeance, and "The Wedding" takes a personal turn when Malachi must confront painful truths while endeavoring to protect his niece from a potentially devastating union. Travel into the Breach with a pair of paranormal warriors who choose to confront overwhelming forces on a battlefield unsuspected by most.

A Ghost of a Chance

6 x 9 Softcover 174 pages

ISBN 978-1-88756-050-4

Jack Brennan, an ambitious high-powered attorney dies, only to find himself constrained to a peculiar afterlife as an earth-bound spirit trapped in an old Virginia farmhouse with a very much living, reclusive writer of campy vampire novels. Hallie Barkly recovering from a painful and disillusioning divorce has forged a career and exorcised her demons by writing under the pseudonym of Sebastian Winters. Their lives intersect, and two unconventional lovers are brought together under insurmountable circumstances. They must battle an unseen force hell-bent on possessing Hallie's life and bridge death itself to make possible what cannot be - to find a chance.

Explanations

6 x 9 Softcover 82 pages

ISBN 978-1-93493-515-6

In this, her second poetry collection, Evelyn Klebert takes us down the intricate path of a personal journey. Life with its particular struggles, pit-falls, and ultimately triumphs clearly begins to mirror a universal path, the quest for answers that we all ultimately pursue. In this reflective, esoteric collection we can all explore and seek some of life's elemental mysteries and hopefully when all is said and done emerge with some *Explanations*.

Breaking Through the Pale

6 x 9 Softcover 92 pages

ISBN 978-1-88756-045-0

Breaking Through the Pale is a compelling collection of paranormal short stories by metaphysical author Evelyn Klebert.

"Contact" is the tale of a woman who life is irrevocably altered when she unexpectedly establishes communication with a spiritual guide.

In "A Grey Mourning," a disillusioned man encounters a mysterious being on the foggy streets of New Orleans.

"Dancing on the Threshold" relates the story of a woman who precariously poised between life and death takes a journey that unravels the true nature of her life.

"Isolation" is the story of a woman who inexplicably finds herself alone and disoriented in an old, quaint house on the edge of a forest. Slowly, she must piece together the past that brought her to this place and the mystical implications surrounding her predicament.

The Witches' Own

6 x 9 Softcover 124 pages

ISBN 978-1-61342-058-4

On the surface things seem quiet and serene in the picturesque coastal village of Kilmarnock, Virginia. But something unseen roams its lush forests as the past and present collide and the unthinkable begins to wreak its vengeance. Young Lucy Bonner is executed for witchcraft in the town's distant and brutal past. Her death triggers an unholy chain of events which grasp at the restless heart of novelist Peter McQuade, spurring him towards a quest to uncover the dark and terrifying truth.

The Broken Vow

Vol. I of The Clandestine Exploits of a Werewolf

6 x 9 Softcover 140 pages

ISBN 978-1-61342-133-8

In the heart of every man, there is a history. In the heart of every monster, there is a story. In this first installment of *The Clandestine Exploits of a Werewolf*, Ethan Garraint is on a vendetta that begins in the heart of the Pyrenees with the fall of Montségur and leads him to the streets of New Orleans nearly five hundred years later. But the person he chases isn't really a man anymore and Ethan has been a werewolf for almost a millennium. With the aid of a gifted seer, he is on a blood hunt that will culminate in a journey that crosses the line between heaven and earth and ends somewhere in between.

The Left Palm

And Other Halloween Tales of the Supernatural

6 x 9 Softcover 104 pages

ISBN 978-1-93493-556-9

Just when all seems well and quiet when all becomes comfortable and predictable then reality bends. Evelyn Klebert takes you to a place where ordinary life fractures into the sphere of the paranormal.

The journey begins with one woman's unstoppable quest for vengeance against a supernatural creature in "Wolves," and continues in an old historical graveyard where a horrifying discovery is uncovered in "Emma Fallon." In "The Soul Shredder" a psychiatrist's unusual patient opens his eyes to a disturbing new view of reality, while in "Wildflowers" a woman strikes up a supernatural friendship with impossible implications.

And in "The Left Palm" a fortuneteller in the French Quarter receives a most unexpected and terrifying customer.

Considerations

6 x 9 Softcover 68 pages

ISBN 978-1-88756-062-7

Sometimes the struggle to understand the meaning and complexities of living comes down to a single moment of introspection or a fleeting yet meaningful reflection. This collection of poetry by Evelyn Klebert takes you down a winding path of self-discovery where the resolution may not always be absolute, but the journey is indeed unforgettable. It a wide and varied map of inspired poetry for your examination and consideration.

Visit Evelyn's website at:
www.evelynklebert.com

Cornerstone Book Publishers
www.cornerstonepublishers.com

www.ingramcontent.com/pod-product-compliance
Lightning Source LLC
Chambersburg PA
CBHW022245020726
47496CB00004B/1073